Lucy
Talk

Also by Fiona Walker

French Relations
Kiss Chase
Well Groomed
Snap Happy
Between Males

Lucy Talk

FIONA WALKER

Hodder & Stoughton

Copyright © 2000 Fiona Walker

First published in 2000 by Hodder & Stoughton
A division of Hodder Headline

The right of Fiona Walker to be identified as the Author of
the Work has been asserted by her in accordance with the
Copyright, Designs and Patents Act 1988.

10 9 8 7 6 5 4 3 2 1

All characters in this publication are fictitious
and any resemblance to real persons, living or dead,
is purely coincidental.

A CIP catalogue record for this book is available from the British Library

ISBN 0 340 76788 X

Typeset by Rowland Phototypesetting Ltd,
Bury St Edmunds, Suffolk
Printed and bound in Great Britain by
Clays Ltd, St Ives plc

Hodder & Stoughton
A division of Hodder Headline
338 Euston Road
London NW1 3BH

For the dazzling 100 Watt guiding light,
whose bright ideas and brilliance
have put Lucy in the spotlight

Lucy started life as the heroine of a fictional weekly column, first suggested to me by the glorious Carol Smith, to whom I am hugely grateful.

My thanks go to all at the Newbury Weekly News, particularly Brien Beharrell, for giving me the opportunity to have such fun every week, and for allowing me the freedom to take Lucy wherever I choose, including into book shops.

I am indebted to all those Internet sites from which I have borrowed pictures and jokes. I'm sorry that I cannot name the locations, but I'm the world's lousiest surfer. For anyone interested, typing 'sheep', 'pantomime horse' or 'beer and babies' into a search engine can provide surprising results.

All other artwork appearing in this book is courtesy of Microsoft ClipArt.

W Microsoft Word – Lucy's bored.doc

Office very quiet today as Slave Driver is in Jamaica for a fortnight
tanning his six-pack, so plenty of opportunity to design party invites
on Apple Mac and illicitly use colour photo-copier.

You see, this morning a lime-green plastic ghoul fell out of my
Honey Puffs cereal packet and I had *the* most brilliant idea. A
Halloween party at Burr Cottage. Was just excitedly deciding upon
a theme ('Come as your favourite creep') when Jane walked into
the kitchen wearing a stained Tesco's bag on her head. Turns out
she's tinting her hair 'Autumn Gold' in attempt to seduce gorgeous
Tim, her riding instructor, who has a thing about strawberry blondes
– or is it roans?

She was in foul mood as her first pupil for a driving lesson today
is Mad Mildred, the sixty-year-old housewife who's failed her test
six times, and still thinks a three-point turn is a ballroom dancing
manoeuvre. Consequently Jane's not as keen on my Halloween idea
as I'd hoped.

'Aren't theme-parties a bit teenage, Lucy? Although, I suppose if
it's come as your favourite creep, Greg won't need to dress up.'

Jane understandably jealous of darling Greg, who is a gentleman
among boyfriends. Am going to call him now, even though I know
he's flying so won't take the call. He's super-efficient. Even his
outgoing message is just five words – 'Greg here. Leave a message.'

'*Greg here. Leave a message.*' *Beep*.

'Darling, it's me – Lucy, that is. We're having a party on the thirty-first. You must, must be there. Please? Love you. Call me back when you get this. Mpwwwwwww.'

From: Lucy Gordon (lucy@widgetex.co.uk)
To: Bella Smith (smithb@st.cuthberts.ac.uk)

11.45
Subject: Party!!!

Hope you get this attachment through okay – never quite trust the capabilities of the St Cuthbert's staff room computer after GCSE Information Technology class hacked into that nudey pic of Leonardo I forwarded. Would value your artistic judgement. What do you think? Let me know and I can run off a hundred copies. Lxxx

Halloween!
COME AS YOUR FAVOURITE CREEP

Friday 31st October, from 9pm.
Burr Cottage, Hart's Leap Lane, Chisbourne, Wexbury, Berkshire
r.s.v.p. to Lucy, Jane or Bella on 01555 350898

From: Bella Smith (smithb@st.cuthberts.ac.uk)
To: Lucy Gordon (lucy@widgetex.co.uk)

11.52
Subject: Re: Party!!!

Fantastic! Make it a hundred and fifty and I'll invite some of my
London mates. Can't wait to dig out my black PVC again.

Been teaching batik all morning. Can't believe the kids here all
have cars and mobile phones. My old comp was so rough
that they regularly ran an obituary column in the school mag. The
only protection rackets here are used to cover tennis equipment.
Must go – head of Geography wants to check online racing
results.
Atb,

Bella
xxx

Monday

Dear Mo,

*I have no idea where to send this, but this is the point in the evening
where you used to bring me a vod and tell me about your day, and I
wish you were here right now. You're so much better at organising
parties than me – and at arguing with Jane.*

*I've just ventured outside with bin-bag and bumped into Big Mike, the
rugby-mad vet from next door (yes, the one who I used to fancy a bit).
He says that it's about time the girls at Burr Cottage had a bash – as
long as we invite him. He pointed out that things have been very quiet
since you left to go on your travels. Made me think how much I miss
you, babes.*

*We both flirtily agree over the wheely-bins that Halloween is very
sexy – all gothic vampires and red velvet. Big Mike took an unexpected
interest in my description of Bella's black PVC dress. I never knew he
was keen on fashion – apart from checked shirts and wellies variety.*

3

Jane is still grumpily anti-party. 'Autumn Gold' has turned out Dennis Pennis red — she hadn't realised it was unsuitable for bleached hair. Apparently Mad Mildred was so horrified at sight of her driving instructor looking like Cilla Black that she flattened fifteen cones on the by-pass roadworks this morning. I'm dragging the sulky redhead out to Cow in Clover with Bella, who has agreed to help talk her round. I really like Bella, and she's a great laugh, but she's not you. And to be honest she scares me a bit.

Almost wish I'd agreed to come with you now, but I know that I'd slip right down the promotional ladder if I took two years off, and I couldn't leave my family or Greg for that long. Besides, backpacks give me a terrible stoop. Remember that summer we spent Euro-railing? You called me Mrs Overall for six months afterwards.

I'll have a TOR for you tonight. Hope you're having fun wherever you are.

Love,
Lucy
xxxx

Posted on the Burr Cottage fridge:

COW IN CLOVER RESULTS
Mon 29th Sept (score kept by Bella):

Number of times Lucy said 'Greg': 15 (still claiming he is her boyfriend despite two-week silence).
Best quote: 'Being a commercial pilot is very demanding.'

Number of times Jane said 'Tim': 3.
Best quote: 'I'll seduce him at the party over fang-shaped canapés. I can always wear a wig — after all, he does.'

Number of times Bella mentioned London: 7. Best quote:
'You know that plastic ghoul you found in your breakfast cereal this morning, Lucy? It's a Tellytubby.'

RESULT: Lucy = washing up (plus bin emptying penalty for leaving early to check whether Greg had left a message). Jane = vacuuming and dusting. Bella = week off.

You have . . . one . . . new message. Message received . . . today . . . at . . . nine . . . fifty-three . . . pee emmmm.
'Lucy it's your Mum. I've kept a recipe for Thai Fish Stew from the *Mail* I think you might manage – it's very simple. You take half a pound of white fish, three peppers, lemon grass, bunch of coriander, two red chilliesgarlicand – brrrrr – fishsaucewithadashof – whrrrrrr – sauteuntiljustbrown – brrrrr – only a pinch, mind you – whrrrr – fifteen min – brrrr – can'tgowrong, can you?'
That was your . . . last . . . message. You have . . . no . . . more messages.

'*Greg here. Leave a* – Hello . . . We're here! . . . Hello? Is there anyone there? Greg, darling, I think it's a crank caller.'

W **Microsoft Word – Lucy's upset.doc**
Aghhhh! My mother used up all our answer phone's tape with some stupid recipe last night. Realising that darling Greg had probably tried to call while it was out of action, I dialled his plush Wexbury Heights flat. A woman who sounds like Mariella Frostrup with a throat infection answered. I hung up in panic. Who is this husky-voiced minx?

Saturday

Dear Mo,
Very productive weekend so far. Have sent out invitations to Halloween party, sorted my tights drawer, thrown everything past its sell-by date out of the fridge and cleaned the bathroom even though it's

Jane's turn on the roster. As you know, she never uses enough Jif. Bella has made up some stupid new points system based on our nights out in the pub, but it'll never catch on. She's getting on my nerves a bit right now.

She says I'm suffering from displacement activity syndrome because Greg hasn't called me. I told her that was rubbish and set about polishing the telephone for the fifth time. She's gone to London tonight to see a band called The Trash Junkie Acid Tabs. Big Mike next door dropped the milk bottle he was putting out when he spotted her setting off in lime-green hot pants. I think he's developing a crush. Men are so shallow.

Jane hogged bathroom for hours this evening then appeared wearing a Stetson to cover the hair-dye disaster, which is now Chris Evans ginger. She tried to persuade me to go with her to a line-dancing night at her riding school, but I was far too busy removing built-in grime from cooker hob, and cleaning lime-scale from the kitchen taps with the toothbrush Greg keeps here for overnight stays. Still don't know the identity of husky-voiced woman who answered the phone at his flat on Monday. Might just tidy my bedroom again . . .

Love,
Lucy
xxxx

Sunday Lunch Menu – 13 Roundhead Avenue, Wexbury.
Chef: Liv Gordon

Soured goat's cheese fondue with sesame melba dipping sticks
Carbonnade à la flamande
Pickled kumquats in sweet horseradish jelly

To be served with a bottle of Nuits Saint Georges, '97
For Mother: Litre of Lambrusco Rosé

Jeremy Gordon
c/o PO Box 2307
Sheep's Eye
New Zealand

Burr Cottage
Hart's Leap Lane
Chisbourne
Wexbury
Berks

Sunday 5th October

Dear Big Brother,

The family was on usual form at lunch. Alice munched a nut cutlet and insisted on describing how cattle are slaughtered while the rest of us tucked into our beef. There was so much garlic in the sauce that Granny required three glasses of wine to 'cool her palate'. I enclose Mum's usual menu so that you know what you're missing out on. She's thinking of entering *Masterchef* next year, and has even sent for an application form from the BBC.

Alice refused to eat pudding (something to do with exploited kumquat-pickers). Instead she turned to me and asked, 'How's Tory Boy?'

Hate her calling Greg that. Having a six CD Blaupunkt in your Mazda doesn't mean you haven't got a social conscience. Know for a fact he votes Lib Dem.

Then she gave me one of her evil looks (you know – the same one she used to give you when she'd covered your essays in felt-tipped scrawls) and she said: 'Only he was drinking in the Mill Arms last night, with a girl who looked like Baby Spice.'

Felt sick afterwards – not sure whether it was the thought of Greg with a nubile blonde or kumquats repeating on me. Mum insisted I take Tupperware container full of leftover dessert home for Bella and Jane to try. Found Dad had cleaned my car, re-filled washer reservoir and put air in tyres. Anything to avoid watching *Antiques Roadshow* with Granny, who still ogles Hugh Scully throughout.

I decided to drive back via Wexbury Heights but Greg's Mazda wasn't parked in its reserved space outside Hogarth House, so couldn't casually pop in and check beneath his bed for blondes.

Then I drove into Chisbourne to find that the Mazda was, in fact, parked outside Burr Cottage. Yes!

Greg was sitting at kitchen table looking divine – all floppy hair and sexy smile (indulge me here, brother dearest – he is your erstwhile best mate so I know you'll understand). He gave me big tartan tin of shortbread with red bow on it. Turns out he had a last-minute booking flying businessmen around Scotland and 'asked that dumb receptionist who lives upstairs to look after the flat while I was away'.

'The one who looks like Baby Spice?' I gulped.

He was really funny, joking that she was more like Baby Elephant, and that he'd come back last night to find she'd muddled up all his CDs and over-watered the cheese plant. She took him out for a drink to apologise, but he's still charging her for the cheese plant.

I gave him huge kiss. Quite a few huge kisses, in fact, until Greg commented on my garlic breath. Thank God he didn't spot Jane discreetly sliding his toothbrush from sink drainer and binning it.

I'm sorry, Big Bruv, but I think Jane is actually over you at last. In fact, she's as dippy with happiness as I am because she spent most of line-dancing party flirting with Horsy Tim on a straw bale. Not so distracted, however, that she didn't have cynical comment ready the moment Greg left.

'If you'll swallow the house-sitting line, you'll swallow anything.'

Since the only thing left in fridge after my clear-out is a tin of cat food and Mum's kumquat mix, I think she's wrong there.

Write soon.

Lots of love,

Lucy

xxx

From: Dave Marks (dave@widgetex.co.uk)
To: Lucy Gordon (lucy@widgetex.co.uk)

10.13
Subject: Boss alert

Arse. Last day of freedom before Slave Driver returns from tanning himself in Jamaica. Fancy a quickie in his office? Leather swivel chair looks well tasty.

From: Lucy Gordon (lucy@widgetex.co.uk)
To: Dave Marks (dave@widgetex.co.uk)

10.20
Subject: The mice must stop playing

Help! We should have completed next spring's brochures by now. What shall we do? Everyone's just been playing Solitaire all week.

From: Dave Marks (dave@widgetex.co.uk)
To: Lucy Gordon (lucy@widgetex.co.uk)

10.22
Subject:

I'm up to $87952 in three card game. Beat that.

From: Lucy Gordon (lucy@widgetex.co.uk)
To: Dave Marks (dave@widgetex.co.uk)

10.25
Subject:

If that were real money it might just cover the repayments on the Focus when Slavey fires you.

From: Dave Marks (dave@widgetex.co.uk)
To: All members of marketing department

11.03
Subject: URGENT!!!!

Emergency lunchtime drinks meeting in The Pitch Inn – 1.00.
Best-proven Solitaire score of week receives drinks from all team
members.

From: Dave Marks (dave@widgetex.co.uk)
To: All members of marketing department

14.39
Subject: Synchronise all stories

There's been a bad flu epidemic in Wexbury, causing almost total
absentee rate from marketing department.
    Lucy is to go to Boots and then distribute tissues around
department's desks for authenticity. Only fair given that she's
been getting free drinks all lunchtime.

Post-card featuring palm trees:

Dear Former House Mates,
Dig this! Have reached the gulf
of Thailand. Will let you know
when I have a permanent
address. Cyber cafés full of
gorgeous travellers, so I hang
out there.
Email me!
Hobo-mojo@Hotmail.com
Lots of love, Mo xxxxx

The 'Girls'
Burr Cottage,
Hart's Leap Lane
Chisbourne,
Nr Wexbury
Berks
UNITED KINGDOM

From: Lucy Gordon (lucy@widgetex.co.uk)
To: Mo Lavender (Hobo-mobo@Hotmail.com)

19.25
Subject: Yesssss!!!!!

Jane's just called me at work to pass on your email address.
Can't believe you're sunning your bot on a fantasy island while
I'm stuck here at work. Actually, I'm just hanging on late in case
Greg phones. He's promised to take me to gorgeous Bistro Etoile
in Fiscombe this weekend and said he'd ring me at work during
week to 'firm up details' (love the way he says things like that).
Well it's Friday and the week's run out. Sure he'll call any minute.

Jane's insisting that I take the department laptop home so that
we can both email you properly later. Must persuade Slavey to let
me have one of my own when he gets back on Monday. Which
reminds me – there's something I've got to do with tissues now.

I'm back! Realised that the cleaners are bound to tidy tissues
away over the weekend, so have dumped a couple of Nurofen
Cold and Flu sachets in office kitchen instead. Need tissues
myself. Greg still hasn't called . . . probably left a message at Burr
Cottage. More later. Lxxxxx

From: Lucy Gordon (loosejuice234x@roamnet.com)
To: Mo Lavender (Hobo-mobo@Hotmail.com)

02.12
Subject: Bloody technology

You will not *believe* how long it's taken me to set up a free email
address (can't use the work one at home). Jane's gone to bed.
Think she was feeling a bit odd.

Gossip! Bella has new boyfriend she met at a gig last weekend.
He's enormous and is called Brick (a nickname to do with
lavatories apparently, but I was too polite to enquire further).

They disappeared into her room with a bottle of tequila around eight and haven't reappeared since, although Prodigy is still playing as I write. Bella must be keen – she even *baked* for him.

Greg still not called. Shared bottle of Frascati with Jane, watched *Friends* and started crying when Rachel and Ross almost got back together and then it all went wrong. Used up entire Boots tissue supply and stole one of Bella's homemade brownies to cheer self up. Very moreish. Jane and I finished the lot during *Shooting Stars*.

Jane thinks I should dump Greg and find someone more sensitive.

'Like David Schwimmer?' I snivelled.

'No, like Big Mike next door.'

Was horrified. Big Mike has none of Greg's sophistication and puts his hands up cows' bottoms for a living.

Jane pointed out that vets are very heroic media-type figures compared to pilots. Told me to think of *All Creatures Great and Small*, *Noah's Ark* and *Vets In Practice* as opposed to *The Flying Doctors* and . . .

Couldn't think of anything else aerial on TV, and both got giggles. Felt very silly for rest of night. Must cut down on wine. Keep having paranoid worry that Slave Driver will not spot Nurofen in office kitchen as he never makes himself coffee, so won't believe we've all been ill in his absence. Feel a bit peckish. Off to make tea and search for chocolate.

Can't wait to hear your news. Lxxxx

Written on the back of an envelope:

Darling Greg,

You are asleep in front of "Match of The Day" as I write this, and look so delicious that I could eat you if I hadn't already eaten so much during our meal (plus Bella's brownies last night).

I admit I had almost given up on hearing from you after your message. But when you rang during "Gladiators" and asked if I was still on for Bistro Etoile tonight, it was worth the agonising wait. So what if I had to drive five miles out of way to fetch you, and you drank entire bottle of burgundy and flirted with waitress all night. You're a red-blooded man and I am, alas, red-eyed woman (think I'm getting conjunctivitis).

I love staying here in your flat. It's so good to be away from cottage. Bella's not talking to Jane and me because we ate her brownies — she says they were v. special Moroccan recipe. I asked if I could have the recipe for Mum in case she wanted to use it on "Masterchef", but she just laughed bitterly and took Brick to Cow in Clover for lunch. I was going to tell you this during our meal, but I know you find my news boring.

Must stop writing and wake you up.

Please ask me to move in here with you. Please, please, please!

Am going to flush this down the loo now. I love you.

To: Bella Smith (smithb@st.cuthberts.ac.uk)
From: Lucy Gordon (lucy@widgetex.co.uk)

09:05
Subject: all tied up

Can't believe he stayed ALL weekend!!! Tell me, tell me, tell me more! Did you shag him???

Having a crap morning. Slave Driver is back from Jamaica and throwing his tanned weight around the marketing department, complaining that we haven't worked hard enough in his absence. I think he's just sulking because his nose is peeling. Tried politely suggesting aloe vera lotion, but he ignored my helpful advice and angrily pointed out that I have yet to start on the electric tie-cleaner campaign. The presentation is next week. Aghh! Lxxx

W Microsoft Word – Lucy's worried.doc

Electric tie-cleaner campaign not going v. well. Was fiddling with the prototype for inspiration, turned it on and it swallowed most of my favourite silk scarf, almost strangling me. Scarf ruined, prototype broken and still no further on in campaign. Should be writing Slave Driver an apologetic email right now, but I'm actually quite angry that I could have been injured and think there is a fundamental design fault.

Haven't been sleeping very well. Am very worried about Hallow-een party. I haven't had a reply to any of the invites I sent out to friends/loved ones/people Jane fancies. Suspect no one will come. Also worried that neighbours will complain (except Big Mike, who is planning to come as Herman Munster). Might invite them all to make up numbers.

Have asked everyone in office, even Spotty Gary and Ambitious Dave. Luckily didn't have to invite Slave Driver, who is in Wolver-hampton promoting nasal clippers and ear de-waxers at a trade fair. Oh – phone! Might be Greg.

*

It was Alice (the first time my little sister's ever called me at work) to say that she will be coming to my party and can she bring some friends? I haven't even invited her.

Can't be bothered to type that memo now. Will photocopy some more invites while Slavey's out of the way.

14

Written on the back of a takeaway pizza flyer:

Darling Greg,

You are asleep in front of "Ibiza Uncovered" and look gorgeous.

I sensed that you were feeling low tonight when we went to see the new Michael Douglas film and you spent the entire film sneering at the star's beer-gut whilst shovelling popcorn into your mouth. Are you frightened of facing the future? At least pointing out that if he could pull Catherine Zeta Jones then you had no worries seemed to cheer you up, if not me. Afterwards, while we spent those hours walking around the ten different car parks in Basborough Leisure Multiplex trying to find the Mazda, it was so sweet the way that you cried because you thought it had been stolen. Glad we finally spotted it between two Range Rovers in first car park we'd looked in.

Have seen a whole new, vulnerable side of you tonight, which I love more than ever.

Please ask me to move in here with you. Please, please, please.

I love you. Am going to flush this down the loo.

From: Lucy Gordon (loosejuice234x@roamnet.com)
To: Mo Lavender (Hobo-mobo@Hotmail.com)

20.52
Subject: Lucy Talk

I've got the company laptop again this weekend (told Slavey I had to work on electronic tie-cleaner campaign). Where are you? Hope you're okay. Thought I'd have heard from you by now.

Bella's new man, Brick, spent this afternoon in front of the *EastEnders* omnibus in our sitting room (I wouldn't normally mind, because I'm a bit of a fan as you know, but this was the flipping UKGold repeat of the nineties). He smoked hundreds of v. smelly roll-up cigarettes and made lewd comments every time Bianca appeared. Bella is so infatuated, she has started wearing lime-green leggings with baby-pink shirts and shouting 'Briiicky!' whenever she wants his attention.

This evening, Jane and I decided to escape to Cow in Clover. Found Big Mike in the lane admiring Brick's motorbike.

'They're classics these old Triumphs.' He then started raving on about it. Jane and I were unimpressed as we both know that motorbikes ruin your hairdo, dirty your boot-cut trousers and haven't got enough luggage space for a decent sized handbag.

We told Big Mike it belonged to Bella's new boyfriend, who is a London courier, and he went very quiet and said he quite fancied a pint in the pub too.

He had several pints. I should have gone home early to work on electric tie-cleaner campaign, but couldn't face returning to sight of Bella and Brick groping on sofa. Jane says that last night she was forced to watch *Blind Date* with them, and that they snogged between mouthfuls of takeaway curry.

Big Mike went even quieter (probably as repulsed by image as I was), so I decided to involve him in conversation by confessing my worries about lack of response to Halloween party.

'Leave it to me,' he winked, then stood up and loudly invited everyone in pub. So embarrassing. Thankfully there were only three other people there – and one of them was old Archie who's stone deaf. Think Big Mike was a bit tipsy. He accidentally knocked Brick's bike over when we walked home, and then got the giggles.

Email me soon. I'm worried about you. Lxxxx

W Microsoft Word – Lucy's operating.doc

Have come in early to prepare for electric tie-cleaner presentation. I really like my idea – it's very original. I came up with it last night whilst watching strange Spanish film with Bella and Jane.

WIDGETEX LTD

Summary of presentation of Electronic Tie Cleaner campaign.

Staff present: Kelvin Hatchard, Managing Director. Gavin Slater, Marketing Director. Lucy Gordon, Marketing Executive. Marie Reiss, secretary to Mr Slater.

- Lucy Gordon presented a 'two-pronged, Y-shaped media attack' with the running theme of 'Tie-Me-Up-Tie-Me-Down'.
- Proceedings were temporarily halted after Mr Hatchard suffered a minor head injury due to a falling flip chart, but were resumed shortly afterwards with Ms Gordon trying to demonstrate a mock-up tie running through the machine. However it would not fit through the device.
- Mr Slater pointed out that the paper tie was of the 'kipper variety', and that no one wears them these days, current sartorial trends favouring a more streamlined style for which the ETC has been designed.
- Ms Gordon responded that lots of people do still wear 'kippers', including her own father and several Geography teachers at St Cuthbert's in Wexbury.
- Mr Hatchard called the presentation to a close after the campaign was deemed unworkable.
- The account has now been given to Gary Best, who wears fashionable bootlace ties and is felt to better understand the product.
- Ms Gordon will be transferred onto a campaign for an automatic tooth flosser.

Sunday Lunch Menu – 13 Roundhead Avenue, Wexbury.
Chef: Liv Gordon

Curried quail's eggs with artichoke caviar
Baby squid stuffed with boiled bacon in black bean and jalapeno puree
Flambéed gooseberry pancake with honeyed mint crown

To be served with a bottle of Chablis Premier Cru, '98
For Mother: Litre of Lambrusco Rosé

Jeremy Gordon
c/o PO Box 2307
Sheep's Eye
New Zealand

Burr Cottage
Hart's Leap Lane
Chisbourne
Wexbury
Berks

Sunday 26th October

Dear Big Brother,

Thanks for the postcard. I showed it to Mum and Dad who were more interested in the comments you made about Greg than the picture. For your information, Greg has changed from the 'fart-lighting bastard' you remember. He is being fantastic and took me out to the opera last night. We had front row seats, which was a relief because that meant that no one could hear his snoring over the orchestra. The poor darling is working so hard that he falls asleep all the time.

I'm just back from lunch at Roundhead Avenue and enclose the menu as usual. Mum was very pleased with the taste, but I think she needs to work on presentation before she enters *Masterchef.* It looked like something Noel Edmonds throws over celebrities in tanks. Alice was thankfully away, attending protest rally for Banana Workers' Rights. Mum took the opportunity to try out recipe for banana and rum stir-fry after her flambéed gooseberries set light to the kitchen blind.

Dad is very excited by the purchase of a new chainsaw. I don't think there's much call for tree surgery in a suburban Wexbury cul-de-sac, but he says it's an investment. He picked it up at a farm auction last week and has spent every evening in his shed since then, reconditioning it (i.e. taking it apart and then reassembling it with two screws and a spring left over). Two apple trees and a willow have mysteriously disappeared from the garden. He asked me if we needed any 'pruning' doing at Burr Cottage. Not liking glint in his eyes, I said I'd consult the girls.

Yes, Jane *is* still over you. You'll have to hurry home if you want to win her heart again.

Bella's boyfriend, Brick, has been here all weekend *again*. He really gets on my nerves with his smelly cigarettes, loud music and unsavoury habit of leaving bathroom door open when having a wee. Greg took an instant dislike to him last night. Told me afterwards he thinks he's a bit druggy. I hope he doesn't start dealing wraps or whatever they're called at our Halloween party.

Lots of love,

Lucy xxxxx

From: Lucy Gordon (loosejuice234x@roamnet.com)
To: Mo Lavender (Hobo-mobo@Hotmail.com)

20.41
Subject: Lucy Talk

Just two days until party! Getting very excited, although now worried that have invited too many people. Went to village stores tonight for bottle of wine to share with girls and Margaret behind the counter said she was looking forward to Friday and should she bring some assorted quiche slices with her? Turns out Big Mike has been inviting everyone in Chisbourne, even eighty-year-old Mrs Brody who took her cat to his surgery to be neutered this week.

Stormed next door to demand that he stops inviting people on our behalf (bit embarrassing actually as caught him in boxer shorts about to take a shower). He says I asked him to. Come to think of it, I do vaguely recall saying something about lack of numbers. Now I think I might have to hire in bouncers and portaloo.

At that point, Dad appeared with box of glasses and two bags of apples. I asked what the apples were for and he said 'bobbing'. God, how embarrassing! I'm trying to aim for an atmosphere of gothic sophistication. Imagine making my guests shove their faces in bucket of wet windfalls? More Brambly choker than Bram Stoker. Dad longingly eyed up the big fir in our drive as he was leaving.

The next moment I overheard him chatting to Mike: 'D'you know much about chainsaws? Just bought myself a new one.'

Mike: 'Petrol or electric?'

Dad, *boastfully*: 'Self-oiling alligator.'

Mike (eyes wide): 'Wow! Fantastic. How long's the arm?'

God, men are so boring!!!! Must go and fiddle with outfit. Have had lots of ideas. Was going to be a vampire, but the fangs I bought in Wexbury's joke shop keep popping out (remember that place where we used to get fart spray to pong out Mr William's History class?). Am now torn between the *Exorcist* (Greg loves that film, but how do I make my head spin around and my tongue flop out?) and Fenella Fielding in *Carry On Screaming* (Mum's idea – she's lent me one of her 1970's velvet dresses). What do you think? Where are you? Are you alive? Lxxx

---

Shopping list – party
Pumpkins for lanterns
Food – some dim sum and stuff
Ingredients for blood punch – white rum, black vodka, Blue Bols, Red Bull
Red wine – 10 bottles
White wine – 10 bottles
Cheap rosé Mum always buys for Granny – 10

Beer – 30 cans (ask Greg what he likes)
~~*Cider – 3 big bottles*~~ *(might encourage Alice to come)*
Carton orange juice
Bottle mineral water
Bottle Coke
Novelty balloons
Joke spider's web spray
Loo roll
Stain Devil red wine remover

Written on marketing department laptop:

W Microsoft Word – Lucy's hungover.doc

~~Ideas for Tooth Flosser Campaign.~~
Party Post-mortem, by Lucy Gordon

Ow, ow, ow! Someone is having a fireworks party outside. They must be the only villagers who didn't come here last night, as the rest of Chisbourne has a collective hangover. Every time a rocket explodes, the entire village shouts 'Shut up!' as one. Jane is wearing fluffy earmuffs to block out the noise while she clears up; I've stuffed cotton wool in my ears and am hiding in my room, too embarrassed to venture downstairs and help. Bella and Brick have gone out, leaving the house full of Brick's smelly motorcycle courier friends from London who are sprawled all over the sitting room, polishing off surplus rosé and watching *Noel's House Party*. I simply can't face them, although I owe Jane an apology.

Everyone else had wonderful time last night. It started a bit ropily. Novelty Halloween balloons had added novelty of being impossible to blow up. When the first guests arrived, Jane, Bella and I were still sitting in the kitchen, adenoids bursting as we tried to inflate the witch's hat-shaped ones. I shot upstairs to get ready and found that the dress Mum had lent me was, in fact, a Laura Ashley maternity smock with faded armpits and twenty-year-old fruit Polos stuck in

21

the pockets. Bella came to my rescue by cutting three holes in a bin-bag and turning it into a vamp's dress. It looked pretty sexy at first – Big Mike's eyes were on stalks which irritated Greg no end – but by the time the house was bursting with a hundred people, I was squelching around in a cloud of steam. Bin-bags smell simply foul when hot. Greg kept his distance once I started reeking of hot Dunlop – deliberately flirting with one of Bella's teacher friends to wind me up. The pig.

The party was a roaring success with punch as spiked as a sprinter's shoe. After four glasses, I decided to flirt with hunky blond to play Greg at own game. Turned out to be Horsy Tim, the riding instructor Jane fancies. Felt awful when she told me, and ignored him after that – determined to be perfect hostess.

But disaster struck when I was fetching dim sum out of oven. The front of the bin-bag dress melted in the heat and fused onto my favourite La Perla bra. I LOVED that bra. Big Mike – who was in kitchen dishing out drinks – thought from my screams that I must be suffering from third degree burns and threw bowl of punch over me before pulling dress off. So embarrassing! I wasn't burnt at all. Have now flashed in front of half the village, my work-mates, friends and my errant boyfriend who – far from rushing over with his coat to protect my dignity – simply got the giggles. I spent the rest of the party in Mum's maternity smock, trying to avoid hot looks from Horsy Tim. Hope Greg doesn't realise it was me who sprayed fake cobwebs all over his Mazda, and stretched a novelty skull balloon over the exhaust pipe.

Ow! Another rocket. Think I might hide my aching head under a pillow for a while – say, a week or two.

From: Dave Marks (dave@widgetex.co.uk)
To: All members of marketing department

11.03
Subject: Flash Gordon

For all those of you who did not make it to Lucy's wonderful party, the design department has put together this mock-up photo image of what our hostess looked like when burning her bra. Germaine Greer watch out!

flashgordon.bmp attachment here

Sunday Lunch Menu. Burr Cottage, Chisbourne.
Chef: Lucy Gordon.

Dips and crisps
Spaghetti con M and S sauce, served with sweetcorn and petits pois
Ice Cream

To be served with that cheap wine Mum buys for Granny

Burr Cottage
Chisbourne

Sunday 9th October

Dear Big Brother,

The family arrived for Sunday lunch at midday to find Jane and me munching our Coco Pops in front of *The Waltons*. I have enclosed my menu for your delectation. Dad spent most of the afternoon pacing around outside prodding our trees and asking if they blocked out light to the cottage. Mum was in v. bad mood as Granny had a raucous Bridge party in the annexe last night, which kept them awake until three a.m. When Mum got up, she found Granny had nipped through adjoining kitchen door in night and 'borrowed' two bottles of sherry as hers had run out. Granny was consequently still in bed with hangover, so couldn't make it for lunch.

At least someone's having a wild social life. I was supposed to be going to fireworks party at posh country house hotel with Jane and Bella last night, but couldn't summon nerve (Horsy Tim, Big Mike and various other friends will all be there). Stayed at home to watch the Chisbourne Village Green display through Jane's bedroom window instead. I lit a sparkler to get in mood, but think I've scorched Jane's curtains.

I was just settling down in front of *Casualty* when Bella's boyfriend, Brick, turned up unexpectedly on his motorbike. Tried hiding, but flickering television gave my presence away and he tapped on the window. I couldn't remember the name of the hotel where the fireworks display was going on, so was forced to share bottle of wine with him and make polite conversation until B and J returned. Despite blue hair and smelly roll-ups, he's quite nice once you get to know him – told me his real name is Phil and that he's only working as a courier while he tries to get a recording contract for his band, Slug. He was very sympathetic about my party trick last weekend – said a similar thing happened to him at Reading Festival this year, involving plastic trousers and a brazier.

He wandered downstairs today just as we sat down to eat, wearing Bella's dressing-gown and smoking a roll-up. Mum politely asked if his hair was 'naturally that colour'. Little Sister gazed at him with her mouth open entire time – didn't even notice that there was bacon in the carbonara sauce. When Bella emerged, Alice kept calling her 'Miss' and sniggering. So embarrassing having a housemate who teaches one's little sister History of Art A level. Bella got quite annoyed after a while and pointedly asked Alice if she'd done her essay on the Pre-Raphaelites yet.

Greg is away this weekend – flying VIPs to Channel Islands. I called him on his mobile to let him know I was missing him, but there was lots of music and chatter in the background. Greg said it was the telly in his hotel room, and that he couldn't find the remote control to turn it down. The conversation was a bit stilted as a result. I asked him if he was missing me too, but I don't think he can have heard me right as he shouted, 'That's fine – I've got it covered this end!' and hung up. The poor thing's very stressed with work.

Give my love to the sheep.

Lucy xxxx

WIDGETEX LTD
Memo
To: Marketing Department
Re: Team spirit
It has been drawn to my attention that some members of staff are ganging up on others and effectively employing bullying tactics more reminiscent of a playground than professional executives. I suggest that we remedy this by collectively bonding on a corporate excursion. Please write down your ideas and leave them on my desk. I will remind you once again that I do NOT 'do' email.
Gavin Slater.

From: Lucy Gordon (lucy@widgetex.co.uk)
To: Dave Marks (dave@widgetex.co.uk)

13.28
Subject: Bonding

This is your fault. Now we'll have to go on one of those naff group excursions in Wales where you all have to wear matching t-shirts, run ten miles together and then make a bridge across a river with two oil drums, a short plank and a ball of string.

From: Dave Marks (dave@widgetex.co.uk)
To: Lucy Gordon (lucy@widgetex.co.uk)

13.31
Subject: 007ing

Would love to tie you up in string, hot stuff.

Hear that boyfriend of yours is away again. Fancy a drink tonight? I've always found you strangely attractive, Ms Moneypenny.

WIDGETEX LTD
Memo
To: Gavin Slater
Re: Team spirit
How about a sponsored parachute jump? I'm afraid that I have vertigo, but I would be happy to be involved at ground level. I know Dave Marks is very keen.

Lucy

WIDGETEX LTD
Memo
To: Marketing Department
Re: Team spirit
Many thanks to all for a wide range of ideas, although I would have appreciated a little less licentiousness, and may I take this opportunity to point out that many of you submitted ideas anonymously which was not my intention?

The marketing department is now booked to do a static line jump at Thrushfield Aerodrome in three weeks' time. Lucy Gordon should be applauded for this excellent idea. ALL members of the team will be expected to jump and I will accept no feeble excuses. Absenteeism from this important team exercise will be looked upon in a very negative light.

Gavin Slater

Cutting from *Wexbury Gazette*:

Local Company to Take the High Jump

Wexbury-based Widgetex Ltd has come up with a novel way of uniting its staff. All the members of the company's marketing team are to take part in a parachute jump next month, and Marketing Director Gavin Slater is seeking sponsorship to raise funds for charity. 'We're all really looking forward to it,' says Slater, 39. 'The idea was suggested by a junior member of staff, and we all leapt at the chance. Any money we raise will go towards the Injured Golfers' Trust.'

W Microsoft Word – Lucy's leap.doc

Can think of nothing but the parachute jump. I know I won't be able to go through with it – I get dizzy going down in a lift. I keep thinking about the girl who drifted in the wrong direction over Salisbury Plain recently, and found herself swinging from power cables for hours before she could be cut down. I have a feeling I'll go one better and drift into the cathedral spire to dangle from a gargoyle.

God! What have I done? Greg's company is based in Thrushfield Aerodrome. Hope he's ferrying VIPs somewhere far away that day – like the Moon. Although on second thoughts, could use his manly support while I plummet to earth.

Haven't mentioned it to him yet as don't think he'll be keen on the idea of his girlfriend falling from the sky above his office at Thrushfield Aerodrome. Was going to say something last night, but he was being so romantic I couldn't bring myself to. He cooked me dinner – yes! This is a first. Admittedly it was only boil-in-the-bag curry while we were watching a video, but I think it's a positive development in the relationship. I now have two jumpers, a tooth-brush, a jar of moisturiser and a pair of jogging trainers in permanent residence at his flat. Am planning to sneak more items in without his noticing over next few weeks in the hope that it will subliminally trigger sense of security and commitment in him. He's off to a stag party tonight, but I'm popping round first to help him on with his cave-man outfit. Think I'll leave my ear-rings there.

From: Lucy Gordon (loosejuice234x@roamnet.com)
To: Mo Lavender (Hobo-mobo@Hotmail.com)

21.56
Subject: Lucy Talk

Have been sulking (in case you hadn't noticed) because I haven't heard from you. But I've got so much to tell that I've decided to forgive you and write another email. I've even bagged the department laptop again, which has the added benefit of making Slave Driver think that I am working like a Trojan – I can DO NO WRONG right now.

He was in an endlessly good mood all week at the prospect of the office parachute jump (Oh yes I have). Kept beaming at me and congratulating me for suggesting it. Only four of us doing it now – Slave Driver, Ambitious Dave and Spotty Gary – everyone else has dropped out. I tentatively put it to SD yesterday that it was no longer much of a 'bonding' session with so few of the marketing team taking part, and that perhaps we should stick to building bridges with oil drums in Wales.

'Nonsense,' he scoffed. 'The rest of the team will come along to support the jumpers.'

Had strange mental image of marketing team holding up huge Arran sweaters for us to land on.

Talking of jumpers, Greg left me a message today. 'You've left a load of stuff at my flat, Lucy – it's looking a bit messy. Could you pop round and collect it some time?'

So sweet. Know this is only an excuse to see me, as I refused to wait in his flat while he was at a stag party last night (Jane and Bella's advice – something they read in *Cosmo* about 'holding back to hold on to your man'). Not that I've seen Bella holding back with Brick much of late – nor Jane with Tim (they're not even going out and she's on the phone to him every ten minutes).

My little sister has persuaded Jane to give her cheap driving lessons. She turned up at the cottage this morning with half an inch of make-up on her face and her hair up in strange Björk horns.

Dad gave her a lift here (she refuses to practise driving in his car because it isn't eco-friendly, but is not averse to begging lifts in it). He told me that Alice has a 'simply awful' new boyfriend who he and Mum have banned her from seeing because he's twenty-nine and has tattoos on his face.

'If only she could meet a nice, sensible boy her own age,' he sighed sadly. 'Someone who'd make sure she's home by ten, like your boyfriends used to.'

'Still do,' I muttered darkly.

He's bought himself a new contraption that sucks up fallen leaves, and spent an hour in our garden playing with it. Poor Jane came back from teaching Alice to find that he'd hoovered up all her winter pansies.

'Your family are a liability,' she told me after they'd left. 'Alice drove as far as the by-pass protesters' camp, parked up and disappeared for an hour, leaving me to listen to the car radio.' Turns out the boyfriend who Mum and Dad don't approve of is a new-age traveller called Scrumpy, and Alice is using the driving lessons as cover for brief romantic trysts. Jane only willing to go along with it as can catch up with *Archers* omnibus undisturbed.

Please email me, just to let me know you're alive. Lxxxxx.

13 Roundhead Avenue
Wexbury

Sunday 28th November

Dear Big Brother,

At parental home, watching rugby with Granny who's fallen asleep with her mouth open, having single-handedly polished off the bottle of wine I brought for Mum and Dad. She said she needed it to get over the shock of my 'news'.

Telling them all about my parachute jump during Sunday lunch not v. good idea. Mum currently crying in kitchen having dropped rabbit, juniper and prune stew over dining-room carpet. Not sure if she's more upset about the stain, the loss of as-yet-untried *Masterchef* recipe, or prospect of daughter plummeting to earth next Friday attached to oversized umbrella. Poor Dad has retreated to his shed to take his beloved chainsaw apart again. Apparently it conked out just as he was half-way through trunk of the Pottingers' diseased lime tree yesterday. The Pottingers – remember? Ardent Lib Dem campaigners next door – are now living under threat of lime tree falling into their conservatory, and Dad's name is mud on the cul-de-sac.

Have to stop writing now. Little Sister keeps badgering me to give her lift to Burr Cottage so that she can have driving lesson with Jane. I've pointed out that she's already had one lesson today (and I know for a fact that she drove straight to protesters' camp to see her new boyfriend Scrumpy – Jane told me she didn't leave second gear once). But she is adamant that she needs a second (proper) lesson as she has already applied for her test. She says Jane has agreed, so I suppose I'd better comply. Is Jane mad? Suspect Little Sister is bribing her.

Written later . . .
Hmph! Was driving Alice through by-pass roadworks on way to Chisbourne when she screamed 'Stop!' and jumped from car. Had to park and go in search, as I was worried that she was going to sabotage a JCB. Eventually found her talking lovingly to tree. For a moment I thought she'd gone potty and become a druid or something, but on closer inspection I noticed there was a dreadlocked man strapped to high branch by webbing harness, wearing sleeping bag and playing a nose flute. Scrumpy.

Apparently they'd had a row earlier and Alice wanted to make it up. When I finally dragged her back to car, I found it surrounded by security guards with walkie-talkies. It took ages to persuade them that I wasn't a radical wire-cutting local. Got to Burr Cottage to find Jane was out riding, so Alice had been lying about the lesson all along. The little monster is now lolling around sitting room with Brick, playing Bella's old Pixies albums. Bella and I are consequently both livid. Would take her home, but Greg (who's in Amsterdam) said he'd call this evening.

Later still . . .
Greg didn't call. Was so annoyed, I made Alice catch bus home.
How are the sheep?
Lucy xxx

From: Lucy Gordon (lucy@widgetex.co.uk)
To: Mo Lavender (Hobo-mobo@Hotmail.com)

11.41

Subject: Portable shirt-collar iron promotion

Excuse the subject title – I'm at work and may be rumbled at any moment.

   Slave Driver is still in a revoltingly good mood. Would normally relish this rare harmony at work, but I'm too terrified about Friday's jump to appreciate his unctuous smiles and constant references to me being the marketing department's answer to Anneka Rice. Am currently working on a fake cold in case I simply can't go through with it and need excuse to cover up my cowardice. Have been sniffing and sneezing since Monday, but SD just thinks I'm even braver, telling everyone that 'Lucy Gordon is the sort of dare-devil girl who won't even let a little head-cold get in the way of her parachuting dream'.

   Greg fog-bound in Amsterdam. Haven't told him about jump. Maybe no bad thing, as with any luck he'll still be there on Friday and will never know that I was dropped from a great height over his office. Am convinced I'm going to land on it, crash through roof, break all the executive toys on his desk and squash his busy lizzie.

   Have psychotic South East Asian brainwashing cult members kidnapped you, or have I got your email address wrong? Jane used your postcard to trap a spider in a glass weeks ago and it's gone missing, so I can't check. Lxxxxx

---

W Microsoft Word – **Lucy's last will and testament.doc**

Spent today at Thrushfield Aerodrome training for the jump. So much to remember and all I took in was that you have to check your canopy has opened five elephants – I mean seconds – after you jump from the plane. Oh God, I feel sick. Slave Driver spent day swaggering around in his jump-suit like a character from *Soldier*

Soldier pretending he knows it all (he bought a skydiving magazine last week and consequently asked lots of questions about the specific brand of altimeter we'll be wearing and the prevalence of north-westerly wind over the drop zone).

Greg is still in Amsterdam. I finally plucked up the courage to tell him about my jump tonight on the phone – casually adding it onto the end of our conversation as a sort of 'By the way . . .' He just thought I was joking, fell about laughing, told me I was 'priceless' and hung up. Oh God, think I *am* going to be sick.

From: Lucy Gordon (loosejuice234x@roamnet.com)
To: Mo Lavender (Hobo-mobo@Hotmail.com)

21.07
Subject: Fall from Grace

I did it! Yesterday, I jumped out of an aeroplane, with a rucksack full of folded nylon on my back, attached to a glorified washing line – and I'm still alive! The world around me has taken on a whole new loveliness as a result. Walked through Chisbourne today, sniffing the lovely air, gazing at the lovely cottages and greeting everyone in sight with a hearty glad-to-be-alive 'hello'. Went into village stores to buy chocolates for Slave Driver and almost hugged Margaret the shopkeeper. Glad I didn't as she's been giving me very odd looks since I accidentally flashed my bra in front of her husband, Ned, at the Halloween party last month.

Visited Slave Driver in hospital this afternoon. His broken leg is in a large tent-like thing covered with a blanket. He was in a very bad mood – kept raving on about freak weather conditions over Salisbury Plain yesterday afternoon. His hurt pride was somewhat soothed by my news that Ambitious Dave landed in a field of sheep, and Spotty Gary managed to float to earth on a housing estate, terrifying the woman who found him wading out of her ornamental garden pond with a plastic lily pad hanging from his harness. SD now convinced that the fact I alone made perfect landing was a 'total fluke' and clearly proves that the cross-winds were far too dangerous to let a bunch of amateurs jump out of a plane at 3000 feet. I didn't like to remind him that the instructors told us it was unusually perfect jumping weather for the time of year. Nor did I point out that despite a day's intensive training, SD completely ignored the fact he'd been told to hold his toggles level until instructed otherwise on the one-way radio. The moment his canopy opened, he was swinging around like a Red Devil and heading towards the aerodrome's epicentre where he crashed into the control tower.

SD has given me long list of instructions for running the office next week and will call every day to 'touch base'. Was tempted to make joke about touching down on an airbase, but thankfully I bit my tongue and fled. Lxxx

---

You have . . . one . . . new message. Message received on . . .
Sunday at . . . two . . . thirteen . . . pee emmmm.
'Lucy, it's Greg. What's going on? I was en route from Amsterdam on Friday night, and my landing was diverted to another airfield at the last minute. I've just heard that it was someone from the Widgetex marketing department who put the Thrushfield control tower out of action. Was it you? Are you okay, my darling? Where are you?'

'Greg here. Leave a message.' Beep.
'Poor Greg . . . you must have been so worried! I'm fine, my darling – I've just been to my parents for lunch. I had no idea you've been back all weekend. You could have come along. Never mind. Um . . . just one thing . . . if you were so worried, why did you leave it until today to call me?'

Written on the back of an old flight plan:

My darling Greg,

You have just popped out to buy some wine while I cook dinner in your flat. This was your suggestion, no less, because you say that we've 'seen far too little of one another recently'. Ah, romance! I am determined to seduce you with my cooking. Chicken curry is bubbling away nicely. Have never made a curry before. Was planning to cook one of Mum's recipes which involves battering breasts flat with rolling pin and smearing them with olives and pimentos, but you looked disgusted when I suggested it. Although now I think about it, I'm not sure you realised that I was talking about chicken at all. Never mind, you love curry — the stronger the better. I hope that means you won't notice the fact that I added three tablespoons of madras powder to the pan before realising that the pot said 'tspns' not 'tblspns'. Easy mistake to make. I've just tried it and it tastes okay. You're bound to love it, as you're being so flattering and thoughtful at the mo.

I loved it when you told me about the drink you had on Wednesday in the Thrushfield Aerodrome bar with one of the parachute instructors who trained the Widgetex marketing department team for our static line jump. Your face went such a funny colour when you explained that the instructor told you that I was the cutest thing he'd ever seen in a jumpsuit and asked if you had my number. He obviously didn't realise that we're going out together. You're now hugely attentive. Must remember to jump out of aeroplanes more often. Am also thinking of buying a jumpsuit to wear casually around Wexbury.

Mmmm. This curry smells soooo good. Am going to try some before I destroy this letter. I love you. Please ask me to move in with you and cook you curry every night.

Oh Christ! Have to stop writing. Mouth on fire! Aghhhh!

Sunday Lunch Menu. 13 Roundhead Avenue, Wexbury.
Chef: Liv Gordon.

Sweetbread ravioli in creamed broad bean sauce
Knuckle of wild boar glazed with molasses and sunflower seeds
Pistachio and grapefruit custard tart

To be served with a bottle of St Pauillac
For Mother: WI gooseberry and pear wine (Sainsbury's out of
Lambrusco Rosé)

Burr Cottage
Chisbourne

Sunday 7th Dec

Dear Big Brother,

I enclose both mother's weekly menu and a cutting from the *Wexbury Gazette* about my recent parachute jump ('Local Girl Shows the Men How To Do It'). Great huh? Ignore the photo of John Noakes in drag; the picture editor got muddled up. It's supposed to go with the piece on the panto coming to Wexbury Corn Exchange.

Talking of inappropriate pictures, I got your postcard of the mooning Maori, but I don't think your 'This is what Greg talks out of' comment was at all kind. He was very sweet about the disastrous curry I cooked him last night. He found me drinking his cold tank dry via the bathroom tap and took me out to eat at Tandoori Tavern in Wexbury instead. He said he'd order me something mild, but I think the waiter got a little muddled up as it tasted a bit fiery, although G says my taste-buds were probably ultra-sensitive and that vindaloo is usually very light and subtle. He poured me lots of wine to soothe burnt mouth. Felt a bit woozy afterwards. Shame as Greg very romantic. Actually said the L-word in bed. At least I think he did – I was drifting in and out of consciousness at time.

Lunch at Mum and Dad's today. There's a bit of an atmosphere there as Alice is still seeing Scrumpy on the sly whilst pretending to be getting driving lessons with Jane. Think Dad is suspicious. He spent a long time in the shed fiddling with his broken chainsaw this afternoon, which is sinister as Scrumpy currently lives up a tree on the by-pass route. Mind you, the Pottingers next door still have a lime tree hanging precariously over their conservatory, so he needs to get it working again soon. Mum says Mr P is threatening to get in a tree surgeon and charge the bill to Dad.

I told her how lovely Greg has been since my parachute jump and Mum suddenly said, 'Why not invite him round for supper next Friday?'

Was certain Greg would be horrified by idea, but I called him – Mum breathing down my neck all the time, mouthing 'Is he a vegetarian?' – and he agreed to come. Yippee! Is this a sign of commitment at last? No, don't answer that.

Blow kisses to the sheep.

Lucy x

W **Microsoft Word – ETF2b.doc**

Outline Notes – Electronic Tooth Flosser Campaign

- Okay budget
- Lay out advert (use old one?)
- Book photographer and studio
- Write update memo to Slave Driver in hospital (NB: more flowers/ a golf mag may be required)
- Possible outfits for next Friday: 1) Pretty dress (too Doris Day?)
  2) Jeans (too casual?)
  3) Borrow something sexy from Bella (Mum and Dad might freak out)
  4) Jump-suit type outfit (requires shopping trip)

● Friday dream scenario:
Greg in casual cream chinos and Arran sweater, calling my Dad 'Mr
Gordon', complimenting my mother on her cooking, asking Granny
about her Bridge parties, flirting mildly with Alice to make her feel
special, and catching my eye over and over again. Plus occasionally
squeezing my hand or stroking my cheek in loving manner. Plus, if
I'm lucky, playing rampant footsie with me under the table. (NB:
Buy sexy boots to match jump-suit.)

From: Lucy Gordon (lucy@widgetex.co.uk)
To: Mo Lavender (Hobo-mobo@Hotmail.com)

10.43
Subject: Please let Mum cook something normal

Hope the cult are treating you well and allowing you access to a
computer to read my emails. I am guessing that you aren't
allowed to write any back, which is why I never hear from you. Do
they make you wear orange robes (I know how washed out it
makes you look) or – worse still – have they shaved your hair?
Can post a hat if you let me have the brainwashing HQ address.

Meanwhile, more news. Am very nervous at the prospect of
Greg coming to dinner at my parents' house tonight. He and my
father have only met briefly since Greg graduated from 'Jeremy's
hell-raising friend' to 'Lucy's boyfriend'. And it wasn't the best of
starts because it was the day that Dad made an unannounced
visit to Burr Cottage with his gutter-unblocking device. He
suddenly appeared at my bedroom window at nine on a Sunday
morning with a large scoop-like implement, and Greg thought he
was a burglar. It was all too embarrassing. After Greg had
stopped screaming that he was calling the police, he tried to
make polite conversation, but Dad wasn't too impressed as Greg
was wearing nothing but my duvet at the time.

So tonight is going to be really special. Darling Greg is
determined to charm my parents – he even asked me what

flowers my mother preferred and whether my father would appreciate a bottle of malt whisky. I hope they like him. Have been worrying about it all day. When Slave Driver called from his hospital bed this morning for his daily report, I was so distracted that I forgot to mention the fact Spotty Gary has got a job promoting a beer festival in the Midlands and has walked out, taking all next year's Widgetex calendars with him. No one is quite sure why he should want three hundred cheap month-at-a-views attached to pictures of a four-storey sixties office block, but perhaps he's very mean and has a lot of relatives to give Christmas presents to.

I'll let you know how tonight goes. Wish me luck. Lxxxxxx

Friday Dinner Menu – 13 Roundhead Avenue, Wexbury.
Chef: Liv Gordon

Pumpkin and pickled walnut soup with mozzarella toast croutons
Roast partridge in sour pear sauce
Tia-Maria-masu

To be served with two bottles of Haut Médoc '94
For Mother: WI Fig and Peach wine (Sainsbury's estimate six weeks
on Lambrusco Rosé)

From: Lucy Gordon (lucy@widgetex.co.uk)
To: Mo Lavender (Hobo-mobo@Hotmail.com)

10.25
Subject: Greg

I know, I know – you and all at the Cult have been gagging for news of Friday night. I'm sorry for the delay, but I don't have email at home and so you've had to wait until I'm back in the office. Have asked Dad for a computer for Christmas to remedy this, but he said he and Mum were thinking more along the lines of a M and S voucher, so I'm not holding my breath.

Anyway, to the important stuff: Greg behaved impeccably all night, although was in a bit of a grumpy mood to start with. When he came to pick me up, he took one look at my ultra-fashionable new jump-suit and asked me whether I'd had a career change and become a car mechanic. But he soon cheered up when we got to my parents' house. Mum excelled herself with her cooking – not as odd as her usual recipes and very tasty. Greg asked for thirds, which means that Mum is now madly in love with him. Dad was more frosty (the Laphroaig was stashed in the drinks cabinet with a terse sniff of gratitude), but soon thawed out when Greg asked if he'd mind very much showing him the chainsaw he'd heard so much about. They were 'bonding' in Dad's shed for almost an hour, while I helped Mum wash up and listened to her telling me what a charming young man he is. Started to feel very odd and unreal. Am certain Greg is in training to be a model son-in-law. Is this a good or bad thing?

Thankfully Little Sister was out with her friends at an anti-bloodsports fund-raising sleepover (or so she told Mum and Dad – I have a feeling she was up a tree with Scrumpy). And Granny only made a brief appearance from her annexe before the start of *Hetty Wainthropp Investigates* to stare at Greg, pronounce him a 'dead ringer for my third husband at that age' and retreat to her lair once more with the half bottle of claret which was left on the dining-room table. So embarrassing family gaffes were kept to a minimum, and Greg was given an unequivocal 'yes' vote all round.

On the way home, he seemed very pleased with himself – kept saying things like 'I think that went well, don't you Lucy?' and 'I believe I pitched that one well'. I was glowing in a haze of claret and adoration, so didn't notice that he was heading for Chisbourne and not his Wexbury Heights flat until he stopped at the end of my drive, pecked me on the cheek and said, 'I won't come in, darling, as I have an early start tomorrow flying jockeys to Longchamps. I'll be in touch. Wrap up warmly.'

Am now a bit confused. Greg is being so attentive and charming at the moment, but at the same time he is treating me like a favourite elderly relative not a girlfriend. I can't figure it out at all. Can you advise? Lxxxxxx

Birthday card post-marked Vietnam:

Dearest Former Housemates,

They don't celebrate Christmas over here so this will have to do. Not coming home for it as totally boracic and afraid my tan will fade. Off to Cambodia and Laos soon, then back to Bangkok in time for New Year (although have just heard they celebrate it in April, so I may be in for a long wait!).

Hope Santa brings you all you dreamed of. Please, please email me if you get a moment. Dying to know how you all are. Give Mike a big snog from me.

Love, Mo xxxxxxxx

WIDGETEX LTD
Memo
To: Marketing Department, all staff
Re: Christmas

Many thanks to you all for the flowers and cards. I have been told that the injury incurred to my right femur during my landing (a result of a freak gust of wind) will require several more weeks to knit and as such I am not planning to return to the office until the New Year.

May I take this opportunity to wish you all a pleasant festive season. I hope you all enjoy the office party tonight, and must remind you that the photo-copier is strictly out of bounds after last year's unfortunate accident.

Gavin Slater

From: Dave Marks (dave@widgetex.co.uk)
To: Lucy Gordon (lucy@widgetex.co.uk)

13.31
Subject: Frankly, my dear . . .

Have I just spotted you feeding all your personal Christmas cards through the office franking machine, Ms Gordon? Naughty, naughty – taking advantage of poor Gavin's injury. I demand a kiss under the mistletoe tonight to keep your secret.

From: Lucy Gordon (lucy@widgetex.co.uk)
To: Dave Marks (dave@widgetex.co.uk)

13.45
Subject: I don't give a damn.

And I was just counting my blessings that I don't have to pucker up for Slave Driver this year. Last year he was on the Bloody Marys all night and my lips burned for days.

From: Dave Marks (dave@widgetex.co.uk)
To: Lucy Gordon (lucy@widgetex.co.uk)

13.56
Subject: Getting lippy

My lips are already throbbing in anticipation. Can we use tongues?

Christmas list:
Mum – Likes cooking. Recipe books, fish kettle, scented kitchen candles?
Dad – DIY. Something technical-looking from B and Q?

Alice – Grieving trees. Jumper (black), skirt (black) or bag (black)

Jeremy – (Missed posting date for NZ?). 'I love Ewe' inflatable sheep as seen on "TFI Friday" (NB: may necessitate trip to sex shop)

Granny – Alcoholic. Gin, sherry or vodka. All three maybe?

Jane – Still trying to woo Tim. Riding gloves?

Bella – Ultra-fashionable. Jewelled stud for her belly piercing/ eyebrow or nose

Greg – Hmmm. Behaving oddly.

W Microsoft Word – Greg's behaviour.doc

1) Calls every day
2) Takes me out three times a week
3) Compliments me on my appearance, although he has banned my favourite ultra-fashionable jump-suit. (NB: wear it to Christmas party tonight.)
4) Took my hand in a crowded restaurant and told me that I had a smile brighter than all the Christmas lights in Regent Street, yet I distinctly remember him once asking me why I had never been given a brace as a child to straighten out my protruding eye teeth.

Present ideas: None.

From: Lucy Gordon (lucy@widgetex.co.uk)
To: Dave Marks (dave@widgetex.co.uk)

15.45
Subject: Gifts

Hypothetically, what do you really, really want for Christmas?

To: Lucy Gordon (lucy@widgetex.co.uk)
From: Dave Marks (dave@widgetex.co.uk)

15.51
Subject: In my stocking

You

Written (badly) on the back of a Christmas card:

Feel a bit dizzy. Office party a mightnare, I mean nightmare. Think I had a bit too much to drink. Bit preoccupied thinking about Grog, I mean Greg. Downed a lot of lukewarm Chardonnays to take my mind off things. Danced a lot – well lurched really. Got a bit flirty with Ambitious Dave during 'Last Christmas'. Very flirty actually. Will never go into stationery cupboard again without blushing. Help! What have I done?

From: Dave Marks (dave@widgetex.co.uk)
To: Lucy Gordon (lucy@widgetex.co.uk)

09.21
Subject: You supply the time . . .

I can't help noticing that you seem to be running short of paperclips. May I suggest a breakfast meeting in the stationery cupboard to evaluate this situation before it gets critical?

From: Lianne Perkins (lianne@widgetex.co.uk)
To: Wendy Timms (wendy@widgetex.co.uk)

09.45
Subject: Office party.

I hate to be the one to break it to you, but I think Lucy and Dave got it together last night. I know you fancy him. It was you who requested 'Last Christmas', wasn't it? She's such a slut. No wonder she's hiding in the loo. I wonder what that lovely boyfriend of hers would say if he knew?

From: Wendy Timms [ACCOUNTS] (wendy@widgetex.co.uk)
To: All Departments

10.18
Subject: Pilfering

It has been brought to my attention that two members of staff were spotted trying to steal office supplies at last night's Christmas party. Lucy Gordon and Dave Marks were both clearly seen stuffing paper and pens into their clothes in the stationery cupboard. In their greed, they started by removing all outer layers so that they could fill their undergarments with stolen Post-It notes (both having ample room therein to do so).

This email is to name and shame. No further action will be taken. Let this be a lesson to us all.

From: Lucy Gordon (lucy@widgetex.co.uk)
To: Mo Lavender (Hobo-mobo@Hotmail.com)

11.45
Subject: Does the Cult need a new member?

Thanks for your card. Why didn't you mention my emails?

There's only one thing to do at times like this. As I can't get a ticket to 'Nam at such short notice, I'm going shopping. Lxxx

<u>Christmas list:</u> The Final Score
(Queues in Boots = 3 miles

Mum — <u>Likes cooking.</u> ~~Recipe books, fish kettle, scented kitchen candles?~~ Ken Hom Wok set (probably the same one that she took back with receipt last year)

Dad — <u>DIY.</u> ~~Something technical-looking from B and Q?~~ Shed dehumidifier (God knows what that does.)

Alice — <u>Grieving trees.</u> ~~Jumper (black), skirt (black) or bag (black)~~ Novelty Slippers

Jeremy — <u>(Missed posting date for NZ?).</u> ~~'I love Ewe' inflatable sheep as seen on TFI Friday (NB. may necessitate trip to sex shop)~~ Smurf CD (easy to post.)

Granny — <u>Alcoholic.</u> ~~Gin, sherry or vodka. All three maybe?~~ Boots smellies (she can always drink them.)

Jane — <u>Still trying to woo Tim.</u> ~~Riding Gloves?~~ 50 hairnets (I ran out of time, had to queue-jump in Boots as it was. Riders wear them, don't they?)

Bella — <u>Ultra-fashionable.</u> ~~Jewelled stud for her belly piercing/ eyebrow or nose.~~ Alice band with diamanté bits (see above)

Greg — <u>Hmmm. Behaving oddly.</u> Aftershave, jockey shorts, cuddly Gromet flying plane.

Written on the back of Christmas list:

My darling Greg,
The Mazda's car alarm has gone off again and so I can write this without you seeing. I know you are trying to be romantic, but I feel so guilty I can hardly breathe. Everything you do reminds me of my sordid little liaison with Dave last night. Why did you have to get a bottle of Chardonnay and put a "Love Ballads" CD on repeat? I've now had to sit through 'Last Christmas' four times, blushing like a furnace. And I'm almost certain you know something's up, which was why you wanted to know exactly what I have been doing today. I can't get over how oddly you are behaving. When I told you I'd bought your

Christmas present, you went all skittish and told me you'd bought mine too. Then you asked me what I thought it was. I guessed perfume or lingerie, but you laughed and kissed me on the nose, saying 'I don't think I'm giving too much away by saying it has several carrots in it.'

I haven't forgotten that on my birthday, you gave me an eye mask, toothbrush, scented flannel and socks all monogrammed with 'Airs and Graces', the charter company you used to fly for. Cheapskate. What have you got me this time? A huge fluffy donkey toy? A pet rabbit? A can of vegetable soup?

Oh! You're coming back! No time to flush this down the loo.

PS (written while you are asleep): It's a three-carat diamond. Attached to an engagement ring. Now on my finger. Oh God! Happy Christmas. Or is it?

To: Mo Lavender (Hobo-mobo@Hotmail.com)
From: Lucy Gordon (juicylucy@webbedup.net))

16.05
Subject: Laptop dancer!

Happy Christmas!

I have my own laptop. Mum, Dad and Granny all clubbed together and bought me a second-hand one. This is soooo fantastic. Excuse the email address with my old school nickname on it – Dad set that up before I got my hands on the thing and I can't work out how to change it. This will revolutionise our lives. Now all you have to do is REPLY!

SO much to tell you. Have never needed you around more.

Am very confused. I think Greg proposed last night – I have a large ring on my finger to partially prove my theory. But first thing this morning (Christmas Day) he suddenly said that he couldn't make it to my parents' house for lunch after all, and was heading for Yorkshire to see his own family instead.

This took me completely by surprise. 'But I thought we were both travelling there tomorrow to break the news? My parents are expecting us for lunch.'

Greg looked strangely shifty. 'Ah – yes, sorry about that Lucy, darling. I think perhaps we should wait until the New Year to make an announcement – get all the festivities over with first, huh? My parents are very old and a little confused. And after all, it's such a happy time already. There's no need to overegg the Christmas pudding is there? Love you, Bunnykins.'

Hmmph. Can't work him out at all. Burr Cottage felt very lonely at 8 a.m. this morning – Jane and Bella have both gone back to their respective families for a few days, so I was left alone with a tree that's already dropping more needles than Snow White's mum. There was a very paltry selection of presents underneath it – some bubble bath from Jane, a pair of Totes toasties from Bella and Brick, a box of orange Twiglets from Slave Driver and a Spice Girls key-ring from Big Mike (we have an ongoing joke that I look like Sporty, remember?).

Have decided to stay the night in my old bedroom here at Mum and Dad's. Cannot face the prospect of Burr Cottage alone. Don't feel very engaged. Not sure I like it very much. Christmas pudding didn't taste overegged to me.

Oh, I wish you were here! Must post this now as Alice wants me to unplug the modem so that she can call Scrumpy at home (his parents live in a gin palace in Croydon. Can you believe it?).

More soon, I promise. WRITE BACK! Lucy xxx

Christmas Lunch Menu – 13 Roundhead Avenue, Wexbury.
Chef: Liv Gordon

Barbary duck baked in sour apple crust with chilli Calvados dipping
*   sauce*
Lime leaf and polenta stuffing
Suckling pig sausages wrapped with Parma ham
Carrots, parsnips and sprouts à la Malcolm Gordon
Roast organic potatoes à la Alice Gordon

Christmas pudding and brandy butter à la Marks and Spencer

To be served with Mumm Napa Valley, Haut Mèdoc
For Mother: Cava, Tesco's Great With Turkey

Jeremy Gordon   13 Roundhead Avenue
c/o PO Box 2307   Wexbury
Sheep's Eye   Berks
New Zealand

Thursday 25th December

Dear Big Brother,

Notice the difference?!? Am writing this letter – the official
Christmas Day missive – on MY OWN COMPUTER, not
Jane's ancient electric typewriter. Look – **bold**, *italics*, **fonts**,
and other things I don't understand – ⌟ 🏛 ♰ 🖳. This has to
be my best present ever. Of course, having you here with us
would be an even better one, but I know what you said about
seeing Mum and Dad again and, don't worry, I'm not going to
have a go at you this time. I now know that you HAVE to
come back to England for at least one day next year – for my
wedding! Greg has asked me to marry him. No, he wasn't
drunk/on drugs/undergoing torture. You just have to face it,
BB. He's grown up. He has the love of a fantastic and
understanding woman.

Got to Mum and Dad's early – well, quite a bit early actually. I arrived at nine to find them all still in bed, apart from Granny who had unwrapped all her presents from under the tree and was grumbling that the only one containing alcohol was the bottle of scent I gave her. She let me in and offered me a sherry. We watched *Dr Dolittle* together and got a bit tight. Quite good fun actually. When Mum and Dad wandered downstairs in pyjamas, they found us cackling on the sofa like naughty teenagers. Granny says I shouldn't marry Greg. She says pilots are unreliable.

'And I should know, darling – I walked out with several during the war. Dreadful charmers, but utterly free spirits.'

When I told my family the news about Greg's proposal, they weren't as excited about it as I'd imagined. Mum was just a bit cheesed off that she had catered for Greg for lunch and he wasn't there (he had to go to his parents at the last minute), Alice snorted with laughter at my announcement and Dad went very quiet. He wasn't even cheered up by the garden shed dehumidifier I had bought him for Christmas.

Mum cooked a v. odd Christmas lunch. The dipping sauce for the duck was so hot that it made Dad cry. At least he said it was the duck, but Granny had put on her *Vera Lynn's Seasonal Carols* album and he started hiccuping sadly during 'Once in Royal David's City'. By 'Away in a Manger' he was sobbing openly and muttering, 'I can't believe my baby is leaving for ever.' I pointed out that I've lived away from home since I was eighteen, but he would not be consoled and disappeared out to his shed to set up his dehumidifier.

Hope you're pulling a few crackers with the sheep. Will enclose present with this letter – sorry it's late. Thanks for the padded bra. Ha ha.

Love,
Lucy
xxx

Oh God, Mo, what have I done? I'm scared!!!

Am staying with Greg's parents for New Year's Eve. They're a
bit strange. His mum is tall and thin and scary and insists on me
calling her 'Coochie', which is her family nickname. It doesn't
seem appropriate somehow as she looks like John Cleese in
drag. His dad is more approachable, but a bit of a roué. He's just
cornered me in the conservatory with a sherry decanter and a
tray of mince pies. I tried to make polite conversation admiring
Coochie's poinsettias, but I'm not sure he was listening. At one
point he leant across to test the soil in a potted palm and his
nose was almost inside the front of my dress. Greg says that he's
become very eccentric as he's got older and that he gets a little
confused these days. But he's only sixty-three, runs a stock-
broking firm, can do the *Telegraph* crossword in ten minutes and
seems sane enough to me, although he keeps muddling my
name up and calling me 'Frances' which is odd.

Greg is behaving impeccably. So impeccably that it's a bit
boring. We're in separate bedrooms at opposite ends of the
house and the only time he's ventured into mine was to offer me
a hot-water bottle. Feel very homesick.

When we broke the news to the Burtons, they seemed really
unsurprised and Pa Burton said 'But I thought you two were
already engaged?' Later, I asked Greg what he meant and he
explained that he has been talking about asking me to marry him
for months and his father must have assumed he'd done it ages
ago. So lovely.

Greg's two elder brothers are staying – they're very sporty and
arrogant and call me 'Frances' as well. Both are married to very
glamorous blonde women who work in 'media' and have very
quiet, well-behaved wipe-down kids with their own personal

nannies. I'm frightened of them – they remind me of Slave Driver's clan. Greg and his brothers keep dashing off to the pub or the golf course leaving me with the women folk. I think we're all supposed to sit around chatting over coffee and petits fours or something, but Coochie seems to spend every other day in the hairdresser's, and the Blondes are constantly yakking on their mobile phones setting up lunches for the New Year. I felt a bit left out yesterday, so I settled in the hall and called Jane who is staying with her parents near Basborough. She says she and Bella are having a party at Burr Cottage tonight. Hate to admit it, but I wish I were there instead of here. Wish you were there too, as would be perfect excuse to rush home. Oh I know I'm being a wimp. This is my future family after all. Can only tell you how confused I feel because you are thousands of miles away. Of course, my Big Brother is thousands of miles away too, and knows Greg better than anyone, but he has always been so disparaging about our relationship that I want to prove him wrong. Am I doing the right thing? Lxxxx

Ruttingdale Hall
Ruttingdale
N Yorks

Thursday 1st January

Dear Big Brother
DID YOU KNOW ABOUT FRANCES?!?

The Burtons' New Year's Eve party was far grander than I'd realised – half the county seemed to turn up in fancy dress to quaff Kir royale and sing 'Auld Lang Syne'. Something very odd kept happening. The drunker people got, the more they called me 'Frances' instead of Lucy. It became a bit silly in the end. I felt like the second Mrs de Winter being compared to Rebecca. But when I asked one of the Blondes who Frances was, she went very pale and muttered, 'Don't you know? She and Greg were engaged for years. Unfortunate business, her swanning off with his best friend like that. Still, he's got you now.'

Greg has never mentioned her before. I was reeling at the news and went in search of him, but Coochie had turned the radio on and we were all listening to Big Ben ringing midnight. The next moment, Pa Burton had cornered me with a sprig of mistletoe and a leery wink.

I thought YOU were Greg's best friend? Oh God, why can't you be on email or the phone – I need an IMMEDIATE response to this.

Please kick a sheep for me,

Lucy xxx

W Microsoft Word – Lucy's New Year's Resolutions.doc

From: Lucy Gordon (lucy@widgetex.co.uk)
To: Mo Lavender (Hobo-mobo@Hotmail.com)

10.03
Subject: Spring Marketing Budget

Excuse subject. As you may be able to guess, I'm at my desk once more and Slave Driver has returned to the office wearing a plaster cast. We're all trying to persuade him to let us sign it.

It might sound odd, but I am SO relieved to be back at work and back to normality. Staying with Greg's family was terrifying, especially as he hardly talked to me all week. He apologised afterwards and said that they always freak him out and that he hoped he wasn't too frosty while we were staying there. Humph! He was positively arctic, and I told him so, then demanded to know why he hadn't told me about Frances, the woman to whom he was supposedly engaged for 'years'. It wasn't a great moment to pick to ask him, actually, as we were in a service station café alongside the M1 at the time and a small boy at the next table was making farty noises with a straw in his milkshake.

Greg went very quiet, mumbled something about it being a long time ago and then stormed off to buy some Murray Mints from the shop. When we got back in the Mazda he kept the stereo on so loud that we couldn't talk. I wouldn't have minded but he'd put six Rolling Stones CDs in the multi-stacker system, which is based in the boot, so I had to listen to wrinkly Mick wailing for four hours solid.

He's now in Germany flying some industrialist bigwig between cities, and I'm back at my desk contemplating the marketing campaign for our new portable lapel de-fluffer.

Oh dear. Poor Greg. I'm not a very good fiancée. Wasted a lot of today thinking bleak thoughts about him in between catching Ambitious Dave's eye and blushing. Feel so embarrassed about snogging him at the Christmas party, but have to admit he's quite sexy in a thrusting, go-getting way.

Must do some work. Lxxx

Written on Slave Driver's plaster cast:
On calf: Get Well Soon. Best wishes, Wendy Timms
On thigh: *When we said, 'Break A Leg', we didn't mean it literally! Lianne xxx*
On ankle: **Can I have a pay rise? Lucy**
On sole of foot: *Lucy Gordon has the sexiest legs at Widgetex. All best, Dave Marks.*

From: Dave Marks (dave@widgetex.co.uk)
To: Lucy Gordon (lucy@widgetex.co.uk)

11.16
Subject: Stationery Cupboard

Did I just see you emerging from our Love Nest with large marker pen? What could that be for, I wonder? Suggest we go back in together and I advise on uncapping.

From: Lucy Gordon (lucy@widgetex.co.uk)
To: Dave Marks (dave@widgetex.co.uk)

11.35
Subject: Go away

Please stop winking at me from behind the filing cabinet. I have work to do.

Posted on the Burr Cottage fridge:

COW IN CLOVER RESULTS
Weds 6th Jan (score kept by Bella):

Number of times Lucy said 'Greg': 28.
Best quote (before eight Whisky Macs): 'The fact that he wants to marry me shows he loves me, doesn't it?' (After eight Whisky Macs): 'He's been a crap boyfriend all year. He only wanted to marry me after I jumped out of a plane. Why d'you shuppose that ish?'

Number of times Jane said 'He's a bastard Lucy': 6.
Best quote: 'He obviously just wants to marry you to get revenge on this Frances woman. Who is she anyway?'

Number of times Bella intervened to stop a fight: 4.

Best quote: 'Can anyone lend us a wheelbarrow? Lucy's passed out.'

Number of drinks Big Mike bought Lucy: 5.
Best quote: 'Lucy, you can't call Germany on that. It's my bleeper, not a mobile phone.'

RESULT: Lucy = vacuuming and dusting (reduced to just vacuuming after crying in loo). Jane = washing up and bathroom cleaning (plus dusting penalty for selecting 'Tainted Love' on the jukebox). Bella = week off. Mike: carrying Lucy home.

From: Lucy Gordon (juicylucy@webbedup.net)
To: Mo Lavender (Hobo-mobo@Hotmail.com)

20.05
Subject: Hungover

Had to take the morning off work today. I must have been very, very drunk last night because I can't even remember how I got home.

Have just encountered Big Mike limping into his cottage looking a bit peaky. Apparently he's had to go to a chiropractor because he put his back out yesterday. Being a vet must be very physical work. He says that a client of his has several kittens that need homes and would I like one. He thought it might cheer me up, as I'd seemed a bit unhappy last night. He's so sweet! Our new addition is arriving next week. Can't wait!

I know you always wanted us to get a cat, and now that it's happening I miss you more than ever and wish you were here to enjoy him/her.

Have just remembered that Greg is allergic to fur and feathers. Oh well. There's always anti-histamine.

There was a funny, crackling answer-phone message when we got home last night (although I didn't get to hear it until this morning for obvious reasons). None of us could make out a word or who was calling. I think it was Greg ringing from Germany, but Jane's convinced it was you. WHERE ARE YOU!? Lxxx

Burr Cottage
Chisbourne

Sunday 11th January

Dear Big Brother,

No menu today because I didn't go to Mum and Dad's. That is because our kitten has arrived! Big Mike brought her round this afternoon, along with a four-pack of Boddingtons and two packets of nicotine gum (he's given up smoking for New Year).

She's tiny, very fluffy and ginger, with big green eyes and white socks. Even Bella's boyfriend, Brick, has gone totally doe-eyed over her, and he used to play bass guitar with a punk band whose lead singer regularly bit the head off live chickens on-stage. Jane suggested calling her Annie, after the orphan in the musical, but Mike and Brick both started making mock-puking gestures and came up with a series of ridiculous bloke-ish suggestions like 'Spliff' and 'Totty'. In the end I liked Bella's comment that she looked like she was wearing Georgie Girl boots, and she's been christened Platforms, because she's a puss in funky boots. I think it's catchy and unusual, even if the rest of the household twirled their fingers around their temples when I announced it, suggesting I've gone barking mad. Or should that be meowing mad?

When she first arrived, Platforms sniffed everything in sight and puffed up like a Flump every time something frightened her. When the video clicked on to record some old war film Greg has asked me to tape for him, she jumped a foot in the air and ran up Brick's trouser leg, ginger tail poking out like a jaunty sock tassel. Then she re-emerged, pummelled the corner of the sofa with her back feet and conked out on a cushion. This nearly spelled an untimely end as she's so small that Big

Mike didn't see her when he lumbered in with a can of Boddington's Draught and he almost sat down on top of her. He joked that we'd have to rename her Flatform. For a vet, he can be very callous. I blame the fact he's so twitchy from packing in the weed.

You still have not written to explain the Frances thing, or congratulating Greg and me. I know the postal service out there is slow, but I cannot believe that it's taken you this long. Mum has taken this as a sure sign that you have had a fatal accident with a tractor and are, as I write, lying in a remote Kiwi ditch gasping your last. Of course, I know that you have a TERRIBLE SECRET. If you don't tell me, I'm going to raid the Roundhead Avenue attic and rip up your *Viz* collection 86–94, including the annuals.

Please apologise to that sheep you kicked on my behalf.

Lucy xxxx

'Hi, you've got through to Jane, Lucy and Bella. We can't take your call right now so please leave a message after the tone. If you're calling to book an appointment with Jane's Driving School, please call 07776 5553078.' Beeep.

'Jane, it's Lucy. Pick up the phone. I know you're there. Jane . . . ? Oh God, maybe you're not there. It's Platforms, isn't it? She's ill – had an accident – stopped breathing. Oh Christ, I –'

'I'm here.'

'Thank God! Why is the machine on?

'Because you've called three times already to check on that precious cat and it's not yet ten. It's my day off, I'm lying in bed trying to catch up on the Sunday papers and I DO NOT want to be disturbed again.'

'Where's Platforms? You mean you're not keeping an eye on her? She might have got out. She might –'

'Platforms is in bed too. Shredding up the Sunday papers.'

'Ah! How sweet.'

'Hmm. Well if that's all, Lucy, then I –'

'Hang on! Dave's hovering again. I have to pretend you're a client or he'll find another ridiculous excuse to stoop over my desk for a chat.'

'What? Oh for God's sake, Lucy. You don't care about the cat at all, do you? Every time you see that cretin approach, you pluck up the phone and speed-dial the Burr Cottage number before shooting him an apologetic "on an urgent call" look, don't you?'

'Not exactly. He's now taken to e-mailing me every ten minutes with lewd suggestions of things we could do in the stationery cupboard.'

'So tell him where to stick his paperclips.'

'I can't! He and Slave Driver are very close. Besides, he has very sexy eyes. Oh dear, I promised myself I wouldn't think about him like that. I'm practically a married woman, after all.'

'Face it, Lucy. Your fiancé hasn't been in the same time-zone since the 5th. You can do whatever you like. Take my advice – run to that stationery cupboard and drape your knickers over the foolscap.'

Written on the back of a phone bill:

My darling Greg,

We were supposed to be going out to dinner tonight, but you're stuck in Stuttgart with a faulty fuel injector or something, so have stayed in and played with Platforms instead. She's so sweet, and has this way of falling asleep in front of the fire with her white paws folded neatly over one another like toasting marshmallows. I can't wait for you to meet her. Despite your allergy, I know you will be kitten-smitten.

Popped out into the garden with her as part of 'toilet training' mission earlier and caught Big Mike having a sly cigarette on other side of the fence. He looked very guilty and threw it into his ornamental pond. I asked him why he bothered to sneak a cigarette outside when he lives alone and he said it was a psychological thing, making him feel as though he's a non-smoker.

If I only eye up Ambitious Dave when you are out of the country, does that make me a non-flirt?

Hurry home. We need to talk. No need to destroy this letter as you are not around to find it and, besides, we haven't paid the bill yet. Jane likes to calculate precisely what everyone owes down to the second. She keeps whingeing about my modem racking up the cost, although I have pointed out that she was the one who surfed the Internet for three hours just after Christmas, looking for the best site to download the "White Horses" theme tune. Stupid waste as I saw it on a television theme tune CD in Woollies for £2.99.

I love you. Lucy xxx

WIDGETEX LTD
Memo
To: Lucy Gordon
Re: Recent work

Congratulations on the success of the electric tooth flosser campaign. I am not unaware of the contribution Dave Marks has played towards the impressive product/client interface you achieved. Dave himself has pointed out how well you two work together and, as such, I plan to pair you up again in future. I must, however, advise caution in regards to internal office dynamics on an intense duo-lateral basis, however effective the combined energy. They must be tempered with caution and professionalism at all times. I'm certain you get my meaning.

   Gavin Slater

WIDGETEX LTD
Memo
To: Hop-along Slave Driver Esq
Re:

What do you mean by product/client interface? That I used the flosser before kissing Dave in the stationery cupboard at the office party? Do you know my shameful secret? Sometimes I wish you'd speak English. Still, you seem happy with my work, which is a good thing. Can I have a pay rise? On second thoughts, I might not send this. Am in too much of a hurry to rush home and tart up for dinner with Greg, who's back from Stuttgart.

The Office Trollop

Written on the back of a Stuttgart Hilton laundry bill:

My Darling Greg,

You are asleep, and look so handsome that my heart is having difficulty fitting in my chest. I don't know why I got so worked up when you were away. You haven't changed.

You insisted that I drive here to your Wexbury Heights flat, because you're allergic to cats. This was actually a good thing, because I was determined to have a quiet chat about 'us'. But as soon as I brought the subject up, you started sneezing violently, and complained that there must be cat fluff on my clothes. Then you started removing them and I rather lost the thread. All my threads, in fact.

I now feel deliciously loved and luscious. You are perfect. I can't wait to marry you.

Am going to hide this under my pillow and flush it down the loo in the morning because last time you woke up and asked me if I had cystitis again.

Note on Greg's pillow:

L. I've gone out to play football. Your clothes are in the washing machine with my shirts. Could you iron those while you're about it? Will be going to pub with lads later, but you're welcome to hang around. Flat could do with a lick and polish if you get bored. G.

Note on Greg's – dusty – sideboard.

Darling G,

When you put my clothes in your machine, you accidentally boil-washed the red angora sweater I got from Granny for Christmas. The colour has run into all your shirts, I'm afraid. No time to iron as Jane has just called saying that there's been some sort of crisis involving my sister and the hunt, so I have to go home.

Love you, L.

PS: Loo is a bit blocked.

Cutting from *Wexbury Gazette*:

Hunt runs into trouble in pub car park

A fracas broke out last weekend when the West Berks Hunt came into conflict with angry protesters at a meet taking place in the car park of the Cow in Clover, Chisbourne. Local riding instructor and assistant field master, Tim Thomas, claims he was attacked by three 'crazed' hunt saboteurs. He was later questioned by police when his horse reared up and injured one of the protesters, who was taken to Wexbury General hospital suffering from minor cuts and bruises.

Protesters Alice Gordon and Carl Rutter, who calls himself 'Scrumpy', were unrepentant. 'They are all murderers,' said Rutter, 29. 'Foxes have rights too.'

The third protester maintains that she is unconnected with the others and had actually attended the meet to support the field. Speaking from Wexbury hospital A and E department, Jane Redven, 24, a resident of Chisbourne said: 'This has all been a terrible mistake. The police thought that I was with Alice and Scrumpy because I know them. I am teaching Alice to drive, but I support hunting. It's a great British sport. Tim Thomas has been my riding instructor for eight years.'

The police are not pressing charges, although the MFH, Rodney Thackery, plans to pursue Ms Redven through the small courts for damages incurred to his Range Rover when she fell on it.

From: Lucy Gordon (juicylucy@webbedup.net)
To: Mo Lavender (Hobo-mobo@Hotmail.com)

20.30
Subject: Horsing around

I have bought myself a scanner this week (am hoping to get it past Wendy from Accounts, but I don't hold out much hope). Attached is a cutting you may find amusing. The picture was taken by an amateur and so is a bit blurry – Jane's the one under the horse, Alice is holding the placard, Scrumpy has tattoos on his face and you can only see Tim's legs (nice thighs though, I hope you agree).

Jane is hugely embarrassed that everyone in the village now thinks she's a protester, and is worried that Horsy Tim will never talk to her again. 'Don't you think your sister owes me an apology?' she huffed afterwards.

I admitted that I didn't really, because I think fox-hunting is cruel. Jane has now sulkily announced that not only is she cancelling all the rest of Alice's driving lessons, but she will no longer feed Platforms while I'm at work.

Not that this will make much difference. Platforms – who is a gorgeous orange bundle of fluff – seems to have doubled in size in less than a week. If she continues to grow at this mutant rate, she'll get stuck in the cat flap before she's fully house-trained. Every time I take her outside to avail herself of the flower beds, I encounter Big Mike smoking a cigarette in his garden. He still thinks he's given up. We've had some quite long chats. He seems very interested in Greg and the engagement. I think he's angling for the job of usher or something.

I'm going to keep this short because I have no idea if you're alive or not. Lxx

hunt.gif attachment here

Sunday Lunch Menu – 13 Roundhead Avenue, Wexbury.
Chef: Liv Gordon

Deep-fried artichoke hearts with vermouth and lime sauce
Broiled whole aubergines with reduced sherry jus, served with garlic
  crust turnip chips
Grape, brandy snap and mascarpone trifle (flambéed)

To be accompanied by: Kent Collective Organic Red
For Mother: Litre of Lambrusco Rosé

Burr Cottage
Chisbourne

Sunday 18th January

Dear Big Brother,

Yes. It *was* revolting, but Alice liked it, as it was vegetarian and consequently made a change from her weekly bean burger. When I told her that Jane has cancelled all their driving lessons, she went very pale, 'But my test is next week!' Then her face lit up and she said, 'Greg could give me some lessons, couldn't he?' Oh God.

64

Will have to finish this letter next week as Jane wants to use the Internet to research slander laws. She says the Wexbury Gazette has ruined her career (see attached article).

Sunday Lunch Menu – 13 Roundhead Avenue, Wexbury.
Chef: Liv Gordon

Black pudding and tripe terrine
Pan-fried veal in ham-stock sauce accompanied by a light salsa
  marmalade
Suet pudding

To be accompanied by Bulls Blood
For Mother: Lambrusco Rosé

Letter continued . . .
Sunday 25th January

There is a reason for Mum's sudden change in culinary style, and it's not the retro bloodthirsty old-world food craze sweeping through the London restaurant scene. Alice reversed Dad's car over the Pottingers' carefully nurtured snowdrop bed yesterday afternoon and decapitated their stone angel. The Pottingers have still not forgiven Dad for almost flattening their conservatory when his chainsaw broke half-way through the trunk of their diseased lime, so the slaughter of the snowdrops is another black mark against the Gordons; he's now convinced that we'll feature in the next series of *Neighbours From Hell*. Alice can't persuade Dad to give her any more driving lessons, nor Greg and I, but she's somehow bribed Granny to take her out this afternoon in her ancient Triumph Dolomite. They were last seen kangaroo-hopping towards Tesco's in first gear, with Granny shouting out of the window, 'So lovely to be chauffeured again – reminds me of my days overseas.'

Afterwards, Greg turned to Mum and said, 'I had no idea Violet lived in the Colonies at one time?' To which Mum gave him a withering look and muttered, 'She's talking about the Saga package tour of Jersey she went on last year.'

I think Mum's in a bad mood with Greg because he refused seconds of her latest recipe – chilli and okra 'salsa marmalade' (sounds like a Motown dance craze). I hardly blame him, as it was so hot one of my contact lenses popped out into the sticky rice, but Mum gets very offended if her cooking fails to impress. She keeps looking at us both with a curious glint in her eye. Warn the sheep.

Love,

Lucy xx

You have . . . one . . . new message. Message received on . . . Monday at . . . ten . . . thirteen . . . ayy emmmm.

'Lucy, it's your mother. Just thought you'd like to know that Alice ploughed through all the crocuses on the Tesco's mini roundabout and then collided with a shopping trolley yesterday. Granny didn't notice at all. When your father went to collect them, she was far more irritated that the supermarket had just closed so she couldn't buy a bottle of sherry and a scratch-card.

Now the reason I'm calling is because I have decided that I should do all the catering at the wedding. Could you pop around this week to talk menus? I know Greg's tastes are somewhat . . . um . . . conservative, but I'm hoping we can both talk him around to a little Salmon Teriyaki. What do you think? Call me when you get in from work.

From: Lucy Gordon (juicylucy@webbedup.net)
To: Mo Lavender (Hobo-mobo@Hotmail.com)

21.15
Subject: Menu Love

Mum is coming around with wedding catering ideas tomorrow morning, even though I've told her that it might be a very long engagement. Oh God, I really have to sort this thing out. I'm not sure I want to marry Greg, especially as he refuses to tell me anything about his mysterious ex, Frances, to whom he was apparently engaged for ages.

At least I've not been distracted by Ambitious Dave, who's been skiing in France all this week.

Have just had long chat with Big Mike over the garden hedge. He was lighting one cigarette from the other. I pointed out that he wasn't doing too well in his attempts to kick the habit, but he says that he has yet to smoke inside the house. I have a feeling he'll end up living in the garden shed at this rate. I told him about my sister terrorising Tesco's when Granny let her drive her there in the Dolomite. He laughed and said, 'You're so different, you and your sister – she's so headstrong, whereas you are gentle and passive.' We proceeded to have v. long and interesting chat about sibling rivalry. Big Mike is the eldest of five brothers – can you imagine? I had no idea.

Not sure I like being gentle and passive, though. It sounds a bit wimpish. When I went inside afterwards, I decided to be more headstrong. Found Jane in the kitchen eating one of my mini Tiramisu pots and smiling at me strangely.

'I thought you were taking Platforms outside for toilet training?' she asked.

'I was!' I said, eyeing the pot with what I hoped was headstrong criticism.

'So why's she still asleep on the boiler?' Jane pointed out.

Thankfully the phone rang at that moment. It was Greg from Birmingham. I was so determined to be headstrong by now that I hardly said hello, just waded in with, 'Tell me about Frances?'

There was a curious fizzing on the line (which sounded suspiciously as though the receiver was being rubbed against a suede jacket) and the line went dead. Maybe it won't be such a long engagement after all. Lxxx

---

Menu plans for wedding reception of Lucy Gordon and Greg Burton.
Chef: Liv Gordon

Need to know:
EDN (Estimated date of nuptials) – consult LG
EB (Estimated budget) – consult MG
EGT (Estimated guest total) – consult LG/GB
EVC/GI/H/K (Estimated vegetarian count/gluten intolerant/
  halal/kosher) – consult LG/AG

Menu Plan 1 – Sit Down
Assuming EDN this Summer, EB >£5k, EGT <100, EVC etc =
  1 (Alice)

*

Radicchio Risotto

Or

Smoked Squid with Japanese cucumber and seaweed salad
*

Poached pigeon breast with mango, cumin and sour cherry chilli marmalade

Or

Noisettes of Lamb with Caper and Lettuce Aïoli
Above served with selection of vegetable tempura in sesame crust
*

Boiled pistachio and mincemeat pudding with sticky caramel cream
Summer Lovin' Puddin' (made with rhubarb, gooseberry and redcurrant)
*

Coffee and petits fours
*

Recommended wines: Veuve Clicquot Champagne, Mâcon-Villages or Chablis
(white), Chateauneuf du Pape or Grand Cru St Emilion (red), Monbazillac
(dessert) Vintage port. For Mother: Lambrusco Rosé.

Menu Plan 2 – Cold Fork Buffet
Assuming EDN this Autumn, EB >£5k, EGT >100, EVC =1 (Alice)
*
Tronchon of Dressed Smoked Eel
(Quince and Thai Basil Dressing)
*
Braised Belly of Pork
(Sage, Pink Peppercorn and Crab Apple Chutney)
*
Turkey, Partridge and White Strawberry Pie
*
Green Fig and Brazil Nut Poached Chicken
With a Curried Courgette Flower Mayonnaise
*
Chickpea and Rum Stilton Quiche
*
Selection of Freshly Baked Bread Rolls
*
Spinach and Dandelion Leaf Salad with Raspberry Vinaigrette
Celeriac and Pickled Ginger Coleslaw
Couscous, Parmesan and Deep-fried Oyster Salad
Penne tossed with Sun Dried Tomatoes, Olives and Marmite
*
Bread and Butter Bavarois served on a throne of Cointreau Clotted Cream
Apricot Frangipan Profiteroles with Blueberry and Guava Compote
Selection of Cheeses

Written on the back of a Wedding Menu Plan:

I need to have emotional mother-to-daughter chat about the state of my relationship with Greg, the mysterious Frances, and the fact that I'm strangely attracted to Ambitious Dave at Widgetex, but Bella and Brick have now wandered into the kitchen wearing towels and complaining that Platforms has just wriggled underneath their duvet at an inopportune moment. Oh great – here's Jane in her dressing-gown, grumbling that there's no breakfast cereal left. I don't believe it! Mum is rising to the challenge and set to perform a "Ready, Steady Cook" miracle with a frying pan, three eggs and half a loaf of stale bread.

I don't want to marry Greg
I don't want to marry Greg
I don't want to marry Greg

Top Table – Bridesmaid, Greg's Dad, Dad, Me, Greg, Mum . . . (Bella was looking over my shoulder there)

I don't want to marry Greg
I don't want to marry Greg
Ha ha! Brick was so impressed with Mum's fry-up that he told her she was a 'Top Dog Cook, mate'. I don't think Mum realised this was a compliment. She's just left, grumbling about the feckless youth of today lounging around in their nightclothes at midday.

Pasted on the Burr Cottage fridge:

> *Lucy,*
> *If your cat mistakes my germinating herb seedlings for her litter tray one more time, then I will personally stuff her with parsley and serve her up at your wedding buffet (given your mother's menu plans, no one will know the difference).*
> *Jane*

Written on the back of a squash court booking form.

> *My darling Greg,*
> *Tonight, you took me to the new Florida Rib Shack in Wexbury. It's jolly hard to have a serious talk with face and fingers covered with sticky barbecue sauce, plus background music so loud that the table rocked along in time. Nevertheless, I tackled you head-on about my worries. I demanded to know why you wanted to get married when you hardly ever have time to see me, and why you hadn't told me that you'd been engaged before.*

You couldn't answer at first because a waiter in a baseball cap came up to read the list of dessert specials, which lasted about half an hour. Then you looked at me with a strange, tearful expression (I think your eyes were watering as a result of your Hot Thing Chilli Burger). I felt so guilty when you said that you had no idea I was harbouring so many doubts and did I want to call it all off and break your heart? That threw me. I'm not sure whether it was the prospect of losing you, or just the fact that I'd drunk three glasses of Californian Shiraz, but I found myself clutching your hand across the laminated cocktail list in its plastic holder and apologising for being so silly and suspicious. Why am I such a wimp?

Am going to feed this into the waste disposal unit as my last letter wouldn't flush – it just floated. When I stuffed half a loo roll on top to try to make it go down, the U-bend got blocked.

I do love you. I think.

Burr Cottage
Chisbourne

Sunday 1st February

Dear Big Brother,

Thank you for the With Sympathy card. Ha ha. You say that you never met Frances, but that doesn't really answer my question. And of course I've asked Greg, but I think whatever happened really hurt him as he refuses to talk about it.

You'll be pleased to learn that he's gone into prospective son-in-law overdrive. This morning, he took Alice out for a driving lesson (in my car), and delivered her back to the parental home in time to accompany Dad to an agricultural auction near Swindon. They came back with a 1950's oil-fired generator and a big box full of rusty scythes and secateurs, which they fiddled with in Dad's shed all afternoon like a pair of schoolboys with a new Gameboy. When they came in for lunch, Greg couldn't eulogise enough about Mum's flash-fried kangaroo steaks. He was being so co-operative that I wouldn't have been surprised if he'd offered to take Granny to the British Legion for a couple of gin slings before *Antiques Roadshow*, but he just looked at me lovingly before announcing to the family that we'd be setting a date in the very near future.

Of course this makes me very happy. You see, he must be over Frances.

Practise your Best Man's speech on the sheep.

Love,

Lucy xxxx

From: Lucy Gordon (juicylucy@webbedup.net)
To: Mo Lavender (Hobo-mobo@Hotmail.com)

22.05
Subject: Panic attack

Aghhhhh, aghhh, aghhhh! Greg is being so repulsive and creepy and smug and unctuous. My family LOVE him. Even my father is now trying out the odd tentative 'son' at the end of sentences. I feel trapped. Help, help, help!!!! Lxxx

---

You have . . . one . . . new message. Message received . . . on Tuesday . . . at . . . seven nineteen . . . pee emmmm.
'Yeah, Lucy babes. S'me Alice. I thought you'd like to know I've passed my driving test, no thanks to Jane. Is that her voice on the outgoing message? Sounds bloody miserable. Anyway, can I borrow your car on Saturday night to go to a party in Swindon? Granny's Dolomite's still at the body shop and Dad won't let me near the Volvo, but your banger's a bit of a heap, isn't it? Not that I'll hurt it. Statistically women who have just passed their tests are the safest drivers. Please? It's not like you'll need it in Yorkshire. Mum says Greg's taking you up to his parents to talk about the wedding, so

72

your car will just be sitting in the drive, won't it? I'll fill it up with petrol.'

From: Lucy Gordon (juicylucy@webbedup.net)
To: Mo Lavender (Hobo-mobo@Hotmail.com)

20.55
Subject: an in-law unto themselves

Oh God, why did I agree to go North on Friday to talk weddings with Greg's parents? They scared me rigid at New Year, but Greg assures me that they think I'm 'gorgeous'. I'll miss darling Platforms while I'm away.

I don't think writing to you, oh incommunicado friend, is doing enough to offload my secret panic. In fact I think I've just committed a major *faux pas*. I met Big Mike by the wheely-bins this evening and, when he said that I was looking a bit distracted, I ended up blurting the fact that I don't feel the same way about Greg now that we're engaged and that he won't talk about Frances. Then I confessed that I have a crush on Ambitious Dave at Widgetex, and told him about the stationery cupboard before Christmas.

I think Mike was a bit shocked at my outburst. He spent a lot of time rearranging back copies of *Veterinary Weekly* in his recycling crate and clearing his throat. Eventually he mumbled, 'If you ask me, you don't sound as though you want to get married at all, Lucy.' And then he dashed inside his cottage. Most odd. I now feel really embarrassed as we've only ever been casually friendly in that way neighbours are – chatting about the state of number 15's fence, borrowing the odd pint of milk or piece of gardening equipment, sharing the occasional chummy drink in the Cow in Clover. Now I've dumped all my problems on him – and all because he innocently pointed out that I'd put three full bottles of wine and a vase in my recycling crate.

Jane says that, being a vet, Big Mike can only offer advice about

73

animal husbandry and is therefore the wrong person to talk to.

'So who should I talk to?' I asked.

'The Samaritans?' she suggested helpfully before racing out to her riding lesson with Horsey Tim.

This is all my fault. Having argued how happy I am to be getting married with my housemates, family and friends, I have now persuaded everyone that Greg and I are the Renee and Renata of West Berkshire. The only person who no longer believes it is me. And now poor Big Mike, who would far rather stick to lancing the odd hamster abscess. Lx.

From: Dave Marks (dave@widgetex.co.uk)
To: Lucy Gordon (lucy@widgetex.co.uk)

12.16
Subject: Lunch

Are you free?

From: Lucy Gordon (lucy@widgetex.co.uk)
To: Dave Marks (dave@widgetex.co.uk)

12.18
Subject: Re: Lunch

I don't have time.

From: Dave Marks (dave@widgetex.co.uk)
To: Lucy Gordon (lucy@widgetex.co.uk)

12.23
Subject: Re: Re: Lunch

When I say lunch, I don't mean sloping out to a quiet country pub far from the Widgetex office for a romantic tryst, alas. I'm off to

M and S to get a triple BLT. I'll treat you. Do you fancy a Big Sausage Filler?!? We can pop open the plastic casing together back at the office . . . in the Stationery Cupboard, maybe?

From: Lucy Gordon (lucy@widgetex.co.uk)
To: Dave Marks (dave@widgetex.co.uk)

12.35
Subject: Re: Re: Re: Lunch

Tuna Salad, no mayo and NO innuendo.

From: Dave Marks (dave@widgetex.co.uk)
To: Lucy Gordon (lucy@widgetex.co.uk)

12.39
Subject: Re: Re: Re: Re: Lunch

Are you sure Tuna Salad is wise? Don't forget the last time you ate one at your desk and a piece of sweetcorn lodged between d, s and e on your keyboard? Don't you have to type the Deeply Delicious Dental Flosser copy this afternoon? Wouldn't you prefer a Big Sausage?

From: Lucy Gordon (lucy@widgetex.co.uk)
To: Dave Marks (dave@widgetex.co.uk)

12.45
Subject: Re: Re: Re: Re: Re: Lunch

Tuna Salad, no mayo and no sweetcorn.

From: Dave Marks (dave@widgetex.co.uk)
To: Lucy Gordon (lucy@widgetex.co.uk)

13.45
Subject: Lunch

You owe me £1.69 for sandwich, and £10.99 dry-cleaning. Why the Hell did you do that?

From: Lucy Gordon (lucy@widgetex.co.uk)
To: Dave Marks (dave@widgetex.co.uk)

13.50
Subject: Sorry

I really am sorry that your suit is ruined. But I thought that we'd worked past the SC incident. Then, when you said that I was the most exciting thing to happen to novelty gadgets since the Ann Summers catalogue I realised that I had to tell you the truth. I'm engaged to be married, Dave. I don't wear my ring to the office because it snags my tights.

From: Lucy Gordon (lucy@widgetex.co.uk)
To: Dave Marks (dave@widgetex.co.uk)

14.06
Subject: Double sorry

Dave, are you okay? I can't help noticing your expression. I'm really sorry that I've hurt you so much. It was all my fault and I'm deeply ashamed of myself. I had no idea that you felt so strongly and that you would be this upset.

The truth is that I'm not convinced I should be getting married at all. And I am strongly attracted to you. Perhaps far too strongly. Can we talk about this over a drink maybe? Or dinner?

From: Dave Marks (dave@widgetex.co.uk)
To: Lucy Gordon (lucy@widgetex.co.uk)

14.23
Subject:

Tights. TIGHTS???!!! Ugh! I'm a stockings man.
    Shouldn't have wasted my time. Your fiancé's welcome to you, Miss Twenty Denier Re-inforced Gusset.

Ruttingdale Hall
Ruttingdale
North Yorks

Friday 13th February (AGHHH!)

Dear Big Brother,

Greg drove here so fast that I still have an impression of the Mazda's headrest upholstery pattern indented on the back of my neck. This time his six CD stacker was lined up with back-to-back Aerosmith to entertain us during the journey. I think my eardrums have slackened like a pair of tea strainers. We arrived at his parents' house an hour and a half before we were expected. Coochie was out at her beauty salon and Pa Burton was practising golf strokes on the front lawn. When I climbed out of the car, a white ball flew past at ear-level, threatening my hearing yet further.

'Frances, my darling!' He bounded forwards and hugged me so tightly that his five iron got stuck up my jumper. 'You look like a new woman.'

'I should do,' I muttered, shooting Greg a dirty look. 'I'm Lucy.'

'Easy mistake,' he squeezed my bottom. 'You really are rather similar. But you're far prettier, my dear.'

I wanted to tackle Greg about this straight away, but he raced upstairs for a shower, leaving my bags on the spare bed.

When Coochie returned from having her cuticles aromatherapy massaged and her roots tinted, she cornered me in the conservatory and said that she refused to let my mother do the catering at the wedding.

'I know a little woman who does wonderful things with canapés,' she announced loftily. 'You must tell Mummy that she needn't worry about the cost. Bernard and I will pay.'

'But Mum likes cooking,' I spluttered.

'Nonsense!' She patted my cheek and winked. 'Greg's told me that your parents might be a little embarrassed financially, so you mustn't feel you have to cover up for them. You're part of our family too now, Lucy. By the way, there are ten of us for dinner tonight.'

Furiously cornered Greg in his bedroom and demanded to know what he'd been saying about my parents. 'I know Dad isn't a Rothschild, but he's not Pa Steptoe either!'

Greg was far more concerned that he was wearing nothing but a towel and that his mother might see us together.

'But we're engaged now!' I stormed. 'And while I'm on the subject of engagements, just how long ago did you and Frances break up?'

He couldn't answer, because Coochie appeared in the door, turned purple with disapproval and announced that the dinner guests had arrived.

So we sat down to eat with a couple of golfing chums of Pa Burton's and their wives, one of Greg's honking brothers and his blonde PR executive 'partner', and a lovely couple whose names I didn't catch because my hearing is still impaired from Aerosmith. He's a farmer, and very dishy. She's a former model – quite ravishing and very, very funny. I liked her straight away, and she had me in stitches describing life as a farmer's wife.

Greg very loving. Kept blowing me kisses across table, filling my glass and calling me 'the future Mrs Burton'. Feel a bit tight now, and very special. Am sitting up in the spare bed wishing

Greg would join me. Have just slipped a Valentine's card under his door, but think he must be sleeping, as there was no response when I knocked.

So you see, all your worries are unfounded. Greg is treating me impeccably and I couldn't be happier. Honest.

Exchange a high five with the sheep.

Love,

Lucy xx

Darling Greg,

Be My Valentine.

Aisle be yours!
Love,
                    ?

From: Lucy Gordon (juicylucy@webbedup.net)
To: Mo Lavender (Hobo-mobo@Hotmail.com)

21.07
Subject: In the Enemy's Camp

I'm here, and it's AWFUL! I have only just realised what a fool I have made of myself.

No Valentine's card from Greg when I got up this morning. He and his father had already left to play golf.

Found Coochie in the kitchen, nursing hangover. We thawed to one another a little. Over M and S truffles, she admitted that Greg's father can be 'a bit of a sod at times'. I said it might run in the family, and that I had to know who Frances was before I exploded with frustration. Coochie looked at me in amazement. 'But you met her last night, darling.'

She was at a dinner party . . . here . . . in the parental home of the man she almost married. What's worse, she's an EX MODEL, Mo. And she acted like she and Greg were just old friends, not exes. They all did, especially her husband who even told me what a 'great bloke' Greg is. What is up with these people? When I said to Coochie that they seemed remarkably unbothered, she said, 'Why should we? We all love Frances', and then she accused me of being 'suburban'. Hmph.

I want to go home. Dearly tempted to call Alice and demand that she drive my car up here to fetch me, but I know I've got to stick it out, if nothing else to prove that I'm not 'suburban'. Lxxx

Written on the back of the Berkshire Wedding Directory list:

My darling Greg,

We have just had an epic talk, although it was slightly odd that you insisted on keeping the television on and pretending it was an ordinary video-and-takeaway night, which it clearly wasn't. The 'Talk' started during "TFI Friday" and lasted until the end of "Frasier" when you paused to call our order through to the Shanghai Hut – exhausting, but very informative. It turns out that your ex, Frances, is now married to your old schoolfriend, Bradley, who is a venison farmer. I can't believe they both came to dinner at your parents' house last weekend without me knowing a thing about it. I feel such a fool, especially as I talked weddings with Frances for at least half an hour – even telling her my worries about Mum doing the catering. She recommended a fork buffet.

'How can you still be friends with them?' I asked you after you'd told me the full gory story of your best friend running off with your fiancée just weeks before the wedding. 'After what they've done to you?'

'Frances and Coochie get on very well,' you said simply. 'Besides which, Bradley's a nice bloke.' Then you went out to fetch two sweet and

sour chow meins and Mars Attacks. I don't really understand the situation at all, nor do I know where it leaves us. When you came back, you said you didn't want to talk about it any more. We just watched the video and I snapped one of my chopsticks in frustration.

I love you. I am going to bury this amongst the take-out bags. The waste disposal makes too much noise.

From: Lucy Gordon (juicylucy@webbedup.net)
To: Mo Lavender (Hobo-mobo@Hotmail.com)

22.18
Subject: Feeling touchy on the touch line

I haven't been able to get Greg to talk about the Frances thing much – every time I try he clams up. I was so eager to pursue the topic that I even agreed to go and watch him play football yesterday, but the only person I ended up chatting to was the girlfriend of one of the centre forwards – a hairdresser called Dawn who told me I needed my roots doing and offered me a discount.

'Are you really getting married to Greg?' she asked, sounding surprised.

'Well we're engaged,' I hedged.

'That's so brilliant – you must have tamed him at long last,' she winked. 'My Nev always said Greg plays the field far too well to marry.'

'Well, he is a very good striker,' I beamed proudly.

'No,' she giggled. 'I mean all those girls. I heard his last fiancée couldn't take it any more and left him.' What does she mean? I cornered Greg about this later in the pub, but he'd had several lagers and didn't seem to understand. He just patted me on the bottom, winked and sauntered off for a game of billiards with one of the defenders. He's flown to Scandinavia this evening, leaving me hugely confused.

Had long talk about it all with Jane tonight. She thinks that

Greg was probably so unfaithful to Frances that she decided not to marry him and to opt for someone safer like Bradley the farmer. 'Country types are much more reliable and loving than slick go-getters like Greg,' she sighed, thinking about Horsy Tim no doubt.

'Greg has never been unfaithful to me!' I huffed. 'I'd know if he had.'

'Does he know you snogged Dave Marks in the stationery cupboard at the Christmas party?'

I had to concede she had a point. Oh God, I think Greg has probably been laughing at me all along. He must think I'm so gullible. Thank God he's going away to Finland until next weekend. It gives me time to think. What am I going to do? Lx

---

W Microsoft Word – Lucy's blooming.doc

Yippee! A huge bunch of red roses has just been delivered to me. The entire office was prairie-dogging their progress through the desks as the florist carried them to me. Ambitious Dave gave me a particularly dirty look over his partition. The attached message is just SO SEXY. My only niggling worry is that I'm certain Greg told me he was going to be away in Scandinavia until next week.

Note posted on the Burr Cottage fridge:

REDECORATION.

Team co-ordinator/designer = Bella
Stripping = Jane and Brick
Filling and sanding = Alice (in return for loan of Lucy's car).
Painting = Lucy and Mike
General carpentry and labour = the members of Slug
Wear casual clothes. Bring a bottle.

From: Lucy Gordon (juicylucy@webbedup.net)
To: Mo Lavender (Hobo-mobo@Hotmail.com)

09.55
Subject: Changing Rooms

Had terrible shock when I walked downstairs this morning to find
dust-sheets all over the furniture and the kitchen full of burly men
swigging sweet tea from mugs. It turns out Bella has decided we
need to completely redecorate the downstairs of the cottage.
She is very organised, enlisting the help of Brick and his band,
Slug – plus my little sister and Scrumpy, and Big Mike from next
door. The plan is to do it all in twenty-four hours. 'There are so
many room make-over programmes on the TV,' she said. 'I
thought it'd be a good laugh to try it ourselves.'

I agreed that it sounded fun, but Jane was less sure when she
surfaced to find the drummer from Slug munching his way
through her Pop Tarts. 'Why didn't you warn us?' she asked
Bella. 'I've got lessons booked all afternoon.' Then she spotted
the lime-green metallic paint that Scrumpy had started slapping
on the banisters, and muttered. 'I can guess why.'

Bella is using the CAD program (which I always thought was
something to do with playboys) on my laptop to redesign the
entire downstairs, so I'll be able to send you email updates
throughout the day.

12.05
I've been helping Alice and Big Mike paint the floorboards of the
dining room – glossy aquamarine. We're going to scuff it later,
apparently. Not quite sure what that means. I'm quite relieved
that Jane has gone out to teach driving lessons, as Bella's colour
scheme is pretty unconventional. Jane's taste, as you know, is
more *Country Living*/Laura Ashley. I must admit, even I have my
doubts about the orange and purple fake-fur sofa covers, but
Bella tells me they're very Conran.

14.13

Dining-room floor took longer than expected and is too wet for scuffing, so we're all trapped in the sitting room stippling the shocking-pink walls; Bella insists bright colours give positive feng shui. Big Mike is now wearing dark glasses.

16.48

Dining-room floor still impassable, and Bella has yet to start on *trompe-l'oeil* wall murals of Las Vegas scenes. She's getting a bit stressed. We've run out of teabags, biscuits and lime-green metallic paint. Alice and Scrumpy were sent out for supplies (in my car) over an hour ago, but have yet to return. Hope they're okay. My laptop is now splodged all over with pink paint.

18.23

Jane has just come in and hit the roof. Admittedly, the place is looking a bit of a mess – especially as the members of Slug have got bored of stippling and are now swigging beer in front of *Ice Warriors* with their feet up on paint cans.

'I can't live with this!' she screeched when she saw the cerise walls. 'I'll get retinal burn-out.' Then she stormed into the dining room to fetch herself a sherry and got stuck to the floor.

Laptop now striped with purple and orange too.

20.27

Brick had four correct Lottery numbers tonight and has taken all the members of Slug – plus Jane – to the Cow in Clover. Bella furious. The dining room is finally passable, but is proving tough to 'scuff'. Big Mike and I have been on our knees for hours with Brillo pads, but the floor paint is some chip-resistant industrial stuff that was left over from the St Cuthbert's art department refit and was designed to stop teenagers daubing it with graffiti. Still no sign of Alice and Scrumpy, or my car.

23.12

Still scuffing. Am exhausted, although it's been fun chatting to Mike. Slug have just come back from pub and are drunkenly trying to help paint Las Vegas *trompe-l'oeil*. Elvis looks like John Prescott. Bella is in tears; Jane in bed. No sign of Alice.

03.06
Still scuffing. I'm sure it's never this hard on *Changing Rooms*. Big Mike asleep on fake-fur sofa with Platforms on his lap. Looks sweet. So does Platforms.

11.56 (next day)
Have had three hours' sleep. Downstairs looks awful. Bella says she'll buy us all a pub lunch to make up for things going so wrong. Alice called earlier to say my car ran out of petrol somewhere near Bath. Dad has gone to fetch it. I'll kill her.

16.08
Have just come back from The Long Barge at Aldersford via B and Q and bought a job-lot of white emulsion. Brick is going to stay at cottage this week and cover up *trompe-l'oeil*/cerise. The sofa covers are now next door, lining Big Mike's dogs' beds. Sadly, I think the aquamarine floor gloss is here to stay. L xxx

---

W Microsoft Word – Lucy's wilting.doc

The roses on my desk have well and truly died. I must throw them out before I go home tonight. I've cut the stems down so much in an attempt to keep them alive that most of the heads have disappeared into the top of the vase. I've re-read the message a hundred times and I still don't understand what Greg meant – 'Let's turn over some new sheets this weekend.' But he's been overseas, working in Scandinavia; I spent last weekend redecorating the cottage with Bella and her army of helpers. All I've heard of Greg in the past week is two short answer-phone messages and a postcard of a reindeer which read 'Looking forward to the rutting season.'

From: Lucy Gordon (juicylucy@webbedup.net)
To: Mo Lavender (Hobo-mobo@Hotmail.com)

19.55
Subject: Homecoming

Greg has just called to say that he's flying back from Finland tomorrow evening. Yippee! He's asked me to pop into his flat and check that it's clean and tidy. Plan to do it tomorrow afternoon and then seductively await his arrival in his bed. Jane says that's hopelessly wet – especially as I agreed to go to the Cow in Clover with her, Bella and Big Mike, but I don't care. Some things take priority and I need to show that I've missed him, despite the Frances thing. I'm going to turn back some clean sheets too – and place myself underneath them for good measure.

I've scanned in some photos of the redecorated cottage to frighten you (taken before Brick covered everything in white). Have given up asking you to write back. L xxx

burr1.gif attachment here
burr2.gif attachment here
burr3.gif attachment here

Written on the back of a gym subscription renewal:

My darling Greg,

Still no sign of you. Feel a bit of an idiot sitting here in your bed wearing nothing but my engagement ring and a fading smile on a Friday night, when I could be in the pub with my friends. Hmmph. Have tried your mobile a few times, but it's switched off so you must be airborne somewhere.

Midnight: What if you've crashed? Oh God.

2.15 a.m.: Have been polishing your squash trophies while watching the all-night BBC news channel on satellite, and there are no reports of a

light aircraft crash over the North Sea. The weather reports are all v. positive, too. Feel a bit better. Might just keep an eye on the news and dust all your CDs ...

'You're listening to Radio UK Global, coming to you twenty-four hours a day. From the heart of England straight into your hearts. And now, with the 3 a.m. world weather report, here is Liesel Washington.'

'Thank you, Peter. Unusually warm throughout Europe tonight, with the Benelux countries and Scandinavia experiencing unseasonal highs as the warm front moves through Northern Europe. Further East, there is little change ...'

You have ... two ... new messages. First message received ... yesterday ... at ... seven ... twenty-six pee emmmm.

'Lucy, darling. It's Greg. I'm ice-bound in Helsinki. You would not believe how cold it is here. Don't bother to go around to my flat, I shan't be back until tomorrow night at the earliest.'

... Second message received ... yesterday ... at ... ten ... thirty-two ... pee emmmmm.

'Hello you lot ... it's me! Mo! Christ, I might have guessed I save together my precious cents and you're all out. I'm in Sydney! It's a beautiful sunny morning. Listen. Have I given you the wrong email address or something? Shit, I'm running out of cash. It's hobo – H-O-B-O – dash – moj—' *Beep.*

Posted on the Burr Cottage fridge:

COW JN CLOVER RESULTS

Friday 6th March (score kept by Bella):
Absentee: Lucy (Excuse: too busy Jiffing Greg's kitchen surfaces)

Number of times Jane said 'paint effects': 9.
Best quote: 'J had to wear dark glasses on Monday to stop my eyes watering, but J kept falling over the furniture.'

Number of times Bella apologised: 41.
Best quote: 'J took inspiration for my design from a box of Quality Street. J should have guessed Chisbourne was more Ferrero Rocher.'

Number of times Big Mike mentioned Lucy's absence: 7.
Best quote. 'Of course J didn't mind lending you my dust-sheets. J was telling a friend only last week that it's about time J turned over a new one.'

RESULT: Lucy = Jiffing all surfaces (as she is so keen).
Jane = week off. Bella = vacuuming, dusting, washing up, bathroom, bins.

W Microsoft Word – Lucy's pennies and petals have just dropped.doc

Oh God. Were my flowers from Big Mike, not Greg? I can hardly pop next door and casually ask him if he had a dozen red roses delivered to my office with an anonymous note, can I? What does he think he's playing at? I'm practically a married woman, even though my fiancé is skating on thin Finnish ice.

WIDGETEX LTD
Employee Holiday

April	15–29 Gavin Slater
May	01–17 Dave Marks
	01–17 Wendy Timms
	20–27 Gavin Slater
June	04–19 Lianne Perkins
July	03–10 Gavin Slater
August	

From: Lucy Gordon (lucy@widgetex.co.uk)
To: Mo Lavender (hobo-moj@Hotmail.com)

16.25
Subject: We got your message!

I HAVE been emailing you, oh beloved friend, but I was using the wrong address. Now I have the right one, we are IN BUSINESS!

I'm at work, so can't write much (more later on laptop, I promise). Must let you know that all is well at Burr Cottage, and we have a ginger cat and Greg and I are getting married. Apart from that no change.

Everyone in the marketing department is leafing through travel agents' brochures and talking about which fortnight they want to book off work this summer. Had sneaky peek at the holiday list this morning and noticed that Ambitious Dave has booked same week off as Wendy from Accounts. Can this be a coincidence? The office gossip is that they are now an item, having been spotted dining *à deux* in Café Blanc on two consecutive nights, but surely it's early days to be planning a holiday together? I'm engaged to my boyfriend and have yet to bring the subject up. Nor have we dined *à deux* for weeks. Come to that, he hasn't been in the same time-zone as me for ten days. He called me from Brussels this morning.

'But I thought you were ice-bound in Helsinki,' I wailed on hearing that he'd be away at least another five days.

'It melted,' he said cheerfully. 'And I got a last-minute job flying MEPs between here and Germany. The money's fantastic.'

Slave Driver caught me surfing the Internet for holiday destinations this lunchtime and asked whether I was looking for a suitable spot to honeymoon with Greg.

'No,' I muttered darkly. 'Just wondering where he is right now.'

So excited that I can contact you at last. Write back soonest! Lxxxx

---

From: Email Post Master (Server@host.com)
To: Lucy Gordon (lucy@widgetex.co.uk)

Subject: Invalid email address
16.36

The following message was rejected (error 345x.5653.SMT/b-yu9) = 'Invalid email address'
Please check the recipient's details.
Post Master

Message reads as: **We Got Your Message!** > > >

Wexbury Veterinary Practice,
Glebe House, Chisbourne Road, Wexbury, Berks
Telephone: 01555 658300   Fax: 01555 658830

Dear *Platforms Gordon,*

Your owner asked us to notify you when you are old enough to be neutered. We have checked our records and found that this is now possible. Please could you request that *Ms Lucy Gordon* makes an appointment to bring you in to see *Mr Michael Ensor* FRCVS at her earliest convenience?

Kind Regards,

Reception

From: Lucy Gordon (juicylucy@webbedup.net)
To: Mo Lavender (Hobo-mobo@Hotmail.com)

09.45
Subject: Email muddle

Okay, Brick (who is surprisingly techy having played computer games for years) says that this MUST be your correct address after all, because my emails don't get rejected as they do with the other address. I must have heard your phone message wrong. He says that some email addresses – especially those ones that people use to pick up family news from Internet cafés whilst travelling like you – are read-only and that is why you cannot write back. Perhaps you could send a postcard or something instead? I'm dying to hear from you. I'm not even sure if you know that I'm getting married. Some time. Maybe. To Greg.

So much has happened:

Platforms the ginger kitten is now so hefty that Bella has cruelly nicknamed her 'Geri'. She no longer needs me to accompany her into the garden for toilet training, which is something of a relief as Big Mike is still smoking heavily outside his back door. She is, however, due to be spayed this week. Have asked both Bella and Jane whether they can take her to the surgery, but they claim to be too busy. I suppose I shall have to finally face Mike who I think sent me a bunch of roses with an anonymous note.

Jane is hugely excited because Horsy Tim has asked her out on a date at last. They're going to the Café Blanc on Thursday night. 'So romantic,' she sighed dreamily.

'Popular choice,' I muttered, wondering privately whether Horsy Tim should show a little more originality. L xxx

---

W **Microsoft Word – Lucy's lightfooted.doc**

Poor Platforms has been under the knife this afternoon – I took her into the surgery during my lunch-break. When I went home to collect her, Big Mike's car was in his drive, and I bolted into Burr Cottage like a burglar. A cat burglar.

Written on the back of a veterinary bill:

My darling Greg,

Welcome back! And thank you for the perfect timing. You rolled up at Burr Cottage carrying a vast box of Belgian choccies just as I was about to set out to collect Platforms. I was secretly SO relieved when you refused to come with me to the surgery, because of your cat allergy. This meant I had an excuse to beg Jane to do it for me and thus avoid Mike. 'You can have as many chocolates as you like,' I bribed her. She's in such a good mood after her date that she agreed without grumbling once, although she did point out that the chocolates you had given me had an M and S price-tag on them, which is odd.

I didn't have time to dwell on this, however, as you then insisted on whisking me straight out to drinks, then dinner at Café Blanc.

'It's the last day of their "eat for a fiver a head" promotion,' you explained, and then told me all about Brussels in such boring detail that you sounded as though you'd swallowed a Berlitz guide. But I can forgive you, because I was very excited by your sudden interest in sightseeing (I know you don't normally leave the airport lounges if you can help it). But when I brought up the subject of summer holidays, you muttered something vague about saving for the wedding.

I was about to mention that you'd just boasted about earning lots of money in Belgium, but at that point I noticed a couple sitting nearby and almost choked on my moules marinière. Two tables from us, Big Mike

was gazing at an unknown petite blonde across a carnation-in-a-Perrier-bottle. He was holding her hand.

What was even weirder was that you went as white as a sheet too. You couldn't wait to race me back here and ravish me, even though I was looking forward to my crème brûlée. Oh God, I have a feeling that not only do you know about Dave, but also that Mike is — might be — sniffing around me. I almost suspect that you've not been in Brussels at all, but here all the time, in hiding, watching my every move.

WIDGETEX LIMITED
Memo
To: Lucy Gordon
Re: March out of March and Spring into Spring Campaign
May I draw your attention to the Spring-Loaded Hit List, which my secretary placed on your desk first thing this morning? I would suggest that this may prove a more productive use of your (wo)man hours than playing card games on your computer.
   Gavin Slater

WIDGETEX LIMITED
Memo
To: Gavin Slater
Re: Time management
I fully appreciate that you do not approve of advances in technology and the 'surplus energy time' that they take up in employees' working hours. I would, however, like to point out that the purpose of the program Solitaire is to improve the user's mouse skills. Mine are, I would estimate, 20 per cent below optimum speed and so the short tutorial that you saw me taking while you were at the photo-copier, was in fact a personal initiative to improve my productivity. I

am fully up-to-date with the Spring-Loaded initiative, and actually in possession of two copies of the list, since Dave Marks shaped his into an aerial office-traversing device in order to speed it onto my desk. As soon as I have finished work on the Collar and Cuff Defluff promotion it will be top priority.

Lucy Gordon

From: Lucy Gordon (juicylucy@webbedup.net)
To: Mo Lavender (Hobo-mobo@Hotmail.com)

21.49
Subject: Another party you're missing

We're having a small St Patrick's Day party in the cottage – canned Guinness and Bella's homemade soda bread cooked to her grandmother's recipe. All very jolly, although the bread is the texture of ceiling plaster. Jane says she invited Big Mike around, but he's busy. I wonder whether he's with the mysterious blonde whose hand he was holding at the Café Blanc last Friday night? Am certain I know her from somewhere. L xxx

---

Burr Cottage
Chisbourne

Weds 18th March

Dear Big Brother,

Sorry I haven't written for ages – I've been really busy being wined and dined by Greg, who has been behaving a bit oddly since he came back from Belgium, especially when he spotted my neighbour wining and dining a mysterious blonde.

Forced to take today off work as a result of food poisoning. It must have been Bella's cooking for our St Patrick's Day

94

party. Had no idea soda bread could be so dangerous. Jane, Bella and I were up all night groaning, clutching our stomachs and fighting over the Andrew's Salts. Feel a lot better now, but cannot face Slave Driver this afternoon so am bunking off. I called Greg to let him know I had experienced close shave with death. He laughed and suggested that Bella had used caustic soda by mistake. Not exactly sympathetic. He's not flying this week, so I was hoping to see more of him, but he claims he has a lot of paperwork to catch up on.

Platforms is behaving very oddly – keeps dashing around the cottage with her tail bushed and attacking the bottom of the stairs. Might have to take her to see Big Mike in case she has food poisoning too. Hope he pops back for lunch.

3 p.m.: No sign of life next door. Phoned Mum to tell her about poisoned soda bread, but her saffron mayonnaise was at a critical stage and she merely murmured, 'I recommend self-raising flour, darling. By the way, I bumped into Sylvia Mackenzie this morning, and she's convinced she spotted Greg in Paris last week.'

'She can't have!' I laughed. 'He was in Belgium.'

'That's what I told Sylvia – he bought you some chocolates back, didn't he?' Mum said and then screamed because the mayonnaise had split.

8 p.m.: Greg's mobile is switched off now. Have located the Belgian chocolates he brought back for me, and Jane was right when she joked that they were bought in M and S. Platforms is still running dementedly around the cottage; I heard Big Mike's Land Rover pull up a few minutes ago, so I might just take her around to be looked over.

8.10 p.m.: So embarrassing! Big Mike examined Platforms in his kitchen and asked me to describe her symptoms in greater detail. When I did, he gave me a sad smile and said she was behaving like any normal, exuberant kitten at that age. 'She's just bored,' he said. 'She wants you to pay her more attention.'

'Poor Platforms,' I sighed, thinking about Greg. I know just how she feels.

I could hear soft music coming from Mike's sitting room which I thought was the television, but the next moment a small blonde head popped around the door and asked whether he was going to be long. 'Oh hello there,' she saw me. 'It's Lucy isn't it?'

I *knew* I recognised her. It's the dim receptionist who lives above Greg – the one who looks like Baby Spice. Big Mike cleared his throat awkwardly and introduced us – she's called Peach (what sort of name is that?). 'Mike's such a darling, isn't he?' she giggled. 'My pet iguana Tyson's had sticky claw. Mike took him in while I was on holiday and has been looking after him ever since.' I asked her where she'd been. Somehow I knew she was going to say, 'Paris'.

I'll finish this letter after the weekend, and hope to have some better news then. I don't want to send it until I have a full explanation of what Greg's been up to. I know you'll think the worst and I'm sure there's a perfectly simple reason behind it all. Besides, I'm sure you'll want to know all about Sunday at Mum and Dad's (!). I've offered to take them all out, but Mum is cooking a specially-themed lunch for Granny Violet.

Sunday Lunch Menu (Mother's Day) – 13 Roundhead Avenue, Wexbury.
Chef: Liv Gordon

Vol-à-violet
Ultra-violets. Flash-fried shiitake and puy lentil rostis in sour lime and squid ink purée
Frosted violets on a jellied pear brûlée

To be served with Pinot Grigio, 97
For Mother: Lambrusco Rosé (2 Bottles)

Letter continued:
I think Granny was quite keen on the idea of eating out once she realised what was on the menu – especially as dessert played havoc with her bridge work.

Mum's daughters proved a lot less thoughtful to her than she was to Granny. I'd popped into a garage on my way to the house to buy a box of Just Brazils, plus the least horrific of the clashing flower bouquets. Alice gave her a Peruvian nose flute and half a bottle of sherry, which mysteriously disappeared when Granny went back into her annexe to catch the end of the rugby match. I don't think Mum had a very good day on reflection. Must try and make up for it in future.

I haven't tried to find out any more about whether Greg was in Paris last week, or Brussels as he said. I have decided that I should trust him. He is going to be my husband after all. Please don't send any more rude postcards about him.

Be nice to the sheep – it's more than you've been to your sister or so-called 'best mate'.

Lucy

xxxx

From: Lucy Gordon (juicylucy@webbedup.net)
To: Mo Lavender (Hobo-mobo@Hotmail.com)

19.37
Subject: Does my breath smell?

Big Mike has just called round to ask if any of us fancied going to the Cow in Clover tonight as he's at a loose end. Bella is stuck into a video about post-modernist artists and Jane has gone out with Horsy Tim, so I'm the only one free. But as soon as I said yes to the offer – thinking that I could grill him on his friend and Greg's over-flirtatious neighbour Peach – he remembered that he had to make some calls at home and hastily retracted the offer. I don't understand what's got into him – only a few days ago I was convinced that he'd sent me flowers and was keeping a low profile, now he seems to be the one avoiding *me*. I blame the loathsome Peach with her big baby eyes and sickly reptiles. When she's not flirting with my boyfriend in the Wexbury Heights lift, she's flashing her iguanas at poor, besotted Mike.

Greg is visiting his parents in Yorkshire, but comes back tomorrow before flying to Düsseldorf. Can't wait to see him. The map of Europe I keep inside my wardrobe to track his progress is now so covered with pins, it looks like a hedgehog. I told him on the phone last week that Mum's friend Sylvia was convinced she spotted him in Paris (the city from which Peach has just returned), although he'd told me he was in Belgium. But Greg simply laughed and said that he must have a double. Then he pointed out that he'd brought me chocolates back from Belgium, not France.

'But they were M and S ones!' I muttered huffily.

'Didn't you like them?' He sounded terribly hurt. 'They have a Marks and Spencers in Brussels. I was pushed for time, darling, but I wanted to buy you a gift that's as sweet and soft-centred as you are.' At that point the second half of the football match he was watching started and the conversation ended as quickly as a paused CD. He can be infuriatingly selfish about sport – even if he does say the loveliest things during half-time.

Am not totally sure that I *do* believe him, however. I know there are M and S's in France because the labels are in two languages, but does that mean they have them in Belgium too? L xxx

---

International Directory Enquiries, what name please . . . ? Marks and Spencers where, did you say? Brussels? One moment . . . No, I'm afraid we have no listing there. I have checked thoroughly, madam. Under St Michael's? One moment . . . No, nothing under that, either, although there is a St Michel church. Yes, I can assure you that our lists are comprehensive and up to date. Very well, I'll have to transfer you to National Directory Enquiries for that. One moment . . .'

Collar and Cuff Defluff – Exploring International Markets

1) Europe

Slave Driver has just caught me calling the press office of M and S trying to find out whether they have a store in Brussels. When he demanded to know what I was doing I had to make up a hasty lie about product research for the new Cuff Defluff campaign. 'I hear they are particularly obsessed with sartorial smoothness in Belgium!' I announced brightly. He looked slightly bewildered at first, but then nodded and patted me on the shoulder. 'Good work, Lucy. I like to see staff grasping the initiative.' Phew. Am going to cook romantic meal at Greg's flat tonight to see him off to Düsseldorf. Might have a sneaky look to see whether his balcony has fire-ladder access to Peach's. Don't think I'll recreate Mum's Ultra-Violet lunch. Nor will peaches feature for dessert. Actually, think I'll just go to M and S for ready meal . . .

The Tenants	Laurence Starling Property Management
Burr Cottage	High Street
Hart's Leap Lane	Wexbury
Chisbourne	Berks
Wexbury	
Berks	

1st April

Dear Tenants,

I am writing to confirm that your residential contract has not been renewed. As you may note on your Assured Short Hold Tenancy Agreement, this contract runs out three days from the time of writing. As you have not contacted us within the specified three month notice period to renew your agreement, we require that you vacate the premises on or before 3rd April.

The new leaseholders, The Redeye Animal Laboratory, are planning to move in as soon as the property is vacant. They have asked us to emphasise the importance of adhering to the specified dates so that three hundred mice, twenty-five cats, seven beagles and a monkey will not be inconvenienced. Should you have household pets that you are unable to relocate, they are happy to take on the responsibility.

Kind regards,

Ron Starling

'You've called Greg's mobile. Leave a message.' Beep.
'Ha ha! I spotted the Dusseldorf post-mark, you rat. Brick's band is playing next weekend. I've said we'll both go. Hope that's okay. Bella's getting us both VIP back-stage passes, so we'll feel like celebs. I love you.'

WIDGETEX LIMITED
Memo
To: All members of staff
Re: Name Change
From now on, our director of marketing, Gavin Slater, would like to be known as Cynthia Slater. This in no way alters his/her position within the company. We would be grateful if you respect his/her wishes and make as little fuss about this as possible. Any disparaging or bigoted reaction to this change will be looked upon very seriously indeed.
The Management

W Microsoft Word – CCD/F5.doc

Collar and Cuff Defluff – Exploring International Markets

2) South East Asia

Christ, the office is murder. Someone has swapped the male and female loo signs around, several pound coins are glued to the linoleum floor of the canteen, and Ambitious Dave has managed to network a faked photograph of my head superimposed on Pamela Anderson's body onto every computer in the office, claiming it was a snapshot from my last summer holiday. I know I should be mad, but actually I thought it looked rather good. Wendy from Accounts has just given me a v. dirty look in the Ladies (or was it the Gents?).

Asphyxia (Supported by SLUG)

Playing at Basborough Civic Hall 4th April
Ticket Hotline: 01555 235000

Written on the back of an Asphyxia flyer:

My darling Greg,
I'm so sorry I ruined your good coming-home mood, especially as you bet a 'monkey each way' – whatever that is – on the Grand National winner today. And I was so thrilled when you suggested we spend your winnings on romantic Easter break next weekend. Yippee!
But it wasn't really my fault that we were late, was it? You were the one who suddenly decided that a YSL polo shirt wasn't right for a rock

concert and started searching through your wardrobe for the denim shirt you bought in Canada six years ago.

By the time we got there, Slug had almost finished their supporting set and the hard-core Asphyxia fans were hurling beer bottles on stage to try and get them off. I felt so sorry for Brick — even though he did look terrifying wearing an undone strait-jacket, with his blue hair punked up in devil's horns to look like Keith from the Prodigy. Bella says he was really hurt that the audience failed to appreciate Slug's music, although from what I heard it seemed to consist of one droning guitar chord, a deafening drum machine, three synthesisers cat-wailing and screaming lyrics about dead junkies. When we went back-stage, our OIP passes allowed us into a sweaty neon-lit dressing-room heaving with bearded roadies and depressed members of Slug. The only refreshments on offer were bottles of warm lager and some curling ham sandwiches covered with cigarette ash. I've never seen you look so disappointed.

I know you couldn't stand Asphyxia (whose lead singer sounded as though he was suffering just that), so I really don't mind that we left early and went for a Chinese meal. I'm almost sure that, as we walked out through the deafening mêlée, I spotted my sister and Scrumpy head-banging at the front. I suddenly feel rather old and boring for preferring Celine Dion.

I'm going to burn this on your fake-log fire. I love you.

Sunday Lunch Menu — 13 Roundhead Avenue, Wexbury.
Chef: Liv Gordon.

Calves liver and goose neck pâté marinated in honey and almond
    vinegar
Tuna loin served extra-rare with nasturtium sauce
Lemon curd and lychee soup

To be accompanied by a bottle of Gaillac perlé
For Mother: Litre of Lambrusco Rosé

Sunday 5th April

Dear Big Brother,

Dad's old workshop in the garden was so full of machinery that he kept catching his beer gut on sharp implements, so he's bought a new wooden extension for 'safety reasons'. He told Mum it was just a 'small additional lean-to' when he ordered it from Sheds-R-Us, but it turns out to be the size of a small bungalow with glass windows, mains electricity and a phone extension. She's furious that it's completely obliterated her herb bed and casts a huge shadow on her favourite, temperamental clematis. Apparently the Pottingers have already called it an eye-sore and are threatening to complain to the council. But Dad is delighted, and has been pottering around inside it labelling shelves and drawing lines around his tools since dawn. He couldn't even be coaxed inside for lunch – I took him out his tuna on a tray in the end. He used it to demonstrate his new industrial shredder.

Alice says that Brick's band, Slug weren't a patch on Asphyxia at a concert the other night, and that Brick looked like a mad budgerigar with his hair peaked up, although she thought his strait-jacket was 'quite cool'. Then she added casually, 'Are he and Bella really serious about one another?' When I said I thought they were, she stormed up to her room in a sulk. I think Scrumpy has a rival in her affection.

I'm not going to even mention Greg after your last rude postcard.

Suggest you ask the sheep what it's like being a higher life form.

Love,

Lucy xxx

Written on the back of a *Guide To Walking In The Dales*:

My darling Greg,

When you said that you were going to take me away for a romantic break over Easter, I imagined you were thinking of Paris, Venice or Barcelona. Not somewhere in England. Not Yorkshire. And certainly not a few miles from your parents' house.

You noticed that I was a bit grumpy when you broke the news last night, but you consoled me with descriptions of idyllic moors, woods, streams and beautiful stone houses miles from anywhere; a place to be pampered and recharged. I envisaged a huge country house hotel dripping with antique furniture and oak panelling, stag-heads looming from every wall, chambermaids whisking silently past with piles of fluffy towels or trays laid with silver tea services, cucumber sandwiches and cakes. I imagined that hidden beyond all this antiquated charm there would be a modern gym, pool and sauna, a treatment room where I could be pumiced and pummelled, clay-wrapped and waxed. In fact I got quite excited at the prospect and even had a sly look through your desk while you were in the bath to see if I could find a brochure for our bucolic haven, but only found lots of flight log sheets and – strangely – a Paris restaurant guide.

So here we are in a small keeper's cottage on the edge of a hunting estate somewhere near Hawes. No chambermaids, saunas or aromatherapists in sight, although there is a very ugly stag's head mounted over the downstairs' loo cistern. You say the place belongs to some friends of yours. The fridge is full of beer, which you think is a 'terrific gesture'. In fact, you're already half-way down your third can of draught Boddingtons. I'm clearly expected to cook tonight – a romantic meal for two, which we can eat in front of an open fire. I'm probably expected to light that too. Feel so mad, I'm tempted to use your underpants as tinder. There isn't even a phone-point for me to send an email to my crap-friend-who-never-answers on the other side of the world.

I am going to use this letter to start the fire instead of your pants,
since you're wearing those and may misconstrue the gesture if I try to
remove them. I'm not sure if I love you very much at the moment.

From: Lucy Gordon (juicylucy@webbedup.net)
To: Mo Lavender (Hobo-mobo@Hotmail.com)

22.18
Subject: We're all going on a . . . !

Having a lovely romantic break with Greg (yes, really!). He's in the bath. I'm going to have to send this later because I can't connect the modem here, but there's no telly so I thought I'd write you a few lines. Greg thinks it's a bit weird that I take my laptop everywhere with me, but I've managed to persuade him that it's because I am such a high-flying executive these days that I have to work every free moment.

Despite the fact that the local walking guide had curiously gone missing, today we hiked for miles through the Dales. Well, jogged really; Greg has decided that he's not fit enough and that we should both start training together.

'Training for what?' I panted as I fought to keep up with him.

'For summer – do you want to look like a King Edward potato wearing a bikini when we go on holiday?'

Consequently didn't see much scenery today, as vision started to blur with fatigue after three miles. Am now convinced that I have the figure of a Tellytubby. Feel so paranoid that I rejected the sexy little mini-dress I'd packed for tonight and wore baggy trousers and a long jumper instead. We ate out in a country pub called The Poacher. I had a small tuna salad. Feel famished, but also excited after long chat with Greg about summer holidays. He thinks it might be fun to get a party of us together and rent out a villa in Tuscany – Jane, Bella, Brick and some friends of his too. God, I hope you can come!!!! It would be so great to see you and

105

it might fit in with you working your way back to the UK (I know you said you were going away for two years, but surely you want to catch up with us/your family, etc.). It's really not worth bothering to visit my brother in New Zealand. He lives in a very boring part – it's flat and wet and there's nothing to do except count sheep.

Oh! Greg's shouting for a towel. Must dash.

Easter Sunday, Ruttingdale Hall:
I ache all over today. Managed to eat practically nothing during Sunday lunch with Greg's parents and his brothers, plus their cool blonde wives and obedient children. Greg's mother, Coochie, had hidden Easter eggs around the garden, but both daughters-in-law announced that the children weren't allowed chocolate, and that their nannies were going to help them decorate free-range hen's eggs instead. I was so hungry that I was tempted to go and hunt out the chocolate myself, but then I spotted the Burtons' Labrador munching through one in the shrubbery and decided against it.

Pa Burton tried to play footsie with me during lunch, and then gave me a lewd Dick Emery wink and asked whether I was enjoying my stay in Keeper's Cottage. 'Good of Bradley and Frances to lend it to you while they're in Barbados, huh?' So we're staying in a cottage belonging to Greg's ex-fiancée and her husband. I can barely believe it. I wouldn't be at all surprised if Greg suggests that they come with us to Tuscany. If he does, then I'm going to invite Big Mike and Ambitious Dave.

Can send this at last – Coochie's very accommodating about my laptop and thinks that I'm 'fritefully jet-set'. Too right. L xxx

From: Lucy Gordon (lucy@widgetex.co.uk)
To: Mo Lavender (Hobo-mobo@Hotmail.com)

15.56
Subject: Desk duty

So many people have taken the week off work after the Easter break that the office is almost deserted. Slave Driver is in Mauritius with Mrs SD (apparently the poor little SDs have been farmed out to stay with a granny in Surbiton). Rosy the lovely new receptionist is in Malaga, so we have a temp – a university student called Camilla. She's so posh that whenever she answers the phone, she says, 'May I help you?' in a sort of duck quack. She's also incredibly blonde and fresh-faced, so Ambitious Dave has been prowling around the reception console like a teenage joyrider eyeing up an Escort XR3i. Consequently his new squeeze – Wendy from Accounts – is in a huge sulk and huffily refused to sign his latest expenses form, which includes a three-hundred pounds claim for 'miscellaneous'. I was wandering past his desk at lunchtime when she steamed in and demanded to know precisely what he was claiming for. He cleared his throat and muttered 'Liverpool' in a sexy undertone, to which she suddenly giggled, winked and signed the form on the spot. When they saw me nearby, they both turned scarlet.

I have a feeling something dubious is going on. L xxx

From: Dave Marks (dave@widgetex.co.uk)
To: Lucy Gordon (luoy@widgetex.co.uk)

16.23
Subject: Cuff Defluff

As you know I am deputising in Gavin's absence. I have just glanced at the Cuff Defluff promotional layouts, and I find that they are far from satisfactory. As such, I must insist that you redesign them all by the end of the day.

From: Lucy Gordon (lucy@widgetex.co.uk)
To: Dave Marks (dave@widgetex.co.uk)

16.28
Subject: Re: Cuff Defluff

I cannot possibly redesign all the layouts in one and a half hours.

From: Dave Marks (dave@widgetex.co.uk)
To: Lucy Gordon (lucy@widgetex.co.uk)

16.31
Subject: Re: Re: Cuff Defluff

I think you'll find that you can, and you will, stay on at the office until they are done. I'm sorry if this inconveniences any arrangements you may have made to meet your jet-setting fiancé, but WORK COMES FIRST.

From: Lucy Gordon (lucy@widgetex.co.uk)
To: Mo Lavender (Hobo-mobo@Hotmail.com)

11.16
Subject: Fraud!

Have just had coffee break with Marlene the Moose, the ancient battle-axe who rules the stationery cupboard with a rod of iron and requires you to fill in three forms if you need so much as a paperclip. I normally avoid her like the plague, but she's very pally with Wendy from Accounts and I was dying to know if she could spill some light on the mysterious Liverpool claim. I didn't want to arouse her suspicions, so I subtly asked whether she knew how Wendy was getting on with Dave.

'Famously – I expect we'll hear wedding bells soon,' she told me, crumbling a Digestive into a cup of dish-water tea. 'He took her to see the Grand National a couple of weeks back. Ever so romantic, it was. They stayed in the Adelphi. You know – where that documentary was filmed. Wendy says she got the function manager's autograph.'

'How thrilling – they could have their reception there.' I narrowed my eyes, realising that Ambitious Dave is filing dodgy expenses claims.

'Oh, I'm sorry, Lucy,' she suddenly gave me a sympathetic look. 'You have a bit of a soft spot for him, don't you?' She then nudged me knowingly. 'That gorgeous fiancé of yours playing you up, is he?' Damn! I forgot that she knows all about my grope with Dave in the stationery cupboard before Christmas. How awful. She probably now thinks I'm pining for him. I haughtily told her that Greg was more than man enough for me, but I don't think she's convinced.

Slave Driver is away for a fortnight, worse luck, so I have to put up with Dave throwing his weight around next week too. Have managed to keep him at arm's length today by deliberately pulling my tights up above my skirt waistband so that he is forced to see them at all times. (My reinforced gusset once saved me from his pre-Wendy lust and is now a vital power tool.) Plan to wear American Tan ones on Monday with lots of wrinkled seam poking out of open-toed sandals. Hope it does the trick. L xxx

From: Dave Marks (dave@widgetex.co.uk)
To: Lucy Gordon (lucy@widgetex.co.uk)

14.31
Subject: Cuff Defluff

It is with regret that I have decided I must take the Cuff Defluff campaign away from you, because – put simply – you are making such a hash of it. Instead, I would like you to lay out copy for the discount hearing aid catalogue.

W Microsoft Word – Lucy hates Dave.doc

Aghhh! Aghhh! Aghhh! Am tempted to expose Dave's expenses scam, but can't do anything until SD gets back.

Poor Rosy broke her ankle para-gliding in Malaga and is also off for another week, so we still have quacking Camilla on the front desk. I noticed that she went for a two-hour lunch today at precisely the same time as AD. I'm pretty certain Wendy noticed too, because she was looking positively evil when I spotted her munching her way through her Coronation Chicken. I just hope he doesn't try to claim the lunch on expenses.

Burr Cottage
Chisbourne

Friday 1st May

Dear Big Brother,

All my housemates have gone away for May Bank Holiday, leaving me home alone with Platforms. Bella and Brick are in Amsterdam together; Jane has booked herself on to an intensive residential dressage course in Kent in the hope that she can impress Horsy Tim when she returns (apparently he criticised her lower leg last month and has not asked her out since). Greg is working in Spain. Even Mum and Dad are away on some coastal break they booked cheaply through Teletext. They've asked me to go around to the house at regular intervals to check that Alice and Granny are not having wild parties in their absence. I thought it would be great fun pampering myself, watching old *Bond* movies and teaching Platforms tricks, but the truth is I'm already bored out of my mind and I left work less than two hours ago. I don't know how I'll get through the next seventy-two hours. May Day, mayday!

Saturday 2nd May, 9a.m.:
God, I'm bored! Was planning a lazy lie-in, but found myself
wide awake at seven a.m., still primed for the working week.
Tried to go back to sleep, but Platforms came into my bedroom
bearing a small, fluffy dead thing, which she dropped on my
pillow. I screamed in horror and she fled, leaving it by my nose.
Spent ages constructing a pair of pincers from a wire
coathanger in order to pick it up and bear it at arm's length to
the outside bin. Dropped it twice on way. It was only when I
saw a small, chewed acrylic label that I realised it was her fake-
fur catmint mouse, not the corpse of a mangled vole. Feel a bit
stupid. Think I need an eye test.

Lunchtime:
Have called all opticians in Wexbury, but no one can fit me in
for an appointment today. I tried to convince a nice
receptionist at On Spec that I was going blind, but she saw
through my façade. She gently suggested I book an emergency
appointment with my doctor or, failing that, go to my local
Casualty department if I was really worried. Guess she realised
that I was just a sad, home-alone hypochondriac with nothing
to do over the weekend.

5p.m.:
Am on third family-sized bag of crisps and second *Carry On*
film of day. There must be more to Bank Holidays than this.

8p.m.:
Have just remembered Mum and Dad asking me to check on
Roundhead Avenue. Will go there straight away. With any luck
there'll be a party on.

Midnight:
I don't know which was worse – Granny dancing to 'I've Got
You Under My Skin' while seventeen assorted pensioners
tucked into the sweet sherry and denture-friendly nibbles in the
annexe, or Alice and Scrumpy snogging on the sofa next door

surrounded by grungy road protesters of indistinguishable sex, all wearing ponchos, smoking dope and listening to dolphin birthing music.

Sunday 3rd May, 4p.m.:
Today was just like yesterday – two *Bond* movies, a *Carry On*, *Lassie Returns*, and a lot of one-sided conversations with Platforms. I was so bored this afternoon that I decided to make a rare foray into the garden (usually Jane's territory) and pull up a few weeds. Almost fainted when I straightened up by the picket fencing to find myself eye-to-neck with Big Mike, who was holding something that looked suspiciously like a dahlia in his hand. I clutched my petunia to my chest and made a friendly comment about green fingers. Turns out we're both a bit bored, so are heading for Cow in Clover tonight. Ideal opportunity to draw him out about Peach.

Midnight:
Feel bit tight. Fab night. Didn't do much drawing out – too busy drawing in breath and laughing. Big Mike v. good company. Says Peach is a bimbo, hee hee. Says she's in Benidorm this weekend sunning her tiny bikini line and dancing in foam-filled night clubs. Oops – must stop writing as room's started to spin.

3a.m.:
Ouch. Hangover. Can't sleep. God! Benidorm's in Spain isn't it? May Day, mayday!
   Baa at a few sheep for me.
   Love,
   Lucy xxx

Written on the back of a *Discover Tuscany* brochure:

My darling Greg,

You are back from Spain at last. It sounds like you had a tough week working for those Japanese businessmen, you poor love. You say they were trying to buy a golf club, and kept changing their return time, so you had to hang around at the hotel while they negotiated in the nineteenth hole. I want to believe you, I really do.

You look very pale – as though you've spent the entire week indoors (what Bella calls a 'honeymooner's tan'). But when I asked you why you hadn't sunbathed while you were out there, you said that you'd been too busy. How can someone who just has to wait around for a phone call beckoning him to an aerodrome be busy? Now that I know Peach was in Spain last week too, am v. suspicious. If you'd said you were trying to avoid the sun for health reasons – malignant melanomas, etc. – or that the weather had been lousy, I'd have believed you. But 'busy'? Were you checking your navigational aids ALL WEEK? I think not.

You say that I seem to be very stressed and need a holiday. I think you're right. Am going to rip this into small shreds and bury it in your window box. I love you.

W Microsoft Word – Tuscany.doc

Tuscany Villa Week

Aims:

Invite lots of friends (note: already mentioned in passing to several)

Make Greg faithful only unto me

Get fantastic tan

Done:

Picked up brochures from Travel-a-Go-Go, Wexbury (note:

only show smallish self-catering apartments, sleeping six or eight at most)
Bought sun cream

To Do:
Get firm idea of numbers (see above)
Ask Travel-a-Go-Go about bigger villas (see above)
Look on Internet

W Microsoft Word – Tuscany2.doc

Tuscany Villa Week

My friends who want to come: 16

1) Definites:	Bella and Brick
	Jane (and maybe Horsy Tim)
	Sally and Dan
	Bridget and Peter
	Madeline and Garth
	Rachel and Andrew
	Fliss, Beth and Zoe
2) Iffy 'sounds good –	I'll think about it': Big Mike.
3) No response:	Mo

Greg's friends who want to come: 0 (note: couldn't get hold of him today to ask who he wanted to invite. The answerphone in his flat is switched on and his mobile is off. *Vive la différence*.)

To do:
Track Greg down
Pop into Wexbury tomorrow for more specialised information (re: bigger villas)
Surf Teletext.

NOTE: Big problem = Money. Most of my friends are broke and can only afford £100 a head – including flights, accommodation and car hire.

Saturday Lunch Menu – 13 Roundhead Avenue, Wexbury.
Chef: Liv Gordon

Selection of dry–cured meats
Cheese board
Bread rolls
Leaf salad

To be served with bottle of Chablis
For Mother: Woodpecker Cider

Burr Cottage
Chisbourne

Saturday 9th May

Dear Big Brother,
Having a bit of a nightmare organising my dream holiday.
I surfed Teletext for so long last night that I developed
double vision – plus an intimate knowledge of half-board
holidays in Lanzarote departing from Stansted next week.
Hopeless.

Travel-a-Go-Go in Wexbury wasn't too hot on large Italian
villas sleeping twenty in deepest Tuscany for less money than it
costs to rent a mobile home in a caravan park in Wales. They
suggested I down-grade to the Lake District. I politely said
pasta off and marched to that very posh speciality travel
agents, Loco Citato – the one in a little cobbled side-street
beside the saddlers and the new Spanish tapas bar. I've never
dared go in there before – just loitered around outside looking
at the pictures of French chateaux available for rent at
FF20,000 a week. You have to ring a bell to be let in. That was
about twenty seconds before I was let out again. A grey-
bunned, snooty woman in a Windsmoor twin-set peered at me
over her half-moons as I spluttered my requirements – hill-top
location, preferably with a misty view over vineyards and olive

groves, four-poster beds, pool, courtyard with dovecote, terracotta tiles, a hundred smackers a head all in – and then she laughed sarcastically and said 'Selwyn sent you in here as a practical joke, didn't he? He's such a wag. Now push off, I'm busy.'

Mum v. sympathetic. Suggests Jules Verne. I think I might just get one of those last-minute Teletext deals to the Canary Islands after all.

Tell the sheep that they're very lucky they don't go on holiday.

Love,

Lucy xxx

✈ **Greg Burton Charter Pilot** ✈

Apartment G, Wexbury Heights, The Wharf, Wexbury, Berks
Hangar 134F, Thrushfield Aerodrome, Swifthill, Salisbury, Wilts

L,

People I'd like you to invite to Tuscany:

Johnny and Julia Exeter
Richard Huntingdon
Baz and Louella Trowbridge
Tank Swindon
Miles and Fiona Rochester
Tristan and Shakira Guildford

G

'*Greg here. Leave a message.*' *Beep.*

'Thank you for the list. If they all agree, that takes the total group up to twenty-eight. Who do you think I am? Thomas Cook? Sorry, darling – ignore that. I'm very stressed at work. Do you really want to invite Tank? Will he behave?'

WIDGETEX LIMITED
Memo
From: Lucy Gordon
Re: New project
I have been most impressed by the diligence you have shown during my recent absence. As such, I would like you to spearhead a brand new marketing campaign for the Stress-free Shirt Press, which as you know is our market leader. Could you come to my office at your earliest convenience to discuss this further? (Please Note: Am playing golf from 1200 hours.)
Gavin Slater

To: Dave Marks (dave@widgetex.co.uk)
To: Lucy Gordon (lucy@widgetex.co.uk)

11.33
Subject: Creep

Are you shagging him or something? Does he know you wear tights? I think he should be told.

From: Lucy Gordon (lucy@widgetex.co.uk)
To: Dave Marks (dave@widgetex.co.uk)

11.40
Subject: Grand National

Does he know about Liverpool?

W Microsoft Word – Tuscany3.doc
Have just called all the people on Greg's list and almost died of embarrassment. First, he hadn't explained that Exeter, Huntingdon, Trowbridge etc. weren't their surnames, but the places where they live. I

117

only found that out after 'Miles Rochester' told me that my 'piss poor market research company have cocked up, now bugger off and don't bother me again'. Which brings me to my second nightmare.

It took ages to explain who I was and why I was ringing; Greg hasn't spoken to most of them in weeks. I can't believe he hadn't even prepared the ground and told them what we're organising. Most of them had no idea 'Play-Away Burton' even had a girlfriend. So embarrassing. I felt like a cold-calling sales representative trying to flog double-glazing. Only three people want to come – a v. posh sounding couple called Baz and Louella, who I've never met, and Greg's loud-mouthed drinking crony, Tank. I'm not sure they'll mix with my lot. At least Rachel has just called to say she and Andy can't get the time off work to come. It's a relief as Tank tried to grope her at the Halloween party last year.

Written on the back of a *Hidden Italy* brochure:

Dear Greg,

I'm sorry I threw prawn korma all over your favourite Hugo Boss shirt. This has been such an exhausting week. I feel totally drained. The new marketing campaign is taking up all my time, and four more people have dropped out of the Italy villa idea (no bad thing as we still haven't got a venue for twenty, and hiring a cheap castle is proving tricky). So, you see, I was really touched when you offered to cook tonight by way of apology. But then you realised that you had no curry powder left and had to pop upstairs to ask Peach for some. You were away AGES. When you came back, you had a really smug look on your face and told me that she'd agreed to come on the Italian week too.

That's why I was so furious, most especially as you ignored all my complaints . . . 'But I hardly know her! We already have more women than men going. It'll ruin the balance' . . . and simply said, 'But she's such fun, Lucy.' You have no idea how much this has wound me up, have you? Now you are asleep with your back turned sulkily towards me because I refused to have sex. Was tempted to agree to a quickie so that

I could have screaming orgasm (faked, naturally) which Peach would overhear, but I'm really far too annoyed with you.

Put off by horrifying mental images of Peach sunbathing topless on the terrace while the rest of us try to eat insalata tricolore al fresco. Have a feeling that you were having self-same images which was why you were so randy.

Am going to bury this in the window box as seems eco-friendly way to dispose of these letters.

Sunday Lunch Menu – 13 Roundhead Avenue, Wexbury.
Chef: Liv Gordon

Chilled melon, crab and black olive soup with gnocchi croutons
Fusilli tossed in Dolcelatte, pancetta, coconut and raisin sauce
Tiramisu 'Liv', made with Arabic coffee and goats cheese

To be served with bottle of Valpolicella, '98
For Mother: Litre of Lambrusco Rosé

Burr Cottage
Chisbourne

Sunday 17th May

Dear Big Brother,

Mum is no longer sympathetic about the Italian disaster. She says it's my own fault for being too ambitious in the first place. 'Why don't you and Greg spend a week in a nice Spanish resort like normal couples do?' Hmph. Was so annoyed with her that I refused to compliment her gnocchi. I'm sure she cooked Italian on purpose to spite me.

Sought solace with Dad in his new, huge workshop. He was supportive in a distracted sort of a way, but was far more interested in showing off the wood sander he's just rebuilt from scrap.

Thank you for the postcard advising that I make friends on the Internet and seek AA's help for my drinking problem. I would like you to know that May Bank Holiday was an isolated moment of loneliness brought about by lack of pre-planning and a last-minute change in Greg's plans. I am a very popular person (twenty-four people want to come on holiday with me). You are the one who talks to sheep.

You can tell them your sister is already a member of the AA and has full road relay protection.

Love,

Lucy xx

From: Lucy Gordon (juicylucy@webbedup.net)
To: Mo Lavender (Hobo-mobo@Hotmail.com)

20.18
Subject: Oh la la!

I can't believe what's just happened. SO glorious! I've had a terrible two days at work struggling with a new campaign, as well as sweating to book an Italian villa for twenty people including Peach (don't ask). Made no progress on holiday front – I even resorted to phoning the Italian Embassy to ask whether they knew of any cheap properties for let. Then I was outside in the garden this evening when Big Mike leant over the fence and asked me whether I was still looking for somewhere overseas for a group holiday. 'I know of a place,' he explained. 'It's not exactly Tuscany – it's in Northern France. A mate of mine ran outward-bound courses there, but he gave it up this spring to go travelling, and the old chateau is more or less lying empty. It's huge. Could it be any use to you? The only condition is that I'd like to come too.'

I wanted to fall to my knees in gratitude. Big Mike is my saviour. Can't wait to tell Greg. This is especially good as predatory Peach seems v. keen on Mike. Peachy!

Am assuming that you do not want to come to Europe. The brainwashing cult will clearly not let you out. Lxxx

Written on the back of the Basborough Leisure Complex Film Listing:

My darling Greg,
You are not as excited as I'd hoped at prospect of going to France instead of Italy. I've told you we'll be staying in a chateau, but you seem to think that it'll be full of boarding-school dormitories because it was once used as an outdoor pursuits centre, and that no one will have cleaned there for months. You were hardly complimentary: 'It's bound to be filthy if it's been lying empty. And what about bedding? I hope there's still some decent sports equipment around. Are there any good restaurants nearby?'
I had to confess that I really don't know much about the place at all. I was so excited when Big Mike offered it for us to use that I didn't ask any relevant questions — like whether there was a state-of-the-art treadmill there. I have a feeling that there won't even be electricity, but I'm keeping quiet about that. Will have to take BM for drink tomorrow evening and find out the low-down. Off to cinema tonight. You want to see some action thing, but I'm angling for the latest Jane Campion. Think I'll use my feminine wiles to talk you around on way to Basborough Leisure Multiplex. Must hurry and bury this in window box before you come out of the loo.

From: Lucy Gordon (juicylucy@webbedup.net)
To: Mo Lavender (Hobo-mobo@Hotmail.com)

00.13
Subject: Not so peachy.

My feminine wiles are not what they once were, as I discovered last night. Greg couldn't hear my flirtatious overtures over the blast of Meatloaf in the Mazda. We saw an action film – lots of people blown apart by major Hollywood star wielding an Uzi. Once the gore started flying, I couldn't bear to look, so concentrated instead on the weird haircut of the man sitting directly in front of us. Looked strangely familiar, with ratty dreadlocks and several long beaded strands poking up to obscure my view of the machine-gunning hero. Soon realised it was Alice's boyfriend, Scrumpy. He had his arm around small, androgynous creature with shaven head and five studs in her upper ear. Definitely not Alice. At a suitable point, I tapped him furiously on the shoulder and asked what the hell he thought he was up to. Then an irritated female voice said, 'Shut up, Sis. What's your problem? We're trying to watch the film.' Oh God. My sister has had a crew cut. She looks like Tank Girl. Apparently Mum and Dad are furious, but Granny thinks it looks 'pretty cool'. After the film, Alice asked if she and Scrumpy can come to France. Greg looked so horrified at the idea that I had to lie and say chateau was very small. 'It's okay,' Alice grinned wickedly. 'We can camp in the grounds.'

Popped into Waterstones after work today to buy several Normandy travel guides. Looks lovely – lots of beautiful towns with restaurant-lined squares. Will take them to Greg's flat tomorrow night and leave them lying around in hope he warms to idea. Will not, however, take the photograph which Big Mike dug out for me to look at tonight. Not because the Chateau Fisquet doesn't look beautiful. It does – all creamy stone, glittering windows and gravel carriage sweeps. Greg would love it. What he would also love is the fact that Peach is in the photograph, wearing a minuscule bikini top and looking up at the camera adoringly. I almost fell over when I saw it. 'I thought you only knew her because she has an iguana with sticky claw?'

'Not exactly,' he looked awkward. 'We went out together for a while.'

I was amazed, and blurted: 'But you said she was a bimbo!' Then I went v. red. Thankfully BM just laughed. 'She is rather. But don't tell her I said that whatever you do. She's good fun when you get to know her.'

I asked whether he minded coming now that Greg has asked Peach along too, but he assured me they're good friends. 'She'll add to the fun. But I think you might be quite grateful to have me around.' He winked. Wish I understood what he meant by that, but we were in the Cow in Clover at the time with Jane and Bella, who started raving about the chateau and demanding the info I should have been asking instead of quizzing him about his ex. No treadmills, the pool will be empty, the stables deserted, cobwebs everywhere, but it is still connected to an electricity supply and – better than anything – it hasn't got dormitories at all. It has huge four-poster beds! L xxx

---

Wexbury and District Riding Club Show

To be held on Saturday 23rd May
at Chisbourne Manor

Many Showing and Jumping Classes
Gymkhana
Clear Round
Terrier Racing
Refreshments

Kindly sponsored by Wexbury Sanitation Ltd

W Microsoft Word – Swimsuit.doc

Jane was competing in a local horse show today, so I decided to go along and offer my support. It was v. hot, but most of the spectators seemed to be wearing several layers of shapeless waxed green cotton. Felt a bit self-conscious in my shorts. Jane looked fantastic in breeches and black jacket, with her red hair in a net. Horsy Tim certainly seemed to think so, and kept patting her cream bottom when they walked the course of the Novice Jumping. I think Jane was slightly distracted by this as she lost her way after the third fence and was disqualified for jumping an oxer the wrong way round. Afterwards, HT consoled her for ages in the horse box while I waited around with three ice creams melting on my hand. Ended up eating them all.

Wish I hadn't as headed into Wexbury this afternoon to look for swimsuit for my holiday. Know Greg wants me to buy a bikini, but I have a feeling I'll look like a trussed chicken. Tried on a couple of flowery ones in Monsoon, but my stomach was hanging out like a Buddha's. Will go back when I haven't just eaten three Flake 99s and a greasy burger from a stand.

Sunday Lunch Menu – 13 Roundhead Avenue, Wexbury.
Chef: Liv Gordon

*Milk-poached baby octopus on wilted rocket leaves, served with
    vermouth mayonnaise and Jerusalem artichoke drop-scones*

*Thai rabbit curry with deep-fried chilli polenta, sautéed sage leaves
    and asparagus bundles tied up with liquorice ribbons*

*Rice pudding ice cream presented in a spun-caramel cendrier,
    accompanied by tuile cigars*

To be served with bottle of Aglianico del Vulture
For Mother: Litre of Lambrusco Rosé

Sunday 24th May

Dear Big Brother,

Today, Mum tried out her competition menu for the Wexbury *Masterchef* regional trials in a fortnight. Her concentration was sorely tested, as Dad appeared outside the kitchen window to noisily strim the weeds just as she was trying to emulsify her vermouth mayonnaise. It separated and Granny said it looked like wallpaper paste (although she polished it off pretty quickly). I think Mum's menu might be a little ambitious. The main course looks sensational, but the combined flavours are v. odd. When Dad asked politely whether they had rabbits in Thailand, Mum was furious, snapping that there are rabbits world-wide. 'After all, they breed like rabbits, don't they?'

Tell sheep to rest assured Mum won't be substituting rabbit for lamb.

Love,

Lucy xx

W Microsoft Word – Swimsuit2.doc

Wandered around shops this lunchtime in search of perfect swim-suit. Tracked down fifties-style navy blue one in trendy new shop, On Fash, and was just admiring its flattering effects in long mirror in changing room, when I heard a vaguely familiar voice on the other side of the curtain. Peeked through crack to see Peach standing in communal area, asking the attendant whether she thought the colour suited her. She was wearing three minute triangles of shiny orange lycra, strung together like bunting on dental floss. My huge navy blue number had about twenty times the fabric. I put it back on the rack and fled. Will go to gym before I buy anything.

Oh God, Ambitious Dave has just sidled up, falling about with laughter, and asked me why I've got a panty-pad stuck to my leg. It's not a pad – it's the sticky strip that shops put in the gusset of swimsuits when you try them on. The one from navy blue monster must have attached itself to me when I was climbing out of it. I've been walking around with it flapping there all afternoon. So embarrassing!

From: Lucy Gordon (juicylucy@webbedup.net)
To: Mo Lavender (Hobo-mobo@Hotmail.com)

20.48
Subject: Alice alert

Alice called round this evening, driving Granny's Dolomite which she parked on Jane's favourite peony. She pretended that she'd come to see me, but I think it has more to do with the fact that Brick is staying at the cottage this week while Bella is on half term. She stayed for ages, eyeing him up lovingly, much to Bella's irritation.

Alice says that Dad has been forced to eat rabbit curry every night this week as Mum is trying to perfect the recipe for the *Masterchef* competition. She's given up on vermouth mayonnaise, though, because Granny keeps drinking the main ingredient. L xxx

---

You have . . . one . . . new message. Message received . . . today . . . at . . . six . . . thirty-five . . . pee emmmm.

'Lucy, this is your mother. I've tried your work number but you're not there either. What is this I hear about you being away on holiday during my *Masterchef* Trial? How *could* you be so inconsiderate? *And* you are taking your little sister with you, much against my wishes. Do you realise this means that I will have *no* daughterly support whatsoever as I slave over my Thai rabbit curry in front of the critical gaze of Wexbury's dignitaries and the chef from the Café

Blanc? I blame you entirely for this, of course. And don't you dare tell me again that Alice invited herself to France and you don't even want her to be there. It will be *all* your fault if my mayonnaise splits. You are *not* welcome at Roundhead Avenue any more.'

'*This is Violet Beasley. I am unable to take your telephone call, so please leave me a message after the tone . . . um . . . Gordon? How do you stop this bloody thing recording . . . ?' Beep.*
'Granny, it's me. I think I left a couple of Normandy guide books in the sitting room. The trouble is Mum's a bit mad at me, so I can't come and pick them up. Could you go next door and see if they're around? Thanks.'

'*You're through to Lucy Gordon's voice-mail. I'm not at my desk right now, but if you leave a message, I'll get right back to you as soon as I can.'*
'Ziz ees Agent Beasley. Ze Normandy mission has been accomplished, comrade. Commandant Liv does not know a theeng. She ees not happy with your behaviour. I would not eat her cooking until she has calmed down, da? Meet me in the Bluebird Tea Rooms in half an hour. Codeword: Snifter. Over.'

W **Microsoft Word – Normandy.doc**
What have I done? My grandmother thinks she is a Russian spy. She has just given me a box of books – mostly Dad's tatty spy thrillers, a couple of Bridge companions and an ancient Ford Popular manual. No Normandy guide. I treated her to a cream horn and then went back to work via Waterstones to buy another copy. Feel really bad about Mum.

'Greg here. Leave a message.' Beep.
'Darling, it's me – um – Lucy. It looks as though I might have to stay here for my mother's trial and then come to France a couple of days late. Do you mind very much? Call me. I'll be home around seven.'

You have ... one ... new message. Message received ... today ... at ... six ... fifty ... pee emmmm.
'Lucy, darling, I had no idea your mother was on trial. Of course you must stay in England until it's over. You can take your car through the Tunnel and meet us there. Or get a ferry to Calais and I'll come and collect you. Don't worry, darling. I'll do everything I can to help.'

'Greg here. Leave a message.' Beep.
'Greg it's me. Lucy. Where are you? It's after midnight. I've only just realised that you think my mother is on trial for something criminal. Oh God. She's not! I hope you haven't mentioned it to anyone. She's mad enough at me already. Mum is going to be competing in a trial for *Masterchef*, not on trial for a crime, and that's why she wants me to stay here. But I'm not sure I do want to stay here when I could be on holiday. After all, she does have Dad and Granny for support. And she's been so horrible about this, when it's not my –' *Beep*. 'Greg? Hello? Has the tape run out? Bugger.'

Posted on the Burr Cottage fridge:

COW IN CLOVER RESULTS
Thursday 4th June (score kept by Bella):

Number of times Lucy said 'cellulite': 7.
Best quote: 'Bikinis are so last year. Everyone's going in for the bathing dress nowadays. Aren't they?'

Number of people who stopped talking when Mike rushed up to Lucy: 34.
Full quote: 'Are you all right? Peach has just called and says that your mother's standing trial for something horrific involving Loyd Grossman.'

Number of times Jane fell off her chair laughing: 3.
Best quote: 'Shhh! Mrs Gordon hasn't actually poisoned Loyd yet.'

Number of torture methods Bella came up with to punish Greg for telling Peach that Lucy's mother is a criminal: 4.
Best quote. 'Cut the fuel pipe in his plane.'

RESULT:
Lucy = week off. Jane = vacuuming and dusting. Bella = washing up, bathroom, bins. Greg = cress planted on carpets/kipper in airing cupboard/phone left off hook to Singapore speaking clock.

You have . . . one . . . new message. Message received . . . today . . . at . . . ten . . . twelve pee emmmm.
'Lucy darling, it's Greg. Er – sorry about the mix-up to do with your mother. I did mention it to a couple of people, but I'm sure they'll be terribly discreet. By the way, I've offered Peach a lift to France now that there's a spare place in the Mazda. She's very sweetly offered to share the cost of the petrol and I'll appreciate the company to be honest.'

Written on the back of Greg's packing list:

My darling Greg,

I've been watching you pack this evening, feeling like a small pet dog that is going to be left behind while her owner goes on holiday. Even worse is that the flirty neighbouring cat – Peach – is also packing and keeps popping into your flat with a pile of skimpy dresses, asking whether you've got enough room in your suitcase for them because hers is full up and 'we're travelling together after all'. Humph. Have pointed out to you that her dresses are very last season, and a couple of them smell of smoky pubs. Can't believe I have to stay here in rainy Wexbury until after Mum has competed on Sunday, and then drive to France straight afterwards, all alone. Don't know what's more terrifying – Mum's nerves, the prospect of you and Peach alone together in the Mazda, or the fact that I have to navigate my way through northern France alone.

The plants in your window boxes are starting to look sick so I'll creep out to the bins with this later. I'll miss you.

Written on the back of a note to Greg's cleaner:

My darling Greg,

You've just left. I'm hugging your Arran sweater in one arm and writing with the other hand. Feel very left out and miss you like mad already. Also feel a bit guilty that the 'travel sickness' pills I gave Peach are, in fact, two of the coma-inducing sleeping pills Jane uses. Called Mum to see how she's feeling about tomorrow, but Dad answered and said that she was in the 'isolation booth' (the kitchen) trying out a new variation on the controversial mayonnaise for the octopus starter. It's now being flavoured with cardamom pods and kumquat zest. Dad says that Scrumpy and Alice set out for France in Granny's Dolomite this morning with the boot loaded up with camping equipment and dried veggie burger mix. Wish I was travelling to Folkestone in the Mazda right

now, listening to Aerosmith at top volume. I'm not going back to Burr
Cottage until after Jane, Bella, Brick and Big Mike set off, so that I
won't have to wish two groups of people bon voyage. I know it's a bit
childish, but I want to hug your jumper some more. Wish I'd never
organised this stupid holiday in the first place.

From: Lucy Gordon (juicylucy@webbedup.net)
To: Mo Lavender (Hobo-mobo@Hotmail.com)

22.07
Subject: Home alone

Trying not to feel miserable that I have to stay in Berkshire for
Mum's cooking competition while everyone else has bon
voyaged. It's very lonely here at Burr Cottage. Jane, Bella and
Brick must have set out for France in Big Mike's off-roader hours
ago, leaving half-drunk mugs of tea which have all grown slimy
films on the surface. At least I think they were all going in one car,
but Jane's Peugeot is also missing which is slightly odd. Bella's
left her camera behind on the kitchen table, along with two
thousand francs and an alternative phrase book, which has
translations for 'Are there any good music festivals nearby?' and
'Where can I score some gear?' Am wearing Greg's Arran
sweater now, although it's a bit hot for the time of year. I think I'll
take my mind off him and Peach by starting to pack tonight. Not
sure what to take, so will empty contents of drawers and
wardrobe on bed and start by process of elimination. Lxxx

Packing List – 1st draft, 10.15p.m.
Skirts – 8
T-shirts – 17
Shirts – 6
Jumpers – 3 (including the Arran)
Dresses – 7

Pairs of trousers – 5
Pairs of shorts – 4
Jackets – 3
New swimsuit
Sarongs – 5
Pairs of shoes – 11 (3 pairs dressy, 2 trainers, 4 open-toe sandals, my flip-flops and my wellies)
Laptop (need plug and phone converters)

To do:
Look for suitable suitcase (NB: might need to hire trailer for car too.)

Update, 1.15a.m.:
Jane and Bella must have made off with all the big suitcases in the house. All I can find is a small sports bag and a vanity case. I suppose I could throw things loose into the boot of the car, but I don't think Bella's phrase book will be much use if French custom controllers ask awkward questions. Will have to create more capsule wardrobe.

3.30a.m.:
Am sure I can hear music coming from Big Mike's cottage; guess he must have left a radio on to deter would-be burglars. Have just tried on clothes I was planning to take, and rejected everything that I think doesn't suit me.

Packing List – 2nd draft, 03.35a.m.
Skirt – 1
Dresses – 2
T-shirts – 2
Pairs of shoes – 12 (found favourite pair of ankle boots under bed)
Laptop
(NB: Can I send emails using Greg's mobile for modem?)
(NB2: I hope there's a washing machine at the chateau.)

Sunday 14th June

Dear Big Brother,

Mum is in the huge kitchens here preparing three courses for
the *Masterchef* trials while her supporters wait anxiously in the
bar. Dad won't stop pacing around and looking at his watch,
Granny is on her third Gin and It, and I keep falling asleep. I
shouldn't have stayed up all last night sorting through my
wardrobe for France. I know it's not Tuscany (we were
desperate), but it's just as difficult deciding what to take,
particularly as Peach has invited herself and has a head start
while I'm stuck supporting Mum. I need a full competition
wardrobe. I only finished packing at six o'clock this morning,
by which time there seemed no point in going to bed. Stayed
awake instead, worrying that Peach is making moves on Greg
in my absence, and that the music coming from Big Mike's
cottage next door might be squatters. Tried to check around
back, but all the curtains were closed. More later.

5p.m., Roundhead Avenue:

Poor Mum. Her Thai rabbit curry was so hot it made one
judge cry, and her frosted crème anglaise mousse was just thin
custard by the time it was tasted because it had melted under
the lights. Thankfully her baby octopus starter was declared
absolutely delicious, especially the 'piquant and unusual'
mayonnaise which she'd cryptically called Sauce Lit de Mer to
hide the fact that she'd finally settled on anchovy, capers and
pickled walnut as flavourings. Unfortunately it wasn't good
enough to swing the vote, so it's a Sloaney interior decorator
from Basborough who's going to take her pistachio and
polenta-stuffed poulet to the regional finals. Mum is v.

disappointed, but philosophical. She thinks her key mistake was not using alliteration in her menu, although Dad's suggestion of Run Rabbit Runs didn't go down too well. I feel absolutely drained. Can't believe I've got to drive to France tonight. Mum's given me a Tupperware container of baby octopus to take with me. Her sea bed sauce is a little too appropriate given that I'm probably going to snooze under the Channel. Wish I didn't have to go on my own. Granny has just announced loudly that if Greg loved me he'd have stayed behind too. I defended him hotly, but secretly I agree.

Tell the sheep that I'm developing a penchant for Arran.

Love,

Lucy xx

To do:
Take Platforms to the cattery
Clear out the fridge
Set the video for EastEnders
Cancel the milk
Check the route to Folkestone on the road atlas
Put the yellow deflectors on the headlights of my car
Lock up the cottage

You have . . . one . . . new message. Message received . . . today . . . at . . . seven . . . o . . . four pee emmmm.

'Lucy, darling it's Greg. I was hoping to catch you before you set out – Christ the reception's murder here. Hang on, I'm just opening a window. Better. Just thought I'd let you know Peach and I arrived safely last night and the chateau's lovely. Not everyone's here yet, but those who are are getting along famously. Nothing much else to say – Jane reversed her car into a millstone. That's about it. Hope you get this message. Er – bye –'

'Greg! I'm here! I was packing the car. What do you mean about Jane? I thought Mike was giving her and Bella a lift? Greg? Hello? Bugger.'

From: Lucy Gordon (juicylucy@webbedup.net)
To: Mo Lavender (Hobo-mobo@Hotmail.com)

22.07
Subject: Something sweet for the journey

I'm eating a packet of Microchips in Big Mike's kitchen while his dogs polish off Mum's octopus. I'm worried it'll upset their stomachs, but Mike assures me it's fine, and he should know, after all he's a vet. 'I was up all last night with a late foal – terrible breech birth, almost lost both of them,' he told me when he called round, not looking me in the eye at all, which is odd. 'It was a last-minute call, and the owner's one of my best clients, so Jane offered to drive the others to France while I stayed behind. Only got back this evening – when I saw your car in the drive, I thought I'd pop round and see if you needed a lift.' Yippee! I told him I'd been a bit confused when I heard his radio on the go last night. 'You heard it?' he suddenly looked really embarrassed and coughed a lot. 'Well, yes. I must have left it on. Had to get to the stables in a hurry.' So glad I've got some company. We're going to drop his dogs off at his friend's farm, buy some sweets for the journey and head for the Channel Tunnel. Life is a sea bed of roses after all. Will keep you regularly updated, my darling, so that you could almost be with us. *Bon voyage!*

From: Lucy Gordon (juicylucy@webbedup.net)
To: Mo Lavender (Hobo-mobo@Hotmail.com)

15.36
Subject: By the pool, Chateau Fisquet

All the men are inside the house watching some football match.
Can't believe that they'd prefer to be there when it's so bright
and sunny out here. Actually it's a bit windy, too, but I'm wearing
a cardigan over my swimsuit and braving it out on a sun lounger
with the latest Jackie Collins and my laptop. Jane and Bella say
that Greg rigged up a television as soon as he arrived, and les
hommes are now watching non-stop World Cup coverage while
les femmes are left out in the cold. The only exception is Peach,
who claims to love football, even though she thinks offside is a
bad profile. All I can hear right now is that Three Lions song, with
Greg shouting 'Eng-er-land!' loudest of all. Big Mike did come
out for a coffee earlier, claiming he was more of a rugby man at
heart, but Jane scared him back inside by making some sort of
joke about foals and goals which I didn't get. I only wish things
were easier for him; I think he's still quite keen on Peach,
however much he says not. On the way here last night, he said he
was hoping for a holiday romance and then blushed like
mad. L xx

Postcard featuring truffle pig:

Dear Mum, Dad and Granny,
Having a lovely time. Weather v. good and chateau
beautiful. Alice and Scrumpy are camping in the gardens
and behaving themselves. Greg sends his love.
Lucy xx

From: Lucy Gordon (juicylucy@webbedup.net)
To: Mo Lavender (Hobo-mobo@Hotmail.com)

17.02
Subject: By the pool again

It's official. I'm a football widow. I had a lovely, romantic image when I started organising this holiday – meals al fresco, tanned faces lit up by flickering storm lamps as we share jokes and stories, laughter and wine. The only meal we share is breakfast, which is dominated by post-mortems of last night's match. Then all the women gather around the pool to uncap the suntan oil, and all the men gather around the television to uncap the beers. Our only communal group trips so far have been early-morning vigils to see battle grounds or military graveyards – very moving, but hardly likely to put you in the holiday mood; Greg's friend Tank is fascinated by battle fields and missile launch sights. Oddly, Peach is suddenly v. keen too, although she keeps getting the wars muddled up, and thinks Dunkirk is a famous Hollywood actor. Lxxx

Postcard featuring military bunker:

To all at Widgetex,
Having a sensational holiday in Sunny France. Weather glorious. Lots of friends, wine, great food and good conversation.
   Regards, Lucy

From: Lucy Gordon (juicylucy@webbedup.net)
To: Mo Lavender (Hobo-mobo@Hotmail.com)

11.27
Subject: In the kitchens

We all trooped to see another military bunker this morning. Greg drove the Mazda like Schumacher when he thought we were going to miss the two-thirty kick-off. Peach and Tank (who were squashed together in the back seat) are getting along v. well, much to my relief. The only trouble is that Greg is so in love with the football, he hasn't even noticed. Might suggest that Tank shows us a battle site of the sexes tomorrow. Hope Big Mike isn't too upset about Tank and Peach. Lxx

Postcard featuring onion-seller on a bicycle:

Dear Big Brother,
We're all having such a fantastic time. Weather miraculous, company heavenly, chateau beyond romantic. Greg treating me like a princess. A holiday none of us will forget!
Love,
Lucy xx

From: Lucy Gordon (juicylucy@webbedup.net)
To: Mo Lavender (Hobo-mobo@Hotmail.com)

01.39
Subject: The kitchens (now nicknamed The Coven by Greg)

Have stayed up giggling with girls. We decided to take ourselves off to the seaside today – La Baule. To our utter amazement the boys wanted to come along too. I thought there must be some sort of WW2 site around, but no – it turned out to be far more exciting than that: the training ground for the England Football Squad. While we played on the beach, gamed the arcades and shopped the boutiques, Greg and his gang of footie fans hung around outside the security-rimmed grounds like lovesick teenagers. Only Big Mike came along with us, and treated me to a huge ice cream to cheer me up about Greg. 'I wish I had an England strip to wear,' I sighed. 'That way he might notice me.' Mike coughed a lot and said he thought I looked much nicer in my swimsuit. He's so sweet like that, even when he's broken-hearted about Peach.

Greg has gone to bed with his mobile under his pillow (he's very mean about me using it for my modem) so will have to wait until he's in the shower to send this.

Twenty hours later:
'Eng-er-land!' They're at it again. Jane stirred a raw garlic clove into each of their casseroles tonight, but none of them seem to have noticed. We're hatching a plan . . .

(Greg took mobile into the shower. Will try to grab it when he's having a swim instead.)

Friday, 6p.m.
The pool: Our final day here, and I'm catching the last of the rays. Tonight, the girls and I are getting revenge. At ten to nine (just before England's last group match), Chateau Fisquet will suffer an unexpected power cut. We will have our candle-lit dinner after all.

(Greg says there's something wrong with his mobile battery and 'face it, Lucy, it's not healthy to keep sending emails to a friend who never bloody answers and might be dead for all you know', so I'll have to send this when I get home. Think he's a bit tense.) L xxx

When we all arrived at Le Shuttle this evening, the Mazda was waved upstairs, while all the other, bigger cars in our group were ferried onto the bottom rank. As a consequence our little convoy has been split up. I'm sure everyone else is having a party down there while I watch Greg eating Duty Free *bonbons* and determinedly not offering me one. Not that I'd want it. Feel really ill. Didn't know it was possible to be *under* seasick, but I think it is. Last night was a disaster.

It seemed like a terrific idea at the time – preparing an aphrodisiac meal for our menfolk and then causing a 'power cut' in the chateau so that they couldn't watch the England/Colombia match. Unfortunately it didn't quite work out that way. A few of them saw the funny side, but Greg was close to hysterical. First, he kept calling England from his mobile to find out the score. Then, deciding that this wasn't sufficiently 'live', he decided to go in search of a local bar to watch it on their screen – even though he'd drunk far too much to drive. Luckily he lurched outside and overheard my sister and Scrumpy listening to the match on an ancient tranny in their tent. So they were invited inside and we ate our sumptuous meal in a candle-lit dining room of baroque splendour, listening to the ghastly, tinny whine of a crazed French commentator. The simultaneous translation was provided by Alice and a French dictionary – 'The ball's just hit the Colombian *poteau de but* . . . hang on, I think that means signpost. Are they playing in the street or something?' Not only that, but she and Scrumpy guzzled so much wine that it ran out during the starter. When Jane insisted that they help us with the washing up afterwards, Scrumpy said, 'We need some light in here, man,' went in search of the fuse box, and discovered that the trip switch had been turned off. At this, all hell broke loose and Greg called me a 'scheming cow' before storming off to sleep in a separate room. I tried to point out that the whole thing had been Bella's idea, but he'd already left the kitchen. Brick hadn't, however, and it was his turn to start yelling accusations. Peach didn't help matters by getting the giggles and dropping a pan on his foot.

So the holiday broke up on a sour note, and now we are travelling back in gloomy silence. Greg is in such a bad mood that he doesn't even want to listen to Aerosmith. Things must be bad.

Sunday Lunch Menu – 13 Roundhead Avenue.
Chef: Liv Gordon
Theme: Welcome Home Les Enfants!

Vichyssoise made with sweet potatoes, baby leeks and rice wine
Seviche 'Chateau Fisquet' avec capers
Crêpes Suzette avec butterscotch Angel Delight et crème anglaise

To be served with a bottle of Crémant de Saumur
For Mother: Litre of Lambrusco Rosé

Burr Cottage
Chisbourne

Sunday 28th June

Dear Big Brother,

Mum cooked an especially themed French meal to welcome us all home today. Unfortunately Alice and Scrumpy have decided to stay on in France another week to travel around, and Greg refused to come to lunch at my parents because he's still mad at me for interrupting his football-watching plans on holiday (he just dropped me off at the end of the drive last night, not even kissing me goodbye or helping me with my bags). Mum sulkily gave me three portions of Seviche, which is basically raw fish. Still feel seasick.

Will write more soon.

Say *bonjour* to the sheep.

Love,

Lucy xx

From: Dave Marks (dave@widgetex.co.uk)
To: Lucy Gordon (lucy@widgetex.co.uk)

09.13
Subject: Welcome back, Slacker

So the Frogs have finally deported you. No wonder, judging by that flaky tan. You must have put them off their snails. Is it an all-over tan? Can I check out your tide-marks?

Nothing dramatic to report, except that as you can see we now have a full-time receptionist. The fat cow is called Ceri (pronounced 'Kerry'). Bloody Gavin employed her because so many man-hours were lost when Camilla the Babe was manning the front desk, and all we discerning male members of staff hung around to admire her. No one would admire Ceri unless they were seriously into flesh.

So you are once again Widgetex's hottest totty. Congratulations! You win a drink out with the company's Most Eligible Bachelor (i.e. me). ;0)

From: Lucy Gordon (lucy@widgetex.co.uk)
To: Dave Marks (dave@widgetex.co.uk)

09.46
Subject: Bikini Lines

Dave, I have a fortnight's worth of post, memos and emails and so much voice-mail that my ear aches. Please keep your sexist, sizeist and tannist comments to yourself. Also, a word of advice: never add silly punctuation faces to emails. It makes you look desperate, sad and talentless.

Surely Wendy is Widgetex's hottest totty?

From: Dave Marks (dave@widgetex.co.uk)
To: Lucy Gordon (lucy@widgetex.co.uk)

09.53
Subject: They're Playing Our Thong

As my girlfriend, Wendy is disqualified. I can wear a disguise. :)

From: Lucy Gordon (lucy@widgetex.co.uk)
To: Ceri Dixon (reception@widgetex.co.uk)

10.09
Subject: Welcome

Hello! Lovely to meet you this morning – I've just heard that you'll
be with us full time. That's great. Hope you're settling in okay.

From: Ceri Dixon (reception@widgetex.co.uk)
To: Lucy Gordon (lucy@widgetex.co.uk)

10.14
Subject: Thanks

That's so kind. Everyone's been really great.
    Couldn't help spotting your engagement ring. When are you
getting married?

From: Lucy Gordon (lucy@widgetex.co.uk)
To: Ceri Dixon (reception@widgetex.co.uk)

10.19
Subject:

The day I learn to love football.

From: Ceri Dixon (reception@widgetex.co.uk)
To: Lucy Gordon (lucy@widgetex.co.uk)

10.23
Subject: Coffee break

Tell me about it! I'm off for a break now. Come along and share my Twix. Sounds like you could use it!

From: Lucy Gordon (juicylucy@webbedup.net)
To: Mo Lavender (Hobo-mobo@Hotmail.com)

19.08
Subject: Feeling Snappy

Have finally got all my holiday photographs processed. Was dying to go round to Wexbury Heights to show them to Greg – especially as there are no football matches on tonight – but he says that he's busy preparing to fly sponsors to the Tour de France, and he won't be through with paperwork until late. This is really annoying, because he was working last weekend too. I haven't seen him properly since we came back from France. The dreaded Peach has, though. I bumped into her by the film counter in Boots this afternoon and she said she was collecting the copies of her holiday snaps that Greg had asked for last week. Last week! She showed me them, and none are of me at all – just lots of shots of *les hommes* playing five-a-side in the long dining hall, and one of Greg standing proudly by the Mazda at Folkestone.

I seem to have an awful lot of photographs of battle-fields. Bella cheered me up tonight by pointing out a shot of Peach in a bikini, taken from an incredibly unflattering angle. Must make sure it's at the top of the pile when I finally show them to Greg. The worrying thing is, I'm sure I didn't take it. I can tell from the ones either side that it was the day I thought I'd left my camera in my room. Maybe Tank borrowed it?

Have new friend called Ceri – the Widgetex receptionist. She is such a laugh and full of wise advice like: 'Not all men are annoying. Some are dead.' And 'Stress is when you wake up screaming and realise you haven't fallen asleep yet.' She says she's picked them up after years of temping. We're going out for a drink tomorrow. I hope it takes my mind off Greg. L xxx

---

W Microsoft Word – Lucy's tight.doc

Think I'm a bit tiddly. Went out for quick drink in Café Blanc after work with Ceri, the cuddly new Widgetex receptionist. Moved swiftly on to the Lock Inn, then to the Battle Arms before catching last orders in Waxy's Wine Bar. Boy, can that girl party. We got chatted up by two apprentice jockeys at one point. Ceri was at least twice the size of her admirer, but that didn't stop them swapping numbers. 'I love small men,' she sighed afterwards. 'I'm a bit of a man-eater, but I prefer little and often – the same with cream cakes.' She's an amazing woman. I was thinking of setting her up with Big Mike, but now I'm not so sure. He's worth an awful lot of cream cakes.

Sunday Lunch Menu – 13 Roundhead Avenue.
Chef: Lucy Gordon

Dips and crisps
Vegetarian Lasagne
Tesco's Finest Belgian Chocolate ice cream

To be accompanied by Lambrusco Rosé

Sunday 11th July

Dear Big Brother,

Mum's gone to stay with an old schoolfriend in Derbyshire
this weekend, so I offered to cook Sunday lunch. Dad must be
the only man in Wexbury who isn't watching back-to-back
sport today – he's holed up in his shed mending an old toaster
and listening to a Goons compilation tape. Scrumpy has taken
advantage of Mum's absence to monopolise our television for
the Grand Prix; Granny is glued to cricket in her annexe, and
Alice is running between the two. No one appreciated my
lasagne – they all ate it off trays on their laps. I should have
just picked up a takeaway pizza like everyone else in the
country. Bella, Jane and I are planning to get *Thelma and
Louise* out on video tonight, then watch it with face-packs on.
Sisterly solidarity.

Tell ewes to treat themselves to a facial and a night on the
sofa with *Babe*.

Love,

Lucy xx

PS I got your postcard. I said I was developing a penchant
for 'Arran', not 'Alan'. I don't know anyone called Alan. Greg
remains the only man for me.

Written on the back of a Boots photo wallet:

My darling Greg,
You are clearly not interested in my beast of a day at work. Slave
Driver hit the roof this morning when caught me gossiping with Ceri
about her jockey; I should have been preparing the slides for a client
presentation at the time. Ambitious Dave smirked all afternoon as a

result, and yawned an unprecedented seven times during the meeting. I could kill him. Ceri says he's got a problem with high-flying women. I said I have a problem with high-flying men — my pilot boyfriend being key amongst them. On cue, you called the office and said you wanted to see me tonight. So I'm here — with my holiday snapshots — but I have to say you're behaving very oddly. You keep 'popping out for a sec' to fetch things from the Mazda, take out half-full bin-bags or see if you've left the bin cupboard open. I think you want to tell me something, but you don't seem to be able to sit down for more than a minute at a time. I'm filled with foreboding. Are you about to confess that you've got cold feet? That you want us to split up? That you've been having an affair with Peach?

Now that the bin is empty, I am going to have to hide this in my handbag. I love you.

From: Ceri Dixon (reception@widgetex.co.uk)
To: Lucy Gordon (lucy@widgetex.co.uk)

10.03
Subject: You okay?

What's up, Lucy? You look like today was a waste of make-up.

From: Lucy Gordon (lucy@widgetex.co.uk)
To: Ceri Dixon (reception@widgetex.co.uk)

10.19
Subject: Badly need advice

I'm too stressed to work. Last night, I was convinced that Greg was going to tell me that he was breaking off our engagement because he's secretly in love with Peach. In the end, I got fed up waiting and decided to help things along by blurting 'Do you want to dump me or what?' He came to sit beside me and gulped, 'What on earth makes you think I'd want to do that, Lucy?'

At this, I attempted to list the several hundred reasons I've accumulated in my head over the past few weeks, but I suddenly couldn't think of any of them – he has this way of looking at me which still makes me feel as though all my clothes are far too tight. All I managed to splutter was, 'Just a hunch.'

And then the truth came out. He doesn't want to end things at all – quite the reverse. He wants me to move in with him! I was speechless with surprise, which he clearly took to be a good thing, as he opened a bottle of champagne. I always thought the living together suggestion – if it came – would be a big, romantic gesture. But he seemed really awkward and embarrassed. I don't get it at all.

He was admittedly a bit miffed when I said that I'd have to think it over for a few days. The truth is, I'm too dazed to decide right now. I keep thinking about poor Platforms – Greg is allergic to cats. And what about Bella and Jane? And Big Mike? And lovely, lively Chisbourne with all its gossip? What do I do?

Would demand coffee break, but Slave Driver's been prowling around my desk all morning.

From: Ceri Dixon (reception@widgetex.co.uk)
To: Lucy Gordon (lucy@widgetex.co.uk)

10.23
Subject:

You want the truth? I think that Greg has a hidden agenda. I know I've never met him, and I'm sure he's a lovely bloke, but from what you've said, he's a crap boyfriend and always will be. Take my advice: dump him.

Am sending over a Caramac with Lianne.

Posted on the Burr Cottage fridge:

COW IN CLOVER RESULTS

Thursday 16th July (score kept by Bella):
Absentee: Lucy (Excuse: too busy playing woolly-pully with
Platforms)
Subjects for discussion: Bella's birthday party. Lucy's continued bad mood.

Number of times Jane said 'I hate parties': 4.
Best quote: 'I don't know what Lucy's problem is, but I'll bet it's
hard to pronounce.'

Number of times Bella said 'I want a party': 11.
Best quote: 'My wardrobe and my body were built to party.'

Number of times Big Mike mentioned Lucy's absence: 9.
Best quote. 'I think a wardrobe's a bit small to hold a party in. It's
my thirtieth just a week after your birthday, Bella. We could have a
joint barbecue.'

RESULT: Lucy = bathroom and bins. Jane = washing up,
weeding. Bella = vacuuming, dusting, party organising.

Written on the back of a *Golf Monthly* questionnaire:

My darling Greg,
You are being so attentive that I feel really guilty for stalling so much.
It was so sweet of you to take me for a meal at the Café Blanc tonight
and insist that I could choose from the À La Carte menu for once. I
could see the love in your eyes when you told me that you can think of
no one you'd rather have looking after your flat for you. This was a bit of
an odd thing to say, but I let it pass. I know you're very old-fashioned
and I don't want to start laying down house rules about sharing the
hoovering right now; it would ruin the romance. You even bought me one
of those red roses in cellophane that are touted around restaurants in a

bucket. You've never done that before. Unfortunately I sat on it in the Mazda on the way back, but I don't think you noticed.

I am going to tuck this behind your framed poster of a Lear Jet. I may remove it when — if — I move in. I love you.

Sunday Lunch Menu — 13 Roundhead Avenue, Wexbury.
Chef: Liv Gordon

Individual chilled taramasalata yoghurts with mini pitta bread
Pigs Trotters baked in green mustard and cumin seed crust,
    accompanied by caramelised gherkins
Deep-fried grapes served on raspberry and rose-petal coulis

To be accompanied by New Zealand Gewurztraminer
For Mother: Four bottles of Orange Hooch

Burr Cottage
Chisbourne

Sunday 19th July

Dear Big Brother,

Greg has asked me to 'co-habit' as Dad puts it. He and Mum are all for me moving in with Greg. Mum said, 'Does this mean you two will finally get around to setting a date?' I hadn't a clue what she was talking about for a minute until Dad added, 'For the wedding, Lucy?' Oh God, I'm not sure this is a very good idea at all. For the best part of a year, I've been dying for Greg to ask me to move in with him, but now that he has I'm not sure I want to go. Worse still, I'm not sure I even want to marry him any more.

Please don't say 'I told you so'. Just ask the sheep what they'd do in my shoes.

Love,
Lucy xx

PS The shoes are hypothetical.

Party invitation posted on the Burr Cottage fridge with message:

Lucy,
What do you think? Sorry, we couldn't figure out anything that you are celebrating, but feel free to add it before I go to the copy shop.
Atb,
Bella

Come and Celebrate With Us!

Bella Smith has her Twenty-Fifth Birthday

Mike Ensor hits the big 3-ohhhhh

Barbecue at Burr Cottage, Chisbourne.

Sat 24th July from 7.30p.m.

Bring a bottle and a sausage
r.s.v.p.

Jane Redven's hundredth learner driver passes test

Slug gets its first festival tour

W Microsoft Word – Celebration.doc
I don't feel much like celebrating. The truth is I've barely been involved in the planning of this party. I can't decide whether to live with Greg or not. I can't decide whether I still love Greg or not. I'm not sure if my final decision will be a call for celebration or commiseration.

From: Lucy Gordon (juicylucy@webbedup.net)
To: Mo Lavender (Hobo-mobo@Hotmail.com)

18.01
Subject: Ready to party

Sorry I haven't written in ages, oh brainwashed one. But now we're about to have a party at Burr Cottage, I am suddenly reminded of your legendary 'Packs a Punch' and The Shed Incident (the secrets of which I will take to my grave). So wish you were here.

Today's been really fun. Have spent most of it splitting baps and tossing salad. Big Mike has invited half the village, plus all of his brothers. Jane is in a state of excitement because she's convinced at least one of them will be single and fanciable (Horsy Tim has recently fallen for an eventer called Victoria). I said, 'What about Mike himself? He's single, and quite good looking in a prop forward sort of a way.'

She snorted, 'You should word his Lonely Hearts ad. He's just not my type. Anyway, he's very keen on someone else.'

I'm sure he still holds a torch for Peach. He watched her v. closely when we were all in France, and must have been as worried as me that she and Greg seemed to flirt all the time. He'd probably be really happy to know Greg has asked me to move in with him, but I can't bring myself to say anything until I decide what to do (that's my biggest news, by the way). Greg is coming later, after he flies back from delivering a DJ to Manchester. I wonder if Mike has asked Peach? Must tart up just in case. Will finish this later.

20.30
Party is well underway downstairs. My sister and Scrumpy have turned up with stacks of veggie burgers. Three of Mike's brothers are here – they all look exactly the same and are lovely. Everyone is rushing between the two gardens via the hole in the hedge, so that all our guests have laurel leaves in their hair like Caesar. No

sign of Greg. Keep feeling stupidly tearful, and have to come up here to my room to calm down. Big Mike asked if I was okay a minute ago and I pretended I had hay fever. He's been really sweet and keeps looking at me worriedly, but that only makes me feel worse.

22.00

Lots of the locals have turned up and are all having heated arguments about how to achieve the best barbecue glow. Big Mike, who has been doing sterling work at the coal-face all evening, has relinquished cooking duties to Tristram, the posh weekender from the Old Rectory. BM's now having a sing-song with his brothers, and is playing the guitar, still wearing his striped apron. They're v. good. When they sang 'Killing Me Softly' a moment ago, I realised that I had tears in my eyes. I think Mike saw, but I pretended it was the barbecue smoke making them water. Have sloped upstairs to redo my eye make-up for fifth time. Wish Greg would turn up.

0 .00

Peach the minx has just arrived looking frantic. She's wearing shapeless old jogging gear, her hair is scraped back in a scrunchy and she has mascara all over her cheeks – not her usual party raver kit. She came marching straight up to me and sobbed, 'I can't believe he's moving to Finland for six months. I only found out tonight.'

I looked at her in amazement, mouthing like a lunatic, 'Finland?'

For some reason I had a sudden vision of Big Mike with his arm up a reindeer's bottom. Horrible.

Peach nodded. 'I offered to look after his place while he's away, but he says you're moving in there. He's parking the Mazda, by the way. I'm the reason he's so late – he didn't want me to come, but I insisted. I can't go on lying to you, Lucy. You're too nice. I have to tell you about us. It's over now, but I still hate myself.'

I gaped at her, realising my mistake. She was talking about Greg, not Mike. He hasn't really asked me to move in with him. Oh no. He just wants me to water plants and house-sit lovingly while he's away. What's more, he and Peach were an 'us'. I'm hiding in my room again, but I know I have to do something about this before Greg comes up and finds me here. He deserves roasting on the barbecue for this.

01.00
I don't think Tristram will ever forgive me for grabbing the fish slice, scooping up several of his perfectly sizzling organic sausages and hurling them at Greg, yelling 'We're Finnished, you adulterous slime!' Still, my housemates enjoyed the show. Bella says I have something to celebrate at last. She says tonight was the best disengagement party she's ever been to. The oddest thing is, I quite enjoyed it too. L xxx

From: Ceri Dixon (reception@widgetex.co.uk)
To: Lucy Gordon (lucy@widgetex.co.uk)

08.32
Subject: Some party

That was so, so fantastic the way you finished with Greg. I can't believe how cool you are. I'll buy you a drink after work to celebrate.

Is the big, sexy vet who lives next door to you single, by the way?

From: Lucy Gordon (lucy@widgetex.co.uk)
From: Ceri Dixon (reception@widgetex.co.uk)

09.29
Subject: Ringing the changes

Can't believe I'm single again. Haven't been able to bring myself
to tell anyone here, except for you (well you know already
because you met Greg for the first time when I was throwing
sausages at him and telling him to take a hike). Can you keep it a
secret for me? No one else here suspects that I've just broken off
my engagement, because I can't get my ring off. Either my
fingers have swollen up in the summer heat (what heat?), or I've
put on a bit of weight lately – all that misery eating while I was
worrying what to do about Greg and The Move. Am determined
to turn over a new leaf and get fit. Also need to take my mind off
what's happened.

  Mike (the vet) has long-distance relationship with a Swedish
model.

From: Ceri Dixon (reception@widgetex.co.uk)
To: Lucy Gordon (lucy@widgetex.co.uk)

10.02
Subject: Exercise your imagination

Ugh! Can't think of anything worse than being trapped on
fast-moving conveyor belt in front of MTV while there are cakes
left in the world. And you are SO SLIM! Still, if you insist upon
personal humiliation and torture on a grand scale, someone
who looked like Jean Claude Van Damme dropped a few
brochures into reception this morning. A new gym is offering
free fitness assessments. They measure how fit you are and
suggest an individually tailored workout regime. Sounds
awful.

Come and fetch one (and me) on your way to coffee. I have a bag of fun-sized Mars Bars . . .

Shame about Mike. I was thinking he might cheer you up . . . !

The Sweatshop

Name: Lucy Gordon
Membership number: 00987K
Joined: 29/7

W **Microsoft Word – Lucy's shame.doc**

Result of tonight's free assessment = I am monumentally unfit. A huge gorilla with muscles as big as bricks took my heart rate, measured my thighs, waist and upper arms with callipers and then tutted like mad, telling me that I'll have to start ultra-slowly as I have no muscle tone at all. No wonder Greg and I are through – he must think I'm a lard mountain. Managed three minutes on a treadmill before feeling dizzy and having to sit down on a nearby bench to recover. Then a second beefy gorilla lumbered over to ask me whether I was planning to use the weight-press or just drape myself over it. I looked up to see fifty kilos of lead above my head. When I got up, Gorilla 2 lay back and pumped them up and down as though they were a gurgling baby. Suitably inspired, I managed another two minutes on the treadmill. Think I'll train on ladies-only morning in future.

Posted on the Burr Cottage fridge:

COW IN CLOVER RESULTS

Friday 31st July (score kept by Bella):
Absentee: Big Mike (Excuse: collie with broken leg)
Subject for discussion: Lucy's love-life.

Number of times Lucy said 'Greg': 28.
Best quote: 'He hasn't even tried to call since I broke it off. You'd think he'd check that I meant it, try to win me back.'

Number of times Jane screamed in frustration: 6.
Best quote: 'Your engagement wasn't the only thing you should have broken off. I can think of at least one unwanted appendage Greg would be better off without.'

Number of times Bella told Lucy she wasn't fat: 9.
Best quote. 'Remember, you were the one who told him to take a hike, so he can't have thought you were a lard mountain.'

RESULT: Lucy = bathroom, bins, washing up, weeding, vacuuming and dusting (needs distracting, also good for stamina). Bella and Jane = week off.

✗ Greg Burton Charter Pilot ✗
Apartment G, Wexbury Heights, The Wharf, Wexbury, Berks
Hangar 134F, Thrushfield Aerodrome, Swifthill, Salisbury, Wilts

Dear Lucy,

As you know, I am not given to writing letters. In our entire relationship I think I have sent you just three postcards. Now I am putting pen to paper and pouring out my heart, so please bear with me if I am not as eloquent as the heroes in all those slushy books you read. Nor am I quite as perfect. But I do love you and I am very sorry for what has happened.

I know that I am responsible for causing you a great deal of unhappiness. It was wrong of me not to tell you about the job in Finland. I did try to – the night you came to my flat to show me your holiday photographs. But then you asked whether I wanted to break off our engagement and I panicked, asking you to move in here instead. The truth is I couldn't face the idea of leaving you behind, but I knew you would not leave that high-powered job you love so much just for me. Nor was I certain that you would be willing to wait for me to return. I was in a terrible dilemma. I have even seriously considered turning the job down (even though it is extremely well paid and would secure our future for years to come).

And so I asked Peach for advice. I was simply looking for a feminine perspective, quite innocently asking how she thought I should approach you. I will not deny that there has always been attraction between us, but we have always resisted. However, you were pushing me further and further away and Peach was there for me. I regret letting it go too far. I never wanted to hurt you.

In my defence, I must add that your behaviour has been more than a little odd since we became engaged. You have been distracted and edgy and have displayed some worryingly destructive urges (your abuse of my plumbing system, waste disposal unit, window boxes and log-effect fire have not gone unnoticed). I have felt both concerned and neglected. Some would say that you pushed me into Peach's arms.

But I do not want this to be the end. I believe that we do have a future together and that, in time, you could become a good wife to me. I should like to discuss this and other matters further if you will allow me to buy you a drink somewhere quiet and neutral (I hear the new Vats Wine Bar is very good and has a half-price happy hour between six and seven on weekdays).

Awaiting your response,

Greg x

From: Lucy Gordon (juicylucy@webbedup.net)
To: Mo Lavender (Hobo-mobo@Hotmail.com)

18.46
Subject: Letter

Yes! Long letter from Greg in this morning's post. I've scanned it
in so that you can read it too (daren't show it to Bella and Jane
who I know will fight to get to the matches first). Feel really quite
guilty when I read it (which I have done five times so far).
Although I have to say the bit about innocently seeking Peach's
feminine perspective annoys me. If he'd gone to Claire Rayner for
advice, would he have ended up going 'too far' with her? I doubt
it.

Have hidden letter in my bedroom linen basket so that Bella
and Jane can't read it and start picking him to bits. I think it's
very moving, and although I won't call him – yet – I shall treasure
it. At least it shows he cares. L xxx
letter.doc attachment here

Sunday Lunch Menu – 13 Roundhead Avenue, Wexbury.
Chef: Liv Gordon

Asparagus in garlic butter
Roast beef, Yorkshire pudding, glazed carrots, mange touts, baked
*   potato skins*
Strawberries and cream

To be accompanied by bottle of Bordeaux, '97
For Liv and Mother: 2 Litres of Lambrusco Rosé

Monday 3rd August

Dear Big Brother,

I am no longer engaged to be married to Greg. We are no longer together. We are finito. You were right all along. Now stop gloating.

Mum and Dad are obviously still in shock (see attached menu – surprisingly normal). They can talk about nothing else but my broken engagement, asking constant questions: 'Is it really over between you two?'; 'What did he do that was so awful, Lucy?'; 'Why are you still wearing his ring?' Thank heavens for Granny. All she said was: 'Who is this Greg person? Have I met him?'

Please tell the sheep that celibacy is the latest craze.

Love

Lucy xx

W **Microsoft Word – Lucy's resolve.doc**

Still can't get my engagement ring off despite several attempts with washing-up liquid. Have just re-read the letter that Greg sent me. Am only reading it four or five times a day now, which is much less than at first. Haven't heard from him since I received it. Could he have gone to Finland already? Am tempted to call Peach to ask whether she knows, but cannot bring myself to. Must be strong.

Went to ladies-only morning at The Sweatshop today in hope that I could sweat out my twenty minutes on the Stairmaster away from the critical gazes of the beefy gorillas, but it was even worse. Was surrounded by women who looked as though they had just walked into the gym from the set of *Baywatch*. I was wearing my old leggings and Purple Ronnie t-shirt of Bella's. All the babes were in g-string leotards over cycling shorts in the latest fashion shades. Not only that, but they seemed to manage hours at a time on the rowing machine without breaking into a sweat, while I only lasted five on the treadmill at the lowest setting. Ache all over now.

From: Dave Marks (dave@widgetex.co.uk)
To: All staff (mailall@widgetex.co.uk)

09.04
Subject: Feeling mean? Feeling artistic?

Dear All,

Picture the scene – Ceri the receptionist belly-up in a slowly spreading red pool; Lianne slumped in the undergrowth, eyes rolling back in her head; Lucy as limp and lifeless as a rag doll, hanging over a tree branch, her pert little bottom poking in the air.

This is your mission, should you choose to accept it:

The day: Bank Holiday Sunday (30th August)

The venue: Shoot'n'Kill, Lower Dinfield Airbase

The aim: To splatter the other team to kingdom come

Yes, we're talking PAINTBALLING! At just fifty quid a head including refreshments, it's the best fun you'll have this side of being tied in a sack with Britney Spears.

Please email me back on this, or sign the list on the staff notice board.

Chz,

Dave 'the marksman' Marks

From: Lucy Gordon (lucy@widgetex.co.uk)
To: Dave Marks (dave@widgetex.co.uk)

09.23
Subject: Re: Feeling mean? Feeling artistic?

Er – why?

From: Dave Marks (dave@widgetex.co.uk)
To: Lucy Gordon (lucy@widgetex.co.uk)

09.27
Subject: Re: Re: Feeling mean? Feeling artistic?

So that I can shoot you, of course. Warning: Dave Marks shoots to lady-kill, licensed to thrill.

From: Lucy Gordon (lucy@widgetex.co.uk)
To: Dave Marks (dave@widgetex.co.uk)

09.41
Subject: Re: Re: Re: Feeling mean? Feeling artistic?

Not if I shoot you first – you're a far bigger target than me, and 90 per cent of that is head.

From: Dave Marks (dave@widgetex.co.uk)
To: Lucy Gordon (lucy@widgetex.co.uk)

09.44
Subject: Re: Re: Re: Re: Feeling mean? Feeling artistic?

You're the best-shaped target in this office. Is it true that you and Greg have split up? If so, can we schedule a meeting in the stationery cupboard? Fna fna.

From: Lucy Gordon (lucy@widgetex.co.uk)
To: Dave Marks (dave@widgetex.co.uk)
cc: All Staff

09.52
Subject: Re: Re: Re: Re: Re: Feeling mean? Feeling artistic?

My broken engagement is none of your damned business.

Incidentally, what happened between us in the stationery cupboard was the worst executive decision of my life. I am only grateful that you have now so foolishly handed me the opportunity to get my own back for being exploited when I was drunk and vulnerable. There is a paint-ball with your name on it, Dave 'brown-Y-fronts' Marks. Go on, punk, make my Bank Holiday.

  Lucy 're-inforced gusset' Gordon

From: Lucy Gordon (lucy@widgetex.co.uk)
To: Ceri Dixon (reception@widgetex.co.uk)

10.01
Subject: Black marks

Was it you who told Dave Marks that Greg and I have broken up?

From: Ceri Dixon (reception@widgetex.co.uk)
To: Lucy Gordon (lucy@widgetex.co.uk)

10.05
Subject: Guilty as charged

Sorry, sorry, sorry! I owe you three boxes of Milk Tray and a family-sized Galaxy. He was feeling really miserable and I took pity on him. I shouldn't have said anything, but he and Wendy from Accounts aren't getting on too well after their holiday together and I thought it might help. Did you know she was stung by a jellyfish and had to lie in bed all day while he went out jet-skiing? She made his life hell.

From: Lucy Gordon (lucy@widgetex.co.uk)
To: Ceri Dixon (reception@widgetex.co.uk)

10.12
Subject: Hell as in hot and immoral

Yes, I bloody did know. Rumour has it his jet-ski instructor was a Pam Anderson lookalike. She probably trains at The Sweatshop.

And that's no reason to tell him about me and Greg. Who else have you told? I've suddenly started getting lots of emails offering me sympathy and wanting to know what happened. This is all your fault for being unable to keep a secret.

From: Ceri Dixon (reception@widgetex.co.uk)
To: Lucy Gordon (lucy@widgetex.co.uk)

10.15
Subject: More than 10CC

I really am sorry I told Dave. But I think you'll find you were the one who told everyone else in the office. You just cc-ed your 'brown-y-front' message to the whole building. Bad luck, re-inforced gusset. Snickers bar waiting in the staff room if you need it.

W Microsoft Word – Lucy's resolve2.doc

Went to sports shop and bought trendy pink leotard and cycling shorts today. Tried them on at home and looked surprisingly good, although leotard is a bit tight. Was just trying out a few high kicks in the garden to test out their elasticity when Big Mike leant over the fence and wolf-whistled. I almost fell into the pond in surprise. Very hard to make neighbourly small talk when red in the face and aware that your g-string leotard has risen up dramatically. Had to stand on tip-toes to stop it digging in, and found myself bleating, 'Have you seen Peach lately?'

He looked a bit embarrassed. 'I think she's overseas.'

I knew it! She's followed Greg to Finland, the besotted fool. He probably asked her to join him there after I told him to get lost. I stormed inside ready to dig his letter out of the laundry basket and burn it, but it was missing – along with all my white washing. It turns out Jane had some space left in the machine and put my stuff in too. Greg's letter is now a mulchy white crust on several t-shirts including Purple Ronnie. I was just screaming at her to leave my washing to me, when the phone rang.

'Lucy, darling, we have to talk. I'm so miserable without you.'

I tried to be cool and distant, I really did. But Greg's not in Finland after all. He's in Wexbury and he misses me like mad. Meeting him for a quick drink can't hurt can it? Must get the engagement ring off first, though. Either that, or wear gloves.

From: Lucy Gordon (juicylucy@webbedup.net)
To: Mo Lavender (Hobo-mobo@Hotmail.com)

21.56
Subject: Letter

Can you email me back the scanned letter I sent you asap? The hard copy has been destroyed, I can't get the computer to open the file and I need to have another look NOW. Hope you're well. L xx

---

W Microsoft Word – Lucy's resolve3.doc

Got up at six so that I could spend an hour in The Sweatshop, concentrating on their brand new, state-of-the-art Lateral Ski-swing (known as the 'Latski' to regulars). It's supposed to blitz your thighs into shape ultra-fast. I think I was being a bit ambitious, however, as I couldn't get any swing at all on the skis. I was about to give up when an instructor came up and told me that the tension was turned up far too high and showed me how to reduce it. The next moment I was shooting around on the skis like Eddie the Eagle on a jump ramp, totally unable to stop. It was so humiliating. I was trapped, swinging uncontrollably for the best part of an hour before anyone noticed my distress and came to rescue me. Even then I got no sympathy as I was ticked off for threatening to damage The Sweatshop's latest bit of high-tech equipment. I can't believe that they charge me seventy pounds a month to tell me off for almost killing myself. I was on the verge of resigning my membership, when one of the instructors suddenly whooped, 'Look at those sexy quads!' I hadn't a clue what a quad was, but followed her gaze to the area of my lower thigh at which she was pointing. To be honest, I couldn't see a lot of difference, but she was entranced. 'Latski's done it again. That's muscle-tone!' Feel fantastic as a result.

And that is why I treated myself to a haircut and manicure this lunchtime, plus a new short, flimsy dress from Monsoon. It has nothing to do with meeting Greg this evening. I have muscle-tone. Whether Greg gets to see it or not is immaterial. I want to show it off to the world. I'd do the same if I was meeting my mother for tea. Besides which, it will do him no harm to see me when looking my best. He'll realise that I'm not grieving without him, that I am getting on with my life and developing muscle-tone. Jane and Bella think I'm mad, but I've told them it's just a casual drink with my ex, nothing major. Modern couples – or former couples – do it all the time. Might need a quick drink first as Dutch courage to get through main drink, though.

W Microsoft Word – Lucy's resolve4.doc
I hate Greg! The pig didn't turn up. I sat alone in the Café Blanc, two gin and tonics up, and waited for almost an hour. Just as I finally realised that I'd been stood up, Ambitious Dave walked in with Wendy from Accounts. They looked very smug when they saw me. Had to get a taxi home, leaving my car at the office which means I'll have to get up extra-early tomorrow and take the bus. Can't even beg a lift into town with Bella as St Cuthbert's have broken up for the summer.

From: Dave Marks (dave@widgetex.co.uk)
To: Lucy Gordon (lucy@widgetex.co.uk)

09.44
Subject: Eleanor Rigby

Late night, Ms Gusset? Is that why you are so late? It's so sad to see a woman drinking alone.

From: Lucy Gordon (lucy@widgetex.co.uk)
To: Dave Marks (dave@widgetex.co.uk)

09.50
Subject: Mr Rigsby

I have already told you that my love life is none of your business, but since you are so worried about my mental health, you will be reassured to know that I had in fact been out for a drink with my new lover, Latski. He is a fire-fighter and was called away to a major incident that evening, which is why I was alone.

Posted on the Burr Cottage fridge:

> ## COW IN CLOVER RESULTS
> Friday 14th August (score kept by Jane):
> Absentee: Bella (In pub, but serving behind bar most of evening)
> Subject for discussion: Lucy's 'quads'
>
> Number of free rounds Bella managed to pass over without landlord noticing: 6
>
> Number of free packets of peanuts Lucy ate: 12.
> Best quote: 'Can you get post-traumatic shock from peanuts, or just the regular anaphylactic kind?'

Number of pints Mike drank: 8.
Best quote: 'So who is this Latski bloke you're dating,
Lucy? Is he Polish?'

Number of times Jane asked Lucy if Greg had been in touch: 3.
Best quote: 'I bet he has – you have that guilty hamster look
on your face.'

RESULT: Lucy = bathroom, bins, washing up, weeding,
vacuuming and dusting (needs to work off peanuts, also
punishment for lying). Bella and Jane = week off.

---

*You have . . . one . . . new message. Message received . . . today
. . . at . . . ten . . . fifty-seven . . . pee emmmm.*
'Lucy, it's Greg. Where were you last night? I waited in the Café
Bleu for two hours. You could have at least called. Were you meeting
Latski, is that it? Who is he? Call me.'

WIDGETEX LIMITED
Memo
To: All Staff
Re: This Week
In our ongoing effort to make Widgetex Ltd as productive
and efficient as possible, we have engaged in a specialist
consultancy to observe the company and its workers in
action for one week. In this way we hope to maximise
productivity, minimise waste, downsize workspaces and
upgrade mental efficiency. Wize-up is a dynamic, pro-active
American company who have just opened offices in Slough,
and whose reputation for hard-hitting and radical yet
employee-friendly change have earned them blue-chip
clients world-wide.

Their representatives will be present in the office from this morning. Please be polite, but otherwise continue as though they are not here. I cannot stress the importance of carrying on your day-to-day work as per normal. These people need to see us in all our dimensions, good and bad, in order to provide a full and realistic report.

Gavin Slater

From: Ceri Dixon (reception@widgetex.co.uk)
To: Lucy Gordon (lucy@widgetex.co.uk)

10.30
Subject: Wize-up guys

Yeah, I believe it – not! There goes the Lottery Sweepstake, the Busy Lizzy Rota, the KitKat Kitty and the Rude E-mails Run. Still, the short blond one is BEYOND CUTE. I love Americans. I'm going to get his number.

From: Ceri Dixon (reception@widgetex.co.uk)
To: Lucy Gordon (lucy@widgetex.co.uk)

11.41
Subject: Wize this going on?

Now I know this week is literally ball-breaking. Ambitious Dave's executive desk toy (the one with steel spheres on strings which clack against one another) has collapsed under the strain! Have you noticed he's been getting in before eight? So much for Slavey's carry-on-as-normal lecture.

What's that funny smell?

From: Ceri Dixon (reception@widgetex.co.uk)
To: Lucy Gordon (lucy@widgetex.co.uk)
11.45
Subject: Wize it that the best ones are taken?

The air conditioning's been aromatherapied. Short-arsed blond one is married. Huff. Shall I go for the stiff in a suit and specs or the swarthy latino one? Fancy a Walnut Whip?

From: Lucy Gordon (lucy@widgetex.co.uk)
To: Ceri Dixon (reception@widgetex.co.uk)

09.07
Subject: Wize my wardrobe not better organised?

Have you heard about 'Casual Friday'? Christ – I have enough trouble deciding what to wear into work as it is. I'll never make it into the office. Dave has been here since six, by the way. The cleaners let him in.
    Why are they moving the pot-plants around?

From: Ceri Dixon (reception@widgetex.co.uk)
To: Lucy Gordon (lucy@widgetex.co.uk)

09.12
Subject: Wize-up your wealth corner

We're being Feng Shui-ed.
    I blame Mrs Slave Driver. She's heavily into business consultancy evening classes at Wexbury College while all the little Slave Drivers are away at summer camps, crammers and grandparents. We sometimes have a chat when she's on hold for Gavin and the switchboard's quiet. I'm hoping for some serious gossip, but so far she's only let slip that SD thinks Lianne is 'a bit flighty'. Big deal. She's bloody Aeroflot.

09.17
Subject: Wize idea

In that case, tell Mrs SD that he's on another line more often, so that you can extract more relevant bits of information – such as when his efficient young marketing executive, Lucy, is due for a pay rise/company car/better computer.

From: Lucy Gordon (lucy@widgetex.co.uk)
To: Ceri Dixon (reception@widgetex.co.uk)

13.48
Subject: Aghhh!

One of the Wize-up consultants (the stiff in a suit and specs) seems to rather like me. Thank God they didn't come into the office until lunchtime today (in case you were wondering, I spent most of the morning in the loos trying to remove my engagement ring with the aid of the battery-operated Widgetex Oral Gum Polisher and a bar of soap). You'd think it would drop off now I've lost some weight, but my father doesn't call me mallet-knuckles for nothing. I'd given up in defeat and was sitting despondently at my desk munching on an M and S roasted vegetable sandwich (v. low cal to make up for the fact I skipped a session on the punishing Latski at my gym this morning) when a grinning goof in a baseball cap bounced up and said, 'Hi, I'm Bud. Great blouse.' It was the Wize-up stiff out of uniform.

This 'Casual Friday' thing is the pits. I'm wearing shorts and an ultra-fashionable draw-string gypsy shirt which slips off my shoulders all the time. It's supposed to reveal a lot of smooth, bronzed skin, but actually just flashes my grubby bra straps. Is Bud blind? (Actually given the thickness of his glasses, I think he may be more Mr Magoo than Steve Austin.) Still, I was grateful for the compliment and grinned back at Blind Bud. He's rather sweet in a speccy, Ivy League sort of a way, isn't he? He was just saying that he'd put in a good word with SD for me, as I clearly 'mousepad-lunch', when he spotted my reddened ring finger and dropped the grin. 'You got an allergy to that big rock, Ms Gordon?'

I took a deep breath and spluttered the truth: 'My fiancé and I are through; I'm finally meeting him for a post-mortem drink tomorrow afternoon, and I want my ring to be off my finger before I do so that he doesn't think that I want to get back with him.' Was convinced I'd just jettisoned my chances of promotion, but quick as a flash, my Yanky chum whipped the cursed ring off with one swift, deft tug. 'How did you do that?' I gazed at him in awe as he offered me Hatton Gardens' finest carats back as though it was a 7UP ring-pull. He shrugged and winked. 'Because I wanted to, I guess. You free tomorrow night – after you meet your ex?'

From: Ceri Dixon (reception@widgetex.co.uk)
To: Lucy Gordon (lucy@widgetex.co.uk)

14.02
Subject: Fworrrr!

I am so jealous! That is just totally bloody sexy.

I'm definitely going to ask the Latino out. Maybe we can double-date?

Rats, I've just remembered I'm taking my little brother to Legoland tomorrow afternoon. Anyway, you're already double-dating. Good luck!

Got up early to blitz Basborough Retail Village, and returned with the sexiest little black dress imaginable, plus new heels and earrings. Unfortunately I didn't manage to smuggle my treats upstairs before Bella spotted me. She's on her own this weekend because Brick is playing a festival gig, and I think she's in a ratty mood because she immediately started having a go at me for buying a new outfit to wear to meet Greg. 'He'll know you've made a big effort and he'll think you want him back.'

'I don't,' I huffed, not quite catching her eye. 'Besides, I'm only meeting Greg for a quick drink before I go out on a date with someone else.'

To my shame, Bella thought I was talking about Latski, and when I said I was actually meeting Bud the Wize-up nerd (although I told her he was a whizz-kid, not a nerd), she clapped her hands together happily and apologised for misjudging me. At that moment, Jane let herself in from teaching a driving lesson and said that she'd bumped into Mike and asked him in for coffee. Bella was still clapping her hands and turned to them both with a wicked smile.

'Guess what? Lucy's playing the field. Not only is she having an affair with Latski the muscle-man, and meeting her horrible ex tonight, but she's also got a hot date with an American millionaire later.'

I'm not sure where she got the millionaire bit from, but I didn't correct her. Jane and Big Mike looked staggered. I don't think they were as delighted by reports of my wild love-life as Bella, who is far more of a free spirit. In fact, Mike looked really uncomfortable.

'Don't you think it's a bit soon to be seeing other people, Lucy? After all, you've only just broken off your engagement.'

He must think I'm such a trollop. I went very, very red and couldn't say anything. I suppose Bella had made it sound a lot racier than it is (Latski doesn't exist after all), but the truth is, it *is* too soon to be seeing anyone new and I don't fancy Bud at all. I think he's a complete anorak. I only agreed to go out with him because I was grateful that he got my ring off and because I want to make

Greg jealous. I've arranged for him to come to Café Blanc an hour after I've agreed to meet Greg. Now I don't want to see either of them.

Jane has suggested I stand them both up and go to the pub with her, Mike and Bella instead. She's probably right.

*

Have put my new dress on and it really is far too sexy to waste on the Cow in Clover. I want to see Greg one last time, and for him to see me with muscle tone and with a new boyfriend (although I hope Café Blanc is dimly lit and that Bud doesn't wear his baseball cap/glasses/Dilbert t-shirt). I want him to see that I don't care about him any more. Must just apply another layer of mascara. Wearing waterproof just in case.

Sunday Lunch Menu – 13 Roundhead Avenue, Wexbury.
Chef: Liv Gordon

Escargots in rich sherry vinegar aspic with salmon skin crisps
Whole butternut squash boiled in goose fat, served on a bed of spicy
rice
Strawberries and cream

To be accompanied by bottle of Australian Shiraz
For Mother: Litre of Lambrusco Rosé

Burr Cottage
Chisbourne

Sunday 23rd August

Dear Big Brother,

Oh bum. I get one chance to sort things out between Greg and I, and I ruin it by arranging for a decoy to arrive in the bar where we'd met. How was I to know that Greg would mistake the decoy for a piece of exercise equipment?

I'm such an idiot. Mum just laughed as I wailed my tale of woe, but I'm *so* embarrassed. Last night, Greg thought that goofy Bud from work was Latski, my fictional gym lover. Either the lighting in Café Blanc was dimmer than it seemed, or Greg was, because Bud looked squittier than ever to me. I know I wanted to make G jealous. But not *that* jealous. We'd been getting on pretty well and Greg said some very nice things about me (although I noticed he kept eyeing up the waitress while he did it), and he even said he would stay in the UK if I asked him to. That was when Bud arrived carrying a huge bunch of flowers. I guess they hid his weedy chest because Greg looked murderous and said, 'You must be the bastard Pole who's trying to get into my fiancée's knickers.'

'Hey, calm down, buddy.' When Bud – who looked a bit confused at the Pole bit – put out his arm to shake hands, Greg tried out a spectacular judo move which didn't quite come off and they both ended up lying on the floor covered in flowers. They looked so silly, I found myself bursting out laughing. At this, Greg stood up, brushed down his cream chinos and huffily told me that he couldn't think what he ever saw in me and that he's going to Finland after all. As he left the restaurant, he shouted over his shoulder, 'And you can go to Hell, Lucy Gordon!'

Quick as a flash, I shouted back, 'And you can go to Helsinki, you rat-bag!' But he'd already left. Typical. The first time I think of a brilliant put-down, and Greg doesn't hear it. That might be the last time I see him. Am fighting urge to send postcard with my pithy little phrase on it, but Mum says it wasn't that funny.

So now Bud is going back to Slough with broken specs, Greg is going to Finland with a broken engagement, and I still have a broken heart. It's not just balls that are cracking under the strain this week. I think I need to Wize-up fast.

I know you won't understand much of this letter, but I need

to get it off my chest and if you read it out to the sheep I'm sure they'll explain.

Love,

Lucy xx

From: Dave Marks (dave@widgetex.co.uk)
To: All Staff (mailall@widgetex.co.uk)

16.09
Subject: Paint-balling

Before you all slope home early for the Bank Holiday, can I remind you all that we are meeting at Lower Dinfield Airbase at 10.00 hours prompt on Sunday? Wear sensible shoes (no that's not lower stilettos, Lianne). Lucy Gordon's excuse that she has a last-minute lunch date with a Great Aunt has been rejected. I am sure I'm not alone in noticing the attentions of a certain American gentleman and I know Lucy is heart-broken to see the Wize-up team leave. (For those of you on other floors, Bud Lightweight has been shooting Lucy loving looks over his sellotaped spectacles all week.) And I know we would all like to shoot him and his team back with lime-green paint in a pellet, but poor Bud's declined to join the war games because he's hyper-allergic and thinks that he might develop a skin rash if he's splattered. Shame.

From: Lucy Gordon (juicylucy@webbedup.net)
To: Mo Lavender (Hobo-mobo@Hotmail.com)

23.45
Subject: Horsing around

Sorry I haven't emailed in ages, my darling brainwashed ex-housemate. I was a bit annoyed that you didn't send back the scan of Greg's letter. All sorted now (I'm as single as a seven inch

176

again, by the way, fna fna). Greg now thinks I am getting a lot of horizontal action with a body-builder called Latski, which indeed I am. It's a type of skiing machine, although poor Greg doesn't know that and I didn't really get the chance to tell him when we met up for a drink to talk things through.

Just had a fantastic day. Went to support Jane at some horse trials in Wiltshire. She was riding Zak the Yak, a big, boisterous youngster that Horsy Tim has trained and is now selling. Apparently he's destined to be something of a superstar, and Horsy Tim's new girlfriend is really jealous that he asked Jane to compete him, not her.

I got to hold the bucket and sponge to cool his legs between the phases, so I felt very important, even though Zak bit me twice on the bum. Am convinced that my contribution is one of the key reasons he and Jane came third overall. Everyone was really chuffed; Horsy Tim says the success will put up Zak's asking price. Jane looked really glum at this, and when I asked her what was wrong, she said, 'I was hoping to buy him, Lucy, but I simply can't afford to now. I really need a co-investor, but no one I know rides.' She gave me a meaningful look, but I ignored it as Zak had just bitten me again. I haven't been in a saddle since I was thirteen, and I was pretty hopeless then. If I ever take it up again, it certainly won't be on board seventeen hands of spring-loaded, loony horsepower which costs as much as a BMW.

Heading home in the horse-box, Jane confessed that she was the one who had told Greg about Latski and that it was Bella who told him to meet me in the Café Bleu not Blanc the first time we were supposed to meet up (when you didn't send me back his letter).

'Do you really hate him that much?' I asked sadly.

'More,' Jane gave me a hug. 'You deserve much better, Lucy. If I ever start going out with someone who treats me like Greg does you then I hope you'll do the same for me. Lock me in the house if necessary.'

I found myself catching Horsy Tim's eye and went pink. But HT is nothing like Greg – he's kind to animals and has told Jane all along that he only wants a casual fling. Greg said he wanted to marry me. I feel so stupid for ever believing him. I hope he falls down a fjord. Managed to cry quite a lot tonight, which Jane says is a good sign, that I'm accepting things at last. She says she, B and Mike were worried about how positive I seemed after the break-up and they thought I was in denial.

'Have you been talking about me to Mike?' I sniffed when I heard this.

Jane looked guilty and said that he asked after me a lot.

I suppose he would do. After all, he must want to know what's going on between Greg and Peach, although Greg swore to me at the Café Blanc that he hadn't seen her since the night of the barbecue. I don't think Big Mike stands much chance of getting her back, though.

'Is Mike very upset?' I asked Jane.

She laughed in amazement. 'Why should he be? He seems happier than he has in weeks, actually.'

Men are so callous. I hope Greg is at least shedding the odd tear, even if it's only from frostbite. L xxx

---

Sunday Lunch Menu – Dinfield Airbase.
Chef: 'Slab'

Meat in fat, vegetables in fat, baked potatoes 'bullet'
Something that could be crème caramel or phlegm

To be accompanied by stewed tea or lukewarm Fanta

Sunday 30th August

Dear Big Brother,

Ouch, ouch, ouch! I am covered in little circular scars which
are starting to bruise up really badly. Spent entire day sweating
beneath camouflaged combat gear and itchy plastic face mask,
chasing other masked militia (aka Widgetex work-mates)
around a wood near the Basborough Industrial Estate.
Actually, I spent more of the day squatting behind large trees
trying to hide, but I was shot to pieces none the less. One very
short, evil-looking wannabe Rambo unloaded their paint-ball
canister into me as often as possible – aiming cruelly at my
horse-bitten bottom. It's hard to tell who's who under the
masks, but I'm almost certain it was Ambitious Dave's
girlfriend, Wendy, as I spotted the blue eyeliner.

Afterwards, we all compared scars and I had about twice as
many as everyone else, although most of them were in a place I
wouldn't reveal. This is absolutely the last time I ever go paint-
balling. I'd rather be bitten by crazy Zak (the horse Jane loves)
any day.

Monday:

Mum and Dad were horrified at all my scars, which look even
worse today, as the bruising has spread and turned spectacular
shades of purple. I tried to take their minds off them by telling
the story of Jane and Zak the Yak. Yes, I am afraid she loves
another, and although it pains me to tell you this, Zak is
considerably better endowed and marginally more intelligent.
He is, however, a great deal more expensive and she can't
afford the asking price. Afterwards, Dad adopted that funny
look he sometimes gets when he's seen a new and impractical
piece of equipment he wants to buy – a steam engine or

something. I hope he's not thinking of taking up riding. He'd look ridiculous in breeches for a start.

Give a sheep a high five.

Love,

Lucy xx

W Microsoft Word – Zak.doc

Jane has been badgering me all week to buy a half share in Zak the Yak. I've pointed out that I already cater for one large furry animal – Platforms, who is almost the size of a lion cub nowadays, and extremely violent around the house. I have no urge to possess another antisocial beast – especially one that is even larger, more expensive to run and doesn't seem to like me very much. My bruises are finally starting to fade to yellow, but the ones Zak made when he bit me are still a vivid purple, and I can distinctly make out the teeth marks. I've suggested Jane asks Big Mike if he wants to co-own Zak. I'm not sure if he rides, but he must like horses – after all he's a vet. So Jane has asked him to come with her to the stables tomorrow afternoon to 'look him over' in the hope that Mike suddenly finds himself blown away with the urge to own a budding event horse. For some reason, she wants me to come along too.

'Because Mike likes you,' she pleaded. 'If you tell him how wonderfully Zak did at the trials last weekend, he'll see what a great investment he is.'

I hardly see that my word is going to make a lot of difference. Mike knows I'm completely ignorant when it comes to anything with four legs. When Platforms had her first dream, I bolted round to his back door and said I thought she was having a fit.

W Microsoft Word – Zak2.doc

Zak was as friendly as usual – he bit me on the arm the moment I reached up to pat him 'hello'. After that, I kept my distance. When Jane rode him over a few jumps in a field, I sat beside Mike on the gate and told him about paint-balling last weekend. He seemed really surprised that I'd do such a thing, and told me that he thought I was too 'girly' to run around in full combat gear. For some reason this really annoyed me, and I found myself boasting that I was fearless and a crack shot. 'Besides I've done lots of adventurous things,' I pointed out, 'I jumped out of an aeroplane last year.'

'I generally wait until they land,' he said idly, grinning at me. 'If you're such a dare-devil, why are you frightened of that big fellow?' He nodded at Zak who was towing Jane around the field at high speed, eyes rolling menacingly.

'I'm not!' I huffed. 'He just doesn't like me.'

'He doesn't respect you,' Mike corrected, sounding unpleasantly pompous. 'You have to show him who's boss. Why not take him for a ride?'

I made a lot of fuss about not wearing the right gear, and not having ridden in years, but Mike had thrown down the gauntlet – or riding glove – and I felt I had to prove something. I couldn't admit how terrified I felt, so I tried to look cool and unbothered and muttered something like 'piece of cake'. Jane was really keen to hand over the reins, and before I knew it I was being given a leg-up and suddenly the ground was a long, long way below me. I wanted that parachute again. As I clutched on to Zak's grey mane, I'm sure I saw Big Mike and Jane exchange a victory high five.

I'm not sure I showed him who was boss at all – in fact I'm pretty certain that he was just too shocked to misbehave as I bounced around in the saddle with pitiful lack of control and pretended to be enjoying myself for my audience's benefit. Thankfully, I managed to stay on, and Big Mike even said he was impressed by my riding, which I'm sure was a kind lie. Unfortunately for Jane, he's turned down the chance to invest in Zak because he wants to buy himself a motorbike: 'more horse-power, more pulling-power, more staying-power, less girl-power.' Sexist or what?

I now ache all over, and Jane has trebled her attempts to get me to drum up some cash. I've said no, absolutely not. I'd rather sign up for another parachute jump. Without the parachute.

20.23
Subject: Burr Cottage Latest

Thankfully Jane seems to have shut up on the subject of her dream-horse (she wants me to 'co-invest' in the thing with very large teeth called Zak which I told you about last time). She is currently completely distracted by the renewed passion of her dream-man, Horsy Tim, whose girlfriend is apparently laid up at her parents' Suffolk farm with a broken collarbone, poor thing. I can't say I approve – his behaviour reminds me too much of Greg's – but at least it's kept Jane busy. The new school term has brought her lots of evening driving lessons, and after that she dashes straight to the stables to parallel park in Tim's bed. Perhaps old Zak is feeling as neglected as HT's girlfriend. I almost feel sorry for him too.

In contrast to Jane's current love-fest, Bella and Brick seem to have hit a rough patch. They argue all the time at the moment, which is a bit distracting when he comes to stay at the cottage at weekends, especially when *Friends* is on the television. I had to watch it at Big Mike's cottage tonight, which was quite good fun as he opened a bottle of Merlot and told me that he thinks Peach has started dating another vet in his practice. Big Mike says the enamoured vet is continually late for work as a result of midnight consultations with 'a certain iguana owner'. He can be very dry and funny, although I'm not sure he's the 'big fan of *Friends*' he promised he was earlier. Half-way through tonight's episode, he pointed to Joey and said, 'Good grief – that guy from *Lost in Space* is making a guest appearance.'

Am v. worried about Bella and Brick, though. She says he is under stress because his band is on the verge of splitting up. It seems their bass player went to Reading Festival to play for a rival group in an outside tent, and is now signed up for some multi-million pound record deal with them. 'And the rest of Slug are so disillusioned they can't bring themselves to rehearse any more.' I made a joke about pulling the plug on Slug, but I don't think she found it very funny. Hope they work it out. L xxx

---

Burr Cottage
Chisbourne

Sunday 12th September

Dear Big Brother,

Just as I thought I was safe from all things equine, Dad has decided to take a passionate interest in the future of Zak the Yak. Honestly, I don't know what's got into him. He was holed up in his shed trying to strip down the lawnmower engine when I arrived for lunch, but within five minutes he popped his head through the kitchen window and asked after Zak. They next thing I knew, he was up to his elbows in Swarfega and quizzing me about how much a horse like Zak costs. I told him it was thousands and thousands and he went pale. Later spotted a copy of *Horse and Hound* on the coffee table. Hope he's not trying to find healthy hobby for wayward Alice.

She is in serious trouble as she returned to school last week and promptly got suspended for wearing her tongue stud at assembly. Mum hadn't even known until then that her youngest's tongue was pierced, although she now says she had noticed that Alice had been very quiet and eating a lot of soup. Alice has tried to pacify her by pointing out that Princess Anne's daughter has one, so it's v. classy, but she was not convinced. Mum's banned Alice from seeing Scrumpy, and is making her redecorate Granny's sitting room as a penance while she's off school. Some penance – Alice told me earlier that this was in fact 'really cool', as Granny has filled the fridge with hooch, watches daytime TV non-stop and lets Scrumpy in through the back door.

Mum asked me what I wanted for my birthday today. She gave me one of her wise, kind looks and said, 'Your father and I want to get you something extra-special this year, as you've had such a rotten time with Greg and everything.'

I felt strangely tearful at this. I don't care what you say, our parents are so fabulous. I mumbled something about not wasting their money on anything extravagant, and said that I'd be more than happy with a book voucher. Perhaps I should buy *Men Are From Mars, Women Are From Venus* with it?

Do sheep count humans when they're trying to sleep?

Love

Lucy xxx

W **Microsoft Word – Lucy's intrigue.doc**

Something odd is going on, and I'm almost certain it's to do with my birthday on Saturday. Bella and Jane are behaving very oddly, and even Big Mike seems to be in on the act. When I came home from work this evening, he was sitting in our kitchen with Jane, chatting nine to the dozen. They both shut up the moment I walked in and looked very furtive. I'd been to Waitrose to pick up some groceries which I tried to put down on the table, but Jane had a lot of papers spread out which she didn't seem to want me to see as she grabbed my shopping bags from me and insisted that she'd put my stuff away while I watched the news in the sitting room. 'I'll bring you a glass of wine through.' She practically elbowed me out of the door.

'But I don't want a glass of wine,' I grumbled, watching her whisk away the bag with my salsa and Doritos inside. 'I was going to eat something.'

'Fine!' She reached inside the bag and pulled out a packet of Hobnobs. 'Nibble on those.'

In the sitting room, Bella was planning a lesson for the next day with one eye on *EastEnders*. When I asked her what Jane and Mike were up to, she shrugged and mumbled something about a pre-sale vet test, but I'm convinced she was lying as she instantly went pink and changed the subject to my mother of all things – asking after her latest cooking enterprise; Mum is writing *The Adventurous Housewife's Cookbook* with the aid of a nineteen-fifties typewriter, and is convinced that she's destined to be the next Delia Smith. She's roped poor Bella in to do the artwork in exchange for unlimited home-made freezer food.

I think Bella is a bit down at the moment, because Brick is being such a pig. He hasn't called her all week – not since they had a huge row on Sunday night. I asked whether he'd be around for my birthday as I'm planning to get some friends together for a night at the Cow in Clover. Bella pulled a face and said she wasn't sure. Then she went all Miss Marple and started grilling me about who I'd already asked and at what time. The next moment she'd sloped into the kitchen and I could hear her whispering with Jane and Mike. I don't want to be presumptuous, but I'm starting to think that they may be planning a surprise party. Yippee!

The Adventurous Housewife's Cookbook

What every married woman should know

about spicing up her tired meat and two veg

Recipes devised by

LIV GORDON

Publisher's Name

Burr Cottage

Chisbourne

Saturday 18th September

Dear Big Brother,

I'm supposed to be tarting up for a meal out with the family and my housemates, but I have to sit down with my computer for five minutes to confess the awful truth. I'm not getting the surprise party I was beginning to expect, but I've certainly had a huge birthday shock.

When Big Mike drove a horse-box up the drive of Burr Cottage this afternoon with a red bow on each wing mirror, I thought I was seeing things – Mum and Dad were sitting in the cab beside him looking extremely pleased with themselves. Inside, Zak the Yak was kicking merry hell out of the panelling. Then, while everyone sang 'Happy Birthday dear Lucy' in the driveway, Jane shoved me up the ramp and he rolled his eyes menacingly before biting me on the arm. How generous, how loving and how utterly misguided can you get? Poor Dad must have forked out most of his savings on the only thing that terrifies me more than the Alien trilogy. I've tried to smile and laugh and be happy all day, but I feel like screaming. We all headed to the stables together, where Horsy Tim was waiting with a birthday cake in the shape of a horseshoe. Everyone wanted to see me riding, but I managed to persuade them that I preferred to watch Jane show off his talents instead. How could I admit I was scared stiff?

So I've been given a half share in the big equine brute for my birthday. I'm not sure which half – the one that bites or the one that kicks, but I hope it's the latter as I'm fighting a terrible temptation to look this particular gift horse in the mouth.

I know I must seem horribly ungrateful BB, particularly as I got a laptop for Christmas and now this. Mum and Dad have come a long way since you and I were given one adjustable roller-skate each. The trouble is, I'd rather they had done that – maybe one riding boot for me and one for you (I'd also have to have thick socks, of course, because you have such big feet these days). You see, I know why they are doing this. It's to make up for the fact that you have gone away, that I miss you so much and that they blame themselves for you leaving (as, I know, you do). The best present by far would be to see you and them reunited and they simply can't give me that. Can you?

Talk it over with the sheep.

Love,

Lucy xx

Posted on the Burr Cottage fridge:

Dear Jane,

Am in a v. bad mood with you. No, it's more than that; I'm fuming, spitting and hopping mad at you. I now know that you are entirely behind my parents' potty decision to blow their hard-earned savings on half a misanthropic horse for my birthday. Somehow you convinced them that, after my appalling attempt at riding Zak a couple of weeks ago, I was swept away with equestrian enthusiasm. Even more conniving is the fact that you've clearly told them you think it will help me 'get over Greg'. They could talk about nothing else at lunch yesterday — even Granny was full of horse stories from her childhood days before the war when she claims she 'was something of a latter-day Marion Mould', whoever that is. Alice is hugely jealous and can barely bring herself to talk to me at all, although she did manage to mutter that if she doesn't get a car for her birthday next January, she'll torch Dad's precious shed.

I have noticed that you are avoiding me this evening. Guilt, I guess. I've been pacing around the house awaiting your return so we can have it out, but you seem to be teaching an awful lot of late driving lessons. Either that, or you are riding 'our horse' in the floodlit manege. Or perhaps even having a secret liaison with Horsy Tim while his poor girlfriend is still in Suffolk recovering from a broken collarbone? Whatever you are doing, you have behaved despicably. I think I'll send you to Coventry. I'm going to bed.

Lucy

W Microsoft Word – Lucy's lonely.doc

Haven't exchanged a word with Jane all evening, which was quite tough as she kept asking me what was wrong. I think sending someone to Coventry is actually harder for whoever is forced to stay behind as there's no one to talk to. It wouldn't have been so bad if Bella were here, but she's gone to London to talk to Brick, who hasn't been in touch since their last big row.

From: Lucy Gordon (lucy@widgetex.co.uk)
To: Mo Lavender (Hobo-mobo@Hotmail.com)

16.05
Subject: More splits

Bella was in an awful state last night. She says that she and Brick are through. He was too much of a coward to tell her to her face, so when she turned up at his London flat, he pretended that he had to go out and then called her from a phone box around the corner to say that he didn't want to see her any more. She needed to talk last night, which was fine until Jane came home, wearing breeches and smelling of Zak. She tried to offer sympathy too, but there was obviously a lot of tension in the air as I'm not talking to her because she has conned my poor parents into buying a half share of Zak for my birthday. Poor Bella went to bed early. L xxx

W Microsoft Word – Lucy's feud.doc

Jane cracked under pressure tonight, burst into tears and said, 'Forgive me, Lucy. I was desperate.' I was dying to start yelling at her that she had probably bankrupted my parents and that Dad would now never be able to afford the steam engine he so longs to own, but I couldn't bring myself to. She was crying too much, and her nose had started to dribble. 'It's the only way I could see to keep

189

him,' she sobbed, 'and I love him so much. I'm so sorry. I had no idea your parents were spending their savings.'

I fetched her a tissue and sort of stood nearby as she wailed on guiltily, 'I thought it would make him love me, Lucy, but he's just as cruel as ever. It doesn't seem to have made any difference.'

I tried to point out that horses don't actually know when they've been bought, and that Zak was basically just a human-hater, but she didn't appear to be listening. Now that I mull it over, I think she might have been talking about Horsy Tim. So there are two heart-broken women in the house. I suppose the one consolation is that it has made me realise that I'm no longer broken-hearted over Greg. Maybe Jane's plan has worked after all.

From: Ceri Dixon (reception@widgetex.co.uk)
To: Lucy Gordon (lucy@widgetex.co.uk)

18.05
Subject: Don't you have a home to go to?

Why are you still here? I'm on a late shift, but you have no excuse.

From: Lucy Gordon (lucy@widgetex.co.uk)
To: Ceri Dixon (reception@widgetex.co.uk)

18.09
Subject: Black marks

Just finishing up a few bits and bobs. I might be here until seven or so, which is a shame because Horsy Tim offered me a free lesson on Zak at six-thirty, if I 'have the time'. I simply don't see myself getting through all this photo-copying. Plus my pen drawer needs tidying and I have to type a couple of memos for next Monday.

You have . . . one . . . new message. Message received today at . . .
six . . . fifty-seven . . . pee emmmm.
'This is Tim. I'm really sorry about last night. The thing is, I – er –
I need to talk to you fairly urgently about Zak's livery fees. Could
you give me a call? Thanks.'

Posted on the Burr Cottage fridge:

> *Jane,*
> *Tim's left a message on the answer phone. Not sure if it's*
> *meant for me, or you?*
> *Lucy*

W **Microsoft Word – Lucy's cowardice.doc**
Jane listened to Tim's message when she came in, muttered a couple
of unrepeatable oaths under her breath and then charged upstairs,
so I guess it was for her. Things are very awkward between them at
the moment because Tim's girlfriend has come back from Suffolk.
Jane wants to ride Zak as much as possible, but can't bring herself
to risk seeing them together at the stables. In contrast, I can't bring
myself to ride Zak at all.

Post-it note on Lucy's computer at work, Friday morning:

> Lucy,
>
> Hear you've got yourself
> a nag. Great stuff –
> very gutsy. Always
> fancied a go at that
> lark myself.
>
> GS

Post-it note on Slave Driver's framed photograph of Sir John Harvey-Jones, 11a.m.:

> *Be my guest!*
> *He could certainly use*
> *the exercise.*
>
> *Atb,*
>
> *Lucy*

Post-it note on Lucy's monitor, lunchtime:

> Very generous of you!
> Does one require
> specialist equipment
> and/or insurance?
>
> Gavin

Post-it note on Slave Driver's Ronson pen-holder:

> *Suggest you might want*
> *to take lessons first,*
> *maybe?*
> *Can provide telephone*
> *number.*
>
> *Lucy*

From: Anon
To: All staff (mailall@widgetex.co.uk)

17.04
Subject: Murder plot

Insider information reveals that ambitious Lucy Gordon is trying to murder marketing director, Gavin Slater, in order to advance her career. Not content with gradually poisoning his coffee/wiring his executive chair up to the mains/loosening the light fittings in his office, luscious Lucy has hatched a more sinister plot by specially training her horse to throw our beloved director of marketing. Poor, unwitting Gavin has no idea that his days are numbered. Her feeble excuses ('He's my boss and he asked – I could hardly tell him that the horse is a nut-case, could I?') are not to be believed.

Who will be Lucy's next victim?
Signed,
A friend

From: Lucy Gordon (lucy@widgetex.co.uk)
To: Dave Marks (dave@widgetex.co.uk)

17.13
Subject: Re: Murder plot

Bastard.

From: Lucy Gordon (juicylucy@webbedup.net)
To: Mo Lavender (Hobo-mobo@Hotmail.com)

20.23
Subject: More Burr Cottage Latest

Bella is painting the house in an attempt to get over her broken heart, and Jane has joined in enthusiastically. The last time any redecorating went on, as you may recall, it was a disaster, but this seems to be going pretty well – lemon-yellow and terracotta are the main themes, which are remarkably restrained for Bella. I offered to help out today, but I couldn't sugar-soap another skirting board after 'I Will Survive' had been played for the fifth time on the trot, so sloped next door to see Big Mike. He was watching the racing with his dogs on his lap, and seemed really pleased to see me. He asked me if I was enjoying Zak and was amazed when I confessed that I hadn't ridden him once since my birthday. 'I did visit him last weekend and offer him a few carrots,' I said to make up for it. To my surprise, he started to laugh.

'I knew you didn't really want that horse. I told Jane as much, but she was determined to go ahead and somehow managed to convince your parents to buy.'

'I don't think they needed much convincing,' I said. Mum and Dad are really into the horse-owning thing and have already bought themselves Barbours and green wellies in the hope of supporting me at forthcoming events. I feel awful about it.

Big Mike was really sweet about my stupid fear of Zak and told me that I should just go on visiting him with the carrots until I felt more confident around him. He's said he'll come too if I like, which is really kind. And he even said that he thought my parents had spent their money well, whatever the outcome. 'Zak is an investment – he's a really talented young eventer, Lucy. They'll get every penny back plus some if they ever sell. You haven't bankrupted them. Besides, they seem happy enough with their spending spree.' Big Mike can make me feel so good at times; I really like him. L xxx

---

Postcard featuring Wexbury Museum:

Dear Big Brother,
Mum and Dad have bought a
large hunting print to hang
above the fire, and have cleared
the mantelpiece 'for trophies'.
Oh God.
Want to be a sheep.
Love,
Lucy xxx

Jeremy Gordon
c/o PO Box 2307
Sheep's Eye
New Zealand

W Microsoft Word – Marketing Ideas23.doc

~~Bringing Widgetex's Products Up To Date~~

Slave Driver is being incredibly nice to me at the moment; I really hope this means I'm in line for a promotion. Perhaps it wasn't such a bad thing telling him that he could ride Zak after all? It's not as though he's taken me up on the offer – he probably just thought the gesture showed incredible generosity of spirit and management potential. I'm glad I didn't tell Jane about it – she'd have blown her lid. With any luck SD will forget all about his equestrian urges and just settle for restructuring the marketing team with me at the helm.

From: Lucy Gordon (juicylucy@webbedup.net)
To: Mo Lavender (Hobo-mobo@Hotmail.com)

21.16
Subject: Burr Cottage Goss

Bella and Brick are supposed to have split up, but he turned up here tonight on his smelly motorbike and demanded to see her. At first, she refused to let him in, then she relented and marched him into the sitting room for a 'talk'. Jane and I hid in the kitchen and tried to listen in, but heard nothing until Bella popped in to fetch a bottle of wine from the fridge before they both headed upstairs to her bedroom. They've been there ever since. I'm rather perplexed as Bella told me to refuse to see Greg after we split up, and insisted that I should never use his body for occasional wanton pleasure. As far as I can tell from the sound effects, it seems she has done just that with Brick.
L xxx

Notes on Burr Cottage fridge:

Don't Forget!

Lucy,
I have just realised that I
have to teach a driving lesson
this morning. Can you exercise Zak? I will try to come to
the stables later.
Jane

Jane,

Have been to the stables. Unfortunately I managed to forget
my boots and hat. Tim's girlfriend offered to lend me hers, but
very regrettably our feet are different sizes and I have an odd-
shaped head. I waited for you, but came back when it got dark.
I know that you still can't bring yourself to go to the stables
while Horsy Tim and his girlfriend are there together, but I
really think this is excessive behaviour. We both know Zak
needs lots of exercise to stop him being so evil. Am going to
Mike's to watch video (Brick and Bella in front room — do not
disturb unless you like the sight of naked flesh).

Lucy

Don't Forget!

Lucy,
How could you have forgotten
your boots and hat when they
are clearly sitting on the parcel
shelf of your car?
For your information I had to
put in extra hours to overcome Mad Mildred's three-
point-turn phobia.
Are Brick and Bella back
together then?
Jane

Lucy and Jane,

Just because Brick ended up staying all weekend, it
is NOT just like old times. It's over between us.
He's a pig.
He's leaving his leathers here until next w/e. Hope
that's okay.
Bella

From: Ceri Dixon (reception@widgetex.co.uk)
To: Lucy Gordon (lucy@widgetex.co.uk)

15.05
Subject: Tell!

What did Slave Driver want? I hear you were in his office ages this morning! Did you get the prom-oh-oh-otion?!!

From: Lucy Gordon (lucy@widgetex.co.uk)
To: Ceri Dixon (reception@widgetex.co.uk)

15.12
Subject: I wish

You know, I really thought he might this time. Did you see Ambitious Dave give me that really evil look when I was beckoned in? (I smiled at him smugly.)

Unfortunately, SD was just asking me about the budget for a forthcoming travel iron campaign. BUT, I guessed he was going to mention something casually at the end of the conversation, so I hung around his office for a while to give him plenty of opportunity, but he just started to make a call. A couple of minutes later, he looked up and said, 'What are you still doing here, Lucy?'

At that point, I decided that SD would respect a bit of forthright ambition, so I bit the bullet and asked whether there was anything else he wanted to talk to me about. It was a bit awkward because he was still on his call, but he managed to mutter, 'Such as what?' so quickly I said, 'My career prospects.' At this point whoever he was talking to must have started saying something important, because SD sighed heavily and gestured for me to leave the room, mouthing 'Later'. Have been hanging around his door all afternoon in the hope that he calls me back in, but so far he's been on the phone constantly. Am starting to suspect that I've judged the situation a bit badly. The only good thing to come out of it is that Ambitious Dave is looking really worried.

From: Ceri Dixon (reception@widgetex.co.uk)
To: Lucy Gordon (lucy@widgetex.co.uk)

15.15
Subject: Idea

I've stopped putting his calls through. That way he can pop out for a quiet word.

From: Lucy Gordon (lucy@widgetex.co.uk)
To: Ceri Dixon (reception@widgetex.co.uk)

16.52
Subject: Earache

Ceri, can you cancel the bar on SD's line? SD doesn't 'do' voice-mail, remember? When you pressed 'divert extension' earlier, it means that all his calls automatically come through to my phone. It hasn't stopped ringing for two hours and I've just had a very embarrassing experience with a conference call to a German gadget catalogue.

W Microsoft Word – Marketing Ideas24.doc

~~Making Widgetex's Crappy Products Popular~~

Terrible week at work. After my abortive chat with Slave Driver on Monday about career prospects, he seems to be avoiding me. Every time I get close, he mutters something about making a call and legs it. Ambitious Dave is convinced that something is afoot and keeps asking me what's going on. I wish I knew – SD was being as nice as pie last week and I was sure I was seconds away from a company car and an extra week's annual leave. He hasn't come into the office at all today, and Ceri – who always knows what's going on around here – says that he's gone to check out a training programme in Liverpool. 'Training for what?' I asked excitedly, but she just

shrugged and refused to say. Am taking her out for a drink after
work in the hope of loosening her up.

W Microsoft Word – Lucy's tight again.doc

Ceri can out-drink me any day. Boy is my head spinning. Far from
loosening her up, I just got tiddly myself and told her all about the
fact that I'd offered SD Zak to ride in the hope that he'd break his
leg again. Then I had another Sea Breezer and started ranting on
about how bored I am at work, and how much Ambitious Dave
winds me up. I think I got a bit carried away – I wasn't even aware
that I felt like that at all until I said it. Thank God Ceri is a paragon
of discretion. Would hate any of this to leak out. God, my head
hurts. Must find a Nurofen . . .

From: Lucy Gordon (juicylucy@webbedup.net)
To: Mo Lavender (Hobo-mobo@Hotmail.com)

21.16
Subject: Horsing around

Decided that I really had to try to ride Zak today. Jane hasn't
been to the stables in weeks, and Horsy Tim has been phoning
the cottage to ask if we've both died or something. So I put on as
many thick layers as I could to protect myself against his teeth
and went to Holtdean feeling like a soldier heading to the Front.
When I arrived, I saw the funniest sight ever – Slave Driver was
being led around the outdoor school on the yard's old shire,
Hairy Mammoth. He was wearing brightly coloured golfing
casuals and very shiny new boots. When he spotted me standing
at the rails, he called out, 'Hello there, Lucy!' in a remarkably
cheery manner. But he took one hand off Mammoth's mane in
order to wave and promptly fell off. I think he was a bit
embarrassed about this, because he hastily dusted himself down

and sidled up to me, muttering, 'Don't mention this at the office whatever you do. On balance, I think I prefer golf.'

Was so distracted by this that I forgot how terrified I was of Zak for a while and actually quite enjoyed my ride, although I just pottered around the lanes and didn't try anything ambitious, like trotting. He was remarkably well behaved – I think Horsy Tim must be drugging him. The only time he nearly exploded was when SD drove past in his shiny Merc and tooted the horn. I'm sure he was trying to get his own back.

Brick is yet again staying at the cottage this weekend, although Bella claims they are still not officially back together. Have never seen exes kiss as much as they do, or monopolise the television to watch sloppy videos, or go to bed early and then creak rhythmically until dawn. I hardly slept a wink last night for the sound of bedsprings. Jane and I met up in the kitchen at six, both looking baggy-eyed and irritable. Both agreed we're turning into bitter old spinsters. She's v. heart-broken over Horsy Tim although says he was very decent about it and that she hasn't given up hope. L xxx

---

Sunday Lunch Menu – 13 Roundhead Avenue, Wexbury.
Chef: Liv Gordon

Pickled quail's eggs stuffed with cod roe, served on blanched Chinese
  cabbage
Broiled ox tail in port, watercress and juniper sauce
Raspberries and cream

To be accompanied by Evans and Tate Merlot, '93
For Mother: Litre of Lambrusco Rosé

Sunday 18th October

  Dear Big Brother,

Mum is livid because she caught Alice trying to smuggle
Scrumpy into her bedroom last night. She has banned them
from seeing one another again (she bans them about once a
month and they take no notice). Alice consequently in hugely
black mood and refused to come down to lunch. We ate to the
thumping sound of Nirvana overhead. Granny started tapping
her fork in time and said she thought it was rather jolly. Mum
and Dad very po-faced. I tried to cheer them up by describing
Slave Driver falling off horse, but Dad said that he thought it
was very unwise of me to offer him Zak to ride because it
could be construed as bribery. I sulkily pointed out that Slave
Driver is far too hopeless to ever manage to ride Zak. Come to
that, so am I, but I didn't say that. Trophy shelf is still empty,
and Mum keeps looking at it and sighing loudly.

  Q: What do you call a sheep with no legs? A: A cloud.

  Love

  Lucy xx

From: Lucy Gordon (lucy@widgetex.co.uk)
To: Ceri Dixon (reception@widgetex.co.uk)

09.22
Subject: Prom-oh-oh-otion

The best thing has just happened! Slave Driver called me into the
office first thing and asked me to attend a three-day
management training course in Liverpool. Victory! Am going to
hang around the stables more often in future. Am all for bribery.

From: Ceri Dixon (reception@widgetex.co.uk)
To: Lucy Gordon (lucy@widgetex.co.uk)

09.25
Subject: Stable career

But I thought he was only going to send Dave on that course – I heard him booking it last Friday. Besides, you don't want to go do you? You said you were bored stiff here and hate Slave Driver.

From: Lucy Gordon (lucy@widgetex.co.uk)
To: Ceri Dixon (reception@widgetex.co.uk)

09.27
Subject: What????

Meet me in the loo. Urgent.

From: Ceri Dixon (reception@widgetex.co.uk)
To: Lucy Gordon (lucy@widgetex.co.uk)

09.40
Subject:

Shit, I'm sorry. How was I to know Wendy from Accounts was in the cubicle while I was joking about you having a secret hold over Slavey? You don't think she'll tell Dave, do you?

WIDGETEX LIMITED
Memo
To: Lucy Gordon, Dave Marks
Re: Management training
It has been brought to my attention that you are both treating the forthcoming course as a competition. This is most definitely not the case. Whilst I like to encourage a

dynamic and striving team, I cannot condone two employees going head-to-head in this fashion.

I must also add that there has been no coercion involved in my decision to add Lucy's name to the list. Any suggestion of this nature will be treated very seriously indeed. Lucy is on the course as a result of merit alone, plus the fact that there has been a group cancellation and we were offered a second place at a beneficial discount.

Gavin Slater

From: Dave Marks (dave@widgetex.co.uk)
To: Lucy Gordon (lucy@widgetex.co.uk)

16.34
Subject: Score

Dave 1, Lucy 0. And we're still weeks away from the course, Lucretia de Borgia. Just watch The Marksman go into action . . .

From: Lucy Gordon (lucy@widgetex.co.uk)
To: Ceri Dixon (reception@widgetex.co.uk)

13.43
Subject: The War

Ambitious Dave is being so competitive, it's driving me mad. He's been getting into the office earlier and earlier in the morning in an attempt to outdo me. Apparently he was in at ten past seven this morning – Reg the security guard told me. At this rate, AD will be staying the night here with a sleeping bag. I refuse to rise to his challenge.

~~What I would like to do to Dave Marks with a Travel Iron~~

0630 hours: God, it's lonely here first thing in the morning – just me and the office cleaners. Still, I'll be able to get lots of work done, plus I can't wait to see the look on AD's face when he walks in to find me already here. Am bound to gain lots of brownie points with Slave Driver.

1100 hours: Hmph! Apparently, Slave Driver has taken the whole of today off to organise a Halloween murder mystery weekend for the Rotary Club. AD rolled into work late, grinning from ear to ear to find me half asleep at my desk. 'Didn't I mention that the boss is off today, Lucy? Must have slipped my mind.' The pig.

Cutting from the *Wexbury Gazette*:

First Meet of the Year

Members and followers of the West Berkshire Hunt will meet this Saturday in a secret location in order to avoid the clashes with protesters that marred the previous hunting season. All those wishing to attend have been given a telephone number to ring to get directions. 'It's a sorry show when sportsmen and women have to resort to the tactics of illegal rave parties,' says keen hunting enthusiast Jane Redven (pictured, right), who intends to ride out with hounds this Saturday on her horse, Zak.

From: Lucy Gordon (juicylucy@webbedup.net)
To: Mo Lavender (Hobo-mobo@Hotmail.com)

20.36
Subject: Baying for Blood

Can you BELIEVE the attached cutting (I've scanned it in – sorry about the creases, but I threw it in the bin earlier). Ignore the photo – the *WG* picture editor got it muddled up with a record-breaking marrow.

Jane decided to tell me at the last minute that she was taking Zak. I don't really approve of hunting, so I told her that I'd rather she didn't. I thought that she'd understand, but instead she flew completely off the handle and started yelling all sorts of clever arguments at me about how good it was for Zak's cross-country training, how necessary the culling of foxes is and how childish I was for asking her to leave my share of the horse out of it, 'What am I supposed to do, Lucy, tie his hind legs together to stop them joining in?'

In the end, I realised I wasn't going to win the argument without losing a friend, so I let her get on with it and stayed behind at the cottage to sulk. But then Bella returned from a morning's shopping and started lecturing me for 'condoning the most barbaric and brutal pastime ever invented'. Sometimes I just can't win. We did, however, find the hunt's 'batphone' number scribbled on one of Jane's comp slips and Bella called Alice to give her directions, disguising her voice with a Glasgow accent (she might jeopardise her position as Alice's art teacher if she were seen as colluding with potentially illegal protests).

When Jane came back hours later she was covered in mud and blood, which made Bella tut and pull a face before pointedly walking out of the kitchen without saying a word. I tried to ignore her too, but in the end curiosity and morbid fascination got the better of me as I remembered what the huntsmen are supposed do after a first kill. 'Have you been blooded?'

She looked horrified at the notion. 'God, no! We met at the

racecourse, but there were so many antis around waggling leaflets that Zak took fright and bolted. I fell off half-way along the finishing straight and cut my hand, but he carried on for a whole circuit of the steeplechase course.' Then she started laughing rather maniacally. I was just beginning to wonder whether she had concussion when she clapped her hands together in glee. 'You should have seen him, Lucy! He's a natural. We have to use his talent, don't you see? Only I'm going to need your help.'

I didn't like the look on her face at all, but managed a humouring smile. 'Yes?'

'I think we should take him point-to-pointing this winter,' she took me by the hand and squeezed it hard. 'The only problem is, I'm really far too tall to be a competitive jockey. He needs someone smaller and lighter, someone more aerodynamic. Someone like . . .'

'. . . me?' I gulped.

'Brilliant! I knew you'd agree,' she hugged me tightly, 'that's why I've entered him for the novice race at the Stockridge Meet next Sunday. You've lost so much weight since you've been working out at the gym, and you're jockey height. You'll be perfect.'

I opened my mouth to turn her down point blank, but she gave me one of her wise looks and said, 'When I told Big Mike about it this afternoon, he said you were still terrified of Zak and would refuse. Fancy that, huh!'

Why oh why am I so proud? Instead of nodding and agreeing that I was a hopeless coward, I lifted my chin high and pooh-poohed the notion. 'Me? Terrified? You must be joking!' Oh God. Will have to eat non-stop between now and Saturday in order to disqualify myself. If I'm fat and no longer aerodynamic, Jane might decide to ride him herself. Must find some chocolate . . .
L xxx

wexgaz.bmp attachment here

~~Why no Bathroom should be without a Battery Operated Ear De-waxer~~

Still getting up really early in order to arrive at the office before Ambitious Dave, and then staying late after work. Our management training course is fast approaching, and I'm determined to win the psychological advantage.

Unfortunately, Jane is convinced that I've been madly working out at my gym in order to get race-fit for Sunday. I've tried to tell her that this isn't true (actually I've been eating five Mars bars a day in order to fatten up to my old un-racing weight) but she will not be dissuaded. Tonight she came home with a bright green polo-neck and matching helmet silk. 'Your racing colours.' I pointed out that green makes me look drained, but she just laughed and said, 'It's not a fashion show, Lucy. This will be covered in mud, rain and God knows what else by the end of the race.'

'My blood probably,' I muttered weakly. 'You know what they say – red and green should never be seen without a colour in between.' Coward's yellow maybe?

WIDGETEX LIMITED
Memo
To: Lucy Gordon
Re: Work [Private and Confidential]
I am deeply concerned that several members of staff have reported that you are, as they put it, 'hanging around' the building outside office hours. Much as I appreciate your diligence and enthusiasm, this is not healthy. Research has shown that staff who fully utilise their recreational windows are more energised and productive in the workspace.
Gavin Slater

Pinned above bar in Cow in Clover:

Support Our Local Girl:

Lucy Gordon will be riding
promising newcomer Zak the Yak
in the third race at Stockridge
Point-to-Point on Sunday 1st Nov.
Please support her by coming to
the Meet and having a flutter.

Mike Ensor

From: Lucy Gordon (juicylucy@webbedup.net)
To: Mo Lavender (Hobo-mobo@Hotmail.com)

23.13
Subject: Scared

Went to the Halloween party in the Cow in Clover tonight – a bit
of a half-hearted affair with locals in plastic Frankenstein masks.
Everyone seems to have heard about my race tomorrow and, to
my horror, most of them said they'd come along to have a bet
and cheer me on.

I think Big Mike must have spread the word; he's such a
gossip. I finally tracked him down behind a Dracula mask and
asked him why he'd told so many people, 'It's going to be twice
as hard trying to stay on Zak if I know the fortunes of so many
Chisbourne villagers are riding on my back.'

Ladies Open Race

- A Challenge Cup presented by the late Hermione Trott-Fulmer, a Memento and £150 to the winner; £70 to the second; £30 to the third. A cup will be awarded to the first Owner/Rider past the post.
- For Horses which have a current Hunter Certificate issued by any recognised Hunt in Great Britain. To be ridden by ladies.
- Weights: 11ˢᵗ for Horses and Geldings of 6 years and older; 10st9lb for Mares of 6 years and older; 10st7lb for 5-y-o Horses and geldings; 10st2lb for 5-y-o mares.   **No Penalties.**

This race is sponsored, and the Memento presented to the winner, by Delaware Security Ltd

1. SLAMONTHEBRAKES (IRE)   11–00
9 b. g. Hairpin – Flyingbird (Flyingstart)
L. Frances – Taunton V. . . . . Miss B. Cooper
Scarlet, black diamond, white sleeves & cap
1/r3p-p1 Won confined at Banbury April 15; useful; g-g/s (r14 w5) 76

2. WINDY MILLER   11–00
11 g. g. Trumpton – Sweet Geisha (The Porter USA)
R. A. Kline – Beaufort (Ali Dunn) . . . . Miss S. Vicarage
White, gold hoops, scarlet cap
p2114-u Won intermediate at Larkhill Feb 19; improving; g-hvy (r10 w3) 63

3. CASTLE MONKEY (5a)   10–09
8 c. m. Castle Keep – Red Lolly (Fresley Lad)
Mrs H. U. Wilson-Rutt – V.W.H. . . . . Mrs P. Savage
Black, royal blue sash & armlets, maroon cap
1f13–41 Won ladies Erw Lon 2000; stays well; g-firm (r7 w3) 89

4. ZAK THE YAK   11–00
7 g. g. Lazy Herbert – Gull Maiden (Mr Gull)
Miss J. Redven – West Berks . . . . Miss L. Gordon
Green, Royal blue half sleeves, green cap
pp-3 Lightly raced; promising newcomer; g/s (r5 w0) 64

5. FLUMP   11–00
6 b. g. Gizaquid – Welcome Home (Mattastic FR)
Col T. K. Bridges – Ledbury (Maurice Sich) . . . . Miss G. Wilks
Brown, orange epaulets, orange star, brown cap
ppfp1-ur Maiden winner 1999; shown little since; hard to steer (r12 w1). 67

He had a bit of difficulty talking because his fangs kept falling out, but I'm almost sure he said, 'That's why I told them, Lucy. I want you to pull out while you still have the chance. I care about you. I don't want to see you getting hurt.' I longed to hide under his big cloak and ask him to help me, but Vic chose that moment to turn off all the pub lights so that he could run around in a sheet pretending to be the Clover ghost. When they went back on, Mike had disappeared with his pint, although he'd left his fangs on the bar. L xxx

Written on the back of a race-card:

Wexbury District Hospital Accident and Emergency Department must be very short-staffed. They make you wait for ages here to be seen, so I'm writing to pass the time. Poor Mike is sitting beside me with his arm in a makeshift sling; I have two black eyes and a cut lip, and Jane thinks she's broken a rib. Meanwhile, lots of Chisbourne locals are furious about losing their each-way wagers.

Everything was going okay as we lined up at the start. Zak was behaving pretty well and I'd even begun to wonder whether I was going to enjoy myself. Then I suddenly spotted Mum climbing over the course ropes waggling a betting slip and screaming, 'Good luck, darling!' She was wearing a huge waxed mac that flapped around in the wind like a sail. The next moment, Zak bolted in terror – straight towards Jane and Mike. I'm not quite sure what happened next, but I ate a lot of mud and I distinctly heard Big Mike muttering, 'Your riding crop's in my ear, Lucy.'

From: Ceri Dixon (reception@widgetex.co.uk)
To: Lucy Gordon (lucy@widgetex.co.uk)

09.04
Subject: Black eyes

What happened???!!! Don't tell me AD cornered you in the parking lot and duffed you up?

From: Lucy Gordon (lucy@widgetex.co.uk)
To: Ceri Dixon (reception@widgetex.co.uk)

09.13
Subject: Looks better on a Panda

Riding accident. When Slave Driver spotted my black eyes this morning and asked what happened, I smiled as sweetly as I could and said, 'I simply utilised my recreational windows to the full.' Ambitious Dave can't stop laughing, the swine.

W Microsoft Word – Marketing Ideas38.doc

~~Research Shows that the Portable Face Massager is useless for Black Eyes~~

Ambitious Dave and I are due to go on our two-day management training programme next week. I'm hoping that my black eyes will have faded by then, because I currently look like a battered wife and am having to wear dark glasses to the office. Big Mike has given me some cream called Arnica, which he says is brilliant; his arm was black and blue on Monday and has already faded to yellow. Thank God it wasn't broken – he might have sued Jane and me, and my poor parents, as co-owners of Zak.

Jane's also still quite sore after Zak ploughed into her at the point-to-point. She says her ribcage is agony when she laughs, which hasn't been too often this week – not that it ever is. She now thinks

Zak requires some intensive schooling from an expert and she's researching different horse trainers to send him away to – a sort of equine crammer. I've suggested a very long course, possibly overseas.

Burr Cottage
Chisbourne

Thursday 5th November

Dear Big Brother,

Mum and Dad decided to hold a bonfire party this year, and I reluctantly agreed to come along to help them out with the nibbles. Mum's gone off cooking a bit since she failed to get through the qualifying rounds for *Masterchef*, and so all she'd done when I arrived was defrost several hundred ready-made vol-au-vent cases, and bulk-buy mini pizza slices from Tesco's. She seemed very relieved to see me and immediately dashed off to 'do her face', leaving me with a large jar of mayonnaise and five cans of tuna. I set about mixing and watched through the kitchen window as Dad made preparations for the firework display in the garden. It looked more like a military rocket launch site than the setting for a suburban bonfire party by the time he'd finished half-burying metal tubes, poles and emergency anti-fire water supplies in the flower beds. When I wandered outside to see how he was doing he yelled, 'Get back into the house, Lucy, I'm burying the incendiary box. I'll tell you when everything's made safe!' It all seemed a little excessive for a tenner's worth of Roman Candles from the local newsagent, especially as it has been raining all week so most of them damply refused to go off later.

All Mum and Dad's old friends came along bearing medium-sweet wine and sparklers. Alice wisely chose to stay away, apparently spending the night with her friend Stef (I'm sure she's with Scrumpy in his squat, but I said nothing). Granny had invited a few cronies along and they all perched on

213

shooting sticks, swigged sherry out of hip flasks and complained that the fireworks were dreadful, not seeing all the colourful explosions overhead because they were huddling under golfing brollies. As Dad was trying to light the Catherine Wheel on the oak tree for the fifth time, Granny said, 'This is absolute rot. Come on chaps, let's crack open another Crofts and watch *EastEnders*,' and they all trooped inside.

The trophy shelf has gone, I notice, and Mum has put her Lalique vase collection back on it. Huge relief.

I wish Mum and Dad's friends would stop telling me how sorry they were to hear about my break-up with Greg, and asking me whether I've met a 'nice young man' yet. Isn't it obvious that any woman attending her parents' bonfire party is unlikely to be in the first throes of a passionate love affair? I'd be somewhere else with him, wouldn't I? Older people can be terribly dense. They even believed me when I told them that my Arnica cream was a trendy new shade of eye make-up.

All this talk of Greg has made me think about him. I can't help missing him sometimes and wondering how he's getting on in Finland. I still have his engagement ring at the cottage and every so often I get it out of the box and remember how much I loved him. I never try it on, though – just in case it gets stuck.

Q: What did the sheep say to the other sheep? A: After ewe.
Love,
Lucy xx

From: Lucy Gordon (juicylucy@webbedup.net))
To: Mo Lavender (Hobo-mobo@Hotmail.com)

23.24
Subject: We're all going into training

Zak and I have not exactly turned out to be the Aldaniti and Bob Champion of the racing world, so he is going back to school while I am being coached for high-flying career advancement (thus enabling me to afford better insurance). Jane is very excited about an equine trainer she's found in Gloucestershire. He's one of these horse whisperer people, like Monty Roberts, who get crazed animals to do what they want by blowing in their noses and following them around all day. I was all for it until Jane told me what he charges. Considering I want Zak to go away for several weeks, I could never afford it – it costs more than a five-star human holiday and I'm quite keen on having one of those myself soon. Must buy a Lottery ticket. Contemplated selling engagement ring, but can't bring myself to do it. L xxx

From: Lucy Gordon (lucy@widgetex.co.uk)
To: Ceri Dixon (reception@widgetex.co.uk)

18.09
Subject: Will you miss me?

Ambitious Dave and I are off on our management training course in Liverpool tomorrow so I'm staying late in the office tonight trying to clear my desk. Not that there's much to do; I've been putting in so many early mornings over the past few weeks that I've pretty much done all November's work already and we're not even half-way through the month. Feel very satisfied and am consequently certain that I'll impress everyone at Pro-active Management Training no end. Have just taken sneaky peek at AD's desk and it is a mess – all his paperwork is overdue, his pen-lids are all missing and his pot-plant is dead. Brilliant.

Midlands Motivation Limited

Presents:

PRO-ACTIVE MANAGEMENT
TRAINING

Two-day work-shopping skills course

Mersey Travel Lodge.

Course leaders: Keith Kendell/Beverley Champion

Schedule Day 1: **Thursday 12th Nov**

09.00   Paul McCartney Suite
         Meet and Greet. Please collect name badges from reception.
09.30   Group I – Paul McCartney Suite
         Group II – Ringo Starr Lounge
         Interactive workshop: 'Climbing the Corporate Ladder'
11.00   Jimmy Tarbuck Café Bar
         Refreshment break and chance for informal q's and a's with course
         leaders
11.15   Groups as before.
         Discussion Forum: 'Why I Want To Be A Super-Achiever'
12.30   Cilla Black Carvery
         Lunch and chance for informal q's and a's with course leaders
13.45   Groups as before.
         Role-play
17.30   End of session. Please return name badges.
18.30* Brookside Tapas Bar
         Bonding session   ***optional**

~~Notes and Observations - Day 1~~

I'm totally exhausted. Had to get up at five this morning in order to catch early train to Liverpool. Only just made it to the PMT Meet and Greet in time, to find that AD had travelled up last night and had just come from his hotel room, freshly washed, shaven and continental breakfasted, the pig. When I panted in, he shot me a big, self-satisfied smile and called out, 'Leaves on the line, Lucy?' I grumpily ignored him.

The course is being run by a man called Keith, who wears red-framed glasses and matching braces. This morning, he made us climb up stepladders, shouting out a personal ambition each time we ascended a rung, then climb down shouting out a personal fault each time. I asked what the point was and Keith got very huffy and said it was symbolic. Thankfully his attention was then distracted by Ambitious Dave (who was still at the top of his ladder because he couldn't think of any personal faults) having a panic attack. I had no idea he's afraid of heights. Keith gently helped him down, cooing, 'I've got a firm grip on you.' He certainly had. AD almost jumped.

After lunch, we had to 'role-play' which was even sillier than the ladder thing, although I quite enjoyed pretending to be AD's boss and wasted no time telling him off about the state of his desk. Keith seemed quite impressed by my assertiveness and said that he liked strong women because they 'remind me of mother'. He went a bit quiet after that and just looked at Dave sort of wistfully. We're all going out for a 'bonding' dinner tonight at a taco bar. Am certain that it'll be tequila slammers until dawn.

1a.m.: God, my head hurts. We've been inventing cocktails in the hotel bar for two hours. I gave up after Ambitious Dave created a 'Birkenheadbanger' from vodka, rum and ginger wine. I've just left him and several others heading towards the hotel swimming pool. Keith was amongst them. Trust AD to suck up. He's bound to get the recommendation for management now.

2a.m.: I don't believe what's just happened. About five minutes ago, there was a furious pounding on my door and I distinctly heard Ambitious Dave yelping, 'Let me in, Lucy, please!' Naturally, I refused. I know the way his mind works and I wouldn't put it past him to try his luck, even though he is now practically married to Wendy from Accounts. Then he wailed, 'For God's sake, Lucy, let me in before he finds me out here.' Intrigued, I opened the door a fraction and he burst inside, dressed in wet clothes and white in the face.

'Thank you so much!' He almost cried as he slammed the door behind him. 'It's Keith. I came upstairs to find him lying in my hotel bed wearing nothing but a pair of orange specs. Can I sleep in here tonight?'

I am pretending to write a confidential course report for Slave Driver in the hope that he will eventually fall asleep (he has pushed the vanity pouffe against the television chair). Thought telling him about my 'confidential report' would wind him up, but he says he couldn't care less, that the course is a nightmare and would I mind very much if he watches Eurosport? He's currently catatonic in front of live tractor-pulling.

W Microsoft Word – Management Training2.doc

~~Notes and Observations – Day 2~~

I'm sitting on the London train with my laptop wedged on a Virgin Express table between five McDonalds take-out bags, an Upper Crust wrapper, two empty cans of Special Brew and a suspiciously soggy copy of the *Daily Star*. Do the privatised rail networks have no idea of the needs of the high-flying, soon-to-be-promoted marketing executive?

Dave refused to come to this morning's session. I noticed Keith was in a v. bad mood (metal frames, no braces). He clearly didn't believe me when I said Dave had food poisoning. But then, at the end of the course, he patted me on the back and said that I had really impressed him. Perhaps Friday the 13th isn't so unlucky after all?

From: Lucy Gordon (juicylucy@webbedup.net))
To: Mo Lavender (Hobo-mobo@Hotmail.com)

23.21
Subject: Sisterly and Neighbourly Love

Brick is here again this weekend and Bella has finally admitted
that they are officially back together. Phew. Didn't see that one
coming. They were kissing very sloppily on sofa this evening so
Jane and I sloped off to Cow in Clover and had a few drinks with
Big Mike who laughed his head off when I told him about the
management training course I've just been on where our team
leader tried to lead Dave astray (or as Mike put it 'to bat for
another team'!). He says that they are interviewing for a new
partner at the practice and that one of the stars of *Vets in
Practice* came along yesterday, complete with a television crew
to film his interview. I excitedly asked if this means Mike's going
to feature regularly in the show, but he thinks the other partners
prefer a female vet called Rachel. He says he was out on call
when the interviews took place, but that his boss, Martin, was
very hot under the collar when he got back so she must be very
glamorous. Can't think why, but I found this very irritating and
accused him of being sexist. Mike looked stupidly hurt. I came
home early in a grump and saw Granny's Dolomite parked
outside the cottage. A couple were still snogging on the sofa, but
when I checked them out it was Alice and Scrumpy.

'Bella let us in,' Alice explained, not looking remotely guilty. 'We
need somewhere to hang out together. She and Brick were really
cool about it – they've gone to bed. You won't tell Mum will you?'

Was in such a bad mood about Mike and the sexist comment
that I was going to throw them out, but then I checked my Lottery
numbers on Ceefax and realised I'd won a tenner so I told them
to get on with it. I'll buy Mike a pint to apologise soon. L xxx

Burr Cottage
Chisbourne

Sunday 15th November

Dear Big Brother,

Mum has seriously gone off cooking. Today, she insisted
that Dad prepare lunch which, from past experience, Alice
and I know will inevitably lead to carnage. When I arrived
the air was already blue with smoke and expletives. He's
normally such a calm person, but something happens to him
when he dons a pinny and starts chopping up green chillies. I
think it's partly that he feels cooking is 'artistic' and therefore
he should be passionate and flamboyant about it, partly
because he started on the cooking wine at eleven this
morning, partly because Mum interferes all the time, and
mainly because he's just a useless cook. Today he managed
to set light to two tea-towels, blow a fuse on the microwave,
add sugar to the rice instead of salt and then smash the
smoke alarm with a rolling pin because he couldn't get it
to shut up.

So the kitchen now looks like a bomb-site and the front lawn
is currently home to a colander, two saucepans, the 'Gary
Rhodes' professional cooking utensils set Dad gave Mum for
her birthday and most of the curry we were supposed to be
eating. This is perhaps merciful as I spotted the Pottingers' cat
stalking towards the unexpected feast earlier, only to run away

howling the moment it dabbed its tongue into Dad's prawn madras. We finally sat down to eat defrosted fish fingers and peas at three o'clock in the afternoon. Veggie Alice just ate peas and grumbled a lot. Mum and Dad weren't talking at all. I tried to keep the peace until Mum started having a go at me about my non-existent love-life (again). Only Granny seemed really happy, and announced that it was the nicest meal she'd had in years. I might think up an excuse not to come to lunch with the family next weekend; I just can't take the pressure. In fact I might try to think of an excuse to avoid Christmas lunch too.

Q: Why did the sheep call the police? A: He had been fleeced.
Love,
Lucy xx

From: Dave Marks (dave@widgetex.co.uk)
To: Lucy Gordon (lucy@widgetex.co.uk)

08.54
Subject: YKW

Last Thursday night is our secret, yes?

From: Ceri Dixon (reception@widgetex.co.uk)
To: Lucy Gordon (lucy@widgetex.co.uk)

09.25
Subject: Gossip!

So, how did it go??!!

Really boring here without you two last week. The most exciting thing to happen was Marlene's announcement that the date for her varicose veins op has come through at last.

Dave is looking very pale and tense, isn't he? And why has Wendy from Accounts just come storming away from your desk looking like she swallowed your cactus? If I didn't know better I'd say you and Dave got it together . . . !

From: Lucy Gordon (lucy@widgetex.co.uk)
To: Ceri Dixon (reception@widgetex.co.uk)

09.30
Subject: Re: Gossip!

No way! Wendy came bustling up with a query about my expenses just as I got one of Dave's bad joke emails. I think I managed to click on my *South Park* screen saver in time, but I'm not sure and she might have got the wrong idea. She certainly refused to let me claim for three pairs of tights I snagged on the photo-copier paper tray.

Slave Driver has said nothing at all about the management training course. I suppose he can't have got the written report yet, but you'd think he'd bother to ask how it went. I'm so frustrated.

Christmas list:
Mum – Gone off cooking. Perfume? Jewellery? The "Complete Carpenters Collection on CD?"
Dad – Needs to learn to cook. Recipe books? Apron? Smoke alarm?
Alice – Still grieving trees. Year's membership to Woodland Trust? Hammock?
Jeremy – (MUSTN'T miss posting date for NZ this year.) Sheep footstool (as seen in "Mail On Sunday" Novelty Gifts catalogue)?
Granny – Alcoholic. Gin, sherry or vodka.
Jane – STILL trying to woo Tim/calm Zak. Eazee-bum saddle cover? "The Harvey Smith Workout" video?
Bella – Ultra-fashionable. Stick-on Bindi Set? Beaded cuffs?
Ceri – Chocaholic/man-eater. Chocolate penis?

~~Last-minute Christmas Thust for Tweazertorch®~~

Still no mention of the course from Slave Driver. Have booked a day off work next week to go Christmas shopping, but can't muster up much enthusiasm. I suppose I could always get Alice something unusual. I called Mum for ideas today and she said that Alice has expressed an interest in rock-climbing equipment: 'I'm not keen,' she confessed, 'but what can I say? I mean you have that horse which is a quite dangerous sport. I can hardly refuse her.' I don't like to point out that, far from climbing rocks, Alice is going to use the webbing harness to tether herself to the top of trees on road protests with Scrumpy, so I said I'd look into getting her an ice pick.

Mum also announced that she has yet again resurrected her quest to compete in a national television cooking contest. 'Are you going to try for *Masterchef* again then?' I asked, happily realising that she might resume cooking and save us from Dad's curries and Alice's veggie burgers. 'No, dear!' she whispered excitedly. 'I'm entering your father in *Can't Cook, Won't Cook*. I sent the form off this morning. Don't tell him. It's a secret.' There are far too many secrets around at the moment if you ask me.

From: Lucy Gordon (juicylucy@webbedup.net)
To: Mo Lavender (Hobo-mobo@Hotmail.com)

20.29
Subject: Not so house-matey

I went to see Zak the Yak today. Felt really guilty for not having been to the stables in over a week, so took him a huge pile of carrots, but when I got there he ignored me completely. Horsy Tim's girlfriend, Victoria, was in the yard and offered me a cup of tea in the office. Jane's always made out that she's stuck-up, but she was really helpful and gave me lots of names and addresses of trainers who are less expensive than the 'horse whisperer'

Jane's found. She's also offered to give me a few lessons on Zak to improve my confidence, which is incredibly kind. She said it would help her too, as she's training for a British Horse Society instructor's exam.

Told Jane about this when I got home, but she wasn't as enthusiastic as I'd hoped. She just said sarcastically, 'I bet she changes her mind about those lessons when she sees how badly you ride.' Honestly, she drives me mad sometimes. I know she only dislikes Victoria because she fancies Tim, but there's no need to get personal about my uncanny ability to fall off Zak within two minutes of getting on him. L xxx

---

From: Lucy Gordon (lucy@widgetex.co.uk)
To: Ceri Dixon (reception@widgetex.co.uk)

11.30
Subject: Odd

Have you noticed that Slave Driver is behaving really oddly? He still hasn't even mentioned the management training course, and now he seems to be actively avoiding me. Just now, he walked past my desk while I was sneakily calling one of Victoria's suggested horse trainers. The man was on a mobile phone in a lorry and I kept having to shout to get him to hear, so as SD passed I was yelling, 'He's unpredictable and headstrong. It has to stop, do you hear me?' This was obviously a personal call, so when I spotted SD nearby, I turned bright red. But instead of hauling me over the coals, he just backed away hastily, muttering, 'Good work, Lucy. Very assertive.' And he dashed into his office. Weird. I'm glad I've booked tomorrow off.

Christmas list: The Final Score

(Queues in WHSmith's = 2.5 miles.)

Mum — <u>Gone off cooking.</u> ~~Perfume? Jewellery? The "Complete Carpenters Collection" on CD?~~ Jaeger jumper (NB: keep receipt as only had size 18 left.)

Dad — <u>Needs to learn to cook.</u> ~~Recipe books? Apron? Smoke alarm?~~ Ken Hom Wok Set (Mum took hers back again last year.)

Alice — <u>Still grieving trees.</u> ~~Year's membership to Woodland Trust? Hammock?~~ Crampons

Jeremy — <u>(MUSTN'T miss posting date for NZ this year.)</u> ~~Sheep footstool (as seen in "Mail On Sunday" Novelty Gifts catalogue)?~~ Best of Val Doonican CD (easy to post)

Granny — <u>Alcoholic.</u> ~~Gin, sherry or vodka.~~ Tequila Slammer set

Jane — <u>STILL trying to woo Tim/calm Zak.</u> ~~Eazee-bum saddle cover? "The Harvey Smith Workout" video?~~ No-sweat deodorised riding socks

Bella — <u>Ultra-fashionable.</u> ~~Stick-on Bindi Set? Beaded cuffs?~~ Glitter hair-spray

Ceri — <u>Chocaholic/man-eater.</u> ~~Chocolate penis?~~ Milk Tray

---

From: Lucy Gordon (juicylucy@webbedup.net)
To: Mo Lavender (Hobo-mobo@Hotmail.com)

22.43
Subject: Riding high

Fantastic day! I decided to delay Christmas shopping for a few hours and pop to the stables for my first lesson. The last time I was sitting six foot in the air on half a ton of grey menace I ploughed into Jane and Big Mike. This time, I plodded cautiously around the manege listening to Victoria telling me how to sit and where to hold my hands. She's incredibly patient as I know I'm pretty dreadful and I get muddled up easily, but after half an hour I could already feel the difference as Zak went the way I told him rather than any old direction. I was so excited that I didn't notice I had an audience until I rode out of the gate and saw Big Mike sitting on the railed fence. Apparently he'd been filing teeth all morning and had spotted me riding, so thought he'd hang around and see if I wanted a lift. This was a bit odd as my car was parked right next to his Land Rover, but I couldn't point this out because just then Horsy Tim appeared and invited us into the house for soup, doorstep sandwiches and homemade beer. He and Victoria are so lovely that I found myself inviting them – and Mike – around for supper next week. Oh God. I hope Jane doesn't go too mad.

As we were leaving, Mike asked me if I wanted some company Christmas shopping as he hadn't got any appointments that afternoon. So we ended up wandering around Wexbury together. We didn't buy much, but we fell about laughing playing with *South Park* toys and later tried on outrageous furry hats in an outward-bound shop as I tried to find a mountaineering gift for Alice. Ended up buying her some crampons. I apologised for telling him he was sexist in the pub last week and he was really sweet about it, saying that perhaps he was being a bit crass and I was right to stop him. He's offered to bring along a friend when he comes to dinner next week. 'Jane will really like him. It might take her mind off Tim,' he said kindly. I loyally didn't say anything as I know Jane would be really embarrassed to think Mike has figured out her crush. I just gave him a quick kiss on the cheek and then tried on a balaclava to make him laugh. The funny thing is I don't think he noticed I had it on at all. He just sort of gazed at me with a soppy smile on his face. L xxx

Appearing in the *Wexbury Gazette* Situations Vacant section:

WIDGETEX LIMITED

Marketing Co-ordinator

Widgetex is a leading manufacturer of retail electronic equipment, established for over twenty years.

We currently have a vacancy for a marketing co-ordinator. Working alongside our marketing director, you will be responsible for direct marketing, new business development, control of budgets and events organisation across our entire range.

It is essential that you have a high level of interpersonal skills, are self-motivated, conscientious and relish a challenge. In addition, you will be expected to be educated to degree standard or higher and have at least three years' marketing experience.

Attractive salary, company car and generous benefits package

Please send a detailed CV, passport-sized photograph, covering letter and current salary details to: Human Resources, Widgetex Limited, 5 Market Street, Wexbury, Berks RG14 0XX.

From: Dave Marks (dave@widgetex.co.uk)
To: Lucy Gordon (lucy@widgetex.co.uk)

09.01
Subject: Job

Fuck!!!!!!!!

From: Lucy Gordon (lucy@widgetex.co.uk)
To: Dave Marks (dave@widgetex.co.uk)
09.04
Subject: Re: Job

Bollocks!

W Microsoft Word – Resignation letter.doc

Dear Slave Driving Bastard,

This is – to quote your favourite word – UNTENABLE! Now I
know why you have been avoiding both Ambitious Dave and myself
since you sent us on the management training course. It's because
you had no intention of promoting either of us, did you? And you
didn't even have the decency to tell us, you cowardly, Ralph-Lauren-
sports-casual-wearing prat.

You see, I got home last night to find my housemate Jane looking
very uncomfortable. She seemed to be sitting on the Situations
Vacant section of the *Wexbury Gazette*, and when I asked her
whether she was looking for another job, she reluctantly handed me
the squashed paper. One of the first adverts – taking up a quarter of
a page with the Widgetex logo looming large – was for a Marketing
Co-ordinator. My job – or rather the job I am destined for – is being
advertised so that any Tom, Dick or Harriet can apply, provided they
have good interpersonal skills and at least three years' marketing
experience.

Together, Dave Marks and I have awaited your arrival all morning to have it out with you. Alas, that arrival didn't happen as you
have taken the day off work to play golf. I hope you fall in every
bunker on the course.

Yours with loathing,

Lucy

From: Lucy Gordon (lucy@widgetex.co.uk)
To: Ceri Dixon (reception@widgetex.co.uk)

10.21
Subject: Aghhh!

Did you know about this?

From: Ceri Dixon (reception@widgetex.co.uk)
To: Lucy Gordon (lucy@widgetex.co.uk)

10.23
Subject: Sorry

I overheard Slavey saying something about not wanting to cause any more conflict between you and Dave by promoting one over the other. So he decided to advertise the job externally. I'm sure you can apply too.

From: Lucy Gordon (lucy@widgetex.co.uk)
To: Ceri Dixon (reception@widgetex.co.uk)

10.26
Subject: Bosom buddies

More conflict? There is no conflict. Dave and I get on fine – we're great mates! We've made a pact to resign together.
    I refuse to apply. That job is mine by rights.

From: Ceri Dixon (reception@widgetex.co.uk)
To: Lucy Gordon (lucy@widgetex.co.uk)

10.33
Subject: Job

Dave's applying.

From: Lucy Gordon (lucy@widgetex.co.uk)
To: Ceri Dixon (reception@widgetex.co.uk)

10.37
Subject: Re: Job

Bastard! He said he was going to resign too. In that case I'm
staying to fight. How can I get hold of a copy of his CV?

Sunday Lunch Menu – 13 Roundhead Avenue, Wexbury.
Chef: Malcolm Gordon

Chicken Kiev, McCain's potato croquettes, Bird's sweetcorn
Individual Mueller Fruit Corners (assorted)

To be accompanied by Tesco's Great With Chicken
For Mother-in-law: Lambrusco Rosé

Burr Cottage
Chisbourne

Sunday 29th November

Dear Big Brother,

Have calmed down a bit since discovering that the
promotion I deserve is being advertised in the local paper. Told
Dad about it, and he pointed out that I am bound to be better
qualified for the position than anyone who applies externally.
But Dad says that by advertising the post like this, Slave Driver
is making it easier on Ambitious Dave when he doesn't get the
promotion and I do, because this way it won't be such a
personal match between the two of us. Dad is great – he makes
a lot of sense sometimes. Unfortunately he doesn't make very
good chicken Kiev (actually Sainsbury's made it, Dad just had to
put it in the oven). Mum is still insisting that he cooks for Sunday
lunch. Only today's wasn't exactly cooked; the croquettes were

still frozen in the middle and the chicken was suspiciously pink and cold. I feel a bit sick. Can't write any more.

W **Microsoft Word – deathbed.doc**

Oh God, I feel ill. Had terrible food poisoning all last night and most of this morning – salmonella I think. Am so embarrassed, because it must look as though I'm faking it and bunking off work because I'm upset about the promotion thing. Tried to drag myself out of bed just now to go into the office, green face and all, just to prove the genuineness of my affliction, but couldn't make it past the loo. Even feel too rotten to fill in the Widgetex job application form I picked up on Friday. Might try again later.

Later: Have just been sick on the job application form. Will have to pick up another one from personnel. Ceri has just called to say that Ambitious Dave is creeping up to Slave Driver like mad and that she's just overheard him saying that he'd come into work however ill he felt. That's it – I'm going in.

Evening: Managed to get dressed and made it as far as the front door before passing out. Thankfully, Big Mike was parking his car outside the cottages and spotted me slumped over the milk bottles so quickly carried me inside and up to bed. I woke up to find him taking off my shoes and calling for a doctor on his mobile. So sweet. He says no job is worth killing myself for. As I was lying on the stained job application form with a staple sticking painfully into my bottom, I couldn't agree more.

Then he said a really odd thing. He looked sort of red and mumbled, 'This isn't the first time I've carried you up to bed.' Felt far too ropy to argue, but I can't remember another time, and it's not the sort of thing a girl forgets.

Later: Jane has reminded me that Mike once carried me back from Cow in Clover when I was in a drunken stupor and put his back out. Feel thoroughly ashamed. At least I'm a bit lighter now. Must avoid collapsing near him again.

Continuation of last week's letter to Jeremy:

Have been too ill all week to post your letter, so I'll finish it now.

Am still feeling a bit ropy after the food poisoning. Can't believe that Dad's chicken Kiev could lay me so low. Popped to Roundhead Avenue this afternoon to borrow some recipe books from Mum (am having a dinner party tomorrow) and she said that she's hardly eaten a thing since Sunday. Only Alice and Granny were unaffected by the raw Kievs – Alice had veggie burgers and Granny was out with the Pensioners' Sunday Pub Club. Thank God that was the day of her monthly outing, or she might have died; Mum told me this evening that salmonella can be fatal to old people. Unfortunately, just at that moment Dad popped his head around the kitchen door and offered to 'have another go' this weekend. His timing wasn't great – Mum yelled, 'Do you want to kill my mother, is that it?' and stormed out. I don't think they're getting on too well at the moment. Dad sort of hung around after that and asked me whether I'd noticed any changes in Mum lately. Apart from the cooking thing and some blonde highlights, I couldn't think of much. I asked him if anything was wrong, but he shrugged evasively and headed for his shed to hammer something.

I'm a bit worried about them. Please remember to send them a Christmas card. It really makes a difference (and don't send them another rude joke one like the 'How does Santa practise safe sex? Marks the reindeers that kick with a big X' cartoon).

Talking of which, what do you call a Kiwi with a sheep under each arm? A pimp.

Love,

Lucy xx

From: Lucy Gordon (lucy@widgetex.co.uk)
To: Ceri Dixon (reception@widgetex.co.uk)

15.53
Subject: Not a recipe for success

Oh God. Slave Driver has just caught me reading Josceline
Dimbleby's *Complete Cookbook* when I should have been
working on the layouts for the Widgetex spring campaign. And
I'm supposed to be on my best behaviour at the moment
because I've applied for the management job.

    Thankfully, I managed to fool him that I was sourcing some
material for the new Work-top Time-savers range, although he
must be pretty hopeless in the kitchen if he thinks that a Beef and
Olive Pie recipe could help in the marketing campaign for an
electric juicer and a no-spills cappuccino frother.

From: Ceri Dixon (reception@widgetex.co.uk)
To: Lucy Gordon (lucy@widgetex.co.uk)

16.00
Subject: Sounds delicious

Let me know if you need someone to test it!

    I've got nothing planned tonight – do you want to come out for
a drink after work?

From: Lucy Gordon (lucy@widgetex.co.uk)
To: Ceri Dixon (reception@widgetex.co.uk)

16.11
Subject: Busy

Sorry – I'm a bit tied up. Another time?

Shopping list:
Dips and crisps
Ready-made puff pastry
Beef
Olives
Fancy-looking vegetables (ready-trimmed)
Apples
Rum
Wine (four bottles)
Alka Seltzer

From: Lucy Gordon (juicylucy@webbedup.net)
To: Mo Lavender (Hobo-mobo@Hotmail.com)

18.33
Subject: Just like old times!

Lucy Gordon is having a dinner party. Ah, remember the night
of the duck à l'orange . . . ! (Although brainwashing cult may
have removed all memories of that wonderful occasion
by now.)

Can't write much, alas, as guests due any minute, but I'm
waiting for Bella to get out of the bathroom, so can fire off a
quick-e.

Had terrible time in supermarket as spotted Ceri-from-work
wandering around with a reduced-price meal-for-one in her
basket. Was acutely aware that my trolley was loaded up with
most of the ingredients for a dinner party for eight (to which she
was not invited) and felt so guilty that I had to furtively lurk
behind a large display of nappies for almost twenty minutes
and am consequently running late. To make things worse,
Jane is in a foul mood because I didn't tell her until tonight that
Horsy Tim's girlfriend, Victoria, was coming. 'But I bought a
new dress especially!' she wailed. 'Now there's no point in
wearing it.'

I was frantically trying to start the Rum Punch Baked Apples, which take an hour and a half to cook, so I wasn't at my most tactful, and just muttered something about Big Mike bringing a dishy friend along. 'Great!' she snarled. 'So you're setting me up! You could have asked. I'm not a flipping charity case, Lucy.' She's now deliberately wearing her mankiest jeans and no make-up, and has started on the Merlot. Oh! There's the bathroom door. I'll send this later so I can let you know how it goes.

Midnight:

Fantastic night. Feel a bit tight. Mike's friend, Alex, was indeed dishy. Very dishy. He test-drives cars for a living and writes about them in the nationals. So exciting. We had a terrific chat and when I told him I was thinking of changing my car next year, he offered to take me for a spin in his Mercedes SLK to see if I liked it (I couldn't bring myself to tell him I was more in the Citroen Saxo line). I think Jane was a bit annoyed with herself that she hadn't dressed up after all. For some reason she took it out on me. Bella and Brick, and Tim and Victoria seemed to enjoy themselves and they all raved about the pie even though I had accidentally bought capers instead of olives whilst dodging Ceri earlier. Mike was very quiet, which was a shame. I guess he'd just had a busy week. He kept yawning when we were having coffee and pointedly looked at his watch, telling Alex that it was time he left because it's a long drive back to the Chilterns, where he lives in a converted windmill (so romantic!). But Alex said he needed another coffee to make up for the wine he'd drunk and we stayed chatting for another hour. Poor Mike looked really fed up. So did Jane. Party poopers. L xxx

W Microsoft Word – Christmas card list.doc
Work: **Ceri, Lianne, Marlene, Richard, Trisha, Dave and Wendy, Slave Driver (ugh)**
Friends: **Jane, Bella and Brick, Mike, Tim, Sally and Dan, Bridget and Peter, Madeline and Garth, Rachel and Andrew, Fliss, Beth and Zoe**
Greg????? (no address)
Mo (ditto)
Alex?????!!!!!

Haven't heard from Alex since the dinner party, even though he took my number and promised to call me with some advice about buying cars. Perhaps it's no bad thing he hasn't got in touch yet, as I checked my savings account today and realised that I couldn't afford a new wing mirror, let alone a car. If I get the management promotion then I'll qualify for a company VW, or maybe even an Audi. The interviews are next week. Must, must get it. Still, it's disappointing that Alex hasn't called because we got on v. well and he was extremely good looking. It's been ages since I had any romantic interest in my life. I spotted Big Mike getting out of his Land Rover earlier and I dashed outside with a half-full refuse bag as a ruse to hang around the wheely-bins in the drive and casually asked whether he'd heard from Alex this week. But he said he was in a hurry and couldn't chat, then just dashed inside. It's not like him to be so unfriendly.

Have decided to stay in tonight and write my Christmas cards, but I'm bored already. Jane and Bella are both going out tonight, and are currently perfuming and beautifying themselves in their rooms. Wish I was as well – even a night in the Cow in Clover with Big Mike and the locals would be better than staying in and writing 'Sorry I haven't been in touch all year, we must meet up soon for a drink' in fifty Help the Aged cards. Can't decide whether to send one to Greg the ex or not. I don't have his address in Finland, but I could send a card to his parents' house in Yorkshire. Might make up my mind later. Could ask Mike for Alex's address and send him one too . . .

Burr Cottage
Chisbourne

Sunday 13th December

Dear Big Brother,

Mum is going crackers. She cooked lunch for the first time in weeks today. Alice and I were incredibly relieved until we realised that she had removed various breaded foods from the freezer and was frying the lot together. She called it Yummy Crummy, but it was revolting – a mixture of chicken nuggets, potato croquettes, fish fingers and pork balls, all covered with ketchup. When Dad refused to eat his, Mum shouted, 'Well now you know what it feels like!' and threw a breaded broccoli floret at him. Dad was really shaken and said, 'Can't I do anything right?' before storming off to his shed.

When I took him out a coffee, he was jabbing holes into his work-top with the soldering iron. It took me a while, but I finally got to the bottom of the problem: *Can't Cook, Won't Cook*. Mum secretly entered in Dad's name, but he found out when a researcher called him last week to ask for a witty anecdote. Now he's flatly refused to take part and Mum won't talk to him. I told him not to worry, that I'd think of something, but I'm not sure I can. Mum is very stubborn. So is Dad. I can't see either of them budging, and until they do the entire Gordon family faces imminent destruction through poisoning.

I've solved it! Had a brainwave as I wrote that and have just

237

called Alice. I normally wouldn't stoop so low, but I decided that these are desperate times, so I went straight for the jugular saying, 'You want Mum and Dad to talk to each other again, don't you? You want to start eating good food again, don't you? And you don't want Mum and Dad to know that you're still seeing Scrumpy, do you?' It didn't take much persuasion to get her to agree to take Dad's place in *Can't Cook, Won't Cook*. Well, it took a little more work than I'd anticipated. And more blackmail. And bribes. But I'm sure I won't miss my fake-fur coat, or my long snakeskin boots, nor do I mind her and Scrumpy using the cottage to meet sometimes, or the fact that she wants to borrow my car every other weekend. At least the family will be at peace once more. And if Alice trashes my car, I have even more reason to get a new one. And to call dishy Alex the motoring journalist I've just met. More on him soon, I hope . . .

Tell the sheep, I'm sorry about the jokes. I promise to stop.

Love,

Lucy xx

WIDGETEX LTD
Memo
To: Lucy Gordon
Re: Interview
We are delighted that you have chosen to apply for the post of marketing co-ordinator. Interviews will take place on Thursday 17th and Friday 18th December. All candidates are asked to come to the boardroom where our Managing Director Kelvin Hatchard, Head of Personnel Margaret Rowlinson and I will meet them. Please be prompt.

Your interview will be on Friday at 4pm.

Gavin Slater

The interviews for the new management post are taking place today and tomorrow. I'm going to be the last interviewee – tomorrow at four. I had thought this would give me a psychological advantage because I can suss out all the competition, but it's absolutely terrifying. Slave Driver, Hatchet-man and The Blob are conducting the interviews upstairs so I can't spy on them. But afterwards, SD takes each candidate on a guided tour, giving me and the rest of the department plenty of chance to eye them up. Have watched several Mariella Frostrup lookalikes wander through the offices today, wearing smart little suits with too-short skirts. Why are so many women in marketing slim, blonde and called sexy names like Anjelika or Marysia? I bet they just change them from Angela and Mary in an attempt to appear more European and interesting. Might have to start calling myself Luciana or something equally silly in future. May also have to bleach my hair. Apart from AD, there have been no men at all today. He had his interview first thing this morning, and came out looking very smug. When I asked him how it went (purely out of sportsmanlike generosity, not a desperate need to know what questions he was asked) he said, 'I'm not giving you any tips, Lucy. You have to fend for yourself in there. Let's just say I think they were impressed. Most impressed.' The pig.

Dreading tomorrow now. I need an edge. I need to go shopping. Thank heaven for pre-Christmas late opening.

Highlife Highlights

From drab to fab in three easy steps:

1. Wet hair
2. Apply
3. Rinse

So simple, even a blonde could do it!

W **Microsoft Word – Lucy's power helmet.doc**

Only popped into Boots to buy Bella's Christmas present (lots of body glitter and some Velcro rollers). Jane has just caught me looking at a set of bleaching instructions and says that I'll look lovely a bit blonder. I must say I am tempted, but I'm not sure Jane is the right person to advise on hair colour. It wasn't so long ago that she dyed her hair carrot red. Still, it might do no harm to try for a very subtle effect. If I just leave it on for five minutes, the instructions say that the effect will be of 'sun-lightened radiance'. Sounds very good. Very Mariella.

8.45p.m.: 'Three Easy Steps', my arse. Am still pulling strands of hair through the rubber cap with a crochet hook. Agony. The woman on the illustration is actually smiling. What is she on? Prozac? Strong painkillers?

10.30p.m.: Have finally pulled all the required strands through the rubber skullcap and am about to dye and go to heaven. Am starting to have doubts, though. Bella has gone to bed and is not on-hand for advice. Jane is still all for it, but she's half-way down a bottle of Chardonnay and about to watch her *When Harry Met Sally* video again, so I don't entirely trust her judgement. Still, I've got this far . . .

Midnight: No, no, no! I had a glass of wine with Jane while I was waiting for the bleach to take and got rather involved in *When Harry Met Sally*. It wasn't until Meg Ryan was giving it her all in the restaurant that I realised I still had my rubber helmet on. Have now got garish chrome-yellow highlights which stop about three inches from my scalp. And my interview is tomorrow.

From: Ceri Dixon (reception@widgetex.co.uk)
To: Lucy Gordon (lucy@widgetex.co.uk)

10.29
Subject: Mad hatter

Why are you wearing a beret?

From: Lucy Gordon (lucy@widgetex.co.uk)
To: Ceri Dixon (reception@widgetex.co.uk)

10.43
Subject: Interview

It's my 'lucky' hat – I always wear it on a big day.

From: Ceri Dixon (reception@widgetex.co.uk)
To: Lucy Gordon (lucy@widgetex.co.uk)

11.00
Subject: Tip

I always go to Cutz in the Market Place. They have a terrific colouring expert and can usually fit me in at the last minute. I'll cover for you ('terrible crisis at printers, I hear . . . everyone tied up doing interviews . . . willing to risk missing interview to sort it out . . .')

You have saved my life. Have just booked lunchtime make-over and they've promised to turn this yellow string disaster into 'something Ulrika Jonsson can only dream of'. Either that or a Sinead O'Connor crew cut. Anything's better.

I owe you a million drinks.

W Microsoft Word – Lucy's power helmet2.doc

It cost almost fifty pounds and has made me late back to work, but it was worth it. When I returned, no one recognised me – Ambitious Dave gave me one of the sexy smiles he was flashing at the Anjelikas and Marysias yesterday; Ceri asked me what time my interview was. When I said 'Four', she did a double-take and whooped.

Interview tactics – 1. Smile radiantly

2. Shake head a lot and try to catch light through window

3. Mention golf at least once

4. Use the sort of long words SD likes (write on wrist)

5. Try not to stare at Hatchet-man's hairy mole

Stuff it. I'm a blonde! I feel great. Now all I have to do is wow SD. Fingers crossed . . .

WIDGETEX LTD

Memo

To: Marketing Department

Re: Christmas Party

As you know, this year the Widgetex office party will be held at Vats Wine Bar, and our Managing Director, Kelvin Hatchard, has generously hired a karaoke machine. Each department is expected to perform an ensemble piece as well as a number of duets. Unfortunately, time taken up by recent interviews has compromised this department's preparation. As such, I have taken it upon myself to come up with the following running order, based upon well-known songs, which I trust you all enjoy as much as myself:

Ceri Dixon and Lianne Perkins: **'Babooshka'** (Bush)

Lucy Gordon and Dave Marks: **'Islands In The Stream'** (Rogers/Parton)

Gavin Slater and Cynthia Slater: **'I Got You Babe'** (Sonny/Cher)

Ensemble Piece: **'Simply The Best'** (Turner)

I will emphasise that this is not a competition, but I would like my department to show itself to be the professional, talented and organised machine that I have come to expect. In order that you can all enjoy the party to its full, we have decided not to announce the new Marketing Co-ordinator until the day afterwards. I hope this will mean that fewer people develop 'food-poisoning' than last year.

Gavin Slater

From: Ceri Dixon (reception@widgetex.co.uk)
To: Lucy Gordon (lucy@widgetex.co.uk)

15.00
Subject: Tonight

Have you ever heard of 'Babooshka'? I've asked my brother and he says that Bush is a UK grunge band that sounds a bit like Nirvana. If you know the tune/lyrics can you meet me in the loo? What are you wearing tonight, by the way? I've been saving a sparkly top I bought in New Look, but I've just found out Wendy from Accounts has the same one. (Btw, she is so mad at Dave for not refusing to sing that song with you, she's changed her number to 'Jolene'.)

From: Anon
To: All Staff (mailall@widgetex.co.uk)

10.25
Subject: Office party

And the winners are . . .
Best Dolly Parton Impersonation: Lucy Gordon (with thanks to Wonderbra and sports socks)
Most number of Sea Breezers consumed: Lucy Gordon
Most number of compromising dance moves with Gavin Slater: Lucy Gordon (the one where she swung from his Golf Club tie merits a special mention)
Best Cher Impersonation: Lucy Gordon (who claims Mrs Slater had stage fright, but we all know she locked the poor woman in the loo)

Latest betting on the new Widgetex Marketing Co-ordinator:
    Lucy Gordon 5–4
    Dave Marks 12–1

From: Ceri Dixon (reception@widgetex.co.uk)
To: Lucy Gordon (lucy@widgetex.co.uk)

10.29
Subject: Hungover

You okay? What happened? Did you really lock Mrs SD in the loo? I can't remember anything after eleven o'clock. Did I get off with anyone by the way?

From: Lucy Gordon (lucy@widgetex.co.uk)
To: Ceri Dixon (reception@widgetex.co.uk)

10.43
Subject: Very hungover

Oh God! I guess it did look a bit suspicious that I stood under a glitter-ball at two in the morning singing 'I Got You Babe' with the boss, but Mrs SD hid in the loos in a fit of stage fright. I didn't lock her in there. She came running in while I was trying to revive you (you'd passed out under the hand-dryer after you tried to rinse the sick from your hair). When I popped out to tell SD where she was, he just grabbed me and pulled me on stage. I tried to explain that I was looking after you, but he said the department's honour was at stake and I had to 'give it every last ounce you have to redeem our reputation'. It was only when I spotted Mrs SD come out of the loo looking furious that I realised I might have hammed it up a bit too much.

You snogged: Pete from Sales
Ali from Despatch
Ed from Fleet Management
Someone with red hair I didn't recognise
Dave

WIDGETEX LTD

Memo

To: All Staff

Re: New Appointment

I am delighted to announce that Gabriella Peartree will join us in the New Year in the role of Marketing Co-ordinator. Ms Peartree (who prefers to be known as 'Gabby') comes to us from the e-commerce giants BuyItCheap.com, where she was instrumental in developing their marketing strategy. I hope you will all join me in welcoming her on board when she arrives.

Meanwhile, I should like to wish you all an enjoyable Festive Season and to thank you for making last night one of the most enjoyable Christmas parties on record.

Gavin Slater

Stapled to Lucy's copy of the memo:

Invoice:

One Wexbury Golf Club Tie (Life Member).........£17.99

Credit: 30 Days

From: Lucy Gordon (lucy@widgetex.co.uk)
To: Dave Marks (dave@widgetex.co.uk)

11.35
Subject: Silly name

Who???!!!

From: Dave Marks (dave@widgetex.co.uk)
To: Lucy Gordon (lucy@widgetex.co.uk)

11.36
Subject:

Tall, slim brunette. Great pins, medium tits, nice arse. 5–1
    Sorry, Ms Moneypenny. You should never have gone blonde
before your interview. You should know Slave Driver likes them
sultry.
    Happy Christmas.

W **Microsoft Word – Christmas Eve.doc**

A year ago today, Greg proposed to me. I remember lying in bed
saying 'Mrs Lucy Burton' over and over again as I admired my ring
and thought about my future. A year later and I am single again, in
a job that's going nowhere, and blonde. What went wrong? There's
only one thing for it. I have to get very, very drunk.

Posted on the Burr Cottage fridge:

COW IN CLOVER RESULTS

Thursday 24th December (score kept by Bella):
Subjects for discussion: Christmas Carols, Mince Pies and Lucy's
Job.

Number of times Lucy said, 'Gabby Peartree is a silly name': 6.
Best quote: 'I've forgotten to wrap up my Christmas presents and it's
eleven-fifteen!'

Number of times Jane said 'Have another mulled wine, Lucy': 11.
Best quote: 'Thank heavens I'm self-employed. An office is just hell
with fluorescent lighting.'

Number of times Bella sang 'The tart's rich in a pear tree': 7.

Best quote: 'That job was yours until you danced with slavering Gav. His wife clearly thought you were trying to get your Santa claws into him.'

Number of times Big Mike kissed Lucy under the mistletoe: 9.
Best quote: 'Bella's right. No wife would want her husband working closely with someone as sexy as you, Lucy. I'd love you to be my Santa Claus.'

(Note – special bad-taste merit to Vic the Landlord with, 'No, Mike – you should be Santa. Which of these lovely ladies' chimney do you want to come down tonight?')

RESULT: Lucy, Jane and Bella = week off. It's Christmas!
(Vic = pelted with mince pies)

W **Microsoft Word – Christmas Day.doc**

Mum, Dad, Alice and Granny are settling down to watch *Babe* now, but I can't concentrate on the adventures of a small talking pig when I have so much to think about. And it's not the job that's bothering me any more. It's last night. Managed to wrap up all my presents by one in the morning, then realised afterwards that I hadn't labelled them so didn't know which was which. Unwrapped them all, then started all over again and ran out of paper. Was still feeling a bit sloshed, so staggered around cottage looking for more paper and woke poor Jane up. She didn't have any left, so I searched through Bella's room (she's gone to stay with Brick's family). None there. Must have been really tight, actually, because I ended up going around to Big Mike's cottage. Amazingly, he was awake and opened the door so fast that I was still knocking on it and managed to boff him on the nose. Then he said something a bit odd like, 'I never imagined you'd come.' When I asked him if he had any wrapping paper, he looked a bit surprised, but went off to find some. I wandered inside and reeled around for a bit. Decided I wasn't very safe on two legs so slumped onto his sofa while I waited for him. He must have taken ages because I think I nodded off. When I woke

248

up it was pure pantomime. Sleeping Beauty to be precise. Big Mike was kissing me again. It was rather lovely. Better than mince pies and sherry any day.

Jane told me she got up first thing this morning to find the door to Burr Cottage wide open. I went very pink and said, 'Perhaps Santa left it like that?'

Christmas card featuring kangaroo in a Father Christmas hat:

I'm actually in Calcutta, but I bought this card in October, cos I know they don't go in for Santa much in the Indian sub-continent – or sub-incontinent as it has been for me. Had dysentery, but I'm finally over it. Talk about a radical diet.
Hope you're all well. And hey girls, hurry up with those emails.

Dear former housemates and Bella,

Christmas G'day Greetings!

Love,
Mo xxx

From: Lucy Gordon (juicylucy@webbedup.net)
To: Mo Lavender (Hobo-mobo@Hotmail.com)

19.02
Subject: You're alive!

At last – your Christmas card arrived today (30th Dec). Are you free of the brainwashing cult, or do they have temples all over India as well as Australia? Was horrified to hear that you'd been ill. Maybe that's why I never hear back from you? Anyway, I'm sorry I stopped emailing for a bit – I had sort of given up hope. Now I'll have to give you a quick catch-up: I didn't get promoted, but I did have a one-night-stand with Mike-from-next-door on Christmas Eve. Okay, that's about it.

Am now in a quandary about New Year's Eve. I originally agreed to spend it with Jane at Cow in Clover, but Big Mike might be there and am not sure if I'm ready to face him. Am certain he thinks C E was a bit of a drunken mistake. After all, he dashed straight off afterwards to visit his parents in Staffordshire and hasn't been in touch since. If he didn't think it was a mistake, he'd have called me, wouldn't he? Perhaps I should act as though nothing happened. I'm too ashamed of myself to tell Jane, especially as I think she secretly quite likes Mike herself – they seem to spend a lot of time together. Why am I always doing this to her? I'm a terrible friend. And I'm about to behave even more shabbily.

Ceri, the Widgetex receptionist, called me today to ask what I'm up to tomorrow night. I umm-ed and ahh-ed a bit and said I wasn't sure. She's invited me to a huge fancy dress party in Basborough. I asked if Jane could come too, but Ceri says it's tickets only and she hasn't got another spare. L xxx

---

W Microsoft Word – New Year's Eve.doc

1p.m.: I think Mike is back. I can't actually see his Land Rover from any of our windows and I don't really feel brave enough to go outside and look in case I bump into him, but I definitely heard dogs barking earlier and then what sounded like a tail-gate banging. If I do go to the fancy dress party, I'm not sure what to dress as. A big chicken perhaps?

4p.m.: Bella and Brick have just turned up and say that they're going to the Cow in Clover, so Jane will have some company. My mind is made up. Am definitely going to go to the Basborough party. I wish I'd asked Ceri more about the fancy dress part yesterday, though. Can't remember whether it has a theme or not. Have just called her, but her machine is on. It's far too late to try to hire something, so I guess I'll just have to improvise. Quite fancy myself as Cat Woman, since I've got some leather trousers which I can just about fit into, plus my long high-heeled boots, and I can borrow one of Bella's raunchy leather tops. All I'll need to do is make a tail and ears.

6p.m.: My costume is almost complete. Have told Jane and Bella that Ceri is absolutely desperate for someone to go to the Basborough extravaganza with her, so I'm helping out a friend in need. They seem to believe me. Bella has even made me a head-dress, which looks fantastic, with little leather ears, a very sultry feline mask and diamante whiskers. The only trouble is I can't find my long boots.

7.45p.m.: Ceri is due to collect me in ten minutes and I've only just realised that my evil little sister borrowed my boots in exchange for agreeing to appear in *Can't Cook, Won't Cook* in Dad's place. It's too late to change my outfit and my feet are bigger than all my housemates' so am having to wear pair of black wellies. They look ridiculous matched with the sexy Emma Peel leathers.

Later: Terrible party. There was a theme – *Star Wars*. I looked flipping ridiculous dressed as Cat Woman. People kept asking me whether I was Darth Vader. Even worse, just as I was setting out, I spotted Big Mike walking out of his cottage looking really pale. Guilt, I suppose – or fear of encountering me. Thankfully I don't think he recognised me with my kitty head on, so I just leapt into Ceri's car and squeaked, 'Drive!'

Got back to find my housemates plundering the last of the Christmas sherry in the kitchen. Wished them a Happy New Year, and casually asked after the pub.

'Mike was there – had flu all over Christmas apparently,' Bella told me. 'Lost his voice completely – couldn't talk for days. I think he's still quite ill, but he insisted on coming out. He asked after you.'

'He's had flu?' I asked, feeling guiltier and guiltier.

Jane nodded. 'Really bad. He looks awful, poor thing. Although he did say he'd managed to pull a cracker or two this Christmas.'

251

Was about to rush around to Vetch Cottage to offer Florence Nightingale skills when something occurred to me. A cracker or *two*. That means more than one. If, as I suspect, he was referring to pulling me (typically sexist Mike comment) then who was the other cracker? Whoever she is, I hope she's caught flu.

From: Lucy Gordon (juicylucy@webbedup.net)
To: Mo Lavender (Hobo-mobo@Hotmail.com)

22.41
Subject: Pub lick humiliation

Have managed to avoid Big Mike all week, but tonight Jane lured me to the Cow in Clover for a drink and he was in there, propping up the bar with George, the old army Captain who seems to have permanent residence rights to the barstool closest to the 6X tap, under which sits his grey-muzzled Labrador, Monty. I managed to lurk in a dark corner until Jane got the drinks in and then I dragged her to the table farthest from the bar. I know I'm behaving like a child, but I haven't been able to look him in the eye since the Christmas Incident particularly now that I know I am just one of two 'crackers' he pulled. Thankfully Jane (who is still completely unaware of the Christmas Incident) didn't seem to notice that I was behaving oddly. She was desperate to tell me all about a fanciable new client she is teaching to drive – a thirty-something blond-haired yuppie called Charles who has just moved to the village.

'Isn't he a bit old to be learning to drive?' I asked.

'He had no need for a car in London apparently,' Jane told me. 'Now he's bought a cottage here and commutes to the City every day, but he can't get out of Chisbourne to buy groceries because he doesn't drive – he's been getting everything from the village shop, so is living off a diet of Findus frozen food.'

'Poor thing – you should ask him round to supper.' From the corner of my eye, I suddenly caught sight of Mike walking our way. Oh God! He was coming to talk to me and I was totally unprepared. I looked around for an escape route. Then I realised to my relief that our safe haven table was right next to the men's loos. I held a beer mat up to the side of my face and Mike stomped into them without noticing me.

'That's a great idea, Lucy. I could ask Mike along too,' Jane said brightly.

I could tell that she was all set to corner him on his way out of the loos, so I hastily suggested moving closer to the fire and, before she could answer, I dashed to the sofa in front of it, which is hidden from view to both the bar and Gents.

'Are you cold?' Jane looked confused as she followed me, gathering up the dropped crisp packets I had left in my wake.

'Freezing.' I shivered dramatically and huddled lower into the sofa as Mike wandered back from the loos. If I'd been wearing a hat, I'd have tipped it over my nose. I was so desperate not to be spotted that I didn't even make a sound when Monty lumbered over and goosed me for a full minute, snorting furiously.

Really, this avoidance thing is getting too hard to keep up. I must talk to him sooner or later. I'd just rather it was later. Like next year. I can't bear the idea that he took pity on me because I hadn't got the Widgetex manager's job, and because it was a year since I agreed to marry pig-face Greg, in which time I have become a lonely old maid. Or did he just take advantage of me because I was drunk? Either way, I don't want to look like any more of a fool than I already am. I haven't made many New Year's resolutions yet, but one of them will be to avoid being known as Loose Lucy. L xxx

From: Ceri Dixon (reception@widgetex.co.uk)
To: Lucy Gordon (lucy@widgetex.co.uk)

11.09
Subject: First day

I thought the new Marketing Co-ordinator was supposed to be starting today. What's she called again?

From: Lucy Gordon (lucy@widgetex.co.uk)
To: Ceri Dixon (reception@widgetex.co.uk)

11.14
Subject: Re: First day

Gabby Peartree (silly name).
    She's off with flu. What a wimp.
    Slave Driver was revoltingly sympathetic and said that there's a lot of it around. I've told him that people with weak constitutions are particularly susceptible (my neighbour, Mike, had flu over Christmas).
    I've been deliberately bouncing around the office all morning looking as healthy as possible, but I don't think he's noticed.

W Microsoft Word – sick cat.doc

Oh God, I think Platforms is ill. Her eyes are runny, she won't eat and she's been sneezing all evening. Have just got out my *Cat Owner's Guide* and looked up cat flu. After all, if there's a lot of it about then surely cats can contract it too? The book says it can be fatal! Awful. If she doesn't pick up soon, I'll have to fetch Mike. I'll have to swallow my pride and face him. He might be the only one who can save her.

From: Lucy Gordon (juicylucy@webbedup.net)
To: Mo Lavender (Hobo-mobo@Hotmail.com)

18.44
Subject: It shouldn't happen to a vet

Last night was *so* embarrassing. Platforms seemed to be mortally ill, so I raced around to Big Mike's cottage only to find it in darkness. How dare he be out when my cat was dying? I know I've been avoiding him lately, but he chose a very inconvenient – not to mention callous – moment to turn the tables.

Had to phone the emergency vet at the surgery in the end and she arrived about twenty minutes later. Far from being at death's door, it turns out that Platforms has an allergy to the new 'Vacfresh' sachets which Jane has been using in the Hoover. Rachel – that's the vet – was very sweet about the fact I'd called her out, telling me that it was an understandable mistake. I offered her a cup of tea to apologise for wasting her time. She's really nice – about forty and very glamorous for a vet. Apparently she only started working at the surgery recently. I asked her whether she knew Mike.

'Of course, the beefy charmer. He lives around here, doesn't he?'

Beefy Charmer, huh? Hmmm.

'Next door,' I tried to be ultra-casual as I asked her what she thought of him.

'A loveable rogue,' she winked, looking very smug and adding leadingly: 'Bit of a womaniser, I gather?'

Womaniser. WOMANISER!

I wish I'd never asked.

Remembered afterwards that Mike mentioned that the practice was interviewing for a new partner before Christmas, and that he said she was very glamorous. He must fancy his chances with Rachel and might even have had a crack already. Was Rachel the other Christmas Cracker? She certainly seemed quite keen.

Have decided to keep avoiding him at all costs. I had no idea he was a womaniser. To my knowledge, he's not had a girlfriend for years apart from the dreaded Peach. I always thought that was because he was so fussy, but now I'm starting to suspect he just prefers being foot loose and fancy free so that he can indulge himself in one-night stands. Rachel has made me see a whole new side of him. L xxx

---

From: Lucy Gordon (lucy@widgetex.co.uk)
To: Ceri Dixon (reception@widgetex.co.uk)

12.49
Subject: Sick pay

Can you believe Gabby Peartree (silly name) has still got flu? That's almost a fortnight. She must be SO sickly. Bad management choice, I'd say. How can a team pull together when its leader is always ill?

Mind you, I have a lot to thank her for. I've been asked to look after a big new spring campaign in her absence which will promote all the Widgetex products across the board. Very exciting. Better still, Ambitious Dave's nose is thoroughly out of joint because he's still working on the promotion for the desktop diskette holder with integrated pen tidy.

Burr Cottage
Chisbourne

Sunday 16th January

Dear Big Brother,

Thank you for your Christmas card, which finally arrived today, and for the I-heart-ewe knickers in XXXL (ha ha). I'm glad you had a good one.

Not much to report this end. Yes, I'm still 'a single and desperate cocktail of lethal girly-bottom hormones' but no longer as heart-broken about Greg as you suggest (I don't own any Sylvia Plath poems, Alanis Morrisette albums or Germaine Greer books so can't do as you suggest with them). And no, I didn't get the job.

I haven't seen much of Mum and Dad lately (the atmosphere at Roundhead Avenue is still a bit frosty to be honest). And I've passed on your love to Jane, but I fear she is devoted to another. And it's no longer Horsy Tim, thank God, although I'm not sure this one is any better.

Went riding with her today. She took out Zak, who is now booked to stay with a horse trainer in February. It can't come soon enough as far as I'm concerned. I was riding one of Tim's horses, a lovely old plodder called Hobbit, who has only one pace – a sort of slow ambling walk. Jane and I were trying to have a chat about the blond yuppie she fancies, and planning how best to ask him over for dinner. But Zak kept dashing off in different directions, going up on his hind legs and freaking out at every car that passed, so we could hardly talk at all. Most of the time Jane was at least fifty yards ahead of me and travelling at speed.

Tell the sheep the knickers look great – in the duster drawer.
Love,
Lucy xx

From: Lucy Gordon (juicylucy@webbedup.net)
To: Mo Lavender (Hobo-mobo@Hotmail.com)

21.05
Subject: Let tomorrow never happen

Jane was in a furious mood when she came home tonight. At first I thought it was because I had thrown out all her Vacfresh sachets, but it turns out that she took Yuppie Charles out on an evening driving lesson and he turned down her offer of dinner tomorrow night. 'The pig!' she howled. 'The awful thing is that

I've already invited Brick, Bella and Mike, so now I'll have to cook for nothing.'

'You invited Mike?' I gulped, trying hard to think of something social that I simply couldn't get out of tomorrow night. Apart from a much-needed trip to the gym, nothing much sprang to mind. Will have to wear snazziest dress and try not to let personal jealousy get in the way.

Gabby 'silly name' Peartree is starting at Widgetex tomorrow morning. Must wear my snazziest power suit and try not to let professional jealousy get in the way.

It'll be a day for dressing up and feeling down. Wish me luck. L xx

---

W Microsoft Word – Marketing Ideas56.doc

~~Spring Campaign – Making Gadgets This Season's Must Buy~~
~~From Geek appeal to Sex appeal~~

Gabby 'silly name' Peartree finally started at Widgetex today so I deliberately dressed in my nattiest little power suit to show her what a smart professional I am. Unfortunately I took so long getting ready for work that I was late. She was already here, tapping her watch and sporting an identical little power suit. She'd twinned hers with a silk scarf and court shoes; I'd co-ordinated mine with a red polo-neck and knee-high boots, but there was no mistaking that we were wearing the exact same Jigsaw suit – we looked like two air stewardesses. So embarrassing, especially as she is at least six inches taller and a dress size smaller than me.

Thankfully, she spent most of the day in Slave Driver's office, going through the Widgetex marketing history. When I was called in to show her the work I've started on the big spring campaign, I left my jacket behind in the hope that SD wouldn't spot the cloning factor, but alas he is too observant and started to laugh in delight. 'I had no idea you'd asked your staff to wear uniforms, Gabriella?'

I smarted irritably at being described as Ms Peartree's 'staff' –

makes me sound like a cleaning lady. But Gabby was really cool about it, smiling warmly at both Slave Driver and me, and saying, 'I gather that Lucy was a very close contender for the management role, so I'm sure we have a lot more in common than our sartorial style. We're bound to make a good team.' I think she might prove to be quite likeable, even though she does have very long legs and uses flashy words like 'sartorial' which I keep having to slyly look up in the office dictionary.

Thought about working late tonight to impress her, but Jane has demanded that I get back in time to fold napkins or whatever. I'm dreading her dinner party. There's no way I can avoid The Chisbourne Womaniser, as I now think of Big Mike. I tried v. hard to persuade her to cancel last night, but she can be horribly stubborn.

'It's too late for that, Lucy,' she tutted. 'I've already bought the ingredients for Delia's shortcrust tarts. Brick's coming down from London especially, and Mike sounded really excited when I asked him.'

Probably wants a crack at Jane now that he's ticked me off his list. I've hidden Delia Smith under Platforms' basket.

From: Lucy Gordon (juicylucy@webbedup.net)
To: Mo Lavender (Hobo-mobo@Hotmail.com)

00.15
Subject: Dinner party post-mortem

I had been planning to wear a snazzy dress tonight, but decided my 'sartorial' decision hadn't worked earlier (imagine wearing the same suit as my new boss!), so settled for slobby jeans and jumper. Drank two huge gin and tonics to prepare myself for the ordeal, and then the phone rang. Jane was arm-deep in pastry, so I answered it.

'Lucy – is that you?' It was Big Mike on a crackly mobile phone, his voice sort of odd – all shaky-sounding. I didn't hang around long enough to ask whether he was sitting on a tractor or just emotionally overwrought.

'I'll get Jane!' I said with forced cheeriness and, ignoring the fact I could clearly hear him saying 'Wait!' at the other end of the line, I handed the phone to the pastry chef in the kitchen and bolted upstairs. Felt stupidly flustered.

When I came down, Jane was wiping flour from the phone with a cloth and looking at me irritably. 'Mike's been called out to assist another vet at a breech lambing somewhere – he thinks it might take all night.'

'No?!' I tried not to sound too elated, but I almost gave the air a victory punch when I added, 'That's a shame, isn't it?'

Jane gave me an even more crabby look. 'He says the new vet, Rachel, is a bit inexperienced with big farm animals. Said he was really, really sorry – seemed very annoyed.'

'Is that a fact?' I narrowed my eyes. He must have been laying the apologies on thick, the womanising swine. He's obviously still got his sights set on the practice glamourpuss. And she's old enough to be his mother. Well, maybe not quite – his big sister or an aunt or something? Still, has he no shame? I'm sure she'll find that after a night in the Womaniser's company, she's very experienced with big animals. L xxx

---

From: Ceri Dixon (reception@widgetex.co.uk)
To: Lucy Gordon (lucy@widgetex.co.uk)

10.36
Subject: Fwd: Batty

Thought you'd like to know that the male members of staff have gone off Gabby (see below – I hear Creepy Derek voted for NAPAL twenty times, by the way).
C xx

Original message: From <<**Anon**>> To: <<The Lads, cc: Ceri Dixon>>
Subject <<'Batty'>> Date 28/1/** 10.08

>>In the great tradition of Widgetex, we asked you all to vote on a nickname for our latest member of staff, Ms Gabby Peartree. It has to be said that the results for TFWD are somewhat disappointing, but here's the chart:

Fruit-bat 41%
Gobby 35%
TFWD (Typical Fucking Woman Driver) 10%
Nice Pear 8%
NAPAL (Not As Pretty As Lucy) 6%

From: Lucy Gordon (lucy@widgetex.co.uk)
To: Ceri Dixon (reception@widgetex.co.uk)

11.06
Subject: Fruit-bat?

I don't get it. It's not as though she's bossy or rude to them. She was 'Legs' all last week and that doesn't even make it onto the chart.

From: Ceri Dixon (reception@widgetex.co.uk)
To: Lucy Gordon (lucy@widgetex.co.uk)

11.12
Subject: The Parking Lot is not a Happy One

It's because she has just got a company car, of course. And not any old Vauxhall from the pool, oh no. A shiny red BMW, no less. What's more, she has been allocated Ambitious Dave's parking place by the front entrance and he's been demoted to a space right at the rear of the car park by the Security Portacabin. He's livid.

What do you make of her? She just nods at me as she walks past, stuck up cow.

From: Lucy Gordon (lucy@widgetex.co.uk)
To: Ceri Dixon (reception@widgetex.co.uk)

11.06
Subject:

Well, she called me 'assiduous and indefatigable' this week. I looked the words up in the dictionary and they seem to be quite flattering. Can't, unfortunately, say quite the same things for her yet. She still seems to spend most of her time 'liaising' in Slave Driver's office and over long business lunches, leaving me to do all the work on the spring campaign. I know it's early days and she's finding her feet, but I am getting just slightly fed up with her wandering past my desk murmuring, 'Great work Lucy – just off to lunch. My mobile's switched on if you need me.'

W **Microsoft Word – Lucy aches.doc**

Went to The Sweatshop this morning. First gym session since Christmas. Am in agony. Fruit-bat would choose today to suggest new office lay-out, making us all heave our desks around. Ideal excuse not to go to Cow in Clover with Bella and Jane tonight, as can't actually walk. Lay in bath instead trying not to imagine Big Mike – the Womaniser of Chisbourne – chatting up everyone in sight. Needn't have wasted my 'indefatigable' creative energy, however, as Jane says Mike wasn't even in pub. Am sure she's guessed something has happened between us, but am keeping schtum for my pride's sake.

Wexbury Veterinary Practice,
Glebe House, Chisbourne Road, Wexbury, Berks
Telephone: 01555 658300   Fax: 01555 658830

Dear *Platforms Gordon,*

Your owner asked us to notify you when your annual booster is
due. We have checked our records and found that this is now.
Please could you request that *Ms Lucy Gordon* makes an
appointment to bring you in to see *Mr Michael Ensor* FRCVS at
her earliest convenience?

Kind Regards,

Reception

W Microsoft Word – The Womaniser.doc

Have just had first sighting of the Womaniser of Chisbourne for
several days. Was standing in garden admiring snowdrops when I
suddenly spotted him coming out of his garden shed. I ducked down
low like a commando and crept back to the cottage along the line
of the hedge. Made it as far as kitchen door before realising he was
watching me. Feel such a fool although still harbour outside hope
that he might have thought I was checking the crocus bulbs in the
borders.

Platforms is due to have her vaccination booster next week. Can't
bring myself to ask Mike to do it, so have called surgery and
arranged for appointment with Rachel. Hope to do some detective
work to see if he pulled more than just lambs on the night of Jane's
dinner party.

From: Gabby Peartree (gpeartree@gratisweb.com)
To: Lucy Gordon (lucy@widgetex.co.uk)

10.06
Subject: Keeping track

Lucy,
I am aware that you require copy approval for the new catalogues
today. However, I am having a tracking system fitted in my BMW
which necessitates working from home. Can we schedule a
breakfast meeting at 8a.m. tomorrow to go through any
changes? In which case, can you pick me up a low fat plain yog,
banana – no brown bits – muesli bar and a skimmed milk latte
(short) on your way in? I will reimburse.
Tx. Gabby.

From: Lucy Gordon (lucy@widgetex.co.uk)
To: Gabby Peartree (gpeartree@gratisweb.com)

10.12
Subject: Re: Keeping track

You lucky thing. I might suggest I get tracker fitted in the Saxo.
Could use a day off right now!

From: Gabby Peartree (gpeartree@gratisweb.com)
To: Lucy Gordon (lucy@widgetex.co.uk)

10.28
Subject: Re: Re: Keeping track

Lucy,
    This is NOT a day off. I can assure you that people who work
from home OVER-compensate their maximised earning-time by
denying themselves the coffee breaks, personal emails to friends,

idle partition banter et cetera that office employees take for granted.

I've changed my mind about the latte – let's make it a mocha (skimmed). G.

You have . . . one . . . new message. Message received . . . today . . . at . . . six . . . thirteen . . . pee eemmmm.

'It's Lucy. I am shattered! I've just spent the *entire* day trailing backwards and forwards to the printers because Fruit-bat kept noticing errors in my catalogue copy. If she'd given it her approval yesterday when I asked her to, then I'd have been saved the effort. Anyway, Platforms is due in for her booster at Wex Vets tonight and I'm not going to make it back in time. Can one of you two take her? The appointment's at seven. I'd be eternally grateful.'

Posted on the Burr Cottage fridge:

> Lucy, J've changed your appointment to Thursday at six forty-five, with Mike. Hope that's okay? Bxx

---

W Microsoft Word – The Womaniser2.doc

Just back from vet's surgery. While I was sitting in waiting room with Platforms' cat basket on my knee, I could hear raised voices inside the consulting room – Big Mike and Rachel the glamorous vet were arguing. Tried to listen in, but apart from overhearing one juicy line from Mike: 'I have hardly slept this week because of your incessant demands' the rest was inaudible.

Mike looked a bit flustered when he gave Platforms her jab, but I'm not certain because I found I simply couldn't look him in the face, talk to him or – in fact – breathe. He muttered something under his breath like 'That woman!' then 'Sorry, Lucy that's unprofessional of me', then when I said nothing (and was starting to turn purple from oxygen starvation) he asked in a low voice, 'Are you okay, Lucy? I've hardly seen you since . . .'

Not sure whether he was about to say 'since our mistaken one-night stand' or 'since I got it together with man-eating Rachel and her incessant demands' because Platforms chose that moment to attack his stethoscope.

And then I suddenly found I didn't want to do any detective work after all. The truth is too humiliating to face. The Womaniser, it seems, has finally met his match. I was, after all, just a frivolous Christmas stocking filler. As soon as Platforms was back in her pet transporter, I turned and fled. It was only when I got home that I realised a) I hadn't paid and b) Platforms still had Mike's stethoscope in her mouth.

From: Lucy Gordon (juicylucy@webbedup.net)
To: Mo Lavender (Hobo-mobo@Hotmail.com)

18.34
Subject: Best Hoof forwards

Have just returned from taking Zak to the horse trainer in Gloucestershire. Horsy Tim drove us, towing Zak behind in a trailer. Jane acted very strangely throughout, sitting in the back of the car and staring tearfully out of the rear window at the trailer, saying, 'I hope he'll be all right. Do you think he'll miss us?'

I didn't like to point out that we've barely see him lately, since we're both too frightened of the big grey bully to ride him very often. She was like a mother leaving her beloved son at boarding school. I thought the training yard was really nice, with friendly staff, dogs roaming around underfoot, geese waddling through the paddocks and very luxurious stables banked high with shavings. No wonder it's so expensive. If I was Zak, I wouldn't want to come back. He certainly pricked up his ears when he arrived, bellowed out a few 'Hi there' whinnies and totally ignored us when we said farewell. The trainer, Mark, has promised that he'll put in some really intensive work on him this week and let us know how he's progressing. I hope he's a fast learner as I'm not sure we can afford to keep him there long.

We stopped for lunch on the way home, in a little country pub near Chipping Norton. Jane was very quiet, but I had a good old chat with Tim. I asked him whether he'd met the glamorous new vet, Rachel, yet. He rolled his eyes and told me that she was 'very enthusiastic'. When I asked him what he meant, he tapped his nose secretively and said that she seemed to care more about two-legged animals than four if I got his drift. I didn't really, so I had to ask again. HT laughed and said, 'You can be so dim, Lucy. She's a man-eater. Mike warned me, but even I was shocked. I wouldn't bend over in breeches within ten yards of the woman.'

Rachel can't have been trying to chat up Tim can she? What about Big Mike? Do his ovine breech births hold no more charm for her? Feel strangely cheerful. Have rinsed his stethoscope (which Platforms stole) in CKOne bubble bath and posted it through his door. L xxx

---

Burr Cottage
Chisbourne

Sunday 7th February

Dear Big Brother,
Mum and Alice are due to record their episode of *Can't Cook, Won't Cook* this week. They're both very excited; Mum went shopping in Wexbury yesterday and proudly showed me the outfit she'd bought. I think it might be a bit OTT for daytime television – especially the hat – but I said nothing. Alice was in a sulk because she will have to wear chef's whites and a cravat so will not be able to sport her usual punky gear. She seemed to cheer up when I told her that there was no reason not to keep in her nose-ring and lip stud. Mum looked

at me in horror and quickly told Alice that facial jewellery strobes very badly on television.

More later . . .

W Microsoft Word – Spring Campaign8.doc

~~Last minute Presentation Notes:~~

Fruit-bat is improving at work. She spent most of today helping me put together tomorrow's presentation for the Spring Campaign and used only two or three long words which I didn't understand. Afterwards, she took me for a drink at the Lock Inn and told me all about the flat she's buying in Wexbury Heights. It sounded strangely familiar when she described it, and when she said that the vendor was living overseas, I suddenly realised why. It's Greg's old flat. My ex's love-nest. Bizarre. I told her it's lovely, but the neighbours – well, Peach – can be a bit intrusive.

W Microsoft Word – Spring Campaign9.doc

~~Presentation Report~~

Presentation went v. well, although Slave Driver seemed to think that Fruit-bat had done all the work, which was annoying. I waited for her to put him right and give me some credit, but she must have decided to do it when I'm not around. That way she can be even more flattering without embarrassing me. Went out at lunchtime and bought card for Big Mike with big, fluffy sheep on it. Message reads 'Will ewe be my Valentine?' I thought this was nicely ironic, given that I have been passed over in favour of his glamorous (if much older) colleague. Now I'm afraid it might hurt his feelings as nymphomaniac colleague may have started eyeing up another's jodhpurs.

Long, jolly, wine and pizza session with Jane tonight. She has finally given up on Charles the Yuppie. She says she's dropped so many hints now that it's obvious he's not interested. When I sug-

gested she post him a Valentine's card, she poo-pooed the idea.
'That is *so* teenage, Lucy. At our age it seems undignified.' Have
made mental note to rip up card I bought. Big Mike doesn't deserve
it. On second thoughts, I might post it to myself. Nothing undignified
or teenage in that. Just healthy self-respect.

Continuation of letter to Jeremy:

Roundhead Avenue, Thursday:
Dashed around here after work (no easy task as new boss –
Fruit-bat – has given me a stack of paperwork to do). Was
dying to know how Mum and Alice got on as *Can't Cook,
Won't Cook* contestants in Birmingham this morning, but they
were both in very black moods. They don't think their episode
will even be broadcast. Apparently Alice took the opportunity
of appearing on television in front of millions to announce that
meat is murder and that genetically modified vegetables will
cause us all to have three-headed children. Too embarrassing;
I'm sure Scrumpy put her up to it. Ainsley Harriott didn't
know what to do with himself. The contestants had to cook
couscous with Mediterranean vegetables. A middle-aged gnome
enthusiast from Walsall won in the end. Mum says Alice was a
far better cook, but that the Walsall gnome's wife cheated by
peeking out of her mask during the tasting session at the end.
   'But you voted for his couscous too!' Alice pointed out
huffily.
   Dad joked that they should 'cous and make up', and they
both groaned then laughed. At least Alice has got to keep her
chef's outfit. She's planning to tie-dye it purple and use it as a
painting smock for her A level art practical.
   Tell the sheep that lambs have started appearing in the fields
here. So sweet!
   Love,
   Lucy xx

From: Lucy Gordon (juicylucy@webbedup.net)
To: Mo Lavender (Hobo-mobo@Hotmail.com)

00.54
Subject: Funny Valentine

Mark the horse trainer called today and told us that Zak's making progress, but might need another month before he really gets anywhere. The cost is unbelievable.

'A month!' I raged afterwards. 'What's he trying to do? Teach Zak to read?'

Jane explained that these things take time. She's in a very gracious and serene mood at the moment because she received an anonymous Valentine's card this morning. The fact it was postmarked Leicester (where her parents live) was a bit of a give-away, but I didn't say anything and let her enjoy her glory. She's certainly changed her tune about Valentine's cards being 'teenage' and beneath her. I, needless to say, got nothing but a credit card bill. Still have the card I bought for Big Mike. Planned to send it to myself, but I've left it too late. Perhaps I should pop it though the Chisbourne Womaniser's letter-box after all? Shame to waste it.

Brick whisked Bella out to romantic dinner at Bistro Etoile tonight. Jane and I went to Cow in Clover and she told me Bella is convinced that Brick's going to propose. So exciting! Kept thinking about Mike and the card. Every time the door of the pub opened I swung around in case it was him. Jane asked me if I was expecting someone, but I told her I was just annoyed by the draught. He didn't appear. Suspect he was treating Rachel the glamorous vet to romantic meal – possibly at Bistro Etoile.

There was no ring on Bella's finger when we got back to cottage, although she and Brick were looking very loving. Tried not to feel too jealous. Asked them if there were any familiar faces in restaurant. Bella said Slave Driver was there with his wife.

'Anyone else?' I asked leadingly, nudging my eyes towards Mike's cottage.

Bella looked at me as if I was potty. I think perhaps I am. Oh damn it, I'm going to hand-deliver the card. When I thought he was sentimental, reliable old Mike I hardly noticed him. Now he's the village stud I think I've developed a crush.

Ten minutes later: Was just creeping towards end of drive wearing a coat over my pyjamas when Big Mike's front door swung open and he walked out. His security light flashed on and he saw me straight away, so I had to do some hasty thinking. I hid my envelope behind my back and gave him a hearty wave, saying cheerfully, 'Just getting something from the car!'

'Hi Lucy!' He waved back, looking almost as embarrassed as I was. 'Just putting some rubbish out!' The odd thing was he wasn't carrying any rubbish, just something red and square – an envelope, maybe? – which he hastily threw in the bin. L xxx

---

W Microsoft Word – Lucy's loveless.doc

Am home alone. Bella is in London with Brick and Jane is out on a date, lucky thing. When I got back from work this evening, she was wearing rollers and hopping round in a state of delirious excitement. I was a bit surprised that she was going to so much effort for the trip we'd planned to Basborough multiplex to see the latest Keanu Reeves movie. Then I realised that she'd completely forgotten. Apparently Charles the Yuppie – who she'd given up hope of ever noticing her – had just called to ask her if she was free this evening and she'd said 'absolutely'. I nobly told her to borrow anything she liked from my wardrobe, so she swanned off a couple of hours ago in my best seduction dress and a cloud of Chanel No 5. Tried not to feel too resentful that she'd left clothes spread out all over my bed and lid off my favourite nail polish.

Burr Cottage
Chisbourne

Sunday 21st February

Dear Big Brother,

Jane was very hungover this morning, but crazy about
Charles (one of her clients who asked her to dinner yesterday).
She says that he was actually having a dinner party and that
someone had dropped out at last minute. She's the only person
he knows in the village, so he asked her to make up numbers.
The other guests were very London and a bit intimidating,
mostly high-flyers who work in the City. She told me one thing
I thought was very odd. It seems Charles had asked her not to
admit she was teaching him to drive because he didn't want the
others to know, so she'd had to pretend she was an air
stewardess all evening. I asked, 'Why an air stewardess?' She
shrugged and said it was Charles's idea. Sounds a bit suspect to
me, but at least Jane seems happy, and dreamily claims he
cooks like Raymond Blanc.

Unlike Mum, who is still refusing to cook after the television
studio disaster and once again insisted Dad made lunch (the
only man who can burn a pizza so badly he needed to fetch his
axle grinder to cut it out of the oven).

Mum gave me one of her wise-owl talks about my single

272

status today. She thinks I'm not making enough effort to get out and meet people.

'What do you suggest I do?' I asked irritably. 'Walk around the streets with an "available" sign around my neck?'

'Don't be so silly – join a society or an evening class. Develop a hobby. Your father and I were hoping you might meet a nice young country type through Zak . . .'

Had sudden image of Zak at cocktail party, effecting introductions between me and man in flat cap and Barbour.

Sorry about Jane. I'm sure the sheep will be a comfort.

Love,

Lucy xx

CHISBOURNE PLAYERS

Do you enjoy the theatre?

Have you always wanted to tread the boards?

Are you a talented seamstress or carpenter?

New members always welcomed. For details call

the Membership Secretary on: 01555 454367

~~Removing the Stigma of Depilatory Products~~

Boring day sending out mailshots for Spring Campaign. Fruit-bat was supposed to be helping me, but claimed to need progress meeting with Slave Driver which involved boozy three-hour lunch. Afterwards, she took dictaphone and shut herself in boardroom to 'assimilate our ideas'. Have just peeked in and think she's asleep. Guess the pressure of her first few weeks as manager is getting to her, poor thing.

Sloped out at lunchtime myself to raid library and pick up leaflets for amateur drama societies in Wexbury area. There's one under my very nose. The Chisbourne Players. Had no idea there were thespians in the village as have never spotted any shows advertised or encountered luvvie types in Cow in Clover. When I rang the membership secretary this afternoon, she explained that the society – known as the 'Chips' – is just starting up again after a lengthy break without a venue. 'We used to use the village hall, but lost out to the aerobics group on Thursday nights and line-dancing at weekends. We have the use of Lady Gunton's tithe barn now. There's a play-reading on Thursday night. Can I tempt you along? We'd love some young blood.'

If Chips needs young blood then it doesn't sound a very hopeful hunting ground for eligible men, but at least it'll give me something to do, and have always wanted closer look at Chisbourne Manor. Might just pop along for five minutes.

From: Lucy Gordon (juicylucy@webbedup.net)
To: Mo Lavender (Hobo-mobo@Hotmail.com)

23.07
Subject: Lucy's a Luvvie!

Have just got back from my first play-reading with our local drama group, the newly resurrected Chisbourne Players. It took place in Lady Gunton's tithe barn beside the manor house. Was hoping to meet the glitzy Lady G herself, but apparently she and Lord G are away skiing. Am now sitting in our kitchen with feet pressed against Rayburn trying to warm up. The barn was freezing. There was just one tiny plug-in radiator trying to heat entire building, and by the time I arrived the half-dozen assembled members of 'Chips' had all staked a place next to it and were sipping tea from thermos flasks, like miners around a brazier. They'd also dressed for the occasion in thick fleeces, Puffa jackets, hats and scarves whereas I – thinking it would be a social thing with wine and nibbles – was wearing short skirt and velvet jacket.

Was welcomed by the Chips chairman, Ralph, who owns the antique shop on the High Street and once acted professionally (apparently he was in three episodes of *Crossroads* in 1978). He's very dapper and charming, and wears a cravat. He reminded me of Leslie 'Hello' Phillips. When I apologised that I wasn't much of an actress but was willing to help out backstage, or make interval coffee or whatever, he said, 'Nonsense, nonsense, dear child. I will decide whether you can act or not. Tonight you will read the role of Jasmine, the young shepherdess who is mistaken for the long-lost daughter of a powerful duke.' He then thrust a script at me. As everyone else there was over sixty, I guess he was a bit desperate.

The play has been written especially for the society by Lady Gunton – I think that's the reason they are allowed to use her barn. I quite liked it, but my part was enormous. Kept stumbling over my words. My fellow readers were all very sympathetic apart from a woman with bright red dyed hair and too much make-up who kept making a critical little 'tut' noise every time I made a mistake, which was more and more as the night wore on and my teeth started to chatter too much to speak.

Afterwards, Ralph clapped his hands together ecstatically and told me that I reminded him of a 'young Deborah Kerr'. I think he was a bit taken aback when I asked who she was, but then he laughed as though I'd made a very funny joke, and told me that they're auditioning next week and that I must come along, 'Amber Gunton will simply adore you.' The red-haired woman tutted even more at this.

Am hugely excited, although I'm planning to wear at least six layers and my thermal undies next time. Can't wait to meet Lady G. She used to be a top model and once dated Mick Jagger. L xxx

---

Sunday Lunch Menu – 13 Roundhead Avenue, Wexbury.
Chef: Malcolm Gordon

Heinz Condensed Cream of Tomato Soup
Coq au 'Chicken Tonight Spicy' with mashed potato
Individual M and S Trifle pots (assorted)

To be accompanied by Tesco's Great With Chicken
For Mother-in-law: 'Red Square' Tequila and Red Bull mix
   (bottled)

Burr Cottage
Chisbourne

Sunday 28th February

Dear Big Brother,

Mum is really pleased that I've joined a drama group. She's convinced I'm going to be discovered by a talent scout and end up in Hollywood.

Dad's reaction was more circumspect. He asked me how I'm going to find time to ride Zak now I'm treading the boards. I told him that I hadn't actually got a part yet and that I'm pretty sure I won't be asked to play a big role. Besides, I pointed out that Zak is still with Mark the trainer, who called yesterday to say that he thinks he might hold onto him for a couple more weeks and enter him into a small horse trials to try to assess his potential. Dad perked up at idea of his co-investment competing again. He and Mum are planning to go along and support.

Jane has been grumbling about this, however. She seems to think Mark is keeping Zak for purely selfish reasons, but I disagree. Am certain Jane is just in ratty, ungrateful mood because Charles the Yuppie hasn't called since the dinner party, not even to book another driving lesson. I told her she should get out more and suggested she joined Chips (the drama group) too. She laughed and said she's not that desperate yet. Humph.

At least this means that your beloved has not been lured any further into the high-flying world of Charles the Yuppie and his air-stewardess fetish. I'll keep you posted on progress.

Don't forget Mum's birthday is on 18th March.

Tell the sheep that lambs here now all bouncing madly. Too gorgeous.

Love,

Lucy xx

WIDGETEX LTD
Memo
To: all members of the Marketing Department
Re: Office Equipment
Please note that whilst Gabby and I are attending the International Widget Trade Fair in Birmingham, there will be no unauthorised use of office equipment without prior permission.

   Gavin Slater

From: Dave Marks (dave@widgetex.co.uk)
To: All marketing department staff

11.59
Subject: Scoreboard

Best use of phone for personal calls: Lucy calling brother in New Zealand x3

Best abuse of photo copier: Ceri copying all her 18–30 holiday snaps twice (126 copies including enlargements)

Most blatant Stationery Cupboard theft: Marlene (4 multi-packs of biros, 26 marker pens, 2 reams coloured paper for 'the grandchildren')

Most repulsive site found on Internet: Dave – *www.thingsinjelly.com/sanitarytowel*

Most creative use of Word Processor: Equal first –

Dave's CV ('Hobbies: Dangerous sports, spoken Russian, charity field work')

Lianne's CV (Translates 'Girl Friday' to 'Cross-departmental executive assistant')

From: Lucy Gordon (lucy@widgetex.co.uk)
To: Dave Marks (dave@widgetex.co.uk)

12.14
Subject: Career move

So you're looking for another job! What as? Useless desk accessory specialist?

From: Dave Marks (dave@widgetex.co.uk)
To: Lucy Gordon (lucy@widgetex.co.uk)

12.21
Subject: Re: Career move

Assassin specialising in marketing co-ordinators. Plan on taking a course in 'cutting BMW brake cords'. I've tried setting the laser printer to 'stun' but it doesn't work – Fruit-bat lives on. I'm outa here. Lianne agrees – you know The Bat said to her last week: 'What exactly is it that you do here, Lianne?' To which L answered, 'Who, me? I just wander from room to room.' Nice one.

From: Lucy Gordon (lucy@widgetex.co.uk)
To: Dave Marks (dave@widgetex.co.uk)

12.23
Subject: Re: Re: Career move

Actually, I think Gabby is very rewarding to work with.

From: Dave Marks (dave@widgetex.co.uk)
To: Lucy Gordon (lucy@widgetex.co.uk)

12.27
Subject: Re: Re: Re: Career move

I can't believe you're so gullible. You do all the work and she takes the credit.

From: Lucy Gordon (lucy@widgetex.co.uk)
To: Dave Marks (dave@widgetex.co.uk)
12.31
Subject: Re: Re: Re: Re: Career move

No, that's what you do, Dave. Gabby simply recognises my talents and utilises them. That, to me, is good management. I'm sure she will take on more of the workload when she's finally familiar with all our products.

From: Dave Marks (dave@widgetex.co.uk)
To: Lucy Gordon (lucy@widgetex.co.uk)

12.34
Subject: Re: Re: Re: Re: Re: Career move

That's what I've always liked about you, Lucy. You remind me of when I was young and stupid. I'll miss you.

W Microsoft Word – Marketing Ideas62.doc

~~Assessing the need for novelty clocks around the home~~

I'm far too distracted to make much progress through the huge pile of stuff Fruit-bat has left for my attention while she's away. This evening there are the auditions for the Chips summer production, 'Sacrificial Lamb', and the glamorous Chisbourne recluse, Lady Gunton herself, will be there tonight. I can't wait. I'm up for the lead part of Jasmine the shepherdess, so I went out yesterday and bought huge lambswool cowl and long tweed skirt with fringed hem. It's freezing cold in the manor tithe barn as I learnt to my cost last week, so I want to look the part as well as keeping warm. Have been practising looking wholesome and innocent in front of office loo mirror all morning, until Ceri came in and asked me if I had toothache.

You have . . . one . . . new message. Message received . . . today . . . at . . . six . . . twenty-three . . . pee emmmm.

'Lucy, it's Dad. Just called to wish you luck tonight. Or is one supposed to say 'break a leg'? Hmm. No, I think that's just reserved for performances. In which case, twist an ankle! Ha ha! Hmm. Yes. Now your mother is helping out at Vanessa Fluck's OAP whist drive this evening so I'd better mention that I'm rather stumped as to what to get for her birthday. Hmm. Yes. I was hoping you might lend inspiration, Pickle. I'd like to treat her to a day out – something exciting. What do you think? A steam railway ride, or a tank driving day? Something like that?'

From: Lucy Gordon (juicylucy@webbedup.net)
To: Mo Lavender (Hobo-mobo@Hotmail.com)

23.52
Subject: My first role

Lots of people turned up at the auditions – more than thirty. This time, there were five huge heaters in the tithe barn and the place was boiling. I was beetroot-coloured all night. One of the older ladies who'd come along in a mohair polo-neck actually passed out.

Lady Gunton – 'call me Amber' – cast herself in the role of Jasmine. I think she's a little old to play a teenage shepherdess. She's at least forty, but she is very glamorous, with long blonde hair and a model figure, so she might get away with it. She says that as the playwright she has the greatest understanding of the role. There was a lot of disapproving clucking amongst the other Chips ladies, especially the one with the red hair who's called Daphne and teaches elocution. She says Lady G, who comes from Dagenham, has appalling diction. I think Daphne was rather upset at being cast as Jasmine's deaf, toothless grandmother who all the villagers think is a witch.

I have been cast as Jasmine's dim friend, Daisy, who dies in a freak sheep stampede. It's not a very big role – I have just two lines; 'What's that roaring sound?' and 'Aghhhh!', but Ralph the director says that small roles are often the meatiest and reminded me that Holly Hunter had no lines at all in *The Piano*. I'm not disappointed at all. I was a bit frightened at the prospect of being the centre of attention on stage, whereas Amber used to be a model so knows all about it. I've offered to help with the costumes too. That's all I wanted to do in the first place.

The production is still missing a leading man. Daphne's hen-pecked husband, Eric is playing the Duke – Jasmine's real father, and Ned from the Quickfill garage on the by-pass was so funny that he won the part of the shepherd who has brought her up, even though he says he gets stage fright. But there was no one at all in the right age group to audition for Cal, the sexy blacksmith who Jasmine secretly loves. Ralph asked me if I could suggest anyone young and talented in the village. I said I couldn't think of anyone, and almost added that the reason I joined Chips in the first place was in the hope of meeting young talent, but I stopped myself because I didn't want to appear shallow. Promised to keep my eyes peeled. As if they're not already. L xxx

CHISBOURNE PLAYERS

Dear Fellow Thespians,

Please find enclosed a copy of the (working) script for Sacrificial Lamb, a cast, crew and contact list and a rehearsal schedule. Should any dates clash with holidays, school sports days, weddings, funerals etc then please cancel the latter and/or make your apologies. From now on SL is your FIRST priority and, always remember, THE SHOW MUST GO ON!

Regards,

Ralph

W Microsoft Word – Lucy's Theatrical Memoirs.doc

Tonight was the first rehearsal of *Sacrificial Lamb* in Lady G's tithe barn. Ralph the director still hasn't found anyone to play the part of Cal, the sexy blacksmith, so he stood in himself. I think poor Amber Gunton found it quite hard to get into the role of young Jasmine making eyes at Cal, who is supposed to be beefy and irresistible but, in the form of Ralph, is five foot four and as camp as a row of tents.

During the tea break, I chatted to Lady G about her modelling days in the eighties. She's really lovely and says that I have 'classic' bone structure and 'pretty eyes'. I can't believe she's singled me out for friendship. Most of the cast call her 'Your Ladyship' which she finds really embarrassing.

Ralph handed out rehearsal call sheets at the end and I'm not needed next week, which is lucky as it's Mum's birthday so we're having a family dinner at the Bistro Etoile.

You have . . . one . . . new message. Message received . . . today . . . at . . . seven . . . o . . . four . . . pee emmmm.
'Lucy, it's Dad. Rally driving at Silverstone?'

From: Ceri Dixon (reception@widgetex.co.uk)
To: Lucy Gordon (lucy@widgetex.co.uk)

16.34
Subject: Playtime

Want to hit the Lock Inn tonight for a few TVRs? I have heard THE most amazing rumour . . .

From: Lucy Gordon (lucy@widgetex.co.uk)
To: Ceri Dixon (reception@widgetex.co.uk)

16.40
Subject: All work and no . . .

Sorry – have to work late again. Fruit-bat is full of new ideas as a result of attending the International Widget Fair with Slave Driver last week. Ambitious Dave is supposed to be helping, but he keeps taking half days to slope off for other job interviews, the rat.

You have . . . two . . . new messages. First new message received . . . today . . . at . . . five . . . fifty-three . . . pee emmmm.
'Lucy, it's Dad. I hope you're out enjoying yourself. Your mother and I will pick you up at eight tomorrow morning. Have you asked Jane if she wants to come yet? Oh, and one other thing – hope you

can still hear me, Pickle, I'm whispering – what do you think about One Day's Guided Tour of The Hidden Military Bunkers of Wales? It includes the coach and lunch. Shall I book your mother a place?'

Second new message received . . . today . . . at . . . six . . . twenty-seven . . . pee emmmm:
'Hi, Jane. Charles here. On train. You free tomorrow? Racing. Ascot. Same friends, so no L plates, yah? Hats. Pick up midday. Lunch Waterside. *Ciao.*'

Notes on Burr Cottage fridge:

Jane,

I was going to ask you along to watch Mark riding Zak at Gatbury Horse Trials tomorrow, but I guess from the phone message (saved) that you're not free now. You can borrow my black straw hat if you want (assuming you haven't got hold of a British Airways Regulation Issue red trilby?)

Lucy

Thanks for the Memo Re:

L,
Black straw isn't really Ascot.
Have fun in the mud.
Jxx

Crump-Hopkins Department Store
Wexbury

Receipt:

One Lola La Salle hat: £159.99

284

From: Lucy Gordon (juicylucy@webbedup.net)
To: Mo Lavender (Hobo-mobo@Hotmail.com)

23.07
Subject: Hats off all round

Sorry I haven't had time to write for a while.

Mum and Dad dragged me to Gloucestershire today to watch Mark the horse trainer trying Zak out in a small horse trials. He was brilliant. I can't believe the change in him. They came fifth, but would have done even better had Zak not thrown a wobbly in the dressage test when a pigeon flew into the arena. Dad was hugely impressed, and chatted to Mark for a long time afterwards.

Jane had a wonderful time at Ascot with Charles, even though he insisted on putting bets on for her because he claims it's not lady-like. She won almost two hundred pounds, which covers the cost of the hat she'd had to buy. She didn't seem very interested at all when I told her how well Zak had done, and said that eventing was a very 'amateur' sport compared to racing. She says Charles and all his City friends are so rich that they think nothing of buying magnums of champagne at the bar. I'm appalled at how impressed she seems by their wealth. We went to the Cow in Clover with Bella tonight and Jane talked about Charles non-stop, which got a bit dull after a while. She also wanted to know all about Lady G, the Essex girl who married nobility. Oh dear. L xxx

---

W Microsoft Word – Lucy's dilemma.doc

After Sunday lunch today Dad asked me to come and look at the new axle grinder he's bought for his workshop (the old one got mangled on the Supa-Deep pizza). I obliged to humour him, but it turned out this was a ruse to talk to me about Zak. Mark the trainer wants to buy him, and Dad is very keen. He asked if I'd mind very much because I didn't seem to really enjoy riding him. I admitted he was a bit too strong for a cowardly novice like me. It wasn't one of Dad's better birthday presents, and I hope it makes him think a bit harder about the military bunker thing for Mum. I've said I don't mind, but I think Jane, as co-owner, will have something to say about it. I'm dreading telling her, but I know I can't hide up here in my bedroom for ever 'learning my lines'. I only have one, after all.

Later: I'm staggered! Jane's first reaction to me gently telling her of Mark's interest was to ask, 'How much?' She's been on the phone to both Mark and my dad this evening and is now walking around with a smug grin on her face.

Burr Cottage
Chisbourne

Thursday 18th March

Dear Big Brother,

Have just got back from Mum's birthday dinner. Alice typically hadn't got her a present and called me at the last minute to ask if she could go halves on mine. This actually means 'Can I sign my name on the gift tag and then never get around to paying you?' We gave Mum a foot spa. Alice was hugely rude about 'our gift' saying that only old biddies would want to give their verrucas a jacuzzi, but Mum loved it. Alice then swiftly changed her tune and said that she knew Mum would appreciate the chance to pamper herself which was why she'd suggested the idea. The minx.

Was very worried that Dad would give Mum the course of rally driving lessons he's been talking about, but thankfully sense prevailed and he's bought her a week's cookery holiday in Ireland with a top chef instead. Mum is thrilled.

Granny got very confused this evening and thought it was her birthday – a fact she kept telling the waiters at the Bistro Etoile. I think she'd had one too many sherries beforehand.

When they brought out a little cake with candles and a sparkler on top and presented it to Granny, not Mum, there was a bit of a family row. Our fellow restaurant diners listened in with interest. It was only when Granny stood up and started shouting that we had ruined an old lady's happy day that I realised Slave Driver was sitting at a table just a few feet away, looking hugely uncomfortable. Thought, at first, that this embarrassment was just because he was witnessing a Gordon family domestic, but soon realised he was red in the face for quite another reason. His dining companion was none other than Fruit-bat, wearing a very short skirt. Blimey.

Mum appreciated the All Blacks keyring. Hope the sheep are well.

Love,

Lucy xx

WIDGETEX LIMITED
Memo
To: Lucy Gordon
Re: Private and confidential
I must apologise for not saying hello last night, but you seemed a little preoccupied with your family. I was taking Ms Peartree out to congratulate her for coming up with so many inspirational ideas. My wife was supposed to be joining us, but she has a cold. I would appreciate it if you did not mention this informal meeting to anyone in the office. In return you can be assured that both Gabriella and I will not mention your poor grandmother's tragic dementia. You have our utmost discretion.

    Gavin Slater

From: Lucy Gordon (juicylucy@webbedup.net)
To: Mo Lavender (Hobo-mobo@Hotmail.com)

23.21
Subject: The Womaniser makes an appearance

Went to Cow in Clover with Jane tonight. She talked about Charles the Yuppie non-stop again. Yawn. She doesn't seem at all bothered about the fact that Dad is selling Zak to Mark the horse trainer; she's just irritated that the money is taking a long time to come through.

Big Mike was in the pub, standing in his customary spot at the bar chatting to George. It's the first time I've seen him in weeks.

'I hear you're acting in this village play, Lucy?' he asked when I was buying a round. News does get around fast. I mumbled something about only having a small part, and he asked what it was all about. I managed to explain without looking him in the eye once, but I did make him laugh about my dramatic death in the freak sheep stampede, and gorgeous Lady G's Essex accent. Feel less silly and shy of him now, but still go pink when he's near. Can't believe I used to find talking to him so easy, but now I know he's God's gift to women I can't chat over the garden fence. I miss our chummy gossips sometimes. L xxx

---

You have . . . one . . . new message. Message received . . . today . . . at . . . three . . . eleven . . . pee emmmm:
'Lucy, dear girl, this is Ralph Delacroix. Wonderful news! We have a leading man for *Sacrificial Lamb*. Last night, I popped into the village shop for a bottle of Campari and saw a *vision* in checked shirt and Levi's. My dear, he simply *breathes* Cal the Blacksmith. And when he introduced himself as a friend of yours, I realised that my little Daisy had fulfilled her promise to find me a hero. Michael Ensor has star written all over him. You are an angel. *A bientôt, chérie.*'

W **Microsoft Word – Lucy's Theatrical Memoirs2.doc**

Just back from *Sacrificial Lamb* rehearsal. The new leading man, Big Mike, has charmed everyone, even Daphne the Dragon who became positively girlish in the presence of the Womaniser of Chisbourne. Am certain, however, that he only has eyes for Lady G, ex-model, socialite and now his leading lady. He was calling her 'Amber' within minutes, and they sat together chatting during the coffee break. I normally talk to Amber, who is good fun, but I couldn't bring myself to witness Mike's obvious flirtation so I decided instead to talk to Ned the forecourt manager who's playing the shepherd. He's really funny, with lots of gold teeth and Elvis sideburns. He said that if I take the Saxo to Quickfill this weekend, he'll give me a free car-wash token. I thought this was really kind until he told me what he'd once caught a couple doing in there, and suggested that he could accompany me through a full wash'n'wax if I liked.

I choked on my coffee so badly that Ralph had to ask me to step outside the barn until I'd recovered because he wanted to start the rehearsal again, and we'd reached the first love scene between Jasmine and Cal, which requires an intimate atmosphere. I noticed Mike giving me a worried look as I staggered outside, but he was needed on stage to smoulder at Amber. I'm sure he wasn't concerned for my health. He probably just thinks I'm jealous of Lady G. Well I'm not. She may be a stunning blonde ex-model, whereas I am a short marketing assistant whose highlights need retouching, but I am at least fifteen years younger than her. I just think Mike should leave her alone because she's married. None of us have met Lord G yet. Ralph says he's away on business a lot.

After the rehearsal, Mike suggested we all go to the Cow in Clover for a drink. I pretended I had to get home to have a meal with Jane and Bella, but they're both out. I hope to God they're not in the pub. That would be too embarrassing.

Later: Mercifully Jane has been out with Charles the Yuppie (the opera, no less – she's just raved on about it for hours, although I distinctly remember she thought Puccini was a type of pasta dish when I tried to make her go with me once). Bella has been at a parents evening, and is in a very bad mood because the mother of her best artistic protégé wants him to become an accountant, and therefore ditch art A level in favour of Further Maths. I sympathised with her for encountering such narrow-mindedness, but Jane announced that she thought the mother was right, 'There are a lot of opportunities in accountancy. He'll have a secure future, make a lot of money. He might end up in the City.' What *is* happening to her?

W Microsoft Word – Presentation5.doc

~~New Marketing Incentives – The Way Forward for Widgets~~

Slave Driver has sloped off to play golf this afternoon, and Fruit-bat has sequestered herself in his office to prepare our presentation for Monday morning. When I popped my head around the door earlier to say I was going to lunch, I found her holding the framed picture of Mrs Slave Driver.

'What's she like?' she asked, pointing at Mrs SD's dour face which I personally think looks as though it's just been slapped with a wet fish. I said that she's a keen gardener and hates golf. It's all I know really. She never comes into the office and SD doesn't mention her much. And the less said to Fruit-bat about the stage-fright/loo/Cher incident at last year's Christmas party the better.

From: Ceri Dixon (reception@widgetex.co.uk)
To: Lucy Gordon (lucy@widgetex.co.uk)

11.12
Subject: Presentation

How did it go?

From: Lucy Gordon (lucy@widgetex.co.uk)
To: Ceri Dixon (reception@widgetex.co.uk)

11.26

Very well, although Fruit-bat made me do the flip chart because
she had her shoulder strapped up owing to sports injury.
Apparently she got a bit over-enthusiastic swinging a nine iron
during her first golfing lesson on Saturday.

WIDGETEX LIMITED
Memo
To: All members of staff
Re: Sick leave
Next week, our junior marketing executive, Lucy Gordon,
will be going into hospital for surgery. I am sure you will all
join me in wishing her luck and a speedy recovery. Upon her
return, Lucy may look physically different. She would be
grateful if her colleagues do not draw undue attention to
any changes, or make unnecessary comments about them.
These days rhinoplasty, breast augmentation and
liposuction are common practice, although admittedly to
undergo all three at once is a brave decision. We would be
grateful if you respect her wishes and make as little fuss
about this as possible. Any disparaging or bigoted reaction
to these very personal changes will be looked upon
extremely seriously.
The Management

From: Lucy Gordon (lucy@widgetex.co.uk)
To: Dave Marks (dave@widgetex.co.uk)

09.45
Subject: April Fool

Yeah, yeah – I've looked at the calendar. I know you've mentally gone to lunch, gone to the dogs and gone to work for Matthew Freud, but you could have made an effort. It's almost the same as last year's.

From: Ceri Dixon (reception@widgetex.co.uk)
To: Lucy Gordon (lucy@widgetex.co.uk)

10.12
Subject: Gossip!

You are not going to BELIEVE this!!!!! I've just heard from Lance the Rep that Slave Driver and Fruit-bat are having an affair. They were spotted necking at the Novelty Gadget Of The Year Award ceremony last night.

From: Lucy Gordon (lucy@widgetex.co.uk)
To: Ceri Dixon (reception@widgetex.co.uk)

11.06
Subject: Re: Gossip!

Ceri, I am EXTREMELY busy. I have just about had my fill of silly letters, emails and laxative teabags in the office today. Please save your juvenile jokes for the rest of the reception staff. I am no April Fool, okay?

Why did we have to have a Chips rehearsal on April Fool's Day? I know you're not supposed to play practical jokes on people after midday, but that didn't stop leery Ned the Quickfill forecourt manager playing pranks. It was whoopee cushions and fake dog doop from start to finish. I'd already had a belly-full in the office today. Tonight was my first turn on the boards as Ralph blocked the scene where Jasmine tells me, her best friend Daisy, that she is in love with Cal the blacksmith and that she doesn't want to go and live in the big house with her real father, the Duke, because he will ban them from seeing one another. It's very moving. I don't actually say anything in the scene, but I have to nod in the right places and make understanding faces which requires a huge amount of concentration – Ralph says that the actor who is not speaking has to act three times as hard.

Just as we were half-way through the scene and I was timing my facial expressions to perfection, I saw a huge mouse run across the stage and I screamed my head off. All the cast started running around looking for it, except Daphne the Dragon who stood on a chair and shrieked, 'Kill it, kill it!'

Big Mike tracked it down first – I suppose being a vet, he's good at that sort of thing. He calmly picked it up and cupped it in his hand, stroking it and carrying it gently over to me. Then, looking at me very seriously, he said that I had to confront my fear. So he uncupped his hand and the mouse – a wind-up electrical one with a gyrating tail – shot off it and landed in my lap. I was livid, especially as leery Ned was falling about with laughter telling everyone how easy I was to 'wind up'. Even Daphne started to laugh. I felt such a fool and couldn't concentrate on the scene afterwards. Refused to go to the pub again. Hate Ned and hate Mike equally. Need chocolate.

Easter Lunch Menu – 13 Roundhead Avenue, Wexbury.
Chef: Liv Gordon

~~*Mackerel carpaccio on a bed of deep-fried kale*~~
~~*Milk-fed lamb spiced with saki and arrow root and served pink on*~~
~~*radish rostis*~~
~~*Steamed rhubarb with pistachio custard*~~
Can't be bothered. Instead:
Roast lamb and all the trimmings
Rhubarb crumble

To be accompanied by Castagnier, '90
For Mother: Litre of Lambrusco Rosé

Burr Cottage
Chisbourne

Sunday 4th April

Dear Big Brother,

Have just eaten three Easter eggs. Feel such a pig, but a
happy one. Delicious. Mum was a bit annoyed that I couldn't
manage to finish the first lunch she's cooked in weeks (had
already devoured my Galaxy egg and was three-quarters of the
way through a Lindt one). She's off on her cooking course in
Ireland next week and is v. excited. I asked Dad how he'll cope
when she's away but he says he and Granny are planning to eat
takeaways and watch Sky Sport every evening. He seems very
cheerful at the prospect. I think he's up to something.

No time to write more.

Don't tell the sheep about Mum's main course.

Love

Lucy xx

From: Lucy Gordon (juicylucy@webbedup.net)
To: Mo Lavender (Hobo-mobo@Hotmail.com)

19.17
Subject: Wedding bells at Burr Cottage

Bella has just got back from romantic weekend in Edinburgh with
Brick and they're engaged! So exciting. She's wearing a huge
gothic ring shaped like a snake with a ruby eye. It's a bit odd, but
she seems to love it.

Jane is busy cooking celebratory supper for Bella. Brick has
had to go back to London – he's still working as a courier
although Bella says he'll give it up soon and look for something
around here. They split up over the London/West Berkshire
divide last year, but Bella tells me they've talked it through.
Brick's band, Slug, broke up over 'artistic differences' (I
somehow don't think they were arguing whether to go to the
Pollack or the Monet exhibitions) and he wants to start another
one up here. I'm not sure Wexbury is ready for metal thrash
groove, but I kept quiet about that. Bella wants an alternative
wedding in an unusual venue – she's full of ideas. Jane is very
disapproving and says that you can't beat a traditional church
ceremony followed by a country house reception with lashings of
champagne. She's got so stuck-up lately. I suggested she could
wear the hat she blew a week's wages on to go racing with
Charles, but she just said, 'That old thing? Ugh!' L xxx

W Microsoft Word – design notebook.doc

Mum is away on her culinary course until tomorrow. I offered to
cook Sunday lunch for Dad, Granny and Alice but Dad turned me
down. Then, when I said I'd go around there as usual, he told me
not to bother. He was quite adamant that I had to keep away from
the parental home. All very suspicious.

Actually, it's quite useful that I've had the day – and the cottage
– to myself. Bella and Brick have gone to stay with his parents to

break the news of their engagement. They told Bella's parents last week – I don't think they were as thrilled as Bella had hoped; her dad is a bit odd and thinks Brick is the Anti-Christ because of his spiked blue hair and piercings. Apparently her mum just burst into tears.

I'm not sure where Jane is – probably with Charles. She wasn't here at all last night. She doesn't say much to me about the relationship because she knows I disapprove of the fact that Charles has told all his friends she's an air stewardess and that she goes along with him.

I've been asked to design some of the costumes for *Sacrificial Lamb*. I originally just offered to help out with a bit of sewing, but Ralph says that no one else is remotely interested in costumes so he's given me free rein. Very exciting. I've been designing away like mad all day. Bella has lent me some paint and paper and I feel like a kid in one of her classes, although not quite so talented. All my people look like Mr Bean for some reason. Platforms didn't help by walking across the still-wet duke. He now has a footprint on his trousers which looks like an enormous cod-piece.

Design ideas:

Jasmine (Amber) –
Sexy rags until she goes to court. Then pearls and feathers galore.
Cal the Blacksmith (Mike) –
Leather trousers? (NB: Not sure Big Mike has the figure for them.)
(NB2: Need measurements, but not keen on the idea of popping next door with a measuring tape. The Womaniser of Chisbourne might get the wrong idea.)
Perhaps I'll just put him in baggy sack-cloth culottes . . .

From: Lucy Gordon (lucy@widgetex.co.uk)
To: Ceri Dixon (reception@widgetex.co.uk)

12.06
Subject: Need Galaxy

Slave Driver is SUCH a pig. He's just given me an earful about 'personal calls'. I tried to explain that I was checking my parents' line, but he wouldn't listen. (I called my mum last night to see how her holiday was and I couldn't get through – just heard recorded voice telling me that there was a fault on the line. I've just tried again, and the same thing's happening. Hope everything's okay.)

From: Ceri Dixon (reception@widgetex.co.uk)
To: Lucy Gordon (lucy@widgetex.co.uk)

12.12
Subject: Can offer half a Twix

Uncanny that his bad mood coincides with Fruit-bat's holiday to Tuscany, land of the Latin lover, don't you think?

From: Lucy Gordon (lucy@widgetex.co.uk)
To: Ceri Dixon (reception@widgetex.co.uk)

12.21
Subject:

No, I don't. SD's always been a foul-tempered misogynist. I keep getting the sharp edge of his tongue while Ambitious Dave sniggers behind his monitor (probably sending jokey emails to all his mates in Sales). He still hasn't been able to find a new job, although he now claims to have been approached by a headhunting firm. I'll believe it when I see it. I had a sneaky look at his CV the other day and he's spelled communication skills with one 'm'.

W Microsoft Word – Lucy's Theatrical Memoirs4.doc

I showed Ralph my costume designs at tonight's *Sacrificial Lamb* rehearsal and he was most impressed. At least I think he was, because he laughed a lot and said, 'Absolutely unique. You have extraordinary vision, dear child. Now, take some measurements and we'll see about getting you a budget.'

I then had to endure Ned the garage manager's lewd comments about breathing on the end of the measuring tape before calculating his inside leg. It took ages to measure up all the cast while they were off-stage, and I still haven't taken Amber's statistics although she assured me – rather loudly, I thought – that she was a perfect size 10. Felt really embarrassed measuring up Big Mike and did it in such a hurry that I think I wrote my results down wrong – he can't have a twelve-inch waist and forty-inch inside leg, can he? I'll just have to guess them.

Decided to go along to the pub for once, which was really jolly. Big Mike bought me a huge gin and tonic and asked me about Jane and Charles the Yuppie. I found myself confessing that I thought he was a bit of a prat for making her lie about her job to his friends, and that I also thought he was turning her into a snob. Then I told him about her selling Zak the Yak without a single regret.

'She'll have to learn the hard way, I guess,' Mike said rather pointedly. 'We all make mistakes and fall for the wrong people.'

I assumed he must be talking about him and Peach – or even me and Greg, so I agreed whole-heartedly and bought him another pint. It was only when I was queuing at the bar and saw Amber settling beside Mike in the seat I'd just vacated that it occurred to me Mike was talking about her. He has fallen for a married woman and a member of the landed gentry to boot. Tough call, even for the irresistible Womaniser of Chisbourne.

Sunday Lunch Menu – 13 Roundhead Avenue, Wexbury.
Chef: Liv Gordon

Deep-fried geranium flowers in lobster salsa
Mango-stuffed lamb with olive and shiitake sauce
Orange, star anise and coffee bean tarte

To be accompanied by Guinness

Burr Cottage
Chisbourne

Sunday 18th April

Dear Big Brother,

I drove to Roundhead Avenue after work on Tuesday to find
an electrician's van outside and, standing in drive, a strange
man on mobile phone saying, 'We've got a right one here,
mate. I think we'll have to get the crack squad in. This bloke's
a liability.'

When I went inside Mum was having hysterics in the
hallway while Dad, half-way up a ladder, said, 'All under
control' over and over again as sparks flew out of the fuse box.
It turns out he had seen the advert about telephones that ring
with a different tone according to the recipient and decided
that he could set up the same thing but with lights that flash
different colours. I have no idea why – as we both know, he is
grasped by these flights of fancy from time to time. He claims
that he thought it would be a nice surprise for Mum. Instead
she came back from cooking in Ireland to find that there's a
power cut every time the phone rings and that Granny has gone
to stay with Uncle Nigel and refuses to come home until Dad
leaves the house for ever. This seems a bit harsh. Apparently
she's already driving Nigel's wife, Barbara, mad and Barbara
has been calling Mum every day to demand she comes and
picks her up. But Granny will not be budged.

Poor Dad feels very guilty, although no great harm has been done. Their phone is working again now and nothing has exploded since the disastrous experiment where Dad wired it up to the mains, although Mum claims that the television has not been the same since. 'We can get Channel 5 now – never could before.' I think she's quite enjoying not having Granny around. She's full of ideas from her cookery course – she tried some out today. The meal was a bit odd, but it's lovely to have her back to her old self again. She hasn't been this enthusiastic in the kitchen since she entered the *Masterchef* regional trials. She and Dad are thinking of buying a caravan with the money that they got from selling their share of Zak. Alice is complaining bitterly that she will never be able to hold her head up in the neighbourhood again if there is a shiny cream 'gitmobile' parked outside the house, but I think it's a great idea. I know caravanning has a naff image but Mum and Dad don't take enough holidays together so this would mean they can spend lovely weekends away. That said, I suppose I might feel differently if, like Alice, I had to live with the thing parked in the front drive. Dad has hundreds of brochures and is boringly weighing up the merits of different torques and aerodynamics. Mum says she doesn't care what they get as long as Dad doesn't fiddle with the wiring and accidentally set it alight. From the evil look on Alice's face, I have a pretty shrewd idea of who, if anyone, will try to blow it up.

Tell the sheep I'm sorry about Mum's menus. Lamb's very cheap at the moment.

Love

Lucy xx

Postcard featuring sexy Italian man under an olive tree:

Dear All,
He can rub my oil in any day!
Having a heavenly time.
Beautiful landscape,
wonderful food, sexy men.
Out every night drinking
Chianti under the stars.
See you next week.
Gabby

The Marketing Department
Widgetex Limited
5 Market Street
Wexbury
Berks
RG14 0XX

From: Ceri Dixon (reception@widgetex.co.uk)
To: Lucy Gordon (lucy@widgetex.co.uk)

09.52
Subject: Postcard

Don't believe a word. She's there touring churches with her mum.
   Did you notice that after he'd read it, Slave Driver kicked the
partition so hard the poster of Britney Spears fell into Dave's tea
on the other side? Hilarious.

Burr Cottage
Chisbourne

Sunday 25th April

Dear Big Brother,

   Granny has moved back home with Mum and Dad, more by
necessity than by choice. She had drunk Uncle Nigel's wine
rack dry. He and Barbara drove her back today, and they
stayed for lunch while Granny sulked and picked fights with

Dad. We all admired the new caravan – a neat little white one which isn't too embarrassing, although Alice still complains that it's social death and she'll be a laughing stock at school. Mum had to talk Dad out of buying an ultra-luxurious six-berth one with satellite television, microwave and shower. She says their needs are simple and she wants to save money for her new project. She told us all today over lunch – we were munching through braised lamb and baby endives in acorn liqueur sauce when she announced that she was planning to open a restaurant in Wexbury. Dad is really proud of her – she's written up a business plan and is looking for investors. All very exciting.

Not enclosing menu as fear sheep will be too upset.

Love,

Lucy xx

W Microsoft Word – Marketing ideas63.doc

~~The growing Market for In-Car Massagers~~

Fruit-bat is back from her fortnight in Tuscany looking very tanned. Today she's wearing the shortest skirt imaginable to show off her long brown legs and every man in the office has his eyes out on stalks. Slave Driver has taken her to lunch to talk her through new developments. Can't think what he'll say. Nothing much has happened – it's all very quiet at the moment. I have been taking advantage of the lull to photocopy my costume designs for *Sacrificial Lamb* and organise them in a presentation folder. They look great. Must remind Ralph that he has yet to arrange a budget from Chips funds. I've made some rough calculations and I think I can make them all for about five hundred pounds, although I'll need a team of seamstresses. I'm sure there's lots of talent in Chisbourne.

When I told Ralph about my calculations at tonight's rehearsal he just laughed and said he might be able to stretch to one hundred and fifty pounds at a push, but he'd have to okay it with Eric, the society treasurer. He and Daphne are on a caravanning holiday in the Lakes this week. Must introduce them to Mum and Dad.

Amber was very chatty in the Cow in Clover tonight. She asked me all about my love-life and why I don't have a boyfriend. Big Mike was within earshot, so I couldn't tell her that I'd made the mistake of seducing the Womaniser of Chisbourne, so I just said that I was waiting for someone special. At that moment Jane and Charles the Yuppie came into the pub. Charles bought everyone from Chips a drink, which I thought was a bit flashy. Amber winked at me and said that my friend was lucky to 'have found that someone special'. I almost choked on my cider. Then Ralph – who'd had a lot of Tia Maria – asked them if they'd like to get involved in the play. To my amazement I heard Charles saying he'd love to muck in with some set-painting; in the same breath he offered Jane's sewing skills to the 'costume department'. He didn't even ask her! I was horrified and told Jane she didn't have to help if she didn't want to (I know how mad she gets just trying to sew on a button), but she said on the contrary, she loved sewing and that she and Charles wanted to get more involved in the village community. I was speechless.

You have . . . one . . . new message. Message received . . . today . . . at . . . twelve . . . fifteen . . . pee emmmm.

'Lucy, it's Jane – I just tried you at work, but Ceri says you've sloped out to buy sixty ballet pumps, so I thought you might pop home for lunch. If so, you just *have* to go onto the village green and look at the poster that's gone up on the big oak. It's terrible! The "lamb" in the picture is clearly a) male, b) pissed and c) as camp as Ralph. Mad Mildred almost ran over a duck when she saw it. *Ciao!*'

Appearing on trees and lamp-posts around Chisbourne:

W Microsoft Word – Lucy's Theatrical Memoirs6.doc

Terrible rehearsal. I fluffed my one line: 'What's that roaring noise?' over and over again. One reason is because Amber, to whom I am speaking, was making silly faces at Big Mike who was sitting in the front row of the tithe barn. Another reason was because Ralph told me today that he is casting thirty local school children to play the sheep whose stampede crushes my character to death. I simply can't see how the audience will believe it. They'll be howling with laughter as lots of tots covered in cotton wool balls trot on stage and jump on me. Ralph says that their costumes will be very convincing (after all, he added, I am designing them), and that casting children always guarantees a good audience (since their parents and grandparents buy multiple tickets and cam-cord the show). I am still not convinced. When I told Ralph I'd be a laughing stock (failing to see the pun until later), he got into a sulk and snapped 'What do you want, dearie, real sheep?' At this Big Mike laughed like a drain and said that 'it could be arranged'. Am thinking of resigning from Chips. I still don't have a budget for costumes and the first night is just over a month away. They don't appreciate my talent and hard work.

Sulkily refused to go to the pub. Amber's husband is at home so she didn't come and Mike, who clearly didn't see the point in going to the Cow in Clover without her to flirt with, offered to walk me home.

He asked after Jane and Charles the Yuppie again (why is he so interested in them? Is he jealous?) and I said I hadn't seen Jane in days as she now more or less lives in the Old Post Office with Charles. Then Mike asked when Bella and Brick are getting married. When I said September, he fell silent for a while and then asked if I'd decided whether to keep the cottage on or not.

'What do you mean?' I asked in confusion.

'Well Bella and Brick aren't going to live with you after they're married, are they? And you said yourself that Jane has more or less moved out. Are you going to advertise for new house-sharers or find somewhere else?'

It hadn't occurred to me before that I might be left home alone like that. What am I going to do? I can't possibly cover the rent on what Widgetex pay me. Besides, I'd be lonely. But I hate the idea of living with strangers. This is awful. I might end up having to live with Alice in Mum and Dad's caravan.

At least I can talk to Big Mike more normally now, although I still don't trust him. He asked me in for a coffee and said I looked like I needed cheering up, but I wasn't about to fall for that cheesy Womaniser line, and told him that I needed to talk to Bella and Jane about the house. It was only when I waved him goodbye at the end of our respective drives that I realised Burr Cottage was in darkness. My housemates were both out. Walked through the door and knew what it would feel like to return after they have both moved out. Awful. Had to rush around switching on all the lights, the television and the radio for company.

From: Ceri Dixon (reception@widgetex.co.uk)
To: Lucy Gordon (lucy@widgetex.co.uk)

15.22
Subject: Won't take no for an answer

Tonight, Gordon, you are coming out with me on the pull. There's a new club open in Basborough called Moist. I hear it's THE place.

From: Lucy Gordon (lucy@widgetex.co.uk)
To: Ceri Dixon (reception@widgetex.co.uk)

15.25
Subject: Too wet for Moist

I still remember how sick I was last time we went clubbing. Can we go to Basborough Multiplex instead? If we're feeling really racy we can go bowling afterwards. I've never been.

From: Ceri Dixon (reception@widgetex.co.uk)
To: Lucy Gordon (lucy@widgetex.co.uk)

15.32
Subject: Dried up, more like

God, listen to yourself, girl! You've become really boring and heavy lately. You're stuck in a rut because you've joined Chips and now mix with a load of old boffers. Do you want to end up living alone with just a cat and a sewing machine?

From: Lucy Gordon (lucy@widgetex.co.uk)
To: Ceri Dixon (reception@widgetex.co.uk)

15.41
Subject: You've wet my appetite

That might come sooner than you think if I don't find a pile more
rent soon. Can't explain – SD's just walked past and I need to
talk to him about something urgently. Wish me luck.

W Microsoft Word – Marketing ideas65.doc

~~Why you'll never know how you ever coped without a Garden Shed Alarm~~

I have just asked Slave Driver for a pay rise. I know that was perhaps
a bit impetuous, but I was still in a panic about Burr Cottage and
covering the rent on my own. He sucked his teeth a lot and looked
embarrassed and said that there really wasn't provision in the budget
what with the proposed move and everything. When I asked, 'What
move?' he sucked his teeth even more and said that perhaps he
needed Gabby in on this one. Fruit-bat duly emerged and they sat
down to explain that Widgetex is due to relocate to Faulkstone
Business Park at the end of the year. A memo will be going out first
thing on Monday morning announcing it to all staff apparently. I've
been sworn to secrecy and can't even tell Ceri.

I'm not sure what to think. It would be lovely working in purpose-
built offices with air conditioning and a staff canteen, instead of a
cramped old sixties block, but then again I like being in the centre
of Wexbury and popping out to M and S for a sandwich and a bra
at lunchtime. The Business Park is right on the edge of town, miles
from the shops and Café Blanc. If I live alone, I'll never see anyone
except Slave Driver, Fruit-bat, Platforms and my parents. Definitely
not resigning from Chips. They're my life-line.

Am never going bowling again – it's crippling. Convinced I'll get verrucas from the hired shoes. Ceri got very drunk and started necking with a pimply eighteen-year-old called Leigh. I was stuck with his friend – Renny – who kept nudging me hopefully and pinching my bottom when I went to bowl. Deliberately dropped ball on his foot which shut him up. Unfortunately I dropped ball on my own feet by accident several times too. Can hardly walk.

Burr Cottage
Chisbourne

Sunday 9th May

Dear Big Brother,

Have just come back from lunch at the Roundhead War Zone. The good news is that Granny and Dad have made friends again. I'm not sure of the full story, but apparently he forced her into the Volvo yesterday, took her to the Thrushfield Air Show, plugged her into the beer tent with lots of old RAF heroes and they both rolled home best friends. But the bad news is that Dad has now fallen out with Alice over the phone bill. She's been calling Scrumpy's mobile every day. As a result of the row, Alice has moved into the caravan in the drive.

This is really annoying Mum and Dad because they want to take it on holiday soon, but Dad says he can't evict her until she has finished her A levels for fear of disrupting her revision. Not that she seems to be doing much revision in there. When I parked next to the caravan earlier, I could hear very loud music thumping away inside and plumes of cigarette smoke issuing from the window. She deigned to come inside the house for lunch – briefly – and criticised Mum's artichoke heart and kale pie before taking an entire tub of Häagen-Dazs ice-cream back to her lair. I'm convinced she's got Scrumpy holed up in there, but Mum assures me he's still buried under a proposed ring-road somewhere in Somerset. When I asked whether they'd actually checked if Alice was co-habiting in their drive, Mum said they wouldn't dare. Life is so unfair. When I was her age, they insisted I kept my bedroom door open if I asked boyfriends upstairs to listen to records, remember?

I told Mum and Dad about my fear that I won't be able to afford to stay in Burr Cottage once Bella has married Brick and moved out, especially as Jane is more or less living with Charles the Yuppie now. They weren't much help. Dad got rather wistful and said I could move back to Roundhead Avenue any time I liked – especially once Alice has gone to university in autumn and I can have two rooms. Mum, who looked appalled at the thought, quickly suggested I get a mortgage and buy my own place. She's very into loans at the moment as she's in the process of arranging a small business one for her dream restaurant. I didn't have the heart to tell her I couldn't afford to buy a garden shed on my salary. I think I'll have to gather my housemates for a planning meeting.

Mum obsessed by lamb, so no menu again. Have requested trout for next week.

Love,
Lucy xx

WIDGETEX LIMITED
Memo
To: All members of Staff
Re: New premises
We are delighted to announce that at the end of the year, Widgetex Limited will move from its three town centre sites and Basborough warehouse into one purpose-built building in the Faulkstone Business Park.

Plans of the new building have been posted in the reception area of both the central Market Street office and the

Basborough distribution centre. More information will be made available closer to the date, along with details of transport arrangements and relocation packages for warehouse staff. In the meantime, we trust you are all as excited as we are about this wonderful move, reflecting the growing dominance of the company in the widget industry.

The Management

W Microsoft Word – Marketing ideas66.doc

<del>Ten reasons to own a Musical Loo Roll Dispenser</del>

The official memo has just been circulated announcing Widgetex's proposed move to Faulkstone Business Park. Most of the staff are really excited at the prospect of large, air-conditioned offices, ample parking and our near-proximity to the flashy HQ of the Nilson Formula One racing team. That is the biggest selling-point. The men have visions of being spotted driving their Vauxhall Vectras at speed into the car park and instantly offered a job on the team; the women imagine that racing driver heart-throb Pedro Bertolli and his deputy, the craggily hunky Garth Fording, will spot them exiting the building and ask them out for a drink. I have my doubts. The Nilson Team headquarters are hidden behind an electric fence, high cypress trees and CCTV cameras. I think the racing drivers only go there two or three times a year. We're more likely to be spotted by a security guard with a German Shepherd dog. Still, Slave Driver seems delighted with the response and has taken Fruit-bat out for lunch to celebrate, leaving me to write all the copy for the new catalogues.

W Microsoft Word – Lucy's Theatrical Memoirs7.doc

Tonight was the first technical meeting for *Sacrificial Lamb*, which took place in the Cow in Clover. As costume designer, I was at the head of table and felt wonderfully important as I outlined my plans to the crew. My marketing training helped, as I was the only one with a flip-chart and laser pointer. I think everyone was impressed. Then Ralph introduced me to my 'volunteers' – a pretty motley crew, Jane amongst them. She hardly spoke to me all evening, even though Charles the Yuppie, who has offered to paint the set, turned up really late because he had to get back from London. Before he arrived, Jane just sat alone and looked sulky over a gin and tonic. When I suggested that we had a house meeting tomorrow, she snapped that she wasn't ready to face me power-tripping twice in one week. I think maybe she's jealous that I am designing all the costumes. I blame Charles for making her so competitive. She said 'maybe next week' and I had to be content with that because Ralph cornered me to talk about the budget and when I turned around again Jane had left.

Have been thinking about something Jane said to me when I broke up with Greg. She told me that if she was in a relationship with someone who treated her badly, I should step in and try to pull her out just as she and Bella did with me. I'm not sure Charles treats Jane badly, but he does make her lie about her job which is pretty cheap. Want to talk to Bella about it, but she's gone to bed. Am worried that I only dislike Charles because he's going out with my best friend and she doesn't have any time for me these days. More than that, she doesn't even seem to like me very much. Have I turned into a miserable old grouch now that all my friends are in couples? Must try to be more fun.

W Microsoft Word – Lucy's pissed again.doc

Went to Cow in Clover with the Bs tonight. Decided to try to be more fun and less spinstery, so knocked back a few gin and tonics and chatted to fellow Chips members in pub, mostly Big Mike who was really sweet and didn't seem to mind that I was a bit sloshed and had to lean against him to keep my balance. Did notice, however, that he looked very relieved when B and B offered to take me home. Felt about fifteen, but glad to be shaking some of the moths off.

Think I can hear giggling downstairs. Wish I had a bloke to giggle with – preferably one whose name started with L. The Ls sounds lovely. We'd have an L of a time. Oops. Going to be sick.

COW IN CLOVER RESULTS

Friday 14th May (score kept by Bella):
Absentee: Jane Redven (Excuse: Out with Charles)
Subject for discussion: Jane's relationship with Charles

Number of times Lucy said, 'He's changed her': 12.
Best quote: 'She used to think Prada was posh-speak for "prouder".'

Number of times Bella defended Charles: 7.
Best quote: ~~'He hardly treats her badly. She's taken out to dinner or the theatre or a party every night of the week, goes away to Paris or Amsterdam or the races at weekends, looks fantastic, and is clearly very happy.'~~ (Added in Brick's hand-writing): 'Although I did let myself into the cottage for my post this week and found her filling in a British Airways application form.'

Number of times Brick said, 'The geezer's a twat': 7.
Best quote: 'You know the only way to make that Herbert talk sense? Gaffer tape on his gob.'

RESULT: Lucy and Bella = week off. Jane = hire a 'woman who does'

Note added by Jane.

Dear All,
I realise that you were all drunk when you wrote this, but it is still extremely hurtful.
And I was NOT filling in a BA application form. I was simply reading it. J.
PS Actually quite a good idea about the cleaner, don't you think?

312

Written on the back of a *Caravanning in the Cotswolds* guide:

Suggested ways of evicting Alice from the caravan before the Bank Holiday:
Liv: Cut off her electricity supply.
Malcolm: Redecorate her bedroom in the colour of her choice.
Lucy: Torch caravan and claim on insurance.
Violet: What caravan?
Poll results: Offer to redecorate room and await developments.

W Microsoft Word – caravan.doc

This is *so* unfair! Dad said only last week that I could have Alice's room along with my old one if I move back home this autumn. Whilst I'd rather stay living in Burr Cottage, I have made a few rudimentary sketches of possible study/sitting room ideas for my sister's flea-pit should my circumstances change. Could not live with Alice's taste in black and purple fake fur.

W Microsoft Word – Marketing ideas68.doc

~~Why Night Vision Goggles are a Modern Day Must~~

This week just gets better. Am livid with Fruit-bat. I spent ages writing catalogue copy last week while she was out having long lunches with Slave Driver. This morning, I came into work to discover that she changed it all before sending it to the printers. Now it's full of mistakes. The copy for the Plug-in Pet Pong Protector™ should read 'Eradicate unwanted reeks with this handy air purifier' and she's changed it to 'Wreak unwanted eradication of your pets'. I know she likes being clever with long words, but that makes no sense at all. Know I'll get all the blame if the RSPCA complain.

Am so fed up that I'm going to slope off early this afternoon to

313

buy material for the *Sacrificial Lamb* costumes. If Fruit-bat asks where I'm going, I'll tell her I'm popping out to buy a bigger dictionary. A materialist fabrication, she'd call it.

From: Lucy Gordon (lucy@widgetex.co.uk)
To: Gabriella Peartree (gabby@widgetex.co.uk)

14.12
Subject: Catalogue copy

I'm deeply shocked to hear that someone wrote 'bollocks' in the margins of the corrected catalogue copy. I only left my desk unattended for fifteen minutes while I dashed to M and S (mouse-pad lunching again!). Some people can be so childish.

Incidentally, I have noticed that Dave Marks has now passed his fifth deadline for producing an advertising budget for the new Biodegradable Ionic Turf and Clod Holder. I know that he is very preoccupied right now. But since space is at a premium in *Organic Gardener's Weekly* through the summer months, may I suggest the attached media planning schedule?

MEDIABITCH.doc attachment here

W Microsoft Word – Lucy's Theatrical Memoirs8.doc

Held a meeting with my seamstresses in Cow in Clover this evening to hand out fabric and patterns. I've tried to give them all the simple costumes to do while I try to tackle the central characters – Jasmine, Cal the blacksmith and the duke. I'm not sure I was entirely wise giving Jane my character's costume to make, but I was running out of volunteers and at least I can keep a close eye on her and be available for costume fittings. She seemed to be in a better mood today and even agreed to stay in tomorrow night while I cook a meal for her and Bella to discuss the future of Burr Cottage. I tried to be friendly and asked after Charles, getting the usual twenty-minute monologue about his talented gorgeousness. I managed to smile and even laugh at one point, which is progress, although quite why 'making a mint by screwing some German investors' is brilliantly clever, I'm not sure. Have never heard Jane talking like that before. We had a giggle about my forthcoming sheep-stampede death (Ralph is still determined to cast Chisbourne Primary School as flock). In fact, we were getting on really well – almost like old times – when I ruined it all by asking if it was true that she was applying to be an air stewardess. She went pale and said it was a total lie, then looked at her watch, muttered, 'Charles's bourguignon needs to go in the Aga. Must fly,' and ran out.

I muttered, 'Come fly with me' under my breath and finished my shandy alone. Big Mike was at the bar and offered me another, but I was in too much of a bad mood, besides which I have to get cracking on his sack-cloth culottes.

From: Lucy Gordon (juicylucy@webbedup.net))
To: Mo Lavender (Hobo-mobo@Hotmail.com)

22.59
Subject: End of an Era

I know that it's a long time since I've emailed you, my dearest, oldest and tragically brainwashed-by-a-cult/lost-the-use-of-her-keyboard-skills/travelling-the-world-and-has-forgotten-about-me friend, but I NEED TO TALK.

My worst fears have been realised. Tonight, Bella confessed that she and Brick are already looking at property in the area, and Jane says that she thinks it's only a matter of time before Charles the Yuppie asks her to move in with him permanently. Even Bella seemed really surprised at this and said, 'But you've only been seeing him a few weeks!' Jane just sighed dreamily that this is definitely The One, and that 'Charlie' loves having her around to welcome him home with a hot meal, to iron his shirts and to keep the cottage clean and tidy. I was about to say something about her being a glorified house-keeper when Bella looked at me in horror and said, 'What are you going to do, Lucy? You can't stay here on your own.'

Exactly. I felt hugely tearful and said that maybe I could move back with my parents. Expected them to protest that this would be awful for me (which it will), but they seemed hugely relieved at this suggestion and Bella instantly started talking about her wedding. She wants us both to be bridesmaids. As long as I don't have to make the dresses then that's fine by me. Being the Sacrificial Lamb costume designer is a thankless task. Was so upset this evening that I cut out the sleeves of Amber's peasant dress all wrong and she'll look like she's wearing water wings.

I am very, very stressed. So much so that I am going to do something I haven't done in years. Yes, Mo, I'm doing it and you can't stop me – you're thousands of miles away, after all. I'm going to wait until everyone has gone to bed, dig out The Sacred Shoebox, check the coast's clear, creep downstairs and watch every single episode of *This Life*. I've got sewing to do. L xxx

---

You have . . . one . . . new message. Message received . . . today . . . at . . . twelve . . . fifty-four pee emmmm.

'Lucy, it's your mother. Wonderful news. Alice has vacated the caravan. It was terribly easy in the end. Granny talked her into moving back in the house by threatening to cut her out of her will. Alice was up these stairs as fast as her bondage trousers would let her, which was actually about five minutes because she fell back down them twice. Rather amusing. She's now redecorating her room in tin foil and fake leopardskin. Now, darling, I know it was only ever an emergency plan anyway, but I thought I'd better let you know that you can't move back into your old room after all. I've decided to use it as an office to set up my restaurant from. But, don't panic – if it really looks like you might be homeless soon, at least the caravan's now free. Byeee!'

Have been pondering my future homelessness all weekend and come
to conclusion that I should look on the bright side. This could be
the perfect opportunity to meet new people, specifically eligible
men. If I advertise for two housemates at Burr Cottage, I can pick
and choose the best-looking male applicants, who are tidy, good at
hoovering, know how to wire a plug and, most importantly, don't
have a girlfriend. Think it could be quite fun interviewing them, like
Shallow Grave only without the death bit. (NB: Must buy note-pad
and seductive cashmere casuals.)

Draft advert:
*Young, non-smoking professionals (pref m) sought for idyllic cottage
house-share. 5 miles Wexbury, all mod cons. Must be practical and like
cats.*

From: Lucy Gordon (juicylucy@webbedup.net)
To: Mo Lavender (Hobo-mobo@Hotmail.com)

23.07
Subject: Stitched Up

Jane has suffered a set-back in her ambition to marry Charles the
Yuppie. Apparently his dragon of a mother came to stay over the
weekend and spent the entire time criticising Jane's cooking. I
kept my mouth shut because Bella and I spend a lot of time
criticising Jane's cooking too – she's the only person I know who
can burn pasta. Instead I showed her a rooms for rent advert I've
worded for the *Wexbury Gazette*. Jane got a bit huffy and pointed
out that Charles hasn't actually asked her to move in with him yet
and that Bella won't be leaving the cottage until September. I
promised not to run ad for a few weeks, although I pointed out
that I might need some time for thorough selection process.
Could see that Jane was a bit upset so I opened some wine.

We ended up working on the costumes for *Sacrificial Lamb* together, which was strangely companionable – felt like two Jane Austen characters, but suspect Emma and Victoria were better at sewing and far less boozy. Jane kept me in stitches describing Charles's awful mother while I dropped stitches. She says she'll bring Charles round to cottage more so I get to know and like him. She and I are definitely getting along a lot better, although Amber Gunton's peasant dress is looking more and more like a strait-jacket. Think I drunkenly sewed the sleeve to the hem tonight. L xxx

---

From: Ceri Dixon (reception@widgetex.co.uk)
To: Lucy Gordon (lucy@widgetex.co.uk)

10.25
Subject: Swinging his thang

What is that thing Slave Driver keeps waggling around near your desk? It looks obscene. We're laying bets at this end of the office.

From: Lucy Gordon (lucy@widgetex.co.uk)
To: Ceri Dixon (reception@widgetex.co.uk)

10.29
Subject: Not on par

It's his new golf-swing practice toy, which involves twirling a nine iron close to my desk and making loud contact with a ball on an elastic band. I have a terrible headache, so I asked him why he couldn't use it in his office, but he's explained that he tried that and kept knocking over the hat stand.

This is the LAST thing I need. Am totally stressed out because it looks like B and J are moving out of the cottage and I need to find two new housemates fast. Do you know two gorgeous, single men in need of west-facing double rooms (one en-suite)?

From: Ceri Dixon (reception@widgetex.co.uk)
To: Lucy Gordon (lucy@widgetex.co.uk)

10.45
Subject: Housey Housey!

No, but I know one big, sexy, heavy-rock-loving diva with a love-truck of cuddly toys and the Complete Boxed Elvis Video Collection (leather-bound). What'd'ya say, Louise?!? Wanna Thelma to make popcorn with?!? Shit, this is fan-effing-tastico-ho-ho, yeah! I'm SO bored of living with my parents. Can you BELIEVE they refuse to let me bring men home? Losers! Hey, girl, we can SHAKE those rafters every night.

That vet living next door still seeing the Nordic chick, or can I jump him?

From: Lucy Gordon (lucy@widgetex.co.uk)
To: Ceri Dixon (reception@widgetex.co.uk)

10.56
Subject: How lovely

That's a really kind offer. I'll have to think about it, because there are already a couple of people interested, but I'll let you know soon, I promise. Boxed Elvis v. impressive. How do you leather-bind a video?

Vet now engaged to Slavia (ex-model turned physicist) by the way.

W Microsoft Word – Lucy's a liar.doc
Oh God. I like Ceri a lot, but I'm not sure I could live with her. Am thinking up any excuse I can to put her off. Perhaps I can tell her Platforms brings large dead rats into the house on a regular basis?

Jane brings large love-rats into the house on a regular basis. Charles the Yuppie is currently downstairs watching football while

319

Jane uses the sewing machine in the kitchen on quietest setting. She keeps leaping up every two minutes to take him in Italian beer and Kettle Chips. It reminds me of that film – *Stepford Wives*.

Am due to fit Amber's peasant costume at rehearsal tomorrow and it's far from ready, but when I asked Jane if I could use the machine (my machine) for an hour tonight, she had a fit and yelled, 'Do you want me to help or not?' Charles backed her up and gave me a long, pompous lecture about the fact that Jane has volunteered to make costumes out of the kindness of her heart. Actually, he volunteered her, but I didn't say that. He has mad eyes which scare me a bit. Am sulking in my room, sewing by hand. Bella's away for half term so I can't even suggest we escape to pub. Wish Jane wouldn't bring Charles round – am not getting to know or like him at all.

W Microsoft Word – Marketing ideas72.doc

~~The Consumer and Convenience Remote Control Pouches – A Love Affair~~

Slave Driver has taken his golf practice toy into his office again, despite threatening the hat stand with his back-swing. He's currently showing Fruit-bat how to use it. She's been having professional lessons but says her follow-through is terrible. When I popped into his office to offer to fetch them a sandwich from M and S, he was standing behind her with his arms wrapped around her and his bottom wiggling. It looked so funny that I made a joke about them being 'swingers'. They both looked hugely embarrassed, and Slave Driver told me to take the afternoon off because 'you seem tired and drawn, Lucy, and deserve some quality time'. He's so sweet – I did stay up terribly late last night working on Amber Gunton's peasant dress for tonight's *Sacrificial Lamb* rehearsal, but I'm still way off finishing it. Can now go home and use sewing machine. Also means I can avoid Ceri who keeps asking if I've made my mind up about Burr Cottage.

Costume looked terrible. Amber tried it on in her house. It's the first time I've been inside Chisbourne Manor and I was so busy gazing at all the fantastic portraits up the staircase that when Amber emerged from her bedroom wearing what looked like a grubby sack with bat-wing sleeves, I screamed thinking she was a ghost. She was really sweet about it, and has said she'll send it to her dressmaker for adjustment at her own expense, which is a huge relief. She's even suggested she get her other costume made that way if I run out of time. So kind. Amber offered me a G and T and asked me about Greg. I've never told her I was engaged, but she seemed to know all about it. She chatted about her husband, Boffy, who's away on business again. Apparently he's a lot older than her and was a famous playboy in his youth, but now he dotes on her. She cheered me up by saying that she had almost given up hope of falling in love before she met him. Not so cheered by Amber adding that she thinks Big Mike is hugely sexy too. She asked my opinion, and I managed to mutter that he's okay. Wanted to say something to put her off, but couldn't think of anything so just suggested we hurry along to rehearsal. Suspect telling her he's the Womaniser of Chisbourne would have merely encouraged her. Feel sorry for old Boffy, although suspect Amber only flirts with other men because he's away so much.

Ralph in very bad mood – his Shi'tzu, Tallulah, is ill, apparently. We were all v. sympathetic when he burst into tears during the scene where Jasmine confesses to her real father, the duke, that she loves a penniless blacksmith. Big Mike cornered me during coffee break and whispered that Tallulah is not ill, just heavily pregnant by the local canine lothario, Spot, and that Ralph cannot bear the shame. He asked me how his costume was coming along: 'I'm free for a fitting any evening – just knock on my door. I hear Amber's costume is wild – she says she's great in the sack dress.' He laughed loudly at the joke while I turned bright red.

Didn't go to pub. Can't face Amber's double-entendres and Mike's obvious devotion. If he's free every evening, he must be saving himself for her. Plan to make his culottes very tight and restrictive.

Sunday 30th May

Dear Big Brother,

Mum and Dad have taken the caravan to the Cotswolds for
Bank Holiday. They suggested I went along too because I
haven't got anything else planned. The shame! Pointed out that
as costume designer for Chips I have about thirty costumes to
make, including two dozen small sheep ones. Bella and Brick
are helping me by gluing cotton wool balls onto leotards and
leggings. Bella has made some very realistic sheep masks which
I think might be a bit frightening for the children – when she
tried one on earlier, Platforms caught sight of it, fluffed up in
terror and ran out of the room. Still can't find her.

Too busy to write more.

Love,

Lucy xx

W Microsoft Word – Lucy's Theatrical Memoirs10.doc

Everyone in Chips is panicking. With just a fortnight to go to the
first night of *Sacrificial Lamb*, the set is half-constructed, the cast
don't know their lines, hardly any tickets have been sold and my
costumes are nowhere near complete. Those that are finished have
caused huge arguments. Daphne the Dragon refuses to wear her
dress because she says it makes her look fat (she is fat), Ned the
forecourt manager has suddenly announced he's allergic to sack-
cloth, and the Chisbourne Junior School pupils are terrified of Bella's
sheep masks. We had to draw big smiles on them in the end, which
will make my death scene look even sillier.

Was going to head straight home after rehearsal to try to make
Daphne's dress more flattering with aid of whale-bones, but Mike
and Amber dragged me to the pub, insisting that I need to relax. I
don't like the way they seem to think I approve of their affair.

Actually, I'm not sure they're having a fully fledged affair, but they're always talking in a corner and being extra-chummy to me. Tonight, Amber said that I couldn't be expected to make all the costumes myself. Then she winked at Mike who quickly said he'd come around one evening to help, and bring some beer to cheer us along. Not sure whether they are being kind or just want an excuse to meet up without arousing Boffy Gunton's suspicions; he's due back from his business trip tomorrow night. I can't see Mike being much use with velcro fastenings. Told them I'd be fine and that I have lots of helpers in the village, although actually my seamstresses have only made two jerkins and a shepherd's crook so far.

FACSIMILE TRANSMITTAL SHEET

TO: Gavin Slater	FROM: Dave Marks
COMPANY: Widgetex Limited	DATE: 4th June
FAX NUMBER: 01555 5654736	TOTAL NO. OF PAGES INCLUDING COVER: 1
PHONE NUMBER: 01555 6565765	SENDER'S REFERENCE NUMBER: 1
RE: My position within the company	YOUR REFERENCE NUMBER: 1

❑ URGENT ❑ FOR REVIEW ❑ PLEASE COMMENT ❑ PLEASE REPLY ❑ PLEASE RECYCLE

Dear Mr Slater,

It is with regret that I write to tender my resignation. I have been offered a senior position within the marketing department of a big San Diego computer company. They have offered me a simply outstanding package, which reflects my experience, talent and ability. I hope you will understand that this is too great an incentive to deny, although I am obviously happy to discuss this further should you need me to outline the details in confidence.

May I just say what a pleasure it has been working with you and all at Widgetex? My years with the company have been at times exhilarating, at times rigorous, and always a unique inspiration.

Yours sincerely,

Dave

From: Ceri Dixon (reception@widgetex.co.uk)
To: Lucy Gordon (lucy@widgetex.co.uk)

15.00
Subject: The Marksman

Blimey! I didn't see that one coming, did you? Do you suppose Wendy from Accounts will move to America with him?

From: Lucy Gordon (lucy@widgetex.co.uk)
To: Ceri Dixon (reception@widgetex.co.uk)

15.09
Subject: Shooting his mouth off

No wonder he's been off sick all week. Sly bastard. Hang on, Slave Driver's calling me into the Fruit-bat cave.

From: Lucy Gordon (lucy@widgetex.co.uk)
To: Ceri Dixon (reception@widgetex.co.uk)

15.43
Subject: Prime target

I do not believe this. Slave Driver's just said that he hopes I can cover Dave's work until they recruit a replacement, 'Of course it will involve lots of late nights, but I know I can rely on you, Lucy.

You've always put Widgetex first.' Oh God, when will I finish the costumes?

W Microsoft Word – Lucy's Theatrical Memoirs11.doc

Jane says I should get Ralph to hire the rest of the costumes, but I know he's already run out of money paying for the set materials. Apparently Charles the Yuppie spent all Bank Holiday weekend wielding a hammer in the Guntons' pony paddock while Jane held his nails. She says she'll help me with the costumes from now on. She's finished Daisy's dress which is a bit tight and has an embarrassingly low cleavage, but I'm too grateful for her help to complain – will just have to wear a vest and breathe in a lot. Finished Big Mike's trousers tonight but when I popped next door for him to try them on he was out, probably drowning his sorrow in the pub now that Amber's husband is home. Wish I'd asked for his help after all.

Burr Cottage
Chisbourne

Sunday 6th June

Dear Big Brother,

Have got Granny and Alice sewing peasant skirts while Mum makes sheep costumes. Dad was helping her, but he's disappeared into his shed to try to knock together a time-saving device for attaching cotton wool to Lycra. Judging from the sound effects (swear words and much crashing) he's not progressed very far. Mum says they had a lovely break in the Cotswolds and that the house was immaculate when they got back, so Granny and Alice must have behaved themselves. Thinking this was highly unlikely, I questioned Alice who admitted they'd both been away too. She was at a music festival with Scrumpy, and says that Granny has a new pilot boyfriend who took her to Tunbridge Wells. Dying to know more, but A has sworn me to secrecy. Even our eighty-year-old grandmother has a boyfriend now. Feel very single.

Are you dating anyone yet, or is it still just the memory of Jane and the company of sheep? No, on second thoughts, don't answer that.

Love,

Lucy xx

From: Ceri Dixon (reception@widgetex.co.uk)
To: Lucy Gordon (lucy@widgetex.co.uk)

12.47
Subject: Dave's replacement

What's the low-down on Dave? Has he gone to the States already? Has anyone been offered his job yet?

Do you want to come to lunch?

From: Lucy Gordon (lucy@widgetex.co.uk)
To: Ceri Dixon (reception@widgetex.co.uk)

12.52
Subject: Dave

He's supposed to be working out his notice, but he claims to be laid low with gastric flu (and guess who's been landed with all his unfinished projects?).

BUT – you'll love this – I spotted Wendy from Accounts furtively clearing his desk earlier and cornered her by the coffee machine to get the low-down on the move to San Diego, asking whether she'll be going to the States too. She looked very confused. 'What are you talking about, Lucy? Dave's new job is in Slough.' Turns out that although the company is American-owned, Dave is going to be putting together hardware catalogues in their British office.

Can't wait to have a goss, but have no time. Am working through my lunch hour as it is. Need to buy lots more fabric for *Sacrificial Lamb* costumes but can't see myself getting out of here in time. May have to improvise.

Written on the back of Memo from Slave Driver:

Peasant trousers – curtains from dining room.
Waistcoats – sofa throw.
(NB: Sure housemates won't notice they're missing.)

W **Microsoft Word – Lucy's Theatrical Memoirs12.doc**
Am now using my bedroom curtains to make the duchess's cloak. It looks very effective, although I'll have to get undressed with the lights off from now on. Hope Big Mike doesn't spot me flashing past, as window overlooks his garden. We're supposed to be having full dress run at tomorrow night's rehearsal, but I still have about ten to make. Might take a leaf out of AD's book and pretend to be ill. Trouble is, I can't hide in my room with the curtains closed . . .

Jane says that the situation is just as bad with the set, even though it's basically just a wooden platform in a field. The seating rostrum collapsed yesterday and has to be re-built before the weekend, when Lord Gunton has banned Chips from his land while he hosts a clay pigeon shoot.

Note on kitchen table beside paperback book:

Lucy,
    I can't help noticing that you're really stressed. Have been reading this and you are a CLASSIC case of Cinderella complex.
Please read Chapter 6 'Babes with Burdons' (pgs 167–174, marked with Post-it note). You can borrow the book as long as you like.
Bella xx

Note on fridge:

Burr Cottage
Chisbourne

Sunday 13th June
Dear Big Brother

The most fantastic thing happened on Friday night. I got home really late from work, utterly exhausted and dreading another long session at the sewing machine. The house was in darkness so I assumed Jane was staying with Charles and that Bella had gone to London. But when I opened the door, the lights flashed on and I heard loud shouts of 'SURPRISE!' which sent poor Platforms up one of the few remaining sets of curtains.

Big Mike had organised a surprise weekend working party, and half the village turned up to help me finish the *Sacrificial Lamb* costumes, along with Mum and Dad, Alice, Brick and even Ceri from Widgetex. That night was incredibly raucous and late, but we got simply loads done and they all came around again the next day too. By ten-thirty last night we'd finished almost everything and even made it to the Cow in

Clover for last orders. Was so happy when I toppled towards bed that I forgot I had no curtains, so have probably flashed at Vetch Cottage. Must think of lovely way to thank Mike, but don't think that was it.

Had a huge barbecue this afternoon to thank helpers and celebrate completion of costumes in time for Tuesday's technical rehearsal. This weekend has been great fun. I think *Sacrificial Lamb* might be a success after all.

Tell the sheep not to panic – I am no longer contemplating asking you to Fed Ex all their woolly coats here to dress my stampede.

Love,

Lucy xx

***W* Microsoft Word – Lucy's Theatrical Memoirs13.doc**

Sacrificial Lamb technical rehearsal proving a total disaster – costumes all far too tight because I left it too late for fittings and didn't have enough money for fabric. Daphne had an asthma attack when she tried on her dress; Ned says he'll never father another child after wearing his breeches. Have dashed home to try to make alterations while Ralph re-rigs lighting in between tantrums. Big Mike and Amber are also here to 'help', but are busier letting out loving sighs than tight bodices (Lord G is in situ at Chisbourne Manor, so I'm convinced they have only come in order to have short moment alone together). Am currently pretending to look up measurements on laptop. Feel like gooseberry so am trying to leave them to it, but Amber keeps cornering me to tell me how gorgeous Mike is. As if I've needed telling since he arranged a surprise work party last weekend. Am his biggest fan.

Later: Rehearsal lasted until two in the morning. Despite my last-minute alterations most of the costumes are still far too tight – mine amongst the tightest. Amber was also positively bursting out of hers, although I can't be blamed for that since she asked her dressmaker to run them up. They were also the latest hem-length and colour.

Lord Gunton came to watch (and to keep a close eye on his wife, no doubt). He isn't at all as I imagined him. He's nothing like Mick Jagger (Amber's famous ex) – he's much older, blonder and posher, more like Michael Heseltine. Scary, but sexy too. When he asked me in a barking voice whether I was proud of my costumes, I was so tongue-tied that all I could do was shake my head and mutter something about there being no budget for hired ones. He winked a pale blue eye, pinched my bottom and said I looked 'damned choice' in mine. We all ended up drinking cognac in his drawing room. Big Mike kept filling up my glass and saying how talented I am, but I think he was just flirting because Amber was standing loyally by Lord G. The sad thing is, I lapped it up and told Mike he had the best bottom in the cast. Think I had too much brandy.

W Microsoft Word – Lucy's Theatrical Memoirs14.doc

Dress rehearsal went without a hitch – and also without a stitch of clothing made by yours truly. At the last minute, Lord Gunton pulled some strings (and a few corset ties) with his friends on the board of the Royal Opera House, and hired the lot. Such a relief. Tonight I was crushed to death wearing a fetching Vivienne Westwood velvet frock from *Don Giovanni* while the herd of sheep sported fantastic little fluffy leotards once used for a dream sequence in a tour of Handel's *Messiah* directed by Jonathan Miller. Amber says Lord G is 'enchanted' by me. She seems a bit annoyed, although I'm sure it's really just because I flirted with Big Mike last night.

W Microsoft Word – Lucy's Theatrical Memoirs15.doc

Am a bot squaffy so won't right mush. *Sacrificial Lamb* has been huge hit, despite fact that Ned's stage fright rendered him dumb, it rained all three nights, and Big Mike's dogs eagerly joined in sheep stampede last night. After show party great fun. Alex (Mike's dishy friend, the car journalist) came to watch and stayed on for party.

God, he's lovely. Looks like Robbie Williams. He says I was the best thing in it. So flattering. Mike seemed a bit down – probably embarrassed by the dog thing. Also because Amber still acting very loving with Lord G who got drunk and threw a white tiger rug over his shoulders to pretend to be a ram stampeding me to death. V. funny. Alex defended me with antique blunderbuss off wall. Brilliant. Amber and Mike looked highly annoyed, the party poopers. Guess they longed to be alone. Alex has asked me to lunch tomorrow. Was supposed to be going round to Mum and Dad's but don't mind cancelling. They'll just talk about the caravan. Alex will talk about Porsches and Ferraris and ... well ... me. No competition. I've had enough of amateur dramatics; I need professional pulling power. I want to torque dirty. Must stop. Room spinning.

Written on the back of an old costume design:

Lunch With Alex:

Good moments	*Bad moments*
• *Him arriving with flowers and chocolates.*	• *Bella, Jane, Brick and Big Mike being in our kitchen at time (NB they ate chocolates).*
• *Telling me I looked gorgeous.*	• *Me being so hungover that I had to rush off to be sick.*
• *Suggesting we take picnic to river in Merc.*	• *B, J, B & M suggesting fry-up lunch in Cow instead. Alex agreeing (NB too readily).*
• *Inviting himself in for coffee afterwards and staying hours to watch Grand Prix.*	• *B, J, B & M watching too. Me falling asleep and waking up to find A had gone home.*

Sunday 20th June

Dear Big Brother,

Very late so can't write much.

Thought you'd like to see review of *Sacrificial Lamb*.
Fantastic, huh? (Ignore the photo, by the way – the picture
editor got ours muddled with an exhibition of duck and goose
sculptures in the Civic Rooms.) Ralph says that reviews like
this are very good, because it shows that the production
challenged the reviewer (who he calls a 'jumped-up parochial
Kenneth Tynan-wannabe who should stick to writing about
petty crime').

Love,

Lucy xx

Cutting from the *Wexbury Gazette*:

Nothing Sacrificed in Lavish Production

After a long break, the Chisbourne Players recently reformed
to stage the world premiere of a new play, *Sacrificial Lamb*.
It is a simple (and some would say naïve) story of a lowly
shepherdess, Jasmine, who discovers that she is the long-lost
only daughter of a noble duke, but soon learns that to leave
her village for his court would compromise her love for a
local blacksmith. Performed both in the open and in a converted barn, the Chisbourne Manor setting was splendid,
although on the night that I attended the driving rain was
unfortunate and may have contributed to a part of the set
collapsing just before the interval.

The set was not the only thing that creaked in this production, alas. The script was essentially little more than a

string of clichés laced together with awkward phrasing. Its playwright, Amber Gunton, also took the leading role of Jasmine and proved that her talents do not lie elsewhere. Her acting was firmly in the furniture department, not helped by the dated and over-melodramatic direction of local 'celebrity' Ralph Delacroix, a latterday Wolfit in sheep's clothing.

The one redeeming feature of this tortuous production was the acting of local newcomer Mike Ensor in the role of Cal the Blacksmith. Taking the stage with confidence and skill, his emotional range and charismatic talent were both moving and perfectly judged. A shame, therefore, that he was continually upstaged by his leading lady whose obvious maturity stretched the audience's belief in the love affair.

A host of locals (pictured, right) supported the leads with cheerful enthusiasm, particularly the children who stampeded the stage with great gusto in the dramatic 'death scene', beautifully enacted by Lucy Gordon, of whom we saw regrettably little.

An amusing night out, although not, I fear, intended to be.

W Microsoft Word – Lucy's self-helping herself.doc

Gorgeous Alex promised he'd give me a call this week, but I've heard nothing and it's always my mother's number on 1471. Still, I refuse to be one of those women who stare longingly at the phone for hours on end, and have decided to throw myself into making the cottage look wonderful. Have been reading the book Bella lent me, *Totty Power*, and realise that in order to get myself out of the single rut I must first improve my surroundings. The book actually suggests draping brightly coloured feather boas around one's mirrors to promote a positive self-image, but I don't think they'd last five minutes with Platforms in the house. She's already savaged the ostrich hat that Jane bought for Royal Ascot last week. Charles was livid.

I used up rather a lot of the Burr Cottage curtains and throws when making my *Sacrificial Lamb* costumes, and so this is the ideal opportunity to replace them with something modern and chic before I put the sewing machine away. Popped into Wexbury market during my lunch break today and bought several metres of slightly imperfect but v. trendy fabric. Plan to start with my bedroom – it's always been far too girly and I want an air of sophisticated woman.

Ideas for bedroom:

~~Minimalist New York Loft (easy as currently no curtains/duvet cover/clothes)~~ Too plain, would show cat hairs

~~Twenties vamp (Art Nouveau lamps, Beardsley sketches, Jet beads)~~ Too expensive

~~Biba babe (sixties prints, psychedelia, Lava lamps)~~ Would get headache/sister might like it too much and spend more time here

Safari tent (folding chairs, tiger rug, gas lamps) ✓

~~Theatrical dressing room (lights around mirror/wigs/production posters)~~ Would never get to work with brightly lit mirror and have only been in one production

---

From: Lucy Gordon (juicylucy@webbedup.net)
To: Mo Lavender (Hobo-mobo@Hotmail.com)

21.47
Subject: Curtains

Catch-up time: Have decided I fancy Mike's friend Alex, who came to the play and chatted me up at party afterwards. Am redecorating bedroom. Have bought new underwear. The three are entirely unconnected. By the way, *Sacrifical Lamb* was a tour de force (as in the costumes tore when I forced the cast into them, so we hired some in). Mike very good (and strangely sexy in leather jerkin).

When Bella came home earlier to find me hunched over the

sewing machine, she shook her head sadly, 'I take it Alex hasn't called yet then?'

I tried to explain that it was part of the new 'empowered' me to restructure my surroundings, but Bella was running late to get to London and just smiled knowingly.

Big Mike called around a few minutes ago to see whether I wanted to go to the Cow in Clover where a few of the Chips cast are gathering to reminisce over last week's show. I asked whether Amber would be there and he said no, that she and Lord G were staying at their Riviera retreat. He must be missing her like mad (I suspect them of secret trysts). Taking pity, I was about to go along with him when he said that his friend Alex has seemed very taken with my costumes.

'Was he?' I couldn't hide my excitement. 'Have you heard from him then? What did he say?' I almost added 'about me' but managed to bite my tongue.

Mike looked a bit shifty before confessing that Alex had said that I was 'sweet'. Ugh! How condescending. Forfeited pub, and draped mosquito netting around my bed instead to add to sophisticated allure. No wonder he hasn't called – he's a jet-setting motor journalist and I'm just a 'sweet' stay-at-home, obsessed with sewing. Ironic, given the fact that I am still facing the prospect of homelessness. Will have to sew myself a tent soon. L xxx

W Microsoft Word – Alex.doc

Alex has called! Yes! His first words were, 'Lucy, tell me to hang up now if there is some sort of situation going on between you and Mike?' When I quickly told him there was nothing at all going on, he sighed with relief and said he'd have called much earlier but that Mike had given him the distinct impression that we were an item and had actually warned Alex off me, explaining that I am 'too hot to handle'.

What is Mike playing at? I must have terrified him with my ill-judged Christmas Eve seduction routine. On balance, I prefer being 'sweet'. Plan to be as sweet as possible when Alex takes me out to dinner next Friday.

I told Mum and Dad all about Alex over lunch today. Raved on so much, in fact, that they now think of him as the ideal son-in-law. Oops; I have yet to meet him for a proper date (lunch doesn't count because the others were all there).

Bella came home from London this evening and politely asked why I had covered most of the furniture with stained dust-sheets and turned my bed into a shrine. I explained that it's not dust-sheets, it's the latest-look New York Loft hessian and my bedroom is a Safari-themed seduction haven. I couldn't stop dancing around showing my work off. She just raised one pierced eyebrow and said, 'I take it he's called then?'

From: Ceri Dixon (reception@widgetex.co.uk)
To: Lucy Gordon (lucy@widgetex.co.uk)

11.35
Subject: Interviews

Have you seen the one with the bum fluff goatee that Slave Driver and Fruit-bat have just taken in to interview for Dave's job? God, they must be scraping the barrel! Can you believe that they're all spotty school leavers? Have you heard anything about who might get it?

From: Lucy Gordon (lucy@widgetex.co.uk)
To: Ceri Dixon (reception@widgetex.co.uk)

11.39
Subject: Re: Interviews

Not a word. Slavey and The Bat are keeping schtum.
    Wendy from Accounts has just walked past and asked if I was

looking forward to a new work-mate. I wanted to point out that anyone would be preferable to Dave, but bit my tongue and said it would be nice to have someone to 'train up'. Wendy raised a curious eyebrow and said that Dave's vacant position is 'senior exec' whereas I'm just a humble 'exec'. Can't believe an eighteen-year-old will be senior to me! Feel tempted to resign.

AND Wendy told me that there has been 'at least one application from within the company'. How come I don't know? If it's dim Lianne I'm definitely resigning.

From: Ceri Dixon (reception@widgetex.co.uk)
To: Lucy Gordon (lucy@widgetex.co.uk)

11.44
Subject: Your new man

Don't worry, Wendy is such a bitch that she's bound to be lying. How's it going with the sexy boy racer?

From: Lucy Gordon (lucy@widgetex.co.uk)
To: Ceri Dixon (reception@widgetex.co.uk)

11.52
Subject: Date

We're going out tomorrow night. I've been too busy and stressed here to think about it much, which is probably a good thing. It's been so long since I've been out on a proper date that I'm not sure what to do any more. Are you supposed to laugh at all their jokes and ask lots of fascinated questions, or be captivating and entertaining? Help!

11.59
Subject: Re: Date

Take it from the Seductress, if you look good enough, you could talk about your recurring dreams all night and he'll still be on for coffee.

Talking of which – and I'm only pointing this out to increase your chances – the latest eyebrow fashion is narrow curves and yours look a bit bushy. I'll bring my tweezers in tomorrow if you like.

W Microsoft Word – Marketing ideas75.doc

~~The need to re-market the SaunaShed after the well-publicised freak accident~~

Disaster! Ceri has just attacked my eyebrows with tweezers. Now have about three hairs left each side and red swelling. Am trying to cool them with office ice tray.

Fruit-bat says all the job candidates were useless and nowhere near my level. Such a relief. She asked me and Ceri along for a drink after work, which is really rare. When I said I had a date, she gave me a funny look and asked whether I wanted to borrow an eyebrow pencil? Am sure she and Ceri had the giggles when they left.

Rushed out to buy *Chick* magazine at lunchtime, which recommends latest date technique as flirtatious self-grooming (play with hair, stroke neck etc., to draw attention to self), plus engineering a light-hearted debate about politics and/or culture to show intelligence, making certain you let him win. Sounds pretty cool to me.

W Microsoft Word – Alex2.doc

Bella and Brick are looking at houses this weekend and the kitchen table is covered with property details. So romantic.

Think last night went okay. Alex wasn't quite as hunky or tall as

338

I remembered him, but still pretty dashing, particularly as he picked me up in a fantastic Audi TT sports car which he's testing for a magazine piece. It was a gorgeously sunny evening and he took me to the ultra-posh Winery restaurant where he ordered champagne and told me I looked beautiful (I wonder if that's the latest date advice in *Bloke* magazine?). I tried to start light-hearted political debates, but Alex agreed with everything I said, which rather ruined it, so I talked about work instead. He was very understanding about the job thing, although I think I went on a bit long – all three courses, in fact. Also self-groomed which seemed to do the trick as he looked transfixed by the way I stroked my fringe from my face to show off my eyes. That is, I thought he was transfixed by my hair-grooming until I popped to the loo and realised that I'd accidentally smeared my carefully applied eyebrow pencil all over my forehead. This didn't seem to put him off much, as he tried to ask himself into Burr Cottage for coffee afterwards, but I decided I'd play it cool, pecked him on the cheek and told him to call me. I'm not sure how keen I am on him to be honest. He's a bit boring one-to-one. I had a lot more fun when he came to lunch and the others were around. Maybe I'm just too stressed to feel sexy. Is this executive stress, or am I not senior executive enough?

WIDGETEX LTD
Memo
To: All Staff
Re: New Appointment
I am delighted to announce that Ceri Dixon is transferring from reception to the marketing department, where she will be taking over the position recently vacated by Dave Marks. Ceri has impressed us all with her level-headed approach, enthusiasm and energy. I am sure you will all join me in congratulating Ceri and wishing her every success in her new role of senior marketing executive.
    Gavin Slater

~~Face it, Widgetex products are useless, badly made and designed for sad losers~~

I don't believe it! Ceri has just rushed up to explain that Slave Driver didn't want me to know about her application because 'you've been so stressed out, Lucy, and obviously not coping with the extra work-load. He didn't want to push you over the edge.' Then she dashed off to measure up Ambitious Dave's old desk for gonk capacity. Am trying to feign rapture but secretly I'm seething. I can't believe my gossipy, forgetful friend at reception is now senior to me. Wasn't even cheered by huge bunch of flowers arriving from Alex with note asking 'When can I see you again?'

Notice on Widgetex staff board:

(Almost) Leaving Party

Please join Ceri at the Lock Inn on Friday

night, where she will be saying farewell to her

old colleagues on reception and celebrating

her new appointment. Meet 6.00. Those who

want to can come on to the Rib Shack for

food (and the Shack Attack disco).

From: Ceri Dixon (reception@widgetex.co.uk)
To: Lucy Gordon (lucy@widgetex.co.uk)

16.58
Subject: Tonight

I know you said you're busy, but please come! You only need to stay for one drink.

W **Microsoft Word – Lucy's humbled.doc**

Ended up staying for ages at the Lock Inn. Everyone was there – even Slave Driver who never comes for a drink after work, especially not on a Friday. He and Fruit-bat were amongst the last to leave, both as tight as ticks. It made me realise how popular Ceri is, and how silly I'm being resenting her the promotion. She'll be so much more fun to work with than Dave, and I've always thought she was destined for greater things than keeping Mrs Slave Driver on hold for hours while SD is demonstrating golf swings to Fruit-bat in his office.

Feel a lot happier, especially as I came home to find that Alex has called not once, but three times tonight. That's twelve times this week. Guess I should call him back sometime, but Jane has left a note to say that she's in the Cow in Clover with Bella, Brick and Big Mike, so I want to rush along to catch last orders.

COW IN CLOVER RESULTS

Friday 9th July (score kept by Bella):
Late arrival: Lucy Gordon (Excuse: Office leaving party)
Subjects for discussion: Lucy and Alex, Bella and Brick's house hunt

Number of times Jane said, 'She's only going out with him because he drives flashy cars': 4.

Best quote: 'And *she* accused *me* of being mercenary. Charles can't even reverse around a corner without getting a panic attack.'

Number of viewing appointments Bella and Brick have booked this weekend: 10.
Best quote (Bella): 'I prefer a house with more yin, but Wexbury is almost totally yang. The agents have promised to keep a look out.'
(Brick): 'I couldn't care less as long as it's got a bog, a bed and a room big enough for band practice.'

Number of questions Mike evaded about Alex: 16.
Best quote: 'He's just a nice guy. Really likeable. And he's crazy about Lucy, which is totally understandable after all. So do you think she fancies him too?'

Number of times Lucy said 'Alex' after arrival: 0.
Best quote: 'No-one's phoned me in ages.'

RESULT: Lucy = clear away numerous wilting flowers from Alex, empty answer phone of messages from Alex, vacuum. Bella = dust, clean bathroom. Jane = washing up.

W Microsoft Word – Alex3.doc

Alex is taking me out again tonight. He wanted to book a table at the Bistro Etoile, but that place has too many memories of Greg. I suggested that I drive over to the Chilterns and he could cook for me in the windmill he's told me all about (that way I can decide when to leave), but he said that wasn't possible. So we're going out to the Blue Boar in Fulstead Marsham with Bella and Brick instead. Big Mike said he might be at a loose end tonight, so I'm just going to pop next door and see if he wants to come along too. Maybe Jane and Charles fancy it as well? I'll call them.

Midnight: I think Alex was a bit disappointed that there was such a big group of us tonight, but I really enjoyed it, and have started to find Alex strangely sexy – I even asked him in for coffee afterwards. Was rather excited at the prospect of a lovely long kiss, but he seemed to want to psychoanalyse me instead. He knows all about my engagement last year, and kept asking me about the bust-up. Mike must have told him. I didn't really want to talk about Greg, although I've found myself thinking about him a lot since I've met Alex. They don't look very alike (Greg is floppy-haired and public school, Alex is slightly punky and has a touch of a Midlands accent), but there's something weirdly similar about them. In the end, I said I was tired and Alex just pecked me on the cheek and said he'd call. No kiss! Perhaps my friends put him off?

Their conversation tonight was boringly house-dominated. Bella and Brick are all set to make an offer on a place in Wexbury – it's a tiny, tatty Victorian terrace but Bella says it has tons of potential and that it's within walking distance of St Cuthbert's, so she can sell her car to pay for a new kitchen. They were desperate for advice about building societies, solicitors and the like, so asked both Big Mike and Charles the Yuppie. It turns out that Charles bought both his London flat and the cottage in Chisbourne for cash (Jane looked thrilled to hear that), whereas Mike has a mortgage, savings and a pension. He's so organised and middle-aged about things like that.

Then Jane turned excitedly to Alex: 'You live in a windmill near Henley, don't you? That must have cost an absolute fortune!' Alex looked really shifty and said that he doesn't actually own it, he just has use of it. He didn't explain any more, even later over coffee when I mentioned it in order to turn the subject away from my broken engagement. I know he's hiding something. In fact, I'm almost certain that he's co-habiting with a woman, maybe even his wife. So typically like Greg. Will have to ask Big Mike. He was very quiet tonight and looked sort of sad and withdrawn. Perhaps he knows Alex's awful secret, but is too loyal to say? I'm going to ask him round for supper next week and subtly draw it out of him with the aid of lots of wine.

***W* Microsoft Word – Marketing ideas83.doc**

~~Who needs a watch when they can have a pocket sundial?~~

Ceri was an inspired choice as marketing executive. She's so enthusiastic and full of ideas, and she's happy to do a lot of the boring stuff that Ambitious Dave always left to me. Slave Driver is thrilled to bits – he's taken Fruit-bat out to lunch, saying that he knows he can leave the office in our capable hands. Alas, the new receptionist isn't nearly as efficient as Ceri was. She's called Mona which is singularly appropriate because she's already moaned about the fact that the phone system is hopelessly old fashioned, the height of her chair is wrong, the air-conditioning gives her a headache and the flowers on the reception desk give her hay-fever.

Mum rang today asking me if I'd like to bring Alex to lunch on Sunday. Hummed and ha-ed and said I'd think about it. Still don't trust him, and harbour strong suspicion that he's married or living with someone. On impulse I called Big Mike and asked him round for supper tomorrow night so that I can do my detective bit.

From: Lucy Gordon (juicylucy@webbedup.net))
To: Mo Lavender (Hobo-mobo@Hotmail.com)

18.17
Subject: Mike kinda guy

Big changes at Burr Cottage are drawing ever closer. Bella and Brick went to the building society today and found out that they can just about afford the mortgage on their dream house as long as they don't eat for a year. Both are going out for a meal to celebrate, although swear they'll choose cheapest dishes. This suits me because Jane is at Charles's cottage (as usual) so I have the place to myself to embark upon my mission – uncovering Alex's past, otherwise known as The Dark Secret of the Windmill. Strongly suspect that he is sailing too close to the wind by living with one woman and dating another (me).

Have bought a huge luxury pizza to share with Mike because I know he's not keen on fancy food, and besides, I don't want to spend too much time in the kitchen – the more I'm lounging around with him, the more time I get to draw him out about his friend. By horrible coincidence, Alex called me at work today and asked if I was free tonight because he'd just found out there was a comedy cabaret at Wexbury Corn Exchange (actually it's not really a coincidence because he calls almost every day). I felt stupidly guilty about the Mike/pizza/detective-work thing, so I made up a feeble excuse about not going out mid-week, to which he said, 'You are so dedicated to your career, Lucy. I really respect that, even if it means I have to wait. We'll just have to do something fantastic this weekend to make up for it.'

Not really sure I like the way he assumes we're going to spend the whole weekend together after just a couple of dates. Maybe his wife's going away? I didn't mention my mother's lunch invitation for Sunday and instead asked what he had in mind. He said that there's a horse trials at Earlham Dean Hall on Saturday. Can't believe he's a horse trials fan too. Mike must have told him that I love them, and that darling old Zak, my one-time mount is now becoming a super-star eventer. Said I'd think about it, but that I'm very busy this coming weekend. He's just too perfect; it doesn't ring true, does it? Oh, I can hear Mike at the back door. Let the operation commence. Really looking forward to tonight. L xxx

---

W Microsoft Word – Lucy's detective work.doc

I have a terrible hangover. Tried to ply Mike with Merlot last night to get him in confessional mood, but he was on call so I ended up drinking most of it myself. He wouldn't spill much about Alex at all, simply saying that he's a 'really good bloke'. He seemed a bit irritated when I kept asking about him, and specifically about his past relationships (fearing that at least one of them is still current in a co-habiting kind of way). He tried to change the subject, but I was determined to know more. Mike reluctantly confessed that Alex was very like him in many ways and that they share the same passions. He looked hugely embarrassed. I think he was about to tell me something important when the phone rang. It was Alex himself saying that he knows I'm busy at the moment, but he can't bear not to see me this weekend and did I want just to meet up for a quick drink instead? At that moment I smelt terrible burning and yelled for Mike to get the pizza out of the oven. Had to explain to Alex that I'd asked Mike round for a meal. He went very quiet and said he'd call me later in the week.

Mike didn't seem v. keen on his burned pizza and went home early. Not a great night. Bella and Brick rolled home drunk at eleven saying they've decided to call their new house 'B & B'. Think they might be in for a few problems if they do . . .

13 Roundhead Avenue
Wexbury

Sunday 22nd July

Dear Big Brother,
I brought my new boyfriend, Alex, to meet the family over lunch and we're still here. He's been in Dad's shed for hours getting the full guided tour of the lathe/drills/work-mate etc. Mum has just rushed out with mugs of tea and egg sandwiches which is totally weird as she NEVER goes into the sacred shed. Have just spotted Granny hanging around outside with a sherry on the go, peering through the windows at them – she was concentrating so hard she didn't even notice the garden sprinkler soaking her skirt. If Alice were here, she'd probably be in there too, but thankfully she and Scrumpy are back-packing in Ireland. What have I done? I knew it was far too early to introduce Alex to the family. He's probably hugely embarrassed by all their attention, although I have to say he seems to be lapping it up. Even Greg

was never this unctuous to Mum and Dad. It's faintly off-putting.

I know I haven't written for ages, but I've been SO busy. Thank you for the rude postcards and the photographs you sent to remind me that you are still there (the sheep look very nice).

Love,

Lucy xx

You have . . . one . . . new message. Message received . . . today . . . at . . . seven . . . twelve . . . pee emmmm.

'Hi Lucy, it's Alex. Just calling to say how much I enjoyed yesterday. Your parents are utterly charming, and Violet is a marvellous character. Listen, I've just been asked to go to Germany to review a new Volkswagen, but it would mean being away a fortnight so don't worry, I've turned it down. I'll call you later in the week to plan next weekend. Bye.'

W Microsoft Word – Alex4.doc

Q: Why oh why do I wish Alex had said yes to Germany?

And I could think of better descriptions of my family – nutty, drunken and interfering amongst them.

Big Mike has been avoiding me since the burned-pizza supper. Am certain he was hiding behind his Land Rover when I got back from work tonight. Feel really guilty. Called out to apologise, but he carried on hiding. I could see the peak of his waxed hat poking out.

A: Because Alex going away to Germany would remind me of Greg and make it easier to dump him.

*You have . . . two . . . new messages. First message received . . .
today . . . at . . . eleven . . . thirty-nine . . . ayy emmmm.*

'Lucy, it's your mother. I know you're at work, but I want to let
you know that I've just received a beautiful bouquet of flowers from
Alex thanking me for lunch. He is quite the loveliest young man I've
ever met and so much nicer than that ghastly Greg character. Now
please don't let us down this time – you are so lucky to be courting
with someone like Alex. What a catch! He could have the pick of
the girls.'

*Second message received . . . today . . . at . . . three . . . twenty-six
. . . pee emmmm.*

'Hi, Lucy. I won't bother you at work. Just to say I'm thinking
about you. Can't wait for the weekend.'

W **Microsoft Word – Alex5.doc**

Am totally confused. Know I should find Alex hugely desirable, but
the more I see of him, the more he leaves me cold. Every time I ask
someone for an opinion, they eulogise about him. He is universally
adored.

From: Ceri Dixon (ceri@widgetex.co.uk)
To: Lucy Gordon (lucy@widgetex.co.uk)

16.44
Subject: Just me

I've been waiting for The Bat to flap away from your desk all day
to have a gossip about Alex. How's it going? Have you found out
if he's living with someone yet?

From: Lucy Gordon (lucy@widgetex.co.uk)
To: Ceri Dixon (ceri@widgetex.co.uk)

16.52
Subject: Re: Just me

Sorry. I've been working with Fruit-bat on project outlines all day. She can be quite funny when she loosens up, can't she? Slave Driver kept peering at us through his office window. He must have thought we were talking about him, but I was keen to unload my worries about Alex. I still can't work out why I don't fancy him.

I don't know anything about Fruit-bat's romantic track record – she could have been married five times bigamously and murdered all her husbands for all I know – but she looks worldly-wise and self-possessed, so I asked her advice. She cocked her head and said she really couldn't judge without meeting him, but that he sounded sweet enough and perhaps I was still just a tiny bit in love with Greg? I know I'm not, but she has given me an idea. Might ask her round to dinner with Alex and Big Mike next week, then she can suss the situation out, and Big Mike might forgive me for the pizza night. He's bound to adore Fruit-bat, and she says she's had a thing about vets since watching *All Creatures Great and Small* as a child. God, she must be so OLD!

What do you think? Good idea or bad idea?

From: Ceri Dixon (ceri@widgetex.co.uk)
To: Lucy Gordon (lucy@widgetex.co.uk)

16.59
Subject: Good idea

Absolutely. I'd offer to come too, but I'm going to Tenerife next week (yeh hey!) Has Mike broken up with the Swedish super-model girlfriend then?

~~Keeps drinks cool on a ramble with the unique Backpack Fridge~~
Fruit-bat seemed amazingly pleased when I asked her if she wanted
to come to Burr Cottage for dinner with Alex and Big Mike next
week – I don't think she has got to know many people since moving
to Wexbury. In fact she is now acting like my best friend, and even
offered to fetch me a sandwich from M and S this lunchtime. She
seems v. keen to suss out Alex for me, and says she is something of
an amateur psychologist so will relish the challenge. Not quite so
sure this is such a good idea now I've hatched it. I hardly know
Fruit-bat, and I'm not convinced she and Mike will hit it off. I think
he goes for someone more natural and fresh-faced. Fruit-bat wears
a lot of make-up and I'm sure she's been on a sun-bed to maintain
that Tuscany tan.

From: Lucy Gordon (juicylucy@webbedup.net)
To: Mo Lavender (Hobo-mobo@Hotmail.com)

18.49
Subject: Empty nest

Bella and Brick have a completion date already – the day after
August Bank Holiday. I thought these things took ages. Feel very
panicky about future of Burr Cottage. Then Jane dropped a
bombshell and told me that she's moving in with Charles the
Yuppie next weekend! No wonder she was so nice to me last night.
Even more epic is that she's decided to give up driving instruction
and train as an air stewardess. She's applied for a job with BA. I am
appalled, and was going to tell her so, but Alex stopped me. He's
been here all day, sort of getting in the way and watching me. I am
no closer to solving the mystery of the windmill – the pizza-and-
secrets session with Mike was a non-starter.

   After Jane had gone upstairs to start planning her move, Alex
gently told me that she's obviously deeply in love and I shouldn't

stand in her way just because I'm frightened of being left alone. Before I could defend myself, Big Mike popped his head around the door and asked Alex if he could move his car, which was blocking in the Land Rover. There seemed to be a bit of animosity between them, which is odd. However, I immediately grasped the opportunity to tell Mike he's coming to dinner on Wednesday to 'charm my ravishing colleague, Gabby'. I know that was laying it on a bit thick, but I needed to make sure he'd say yes. He didn't have much choice. L xxx

W Microsoft Word – Alex6.doc

Tonight went far, far better than I could have dreamed. For once, my food turned out okay thanks to Delia and a Tesco Premier torte which I passed off as my own. Everyone most impressed. Fruit-bat looked hugely glamorous in floaty silk dress, whereas Mike and I were in jeans. Alex wore a suit which looked a bit pretentious, and he was all over me in the kitchen which was irritating, particularly as it meant we left Mike and Fruit-bat alone for long stretches and I wanted her to analyse Alex, not him. Still, I think everyone enjoyed themselves and once we were sitting down eating, Fruit-bat asked Alex lots of questions to draw him out, and I chatted to Mike about Jane and Bella moving out, and what I'm going to do. He says he'll ask around to see if anyone he knows wants a room, which is really sweet. Also v. worried about Jane, like me. I asked him to help me wash up (leaving Fruit-bat to psychoanalyse Alex uninterrupted). Mike spotted my torte wrapper and teased me mercilessly. We ended up having Fairy Liquid foam fight. In the other room, Alex and Fruit-bat looked hugely disapproving, like two grown-ups at a kids' party.

From: Lucy Gordon (lucy@widgetex.co.uk)
To: Gabriella Peartree (gabby@widgetex.co.uk)

09.12
Subject: Last night

What do you think? He's a bit odd, isn't he?

From: Gabriella Peartree (gabby@widgetex.co.uk)
To: Lucy Gordon (lucy@widgetex.co.uk)

09.18
Subject: Re: Last night

A bit odd? Lucy, I hate to say this, but I think he's awful. He's
really arrogant and childish.

From: Lucy Gordon (lucy@widgetex.co.uk)
To: Gabriella Peartree (gabby@widgetex.co.uk)

09.22
Subject: Re: Re: Last night

Ha! I knew there was something dodgy about him, actually, and I
haven't even seen the childish and arrogant side of his nature yet,
which makes it even worse, doesn't it? It's such a relief to know
that someone else thinks that he's strange.

   That's made my mind up. I've simply got to end the
relationship before it goes any further. Thank you SO much for
your help.

   By the way, did you get the impression that he is living with
someone else?

From: Gabriella Peartree (gabby@widgetex.co.uk)
To: Lucy Gordon (lucy@widgetex.co.uk)

09.28
Subject: Re: Re: Re: Last night

Are we talking about Alex here? Of course he is, Lucy. He lives with his mother. Hasn't he told you?

Written on the back of an electricity bill:

When to tell Alex it's over:
~~Tell him when he rings tonight.~~ *(Too cowardly, plus he's bound to come round and "Hairdressers From Hell" is on TV)*
Break it gently this weekend. ✓

What to say when telling Alex it's over:
My life is very complicated at the moment, i.e.
  i) *The future of Burr Cottage is in the air.*
  ii) *I am stressed at work (okay, so I'm not any more, but he doesn't know that).*
I am still recovering from breaking up with Greg, i.e.
  i) *I don't want to get committed again so soon and Alex coming on too strong.*
  ii) *He reminds me of Greg physically which is upsetting (well, he wears Arran jumpers, doesn't he?).*
My family hate him (not true, but again he doesn't know that and I don't think Alice would like him).

What to say if he thinks up reasons to overcome all above:
I just don't want to go out with a secretive mummy's boy, okay?

W **Microsoft Word – Alex7.doc**
Alex didn't ring last night, which is odd. He's usually so ultra-polite that he calls from his mobile on the way home to thank me for a

lovely time, but it's forty-eight hours since I fed him and still no word. Big Mike has just popped around en route to the pub to say how much he enjoyed Wednesday, and to pass on the news that one of the veterinary nurses in his practice might be looking to rent a room, so he's given her my number. If Ceri still wants a room then I guess that's my problem solved. The trouble is, I'm not certain I want to live with a stranger and a man-eater. Can't ask her until she gets back from Tenerife anyway.

Jane is packing everything in sight. I had no idea quite so many of our household appliances belonged to her. I'm sure Charles the Yuppie already has a toaster and a kettle, but I feel mean asking her to leave them behind. Maybe she's emotionally attached to them? She's very weepy tonight. We're having a Last Supper, with just the three of us. Bella has asked Brick to stay in London.

I would ask Alex to stay away too, but I don't even know whether he's planning to come here this weekend. His mobile is switched off and he's never given me his home number because he was obviously afraid the 'other woman' (Mumsy) would answer if I called. Honestly, he can be so inconsiderate. I really need to see him to tell him it's all over. Bella and Jane are already three gins up and keep pointing out that I'm making a big mistake chucking someone 'so gorgeous, eligible and mad about you'. Almost wish I'd gone to the Cow in Clover with Mike.

From: Lucy Gordon (juicylucy@webbedup.net)
To: Mo Lavender (Hobo-mobo@Hotmail.com)

23.57
Subject: Jane's last night

It's true. She leaves in the morning.

We had a Last Supper which was a bit of a disaster. Just as we were tucking into a vat of cookie ice cream and giggling over old photos, the doorbell went and a ravishingly pretty girl wearing a cropped t-shirt asked if it was 'sorted' to look at the room? It was the veterinary nurse from Mike's practice who's looking to move to the village. On closer inspection, she had a lot of piercings (Bella obviously thought that was a plus point), a barbed wire tattoo (chichi in a mildly grungy way) and a leather jerkin with 'Portishead Massive' written on it. When Bella (who clearly thought she was the height of cool) said, 'I love Portishead too', she sneered (showing three piercings) and said in a broad Bristol accent, 'This ain't the band – this is my home-girls, y'know? My gang from where I grew up. It's rough there – you need protection.' Frankly, I found this scary. She said nothing at all when I showed her round, except when she saw my recently redecorated safari-theme bedroom with its super-chic mosquito net and exclaimed, 'You got an allergy problem?' I don't think she'll fit in. Her stomach is far too flat for a start. Bella, at least, agrees with that point.

When she finally left, we settled down to *Four Weddings* with a bottle of peach schnapps. But we'd only got as far as the opening titles when lights appeared at the window and Alex turned up bearing a vast bunch of flowers. His timing is lousy. I want to call a halt to the relationship, even though I now know that the Windmill's Dark Secret is just that our laddish motoring journo lives with his mother. But tonight is not the night for more heartache.

I am writing this on my laptop in the bathroom, which is the only place I can get some peace and have a cry. Will really miss Jane. It doesn't matter that she'll be just along the lane from me. This is truly the end of something. I'm the only one out of the Lumoja Posse left behind.

Damn. Alex is tapping gently on the door and telling me he's made me a hot chocolate with brandy in it. Will post this later. L xxx

W Microsoft Word – Alex8.doc

Have tried all weekend to tell Alex gently that I don't think things are working out between us, just as I'd planned to, but he didn't get the message at all. He says he knows just how I feel about Burr Cottage, and that he used to live with a mate who turfed him out to move a girlfriend in. His mum is putting him up while he decides where to live next.

Couldn't get out of lunch with my parents today. Of course, Mum was entranced to learn that A lives with his mother. He told her that he doesn't think he'll be living there much longer. When I asked him why, he said, 'Don't you see, Lucy? It's the perfect solution to both our predicaments. I can move into Burr Cottage!' Oh God. My parents are over the moon.

Burr Cottage
Chisbourne

Wednesday 11th August

Dear Big Brother,

Did I tell you that Jane has moved in with Charles the Yuppie?

He is truly horrible. I heard him joking in the Cow in Clover last night that he'd taken Jane on for a free trial loan with an option to own. I think she's made a big mistake, but I know she'll go mad if I tell her straight out so have to be more softly-softly. I suggested we go riding together this weekend, but she says she's booked on an air stewardess intensive training course.

I want you to come over here and rescue her from him ASAP.

I guess I'll have to do something about sorting out the Burr Cottage crisis soon. Alex seems to assume he can move in as soon as he likes and is already sizing up the shelves for his record collection but I am having serious doubts about our relationship, let alone living together. Thankfully Brick has moved into Bella's room and is giving us some rent, so I have a couple more weeks to decide.

Life is so much easier for sheep.

Love,

Lucy xx

From: Lucy Gordon (juicylucy@webbedup.net)
To: Mo Lavender (Hobo-mobo@Hotmail.com)

22.47
Subject: Not so super-stition

The Friday 13th curse is proven beyond all doubt. Bella and Brick are in a total state because they've just been gazumped. A cash buyer has snatched 'B&B' from under their noses. Apparently the estate agent and vendors were unrepentant, saying that it's just par for the course in the current market.

Alex called me at work today to say he can't see me this weekend. Not sure whether to be angry (can't dump him yet) or relieved (saved from upsetting him). L xxx

Burr Cottage
Chisbourne

Sunday 15th August

Dear Big Brother,

Thought Mum would rabbit on about how fabulous Alex is over lunch today, but she is totally distracted because Alice has scraped only two Es at A Level – not enough to get her into Manchester. Dad is locked in shed in foul mood as a result. Alice not helping matters by joking that she can't wait to tell Scrumpy that she has two Es: 'He'll suggest we take them together.' Thank God Mum didn't understand.

Don't worry about saving Jane, by the way. I have found a deputy. And like all good deputies, he's going to gallop to the rescue on a horse (I hope).

Had great fun riding yesterday. Horsy Tim said he'd been asking Mike how I was only last week (bizarrely, Mike told him that I am 'madly in love' which isn't exactly true). Anyway, Tim took me out on a long, lazy hack so we could catch up. The sad news is that he and Victoria have split up – she left him for an equine acupuncturist called Milo. HT seems cool about it, so maybe Alex won't be too upset when I finally chuck him (although I'm having second thoughts about that now that he might be my only chance of staying in Burr Cottage). I told HT about Jane and Charles the Yuppie and he was really concerned. Think I may have over-exaggerated Charles's control-freak side, but I am so worried about Jane. He promised to give her a call. Hence you don't need to leave the sheep.

Love,

Lucy xx

From: Gabriella Peartree (gabby@widgetex.co.uk)
To: Lucy Gordon (lucy@widgetex.co.uk)

14.34
Subject: Getting fit

Do you know of any good gyms locally? I keep meaning to join one.

From: Lucy Gordon (lucy@widgetex.co.uk)
To: Gabriella Peartree (gabby@widgetex.co.uk)

14.42
Subject: Re: Getting fit

I belong to The Sweatshop. It's very good. Which reminds me, I haven't been for ages. If you like, I'll take you there tomorrow and you can try it out.

W Microsoft Word – Marketing ideas85.doc

~~The new face of novelty desktop accessories~~

Went to The Sweatshop this lunchtime – I almost died on the treadmill, but was relieved to see that Fruit-bat was puffing like mad too. She breathlessly asked me whether I've managed to chuck Alex yet and I croakily explained that he's being super-evasive. She was v. sympathetic and suggested I do it by fax as 'it always works for me'. She seems v. bitter, poor thing. Still, not a bad idea. Trouble is I don't have A's fax number. Might draft letter . . .

Written on the back of the Widgetex Autumn Marketing Budget:

~~Darling~~ Dear Alex,

~~I've spent a lot of time thinking this through and~~
~~I have really enjoyed the time that we've spent together, but~~
~~When I was six, my mother asked me who I wanted to marry when I~~
~~grew up and I said 'Prince Charles'. But people change and Charles is~~
~~now a middle-aged baldy with dandruff and sticky-out ears. I'm sure he~~
~~makes Camilla very happy, but the point is that I just saw the prince in~~
~~those days. When I first saw you, I saw a lovely easy-going all-action~~
~~hero, not someone who lives with his mother and~~
~~I know that this is going to hurt you, but I've~~

359

There is no easy way of telling you this. I don't want to go out with you any more.

~~Love~~
~~With affection~~
All the best,
Lucy xx

From: Lucy Gordon (juicylucy@webbedup.net)
To: Mo Lavender (Hobo-mobo@Hotmail.com)

23.11
Subject: Moore news

Fantastic night out with Bella and Brick. I really admire the way they've bounced back over this house thing. One moment they've lost out to gazumpers and their dream is in tatters, the next they are resolved to buy a barn and convert it into Casa B&B. They are full of ideas and have been busily sizing up outbuildings in the area. Apparently a local farmer threw them out of his cowshed this afternoon. The Bs found this v. funny, but Big Mike was less amused when I told him the story in the pub. Apparently that barn has been burned down three times by arsonists. Mike says Brick was lucky not to be shot.

He was v. weird tonight. Asked me if I was still going out with Alex. Said yes, I was, as far as I know (worse luck), although he's in States this weekend. Mike's eyebrow did odd thing – a sort of Roger Moore lift. Never seen it before. Quite attractive. L xxx

---

W Microsoft Word – Lucy's chaperone.doc

Went riding this morning. Really ache. Told Horsy Tim that Jane is having dinner party tonight. She's asked me and Alex, but A away (so selfish not being around for quick pre-chuck inspection of Yuppie Cottage). Think HT was angling for an invite, but I couldn't ask him along to make up numbers, which is rather infuriating as I think he may be the only one who can save Jane from Charles. But I've already asked Mike (after he did the eyebrow thing). Hope he behaves. Hope he does sexy Roger Moore impression too.

Fruit-bat called me at home today (weird!), asking me whether I wanted to come to Sweatshop tomorrow for circuit training. Explained I have to go to parents for lunch (crisis meeting re. Alice's A Level results). She said, 'We should talk, Lucy.' Really think she should confine Widgetex business to weekdays. She's just too dedicated. I need quality time with Platforms and my designer mosquito net.

Dinner Party Menu – Juniper Cottage, Back Lane, Chisbourne.
Chef: Jane Redven

Trout Tartare with Cucumber Crown, Quail's Egg, Caviar and
*   Chilled Gazpacho Dressing*
Spit-roast Chicken Leg Stuffed with Ox-cheek and Black Pudding,
*   with Millefeuille of Apple*
Calvados Pomme Vert Sorbet

Accompanied by a 'pretentiously sexy' Chablis, '97, 'arrogant sod of a'
*   Bordeaux, 'mother of a' Muscat*

Burr Cottage
Chisbourne

Sunday 22nd August

Dear Big Brother,

I never thought I'd say it, but I think Mum has been surpassed in the ostentatious food stakes.

Last night was dire. Jane spent entire time in kitchen slaving over ridiculously complicated Jean-Christophe Novelli recipes. Charles gloated over wine 'I think you'll find this little Chablis rather challenging – it's devilishly sophisticated.' Ugh! Hate him. Thank heaven for Mike who made me laugh by pulling faces. No eyebrow thing, though (he does a very neat trick with one that I can't recommend enough for adding enigmatic charm to your facial repertoire). Shame.

Jane called first thing this morning and asked why I'd brought Mike instead of Alex. Explained that A in States. Jane made long 'ohhhh' noise, eking it out for ages. Then said, 'So we're back in *Greg* territory are we?' Hotly pointed out that I am poised to dump Alex just as soon as he materialises. Have tried to write letter/fax as my colleague Fruit-bat suggested, but can't get beyond 'Dear Alex, It's Over. Love, Lucy x'. Bit brief, and not sure about kiss.

Mum is contemplating selling the caravan to pay Alice through a crammer. She's got lots of brochures, and is ignoring Dad who keeps saying, 'But Liv, the caravan is our little holiday on wheels.' Today she said that if it isn't sold to fund Alice's re-takes she'll sell it anyway as cash capital for her restaurant. Dad has retreated to his shed again.

Mum had a go at me about Alex, saying it was about time I brought him round again. To my amazement, Granny suddenly stood up and said, 'I don't trust that pilot boy – he will hurt dear Lucy. Not like Alice's lovely beau!' Okay, so she got A muddled up with Greg, but I was grateful for the defence. She and Mum had furious row, at end of which Mum threatened to brick up entrance to annexe (cutting off Granny's sherry supply), so Granny belligerently said she'd buy Alice and Scrumpy a camper van.

All fairly normal at home then.

Hope the sheep are behaving.

Love,

Lucy xx

From: Gabriella Peartree (gabby@widgetex.co.uk)
To: Lucy Gordon (lucy@widgetex.co.uk)

09.34
Subject: Running partner

Lucy,

I trust you had an enjoyable weekend. It is a shame that you couldn't make time to meet up. I was hoping to run this one past you first, but since you had other commitments, I have taken the initiative and signed us both up for:

Mini Marathon in aid of Retired Jockeys
24th October.

This gives us plenty of time to train. I feel this will not only boost both our fitness levels (something which we both know we need) but will also be central in creating a team bond. I know that you will not let me down and will respect this initiative.

I've emailed Ceri asking whether she would like to join us, however I have not signed her up at this stage because of her obvious physical disadvantage. Whilst believing that she has an equal right to take part, I would not wish to take responsibility for a colleague's pulmonary incident/chafed thighs.
Gabby

From: Ceri Dixon (ceri@widgetex.co.uk)
To: Lucy Gordon (lucy@widgetex.co.uk)

12.34
Subject: Running away

Ha, ha, ha, ha, ha bloody ha hee hee!!!!! That is so, so funny! You wouldn't catch me NEAR a marathon. How sweet of the Bat to know that. But you're already signed up, my fitness freak chum. Oh poor, poor Lucy.

From: Lucy Gordon (lucy@widgetex.co.uk)
To: Ceri Dixon (ceri@widgetex.co.uk)

12.41
Subject: Got the runs

It's awful, isn't it? Beyond my worst imaginings of awful. I think
I'm going to be sick. Now stuck waiting for Fruit-bat to come out
of meeting with Slave Driver so we can go to gym together. She's
been in there hours, and I'm sure I can hear raised voices. You
don't suppose she's trying to get him to sign up too, do you?
She's mad.

From: Ceri Dixon (ceri@widgetex.co.uk)
To: Lucy Gordon (lucy@widgetex.co.uk)

12.43
Subject: Told you so

Lovers' tiff maybe?

From: Lucy Gordon (lucy@widgetex.co.uk)
To: Ceri Dixon (ceri@widgetex.co.uk)

12.47
Subject: Joke

V. funny. Can't imagine two people less likely to get it together
than FB and Slavey. Except possibly me and Alex.

W Microsoft Word – Lucy's new friendship.doc
Ohmygod! Fruit-bat was really upset at gym – kept bursting into
tears on treadmill. I asked her if she was okay and she said no, that
she's been having an affair with a married man, but recently she's
been seeing someone else too, and that the married man's found out

and now says he'll leave his wife if she stops the other relationship, but that she doesn't want to because she thinks she's in love with the other bloke, but that he's involved with someone else too and . . . well, actually she completely lost me there. Her love-life is *so* complicated. Felt too embarrassed to ask her to repeat it so I could understand, so I just looked sympathetic and handed over tissues. Tried to cheer her up by joking that Ceri thought she was seeing Slave Driver of all people and she said 'But Lucy, I am seeing him – he's the married man.' And she burst into tears again. Feel v. relieved that I just have a boyfriend I don't fancy who I hardly ever see anyway.

Talking of which, Alex got in contact at long last tonight, inviting himself here for Bank Holiday. Now have opportunity to end relationship at long last. Might have to wait till after Sunday, though, as big family lunch planned and atmosphere at Roundhead Avenue already v. tense – Mum not talking to Granny *or* Alice.

Cannot believe Fruit-bat let Slave Driver shag her. *Ugh!*

W Microsoft Word – Lucy's pisde aguin.doc

Feel bit squiffy. Just been pub. Celebration. Bella and Brick bought auction at barn. Mean barn at auction. Going to convent it themselves – mean convert. Feel bit sick. Alex gone to fetch me a bucket. Sweet. Not sure if I will chuck him after all. Ohhhh – head swimming. Might not chuck Alex, but going to chuck up. Can't wait for bucket –

Burr Cottage
Chisbourne

Sunday 29th August

Dear Big Brother,

Sorry this is hand-written. I had a bit of an accident with my laptop last night, but Dad says he has got a marvellous can of special computer keyboard cleaner and has promised to sort it out (I know he hasn't got a keyboard – he uses it to flush dust out of his chainsaw engine or something). That was about the only good thing to come out of today.

Awful, awful lunch at Mum and Dad's. Alex was in foul mood after spending night changing bed/holding bucket for me (too much celebrating with B&B yesterday). Mum was still mad at Granny who is determined to buy Alice and Scrumpy a Dormobile to travel in; Dad is mad at Mum because she wants to sell their caravan. I tried to lift mood by telling everyone about Fruit-bat's affair with Slave Driver. All very shocked, most especially Alex who said, 'I don't believe it. The bitch!' Never knew he was so moral. Rather lovely and old-fashioned if you think about it.

Decided the Bat's affair was a rather dicey subject, so told everyone about Bella and Brick buying barn to convert. Mum asked if that means they're going to stay on at Burr Cottage while they do the work, but I explained that they can't afford to and that they're going to camp in the barn. Mum pointed out that this'll be v. cold and unpleasant through winter, to which Dad suddenly thumped his fist on table and said: 'In that case we have the perfect solution! They must borrow the Gordon caravan to live in!'

What is going on with our family? They are all trying to outdo each other by giving away wheeled accommodation. Don't blame you for leaving. It was only a matter of time before your skateboard got donated to the Pottingers' ageing dachshund.

Alex hardly spoke a word all afternoon. Then he suddenly announced that he had to go somewhere and would drop me home.

'But I thought we were spending Bank Holiday Monday together?' I gasped, as he drove to Chisbourne like clappers and more or less shoved me out of car before pelting in direction of Wexbury.

Think the squabbling Gordon family has put him off me. Maybe he thinks they'll try to give away his flashy sports car? Awful timing, as have decided I fancy him after all.

Join in the spirit of things and strap a sheep to some in-line skates.

Love,

Lucy xx

You have . . . one . . . new message. Message received . . . today . . . at . . . three . . . fifteen . . . pee emmmm.

'Lucy, it's Dad. I've cleaned up your laptop and I'll drop it around tonight if that's okay. Hmm. Yes. Don't come to the house to collect it. I can have a chat with your friends about the caravan while I'm there. Hang on, your mother wants a word . . .'

'Lucy, whatever you do, don't let Bella agree to take the cara— Gordon, let go. I said, Let. Go. Of. The. Phone. Stop it! This is –'
Beep.

From: Lucy Gordon (juicylucy@webbedup.net)
To: Mo Lavender (Hobo-mobo@Hotmail.com)

11.01
Subject: Hacked off

Have just got back from hacking out with Horsy Tim. Big Mike was at the stables vetting a pony for a prospective buyer, but was a bit funny when I said 'hello'. He sort of grunted and ignored me. I asked him whether he'd heard from Alex at all (he hasn't returned my calls all week). But Mike just ran his hands along the horse's legs and snapped, 'You're the one who's supposed to be going out with him, Lucy.'

Afterwards, Horsy Tim explained that Mike's in a foul mood because his new girlfriend's playing him about. This was news to me. Felt strangely irritated. 'What new girlfriend?'

'One of the veterinary nurses at the surgery. Very young. I gather she prefers to go out clubbing with her mates than stay in with old Mike.'

Ugh! Strongly suspect Mike is going out with pierced-belly-button girl who came to look at spare room in Burr Cottage. So the Womaniser of Chisbourne is squiring an employee. Typical. At least he's the one being treated mean this time. Cradle-snatcher.

Unfortunately, HT didn't know any more. Instead he was v.

367

keen to hear all about Jane and Charles the Yuppie. Had to admit I haven't spoken to Jane for ages. Promised to give her a call and report back. Will have to wait, however, as expecting Landlord at any minute to discuss the future of Burr Cottage. Bella and Brick set to move into my parents' caravan after wedding – just three weeks away. The only people who've shown any interest in filling spare rooms so far are Mike's clubbing girlfriend (a non-starter, as refuse to co-habit with skinny, vet-snogging flirt) and Alex (quite tempting if only he'd get in touch).

Do you fancy coming back to live here? Please, please, please say yes. Say anything in fact, just to prove you're alive. A call, a card, a sign – anything!

There's a car coming into the drive. Help! Landlord's here already and I haven't hidden Brick's ashtrays. L xxx

---

W **Microsoft Word – Lucy meets the Landlord, amen.doc**
God! Have just a week to find new housemates or Landlord will put Burr Cottage up to rent. Called Jane to tell her my desperate news, but she was very off-hand and said she couldn't chat as she was taking Charles out for a driving lesson: 'It's his test soon.' Could hear Charles in background, telling her to get off phone. Pig.

Call from Alex at last. He apologised for last weekend and asked if he can see me tomorrow. Such a relief as now don't have to have Sunday lunch with squabbling family, but can see lovely Alex instead and make up for being half-hearted girlfriend.

Possible housemates:

Alice and Scrumpy (no cash, off to university soon)

Ceri (would have to put up with constant influx of small men/chocolate)

Sad Samantha from Widgetex (v. depressed so would stay in her room all the time)

Sunday 5th September

Dear Big Brother,

Missed family lunch today as Alex suggested coming here. But he behaved very, very oddly indeed. Kept looking at his watch throughout lunch, which I had made great pains to create – sumptuous lamb noisettes drenched in truffle and wine sauce to make up for last Sunday's Gordon food feud. I apologised for my family arguing, but to my amazement A said, 'Were they? I didn't notice.'

He still hasn't explained why he dashed off afterwards. He was very on edge. I kept thinking he was about to tell me something important, but every time he opened his mouth, he seemed to bottle out and just made small talk instead. After he'd commented on the weather five times, I got fed up and asked him what was bothering him.

'Lucy, I have to ask you something,' he spluttered, looking deeply embarrassed. 'How do you feel about me?' He looked so worried and hopeful at the same time that I felt a great gush of affection and guilt. Admitted that I had been a bit uncertain at first, but that now I think he's gorgeous and . . . 'in fact I was thinking of taking up your offer to move in here with me!'

Expected him to be elated, but he gulped, said, 'Oh God, I thought you wanted to finish the relationship.' At that moment the phone rang. It was Mum, furious that I'd not come to lunch, and ranting that she's going to brick up the door to the annexe because she hates Granny. By the time I'd calmed her down, Alex had gone. Weird. L xxx

W Microsoft Word – Marketing ideas87.doc

~~Assessing the demand for Microwave Safety Goggles~~

Fruit-bat is really getting on my nerves. Having been oh-so-pally in recent weeks, treating me like her new best friend, she has suddenly changed tack and started bossing me about. Suspect it is because I Know Too Much. Admit I do find it very awkward when she and Slavey are both in the same room as me. Can't keep my eyes off them, certain that they're giving away secret signs of passion, but they are always super-professional and coolly civil with one another. Long to confide in someone, but daren't tell Ceri who is bound to spread it around the office.

Only other person who knows Fruit's secret is Alex, but he's behaving very oddly. Having walked out on me without a word on Sunday, he sent me big bouquet today. Fruit-bat's just angrily asked me to take them home because they're 'provoking office gossip and exacerbating Mona's hay-fever'. Went to loo a minute ago and sure I heard crying in cubicle. Not sure, but think it was Fruit-bat. I cautiously called out to whoever it was to ask whether they were okay, but the loo suddenly flushed and then there was stifled silence. A moment later Wendy from Accounts bustled in and started reapplying her blue eyeliner with a spatula.

Maybe I should tolerate Fruit-bat picking on me a bit longer, as she's obviously in a crisis about two-timing Slavey with the Mystery Man who loves An Other.

W Microsoft Word – Alex9.doc

Alex took me to Bistro Etoile tonight. He explained that he has been behaving oddly because he was convinced I was going to chuck him (which I was but now am not). But then last Sunday, when I told him I'd like him to move into Burr Cottage and he realised I *did* want to make a go of things, he was so relieved he just had to get in his car and drive v. fast. He says it's a 'man thing'. I still think this was a bit of an odd reaction (particularly as he could have taken me

370

with him/driven back afterwards/called me to explain the 'man thing') but am v. relieved that we are still an item. Have worked out that we can just about cover the rent on Burr Cottage if he pays half.

But when I excitedly told Alex this, he chewed his lip and said, 'It's all a bit too soon isn't it, Lucy? I think we should go to Paris together instead.' Tried not to feel too hurt or panic-stricken. Don't want to go to Paris with Alex. Want to keep Burr Cottage.

13 Roundhead Avenue
Wexbury

Sunday 12th September

Dear Big Brother,
The Gordon family feud has reached ridiculous heights. Am being used as mediator because no one is talking to anyone else. Thank heaven I told Alex not to come to lunch today, as would be mortally ashamed of my clan. Mum cooked veal to deliberately annoy Alice; Granny ate in front of television with vast sherry to annoy Mum; Alice insisted on watching *South Park* video to annoy Granny (who has yet to buy Dormobile); Dad retreated to his shed and started axle grinder, which annoyed everyone. Have just looked out of window to see him attaching caravan to back of car ready to tow to Bella and Brick's barn. This annoys me because I was hoping to persuade them to stay on at Burr Cottage for half rent.

Do any of the sheep fancy a spell in Berks? Cheap rent and minimal cleaning.
Love,
Lucy xx

From: Lucy Gordon (juicylucy@webbedup.net)
To: Mo Lavender (Hobo-mobo@Hotmail.com)

22.03
Subject: The box beckons

Not one response to my advert for housemates in local paper. Am desperate. Only call this evening was from Alex, banging on about Paris again – he is driving me in-Seine by suddenly announcing we need to get an Eiffel of romantic sights before we live together. I told him to get off line in case anyone was trying to ring about room. Bella took me to Cow for soothing drink, but then gave me a lecture about only keeping Alex on as boyfriend because I want him to move into house. I hotly denied this. Think he is v. sweet. Just don't want to go to Paris. Very cold at this time of year. Big Mike was at the bar as usual, and asked B about the barn and about the wedding. Both topics cruelly remind me that I'm about to lose my housemates, so I came home early. Wonder if Ceri still looking for room to rent? Not sure if I can live with man-eating Mars Bar addict who was promoted above me, but if it means I get to stay in my beloved old brick-and-flint home I might try. Can't bear thought of Platforms and me sleeping in cardboard box on pavement.

   Still waiting for a sign you're alive, by the way. L xxx

From: Lucy Gordon (lucy@widgetex.co.uk)
To: Ceri Dixon (ceri@widgetex.co.uk)

09.21
Subject: Room to rent

Are you still looking to move out of your parents' house? Only there might be a room free at Burr Cottage soon. Well, this week actually.

From: Ceri Dixon (ceri@widgetex.co.uk)
To: Lucy Gordon (lucy@widgetex.co.uk)

09.33
Subject: Re: Room to rent

Sorry, babes. Just signed rental contract on studio flat in
Wexbury Heights. My marketing executive wages mean I can
afford to live alone and seduce men at will. Wey hey!!!
   Why don't you put up an ad on the notice board?
   I'm thinking of getting fit. Do gyms have snack bars?

W Microsoft Word – Marketing ideas88.doc

~~A New Direction for Unwanted Vermin – the Laser Pest Eraser~~
Fruit-bat has just asked if I'll stay late to work tonight. She deliberately did so in front of Slavey so I had to say yes. Then she gave
me an evil little smile and said 'You don't mind, do you, Lucy?
You're not seeing Alex tonight are you?' Told her that no, I'm not.
In truth have had no desire to see Alex since he refused to move in
with me.

Now Fruit-bat has swanned off to gym with Ceri of all people.
Suspect she will be new victim of two-week best-friend syndrome,
especially now that they will both be living in same luxury mill
conversion. Doubt she'll agree to run mini-marathon, though.

Card featuring wildebeests wearing party hats:

In Kenya.	*Dear Slapper,*
Hot, happy and tanned like you WILL NOT BELIEVE!	
Hope Greg gives you something tasty – like his balls on a plate. Joke.	**It's your Birthday . . . Party on!**
Toast old Burr Cottage from me and give Mike a HUGE SNOG (deliver it personally . . . promise?)	
Love to your mad family, 'specially Jeremy. He's on my list . . .	*Miss you,*
Still got the old email address . . . hint, hint.	*Mo xxxxxxx*

From: Lucy Gordon (juicylucy@webbedup.net)
To: Mo Lavender (Hobo-mobo@Hotmail.com)

22.43
Subject: I got it!!!!!

Thank you, thank you, THANK YOU! It arrived today – on the day itself. You are a BEAUTY! Really cheered me up as Mum and Dad are a bit distracted, so they forgot. So did Alice (she always does), Granny (too pissed to remember), Bella (obsessed with the new barn, bless), everyone at work (well it's a Saturday so they are excused) and Jeremy (post v. slow from Sheep's Eye). My only other card came from Big Mike, but he must have posted it through the door this morning, because by the time I got up his Land Rover had gone.

Had another lovely, chatty ride with Horsy Tim this morning. He wanted to know all about Jane and I realised guiltily that I had promised to find out how she was, but have only had one quick phone call in three weeks. She forgot my birthday too, incidentally. Can't believe we live in same village and never see one another. Think Charles the Yuppie has his driving test this week. Bound to take it in a BMW.

Alex doesn't know it's my birthday because I haven't told him. He's in Scotland on Brick's stag weekend. Was very shocked when he told me he was going. He hardly knows Brick. Bella – whose hen party is next weekend (to allow their married friends with babies to cover sitting duties) – pointed out that he was invited because he was my boyfriend. I grumpily conceded the point, but I still think Brick was unwise to ask him along. We might not still be together by wedding, although having man at side always very useful at these things. Can't decide if we have a future. (By the way, your comment about Greg was odd – I haven't heard from him for over a year.)

Bella got quite stroppy with me, saying that I have turned into a selfish cow lately. I was tempted to tell her that she'd be selfish too if she was facing imminent homelessness, but I held my tongue as I suspect she is only ratty because she's suffering pre-wedding jitters, poor thing. Called Jane tonight, but she was out. So I left a message suggesting a girly night with pizza, wine and Tom Hanks film. She can't refuse. L xxx

---

W Microsoft Word – Lucy vants to be alone.doc

Can't face feuding family Sunday lunch, so called Mum to pretend I have tummy bug. She still didn't twig that it was my birthday yesterday, even though I said 'I got a birthday card from Mo this year.' Things must be bad at Roundhead Avenue. I think I could hear crockery smashing in the background (although it could have been Granny watching a Western because she does tend to have the sound up very loud).

I'm avoiding Bella too, so decided to take a walk. Followed footpath through Chisbourne Manor's big wood. Very muddy. Should have worn wellies as soon it was ankle-deep. Was just squelching through pheasant coops when two horses pounded past splattering me in more mud. They didn't stop, but I had already seen who was riding. Amber Gunton and Big Mike. Ha! The Womaniser is not only squiring his young and pretty veterinary nurse, but also still servicing the local landowner's wife, it seems. Disgusting. No wonder he didn't want to go on stag weekend. Maybe I should move away from the village after all?

From: Ceri Dixon (ceri@widgetex.co.uk)
To: Lucy Gordon (lucy@widgetex.co.uk)

10.17
Subject: The Bat

Honestly, Fruit-bat is a dead loss as a pulling partner. She's got even less stamina than you, doll!!! I took her out clubbing this weekend and she started fading after two Screaming Orgasms. I tried to move her onto Sex On The Beach, but she was off her face and muttering stuff about seeing some bloke who was two-timing 'the sweetest girl I've ever met'. Ended up abandoning her in Gossips when I picked up a well-muscled panel beater called Baz. Fwor!!!!

From: Gabriella Peartree (gabby@widgetex.co.uk)
To: Lucy Gordon (lucy@widgetex.co.uk)

11.34
Subject: Gym

Lucy,

Shall we go to The Sweatshop this lunchtime? I have something of a confession I need to share if you have a window in your diary. Say twelve-thirty at The Sweatshop juice bar (am popping to the w/h first to have a word about catalogue distribution)? My treat.

~~Taking Plug-in Petpong Purifiers into the Twenty First Century~~

It seems I am favoured again. Fruit-bat's new friendship with Ceri has lasted less than a week. I think her initiation into Ceri's dark world of Basborough nightclubbing has taken her to the edge. She's very uptight and can't look me in the eye. And what's this 'confession'? Maybe she and Slavey have broken up? My horoscope says I should avoid conflict with figures of authority. Some hope.

Still no word from Jane, which is odd. Called her again this morning and got Charles the Yuppie who I thought would be at work. He screamed, 'Stop hassling us, you interfering sow!' and hung up. Alarming. Must be nervous about driving test.

Gaunt Ward
Wexbury General Hospital

Thursday 23rd September

Dear Big Brother,

Another hand-written letter, I'm afraid. Not allowed to use my laptop here, as I'm told it may interfere with the equipment (I am lying in a hospital bed, by the way, contemplating Mum's bowl of 'exotic fruit, muesli marshmallows and homemade Turkish Delight Steeped in Lucozade'). I'll explain . . .

Yesterday, Fruit-bat and I were walking along High Street towards The Sweatshop when a familiar driving instructor's car mounted pavement at speed and swept us right off our feet. Fruit ended up sitting in ornamental flower display by bus stop; I crashed right through Debenham's window and was knocked clean out on mannequin wearing casual autumn separates. Very dramatic, I'm told.

All a bit of a blur until I woke up in casualty with the parents peering at me worriedly (although notably not talking to one another). They explained that Charles the Yuppie had lost control of the wheel during his driving test. He caused carnage in the High Street and then had some

377

sort of nervous breakdown, holding the whip-lashed driving test examiner hostage in the car until the police could gently talk him out. Meanwhile the casualties – Fruit-bat and I – were being rushed to hospital. I asked after Fruit-bat in a panic, but Mum said she was fine, and in next cubicle receiving treatment for an 'embarrassing affliction' – she has hundreds of ornamental thistle spikes impaled in her bottom. I am amazingly unscathed apart from a couple of cuts to my arm and a sore head. We're both being kept in overnight and have adjacent beds. Fruit-bat currently conked out on pain-killers. Had no idea she snored so loudly. She keeps muttering 'legs'.

Since Fruit-bat is sleeping, I have just given an 'exclusive' to the "Wexbury Gazette". The reporter – who was about seventeen – said, 'This is like, so cool, because you got run over the day we go to press so we'll have it first.' Photographer kindly shot me from my good side (the one without the huge dressing on my head) and let me borrow her eyeliner and blusher. I'll get Mum and Dad to include the newspaper cutting with this letter – bound to be front page.

Love,

Lucy xx

Cutting from *Wexbury Gazette*:

High Street Comes To A Halt as Learner Fails To Emergency Stop

Tail-backs of more than three miles into Wexbury town centre were reported yesterday when a learner driver lost control of his car whilst taking his test. Charles Carlingford, 38, was just five minutes into his examination route when he suffered what police describe as a 'panic attack', but Carlingford's solicitor, Rudi Goldberg, describes as a 'momentary lapse of focus'. Upon recognising a friend on the pavement, Carlingford's Renault Clio (from Jane's Driving School in Chisbourne) veered left and accelerated dramatically before crashing into a shop window. Two pedestrians were injured, one of them the friend of Carlingford.

After the crash Mr Carlingford is alleged to have held his examiner hostage for twenty minutes before police negotiated for the man's release. However, no charges have been brought forward. 'This is plainly an attempt to undermine my client's reputation,' claims Goldberg. 'Mr Carlingford is a well-known and highly respected lone trader in the City, regularly taking huge risks. Something like this is simply a bad afternoon. He just required a few minutes to gather his composure, as did his examiner.'

The injured pedestrians were both transported by ambulance to Wexbury General where they are described as 'comfortable and not critical'. Lucy Gordon, 26 (pictured left), talked exclusively to the *Wexbury Gazette* from her hospital bed, where she is recovering from mild concussion: 'It all happened so suddenly. Charles had this sort of mad look in his eye. I thought for a crazy moment that he was driving at me deliberately. He's always been a bit odd. He lives with my friend Jane and makes her pretend she's an air stewardess in front of his friends.'

Carlingford's girlfriend, Jane Redven, had the following to say: 'Is this going to be in the papers? Oh no. Charles's friends can't know he's learning to drive. What has Lucy been saying?'

The driving examiner and the other injured pedestrian were both unavailable for comment.

From: Lucy Gordon (juicylucy@webbedup.net)
To: Mo Lavender (Hobo-mobo@Hotmail.com)

18.26
Subject: Crash

All is explained in the cutting which I have scanned in (ignore the photograph – picture editor got muddled up with 'Glamorous Granny Triumphs For Fifth Time').

Such a relief to be home – even if this won't be my home much longer. Now know there is absolutely no chance Alex will move in here. It's all over, kaput, finito.

Today saw the first high drama at *Wexbury General* since the Queen Mother fell over when opening the new maternity wing. I was just having a post-breakfast nap this morning when I heard a kerfuffle in the corridor and Alex's familiar voice saying 'Where is she? Is she scarred for life? I must see her!' To my utter amazement, Fruit-bat positively leapt from her bed crying out, 'I'm here, Alex my love! I knew you'd come!'

There was a ghastly moment when I looked at her, then at Alex, and she looked at me, then at Alex, and Alex just looked cornered, the swine.

It all made sense – his long, sudden absences; the fact they got on so well at my dinner party; Fruit-bat picking on me since Alex and I have tried to make a go of things. She wasn't muttering 'legs' last night, as I thought; she was calling out his name, 'Alex' – her mystery man. And now she was revealing her scarred bottom to the entire ward as she kissed him.

Everyone started shouting at once. Or it might just have been me – I was seeing double, so I could have been hearing it too. I'm not very good at big scenes. My head was pounding and I just felt sick. I think I cried a lot, and swore, and pressed the panic button by my bed several times. Then, like a knight in shining harmony, Big Mike appeared in the ward carrying a fluffy musical cat playing 'My Way'. I begged him to take me home. The nurses were reluctant to let me go as the doctor had yet to give me the all-clear, but I was adamant and refused to let go of Mike's hand. I think Alex was yelling at me to listen to him, to understand that it was all over between them, and Fruit-bat was sobbing that she loved him. But I fled, still wearing my nightie. Passed out in car.

Mike really sweet – he drove me home and tucked me up in bed, then quietly explained to Bella and Brick what had happened. Bella brought me sweet tea and sympathy while Brick manned the phone which rang non-stop as Alex called to speak to me. He came round an hour ago, but Brick barred his way, and eventually Mike appeared and took him next door for a chat.

Bella says Charles the Yuppie is in psychiatric ward suffering from severe stress. Feel like joining him, but not v. fond of hospitals right now. L xxx

wexgaz.bmp attachment here

Alex Harland
The Windmill
Hurville
Nr Henley
Oxon

Darling Lucy,

How can you ever forgive me? Christ, I feel like such a shit. You are so gorgeous, so beautiful, so funny and talented and kind. You are all that I ever wanted and more. The moment I set eyes on you I had to keep reminding my heart to beat. And I've thrown it all away. For what? Nothing. To gratify my own ego because I was a suspicious coward. I am the biggest heel that ever lived. I am nothing. Low, ashamed, beaten, disgraced – nothing without you.

Please let me explain – if nothing else, then at least so that you know the full story. I suspected from the start that you had a greater affection for Mike than for myself, but you assured me that this wasn't the case – that there was nothing between you – so I took your word on trust. I tried not to be hurt when I called to find you cooking for him, or when I heard of the many times you went to the pub together, met up to chat, mentioned one another in conversation. You're neighbours and friends, I understand that. It was only on the night you introduced me to Gabby that my suspicions became darker and more soul-destroying. She told me that you had asked her along to see whether I was 'worth the effort'. But even she could see that you and Mike were better suited and told me so when you were out of the room. I was miserable as hell and she apologised, offered to buy me lunch to talk it over. She promised to find out as much as she could from you. We met later that week.

I guess I was vulnerable and, curiously, so is she, Lucy. We needed one another. We met a few times after that – purely innocently. At first we talked about you – me and you – but that was going nowhere at the time and we found we had other things in common. Soon – and I realised this was happening but did nothing to stop it – we started dropping you as a topic, deliberately avoiding your name. One night, she drove to The Windmill. My mother was away and I was staying up late writing an article. Gabby was terribly upset – I now know that she had argued with Gavin, but of course I didn't know that then. I comforted her and something simply happened. It felt right – pure, white, hot. We became lovers. I could hardly look you in the face afterwards.

Then you told me that she was having an affair with your boss. I was livid. She had compromised all our happiness. I confronted her and she broke down and told me that she needed him but that she loved me. That was a terrible burden. I didn't know what to do. I had no idea that she had grown so dependent on me. And it has simply increased since. She has pursued me relentlessly. She is terrifyingly needy – part Glenn Close in *Fatal Attraction*, part Sharon Stone in *Basic Instinct* – a crazy creature I cannot resist.

I need you to forgive me. If I was asked to choose then I would choose you. But I don't think I have a choice any longer. I don't think that you will afford me that chance.

I saw my future with you. I still wish I had that. It was the best view I have ever seen.

I didn't ever get the chance to tell you that I love you, did I?

Alex

Written on the back of a Get Well card:

Dear Alex,

Christ, you don't half go on! And where are all the motoring metaphors? It might have been a bit more of a racy read if you'd said 'She pursued me like a horny housewife strapped to an Exocet aimed at the planet Clooney.'

Look I'm really sorry you feel bad about this because, honestly, you don't have to. I've been through it all before – I know the ropes 'she wouldn't take no for an answer'/ 'we felt ashamed'/'couldn't resist nature' etc. Greg was just the same. And he used the same "Bumper Book of Excuse Clichés for Boys" when he wrote his letter (shorter and to the point, mind you).

As for getting to choose, well actually you do. In the words of Ewan MacGregor 'Choose Life'. Get one, Alex. Believe me, you'll enjoy it.

Atb,

Lucy

Burr Cottage

Chisbourne

Sunday 26th September

Dear Big Brother,

Any hope that the Gordon family feud would be called to a truce after my accident has been shattered today. All trying to out-do each other in looking after me, so am awash with cups of tea and crammed into the armchair by plumped cushions. Feel very down because have missed out on Bella's hen weekend, but simply not up to it. Don't think Jane went either, but have been unable to get hold of her. Got long letter from Alex yesterday, begging my forgiveness and explaining that Fruit-bat is like Glenn Close in *Fatal Attraction*. Thank goodness she didn't do anything unspeakable to Platforms.

Ripped letter up and wrote very rude letter back, but didn't send it as might start unwanted correspondence. I want him out of my life. Mum says she saw it coming all along because Alex is far too like Greg.

Tell the sheep to avoid wolves wearing Arrans.

Love,

Lucy xx

W Microsoft Word – Marketing ideas91.doc

~~Launching the All Day Breathfresh Tongue Vacuum~~

Fruit-bat still off sick. Huh! I get concussion and manage to struggle back into work, while she just has a few thorns in her backside and qualifies for a long sabbatical. Slave Driver very, very ratty so I assume he must have paid a visit to Wexbury Heights and encountered Alex.

Big Mike told me Alex he has moved in to nurse her and that they are patching things up. I think he expected me to cry, but I just smiled sadly and said I wished them well. Think I treated Alex really badly. Mike argued that Alex has always been weak-willed, but I know who's at fault here. Relieved that he and Fruit-bat are together now. He must go for the rabbit-boiling obsessive type after all.

Ceri dying to know all, but I just recounted barest details of crazed learner driver losing control on High Street, not pointing out that he was my friend's live-in-lover or that Fruit-bat and I had, it transpired, been seeing the same man who visited us both in hospital and caused our boss to moon her bottom. The office has enough to gossip about as it is, particularly as we move to new purpose-built offices in just over a month.

384

From: Lucy Gordon (juicylucy@webbedup.net)
To: Mo Lavender (Hobo-mobo@Hotmail.com)

23.10
Subject: Facing the future – alone again

My last-but-one night sharing the house with Bella and Brick. Went out to Cow in Clover for lovely meal, and persuaded Jane to come along too. She was very subdued, saying that Charles started to change a lot after she moved in, getting more and more controlling and irrational as he headed towards a breakdown. It sounds awful. I suggested she moves back in with me, but she got quite upset, saying, 'Can't you see, Lucy, he needs me more than ever now? He might lose his job. I have to be here for him.' Not a very cheerful thing to talk about just before a wedding. Thankfully Big Mike changed subject with his usual easy wit, telling us about Horsy Tim's new live-in groom who is so madly in love with him that she keeps trying to crawl into his bed each night while he – sleepily thinking it's one of the dogs – shouts, 'Go to your basket!' Unfortunately this didn't make Jane laugh. She really is v. low, poor thing.

Hope the wedding cheers her up. Charles is staying in the psychiatric hospital (or 'clinic' as Jane calls it), but Mike has offered to chaperone us both. Just a quiet day out for the Womaniser of Chisbourne, I guess. L xxx

---

W Microsoft Word – Wedding.doc

Lovely wedding. Cried lots. Drank lots too. Feel slightly squiffy. Just me and Platforms in residence now – one week until we're thrown out. Bella and Brick staying in Honeymoon Suite at Wexbury Hyatt. Ah! Such a gorgeous day. Danced with Jane a lot at party afterwards – she seemed quite happy. Both danced with Big Mike too. He was very sweet, giving two broken-hearted women a spin to Sade and Abba. I told him – rather drunkenly – that he is the loveliest man I know. Not totally sure, as music very loud, but have a feeling he suggested I rent his spare room in Vetch Cottage. What a gent! We're saved. Platforms very happy with idea. I'm going to sleep on it.

From: Lucy Gordon (juicylucy@webbedup.net)
To: Mo Lavender (Hobo-mobo@Hotmail.com)

22.19
Subject: You need friends . . .

This should have been a terrible week – perhaps my worst ever. I am about to be made homeless, my family is at war and my boss is making my life hell. What's more, the notorious Womaniser of Chisbourne wants me to move in with him. On balance, I simply cannot face living with a playboy; Platforms is at an impressionable age.

Yet this has been a great week. I have my best friend back. Jane's been popping around every night, after she's visited Charles the Yuppie in the clinic. We've been working through the last supplies on the Burr Cottage wine rack. I don't think either of us realised how distanced our friendship had become, or how much we'd missed one another until now. Not that she's changed. She's still argumentative and full of crazy ideas, like suggesting I'm reluctant to rent Big Mike's spare room because I'm secretly in love with him, and that I'm wildly jealous of his new Tank Girlfriend, the pierced veterinary nurse. As if! She doesn't know Mike like I do. He's a wolf in sheep's clothing. Well, in a sheepskin jacket.

Was hoping that she'd let me move into her and Charles's cottage in the short term, but she says he could come home any day. I tried calling Mum and Dad again to see if they'd put me up, but when the phone was finally picked up, the sound of arguing in the background was deafening. L xxx

~~Never Miss Again with the Glow-in-the-Dark Loo Light~~

Fruit-bat's atrocious treatment of me since the Alex fiasco is now so obvious that even self-obsessed Mona the receptionist offered me a triangle of her egg mayo sandwich a moment ago and told me, with a sniff, that I could report Fruit-bat to a tribunal.

I'm not going to do anything, however, because I have a sneaking suspicion Slave Driver is already plotting Fruit's demise. He has been holed up in his office all week, looking devious. When I took him through some reports to sign earlier, he was dementedly slamming a nine iron against his golf-ball-on-elastic and I noticed a copy of Fruit's contract on his desk. Have a feeling that fate is on my side. Will trust to it.

Vetch Cottage
Hart's Leap Lane
Chisbourne
Wexbury
Berks

Saturday 9th October

Dear Big Brother,

Came back from riding this morning to find Dad on doorstep with suitcase. He was shivering in cold, and told me with chattering teeth that he is going to solve my housing problems by moving in with me for a while. Over cup of warming tea, he explained that he couldn't cope with atmosphere *chez* Gordon any longer. I tried gently explaining that he should really go home, and that it was too late to keep Burr Cottage on anyway, when doorbell rang and Alice stormed in, announcing that she is moving in too. She looked a bit surprised to find Dad in kitchen, but said she could live with it as long as she could have big room overlooking Mike's garden. Had just made her cup of tea too, when Granny marched in through back door followed by her 'boyfriend', the retired Colonel, who was buckling under weight of four matching suitcases. She ignored us and directed him to carry them upstairs to 'the large room at the front' (mine). I tried to protest when the phone rang. It was Mum, 'Darling, I'm coming to stay with you. We'll be like Thelma and Louise! I can't stand this family any longer. No one compliments my cooking any more.' She hung up with a hysterical sob, before I could explain that the rest of the family was already *in situ*.

Have escaped to Big Mike's. He was v. understanding, and poured me big glass of wine before disappearing to make up the bed in his spare room. He insists that I must stay as long as I like (he's such a joker – 'for ever being one of the options, Lucy'!!). Think I could get used to this, although neighbours are a bit noisy. They argue like mad. Must complain to authorities.

Tell the sheep to cross their hooves for a happy solution.

Love,

Lucy xx

W Microsoft Word – Lucy's squatters.doc

The landlord of Burr Cottage holds me personally responsible for his new squatters. I suppose he has a point, since it is my family who are claiming refugee status in his des res. Thankfully, Mum and Dad have made up their differences and gone back to Roundhead Avenue, but Granny and Alice are refusing to budge until Mum agrees to their 'terms'. Big Mike thinks the whole situation scream-ingly funny, which doesn't help.

Am not sure moving in with him was such a good idea. For one, Mike's dogs terrify Platforms. She spends her time alternating between hiding under the settee and trying to sneak back to Burr Cottage where Granny – who is allergic to cats – throws water over her (at least Granny swears it's water, although I'm sure P smells of

388

gin). My poor little ginger spice is very depressed and keeps giving me mournful, catty looks.

The other big problem is Tank Girlfriend, who is giving me even cattier looks. Big Mike's pierced squeeze clearly thinks I am muscling in on her territory by occupying his spare room (along with a never-used multi-gym, a pile of veterinary books and a large collection of Dinky Toys). She's quite scary. Mike has gone to support her in a regional kickboxing final tonight. Must start flat hunting tomorrow.

Jane popped in after visiting Charles tonight, and we discussed what I should do over a bottle of red. She seems to think I should stay put, and that Mike really likes having me here, but I'm not so sure. Am going to ask Amber Gunton whether any of her estate cottages are free. Must tread carefully, as strongly suspect she and the Womaniser are on-going thing.

From: Lucy Gordon (juicylucy@webbedup.net)
To: Mo Lavender (Hobo-mobo@Hotmail.com)

23.29
Subject: Life on the other side of the fence

Thought I'd better let you know I'm living with Mike. Don't get your hopes up. He has a size eight lover with piercings. I am simply a refugee while Granny and Alice hold my parents to ransom. It's too complicated to explain, but I wanted to let you know that you were right about Mike all along. Enormous. I saw it this morning when his mobile rang and he dashed out of the bedroom stark naked to grab it (the phone, not *it*). I'm getting used to him dashing off at all hours for emergencies – this was a poor cat in a road accident, now saved and recuperating. He is so noble and never, ever complains.

Cow in Clover tonight, with Bella and Brick who were grateful to get out of the caravan and sit near the open fire to warm up. They say progress on the barn conversion is very slow. Alice and Scrumpy were in the pub too, and complained that Granny's boyfriend plays Big Band music too loudly. I asked about the 'terms' they want Mum and Dad to agree to, and Alice explained that she wants a Dormobile, and that Granny wants 'Boffy' to move into the annexe. Fear it'll be a long siege.

Think Tank Girlfriend is staying here tonight. There are big Doc Martens abandoned in the hall, and I can hear loud snoring. L xxx

Vetch Cottage
Chisbourne

Sunday 17th October

Dear Big Brother,

Dad refuses to try to persuade Alice and Granny to come home. He and Mum went back to Roundhead Avenue last week and are getting on really well, and I think they'd rather keep the house as it is – just the two of them. I pointed out that it isn't fair that my old cottage is being used as family feud HQ. He just said, 'Deal with it, Lucy.' Mum looked really proud of him. Am flabbergasted.

I went to see Amber Gunton yesterday after I'd been out riding with Tim and asked her whether she had any property to rent on the estate. She asked whether Mike and I had fallen out. Didn't like to admit that I'm terrified of his new Tank Girlfriend (particularly as Amber might not know about the Womaniser's other dalliance) so I said 'something like that'. She might be able to arrange for me to have one of the holiday cottages, just until I find something permanent.

Rather like the idea as could use a holiday right now. But if I win the Lottery, I'll come to visit you and the sheep in NZ.

Love,
Lucy xx

From: Ceri Dixon (ceri@widgetex.co.uk)
To: Lucy Gordon (lucy@widgetex.co.uk)

08.53
Subject: The bat is flying

Fruit-bat is being transferred to the Birmingham office! She goes in a fortnight. Of course, she's threatening to tell Slave Driver's wife about their affair if he doesn't reconsider, but he's holding strong. Good for Slavey.

From: Lucy Gordon (lucy@widgetex.co.uk)
To: Ceri Dixon (ceri@widgetex.co.uk)

09.01
Subject: Re: The bat is flying

Yippeeeeeeee! I wonder what'll happen to Fruit-bat's flat when she goes?
   Hang on, are you saying that you know about her and SD?

From: Ceri Dixon (ceri@widgetex.co.uk)
To: Lucy Gordon (lucy@widgetex.co.uk)

09.10
Subject: You heard it here first

I've known all along, Lucy. Doh! When will you ever *listen*?!?

W Microsoft Word – Marketing ideas 93.doc

~~Why every home should have a fifty-melody chiming doorbell~~
Fruit-bat in evil mood about her transfer, and picking on me like mad. She's just reminded me about the charity mini-marathon we agreed to run this weekend, saying, 'I can tell you've not been

training, Lucy. Shall I tell the organisers you've had a change of heart?' I ground my teeth and said nothing. Bet she doesn't turn up either.

From: Lucy Gordon (juicylucy@webbedup.net)
To: Mo Lavender (Hobo-mobo@Hotmail.com)

20.55
Subject: The siege is holding – just

Mike in furious mood when I got home tonight, demanding to know why I've asked Amber Gunton if I can rent one of her cottages. I explained that I don't want to get between him and Tank Girlfriend. He looked really hurt and showed off a DIY barrier he's constructed to keep the dogs in the kitchen and protect darling Platforms. It's made out of an old wooden laundry airer, is very lop-sided and poor Mike's fingers are full of splinters. I promised I'd reconsider staying on as his lodger, but still secretly fear that TG will beat me up with her Thai kickboxing moves if I do. She turned up an hour ago and waited until Mike was in the kitchen to say, 'You still here? I thought you were looking for a flat to rent?' Then she gave me a menacing look and fiddled with her eyebrow stud. I fled to Jane's for calming drink.

Jane says Charles the Yuppie is so much better he'll be coming out of his clinic next week, although he won't be going back to work in the City. She is in a quandary because she is happy to support him while he looks for a less stressful job, but to do this she will have to carry on giving driving lessons. Charles's psychiatrist has told Jane that to aid recovery, he must not see her car under any circumstances. She's been keeping it outside Burr Cottage, but thinks our old landlord is about to evict Granny, Alice and her Fiesta. L xxx

Have just come back from horse riding to find that Mike has moved the multi-gym and veterinary books out of my room, and has put the Dinky Toy collection into several shoe boxes. He says I can redecorate any way I like.

Tank Girlfriend is clearly livid. When I asked Mike if Jane could keep her car in his garage, she butted in: 'But he's just filled it with stuff so that you can make free with his spare room. Some people are so selfish!' She has a point. Must be more charitable.

Vetch Cottage
Chisbourne

Sunday 24th October

Dear Big Brother,

Was just about to set out to Mum and Dad's house (after hopeless attempt to persuade Granny and Alice to come too and preferably stay on there) when Fruit-bat's BMW appeared in our drive and she and Alex jumped out. It's the first time I've seen Alex since the hospital thing and he looked really embarrassed, but Fruit had no such humility and said, 'Hurry up and get changed, Lucy. We have a race to run.' Was about to tell her to get stuffed when Mike and Tank Girlfriend came outside to see who had arrived, and Fruit-bat loudly announced that I was running a mini-marathon for charity, insisting that they should come along to cheer us on. Then she started banging on about all the money we were going to raise for 'poor little starving cats'. I had no choice but to fetch my shorts and trainers. Had vague recollection that the event was actually fundraising for a home for retired jockeys, but no time to question this.

Cannot believe I made it around course. Was so slow that I finished behind two men dressed as a pantomime horse. Of course Fruit-bat hardly broke into a sweat and was wearing a tin-foil cloak and laughing delightedly when I finally staggered over the finish line close to death. On the way home, Mike told me that he saw her taking a shortcut through a wood. She cheated! And then, when I was laughing and coughing and crying all at once, he said, 'You will stay with me, won't you Lucy?' He looked so anxious and familiar and friendly that I nodded, unable to speak. I guess charity does begin at home.

Someone should tell that to the rest of the Gordons.

Jog around a few sheep – the endorphin rush is fantastic.

Love,

Lucy xx

Cutting from *Wexbury Gazette* pinned to Widgetex notice board:

Mini Marathon Raises Fun and Funds

The third annual Thrushfield Mini Marathon took place last Sunday, raising funds for the Retired Jockey Fund. The event, sponsored by TeluTalk Limited, was well attended, with many competitors running the thirteen miles in fancy dress costume. Local businesswoman and fastest woman around the course, Gabriella Peartree (pictured right with partner, Alex Harland), said of her run. 'I was very pleased with my time. I have trained hard and fought hard to achieve this. This will be my legacy to Wexbury, which I leave after too short a stay, but which will retain a place in my heart for ever.'

~~Inflatable pet barriers – a kinder way to stop them stray~~

Tomorrow is Fruit-bat's last day before she transfers to our Birmingham office.

Have hardly spoken to her since she cheated on the mini-marathon last Sunday. But this afternoon I'm certain I heard her sniffing tearfully as she packed her photograph of Alex into a cardboard box, along with three executive toys and a lop-sided cactus. Can't help feeling a bit sorry for her. Everyone is talking about the move to the new purpose-built office in Faulkstone Business Park next month. The move was her idea, and she's already had a quiet word with the planners so that her office has direct views over the Nilson Formula One team's HQ. Now she'll never get to ogle Pedro Bertolli or Garth Fording.

Seeing her sad face, I broke my silence and asked her whether she's planning to have a leaving drinks session or anything. Should have kept my trap shut. She said, 'Oh Lucy, that's so sweet of you! I wasn't going to bother, but maybe you could lure me out for a glass of bubbly after all.' Drat! Have asked around and everyone's pretending to be busy tomorrow night. At this rate it'll just be me and Fruit-bat. I put a notice up on the board, but it's already been 'edited'.

Notice on Widgetex staff board:

Leaving Party

Fruit-bat

Please join ~~Gabby~~ at the Lock Inn on Friday night, where

Getting plastered and trying to snog Gavin Slater again

she will be ~~saying farewell to her colleagues at Widgetex Wexbury.~~
Meet 6.00.

W Microsoft Word – Lucy's promoted!!.doc

Managed to bribe Ceri, Mona and Wendy from Accounts to come along to Fruit-bat's leaving drinks in the Lock Inn by promising them that I'll have a word with Slavey about extended Christmas leave. You see, I can now do this because the MOST exciting thing happened today. I was promoted! I have Fruit-bat's job. Yes, yes, yes! Vowed the others to secrecy tonight, but of course Ceri couldn't resist telling Fruit, who went very pale and quiet and wished me good luck, which was very noble of her, I thought. Then she downed her fizzy wine super-fast and explained that she had to get back to packing up her flat as the removers were coming first thing tomorrow. Poor thing. I felt really guilty, but Ceri and Mona insisted that it was the least Fruit deserved and told me that she'd tried to stop Slave Driver giving me the job by saying that I couldn't be trusted and that I'd cheated when running a mini-marathon for charity. I was horrified: 'But she cheated!'

'That's business,' Ceri explained wisely. 'You'll have to toughen up now you're in management, Lucy. Starting tonight. Buy another round of drinks and we'll tell you how.'

Came home to tell Mike what's happened, but Tank Girlfriend was *in situ*, so quickly retreated to my room. But Mike followed me up to tell me that the Burr Cottage landlord tried unsuccessfully to have Granny and Alice evicted this afternoon. Scrumpy's road-protesting experience saved them, apparently. He's now building a tunnel in the garden. It's too dark to see, but I'm sure he's unearthed all the bulbs Jane planted.

Pinned above bar in Cow in Clover:

𝕳𝖆𝖑𝖑𝖔𝖜𝖊𝖊𝖓 𝕻𝖆𝖗𝖙𝖞

(𝕱𝖆𝖓𝖈𝖞 𝖉𝖗𝖊𝖘𝖘)

𝕾𝖆𝖙𝖚𝖗𝖉𝖆𝖞 30th 𝕺𝖈𝖙𝖔𝖇𝖊𝖗 𝖋𝖗𝖔𝖒 7𝖕.𝖒.

𝕱𝖗𝖊𝖊 𝖇𝖑𝖆𝖈𝖐 𝖛𝖔𝖉𝖐𝖆 𝖆𝖑𝖑 𝖓𝖎𝖌𝖍𝖙 𝖙𝖔 𝖇𝖊𝖘𝖙 𝖈𝖔𝖘𝖙𝖚𝖒𝖊

𝕭𝖆𝖗 𝖋𝖔𝖔𝖉

From: Lucy Gordon (juicylucy@webbedup.net)
To: Mo Lavender (Hobo-mobo@Hotmail.com)

23.57
Subject: Spooky goings on

Great Halloween party at Cow in Clover where I told everyone the exciting news that I have been promoted to fill Fruit-bat's Jimmy Choos. I dressed as a pumpkin. Granny and Alice were there (Blithe Spirit and Marilyn Manson respectively). They say Scrumpy's staying put in his tunnel beneath the Burr Cottage garden. Then Jane arrived with Charles the Yuppie. He looks much calmer than before his breakdown, although he didn't seem to know who I was. Jane says it's the drugs. She's delighted to have him home at last, with her car safely hidden in Big Mike's garage. She asked where he was, and I explained that Tank Girlfriend had tickets for the 'Freak Out' party at Basborough's only gay pub, The Rub Bar. He wasn't keen, although she promised there'd be lots of other straight people there.

But just as last orders were being called, Mike himself turned up wearing last year's Dracula mask. I looked around for Tank Girlfriend (who doesn't need to dress up to look scary) but she wasn't with him. He bought everyone a drink and loudly announced that 'Lucy and I are having a bonfire party next weekend and you're all invited!'

This is v. strange. Why me and him, not TG and him? And where is his pierced lover? Can't get answers as Mike came home and promptly passed out drunk on sofa. L xxx

---

W Microsoft Word – Marketing ideas95.doc

~~Cook Vegetables with Ultrasound – the Healthy Option~~

I get to choose my company car this week. Have been poring over brochures with the help of Jane and Big Mike. Jane prefers Golf for handling and reliability; Mike favours Ford Puma as he says it matches my personality – fun and racy.

He has made no mention of his odd behaviour last Saturday, although he claims that he only passed out on sofa so that he was in convenient position to watch Japanese Grand Prix in early hours. Apparently Mike's hero, Pedro Bertolli, was in third place at one point, but then his engine blew. I said I shan't be ordering a Nilson car as obviously very unreliable, but Mike says it's not a make, it's the name of the man who owns the team. When I told him that the new Widgetex office overlooks Nilson HQ, he jumped up and hugged me. I quickly pointed out that there are no openings for a veterinary surgeon in marketing department.

No sign of Tank Girlfriend all week. Mike says they're giving each other 'space'. He has used his free evenings to design an invitation to 'our' bonfire party.

BONFIRE PARTY
Come and have an EXPLOSIVE time with Mike and Lucy!!!!

Vetch Cottage, Hart's Leap Lane, Chisbourne
Friday 5ᵗʰ November from 8p.m.
Bring a bottle

W **Microsoft Word – Lucy lights the touch-paper.doc**

Waiting for our guests to arrive. I have taken charge of catering, while Mike organises 'pyrotechnics' (large box of assorted fireworks bought in car boot sale, minus instructions). Am slightly worried about safety angle, but Mike assures me that the chestnuts I am roasting are far more likely to cause injury than his squibs. I asked him if he's invited Tank Girlfriend, but he says she's going to display in Basborough with her friends. Oh! Someone's arrived!

Have just peeked out of window and seen Amber Gunton wandering to dark end of garden with Mike, both deep in conversation. Can guess why TG needs 'space'.

From: Lucy Gordon (juicylucy@webbedup.net)
To: Mo Lavender (Hobo-mobo@Hotmail.com)

13.42
Subject: Explosive isn't the word

Went riding with Jane this morning. Horsy Tim is away at
Stoneleigh attending big horsy trade fair. We rode very slowly to

accommodate hangovers and conduct full post-mortem of last night's bonfire party. Jane missed out on most of the fun as Charles had a major relapse after Mike asked him to fetch more firewood from the garage. He'd forgotten that Jane is keeping her driving school car there (Charles's psychiatrist has advised her to hide it from him as it triggered his breakdown). They went home early when Charles started crying and muttering, 'Mirror, signal, manoeuvre', although Jane says he's fine now and was happily watching *The Waltons* when she left. She was dying to know what she missed.

So I told her about the 'fireworks' that Mike had bought cheaply at a car boot sale and which turned out to be stolen from a professional display and far too large for a village garden. One rocket set light to the shed, another exploded in a Victoria plum tree, and a third shot over the fence into the Burr Cottage garden. Granny and Alice, who were stuffing themselves with my baked potatoes at the time, watched in amazement as fireball disappeared from view. Then, a few seconds later, we all heard screaming. It turns out the rocket entered the tunnel Scrumpy is occupying to avoid eviction. Thankfully, he escaped with just a few singed dreadlocks, although Alice is threatening to sue Mike for deliberate tunnel-sabotage. He just handed her a sparkler and promised to buy Scrumpy a hat, then shot me a lovely wink. He was, it has to be said, in raring spirits and strangely sexy all night. This, I am certain, was due to the presence of his personal Mrs Robinson – the Womaniser's long-standing married mistress, Lady G – who, like Mike, made a point of hanging around me to deflect attention. This is an old trick of theirs dating back to the Chips production.

Amber Gunton thought the business with Scrumpy and the hat was a scream. Afterwards, she turned to me and said, 'I hope Mike has come clean about how he feels – I've been badgering him to tell you the truth for months.' Am sure she was talking about their affair (and possibly trying to talk me into a more hands-on co-conspirator/ready alibi role). I hastily changed subject to cars (no, I am not mourning Alex – I am celebrating my promotion by choosing my exec mobile!).

Thought Jane would find this particular piece of adulterous party gossip fascinating, but all she said was, 'I hope Amber agrees with me about the Golf.' Daren't tell her I've already ordered Puma in Radiant Red. Rather like idea of being 'fun and racy'. L xxx

---

W Microsoft Word – spaced out.doc

Tank Girlfriend has just paid Big Mike an unexpected visit while he was teaching me to cook sticky toffee pudding (had no idea he was so talented). Think she's a bit fed up of being given so much 'space'. I've left them alone to talk and eat pudding alone. No bad thing, as I'm on a diet. Managed forty minutes on The Sweatshop treadmill earlier, entranced by MTV showing all Spice Girls' solo hits. Was amazed to encounter Amber Gunton wandering around wearing scarlet leotard and strange headphone things. Apparently she's started to teach aerobics lessons there. She says she does it to keep herself occupied while her husband's away. I thought Mike did that (and gets her just as hot and sweaty), but I said nothing. Refused to join her 'Bums and Tums' class.

Later: Heard TG slam door and popped downstairs to find Mike covered with sticky toffee pudding. He was bright red and fled to bathroom. Suspect they were using it as love aid. The Womaniser of Chisbourne has a sinfully sweet tooth.

Friday 12th November

Dear Big Brother,

Lots of good news! I have been promoted, and even better
. . . Granny and Alice have left Burr Cottage and moved back
with the parents. At last! They are both living in the annexe
apparently. Granny's lover has gone back to the retirement
home, and Alice's boyfriend Scrumpy has moved into a squat
in Basborough. I am so relieved that Burr Cottage is finally
empty, and that I can hand the keys over to the landlord. When
I called him tonight, he insisted that I forfeit my deposit to
make up for the inconvenience my family has caused. Big Mike
offered to cook treacle tart to cheer me up, but I explained that
I was going to supper with Jane and Charles.

Charles says he wants to train as a dry-stone-wall builder. I
pointed out that there's not much call for those in West
Berkshire, so he's looking into thatching courses instead. I
quietly asked Jane if they were going to be okay financially on
just her salary, but she says that Charles has sold his London
flat for a huge profit so they can live off that until he finds his
new calling. She's so happy to have him home. I never thought
the relationship would work, but now I see I was wrong. They
are really good together. I'm sorry, Big Brother, but that's the
truth. Going mad was the best thing he's ever done.

Came back to find Mike outside with huge torch and
scrubbing brush, trying to erase something that had been
daubed on the front door. He tried his best to hide it and usher
me inside, but I'm sure I read 'KILL' and 'CAT'. Suspect it's
some loony animal rights protesters mistakenly targeting him
for putting down poor old, sick moggies.

He is also very kind to sheep.

Love,

Lucy xx

402

W Microsoft Word – Tanks but no tanks.doc

Mike has chucked Tank Girlfriend! I only know because her little brother is one of Bella's GCSE students at St Cuthbert's and he told her that he couldn't finish his homework because his psychotic sister had stolen his paints to graffiti her ex's house. Bella says he was really proud of this. Apparently the entire family is 'dysfunctional' and they're on every blacklist going. Hope Mike will be okay, although am certain Amber will comfort him – and protect him with one of Lord Gunton's shotguns.

W Microsoft Word – Lucy's under a death threat.doc

Mike and I were just settling down to watch *EastEnders* to-night when a brick came flying through the window, narrowly missing Platforms. Tied to it was a note 'Your days are numbered.' Awful! I told Mike about what Bella had said and that he might be in serious danger. He went very pale and said, 'No, Lucy, I think you're the one in danger. It's you that she wants to kill. She found this.' He showed me a photograph taken last Christmas Eve. Can't remember it being taken at all. I'm wearing stockings and lying on his sofa. Oh Christ! Platforms and I have a price on our heads.

WIDGETEX LTD
Memo
To: Lucy Gordon
Re: Move to Faulkstone Business Park

As you know, Gabriella Peartree originally held the brief to oversee this department's transfer to the new premises as part of the overall relocation directive for Widgetex. Upon her departure to Birmingham, I was hoping that I would be able to take over. However, I have glanced at my diary and see that there is not sufficient management time in my hectic schedule. As such I am assigning the task to you. I appreciate that you have only just taken over Gabby's role, but I am confident that it is well within your grasp.

Incidentally, I shall be away for the remainder of the week playing golf in Kent.

Gavin Slater

From: Ceri Dixon (ceri@widgetex.co.uk)
To: Lucy Gordon (lucy@widgetex.co.uk)

12.16
Subject: Relocation

Hear that you've got lumbered with the Job that No One Wants, you poor thing (I told Slave Driver that I have an uncontrollable attraction to removal men when he asked me – seemed to do the trick).
Please note:

- My gonks require separate travelling box and cannot under any circumstances be thrown into crates with rest of office paraphernalia.
- My potted fig is ULTRA-sensitive to changes in atmospheric pressure, heat, draughts and light. It will require isolation before and after the move, plus a controlled removal from this office and climate-adjusted introduction into the new one.
- I want a desk by a window (overlooking Nilson HQ if poss). Ta.

W Microsoft Word – Marketing ideas97.doc

~~The Eco-friendly Way to See off Unwanted Cats from Your Garden –Introducing the Rotting Vegweiler®~~

Terrible morning talking through office move with Slave Driver. I have less than a fortnight to organise it. Escaped for sandwich at lunchtime and almost fainted with horror as bumped into Tank ex-Girlfriend loitering by Clintons card shop with huge, tattooed man.

Thought she was about to set him on me like trained Rottweiler, but to my amazement she was really friendly, introducing him as her new boyfriend, Didge. Such a relief.

From: Lucy Gordon (juicylucy@webbedup.net)
To: Mo Lavender (Hobo-mobo@Hotmail.com)

00.27
Subject: Tanks for the memory

Have been living in fear for my and Platform's lives ever since Mike dumped his young scary squeeze and she mistakenly thought I was the reason (as if!). Now mercifully free from fatwa (or in her case, thinwa). Told Big Mike that Tank ex-Girlfriend no longer gunning for my blood, but he said he knew that already, that her new boyfriend Didge has been collecting her from work all week and that she is no longer making threatening gestures at Mike with the claw-clippers in the surgery. Felt v. annoyed that Mike had said nothing about this, and allowed me to carry on fearing for my life – he's even been checking my room for me before I go to bed to make sure there are no venomous snakes planted in laundry basket etc. Suspect he's been too preoccupied by stupid New Year's Eve party to think of much else. Villagers are determined to have a big one to make up for the Millennium Party, which was cancelled at the last minute because an 'unexploded bomb' was discovered under the village green (turned out to be an old petrol tank from a Morris 8).

Talk was of nothing else tonight in Cow in Clover. Village Hall committee are dead set against one, fearing 'unruly element', and pressing for pathetic sing-song thing on New Year's Day (as if anyone will want to go to that with the hangovers we're all planning). Mike says that if they won't change their minds, 'We'll have a party at Vetch Cottage!' (*Why* is he always doing this? He has more parties than Elton John and ropes me in as his Kiki Dee.) Cheers greeted this, and his glass wasn't empty all night, but I fear he might have over-stretched himself on this one. The bonfire party was chaotic enough, especially the firework display, and there's no way I'm doing the catering. L xxx

---

Sunday Lunch Menu – The Annexe, 13 Roundhead Avenue, Wexbury.

Starter (Chef: Violet Beasley)
Bloody Mary Soup with Lime Tequila Cream Swirls and Chilli Gin Croutons

Main Course (Chef: Alice Gordon)
Flash-fried Aubergine steaks, marinated in Merrydown, topped with Lentil and Mung Bean caviar and served on a bed of Spicy Smash

Dessert (Chef: Violet Beasley)
Sherry Trifle with extra Sherry

Accompanied by five bottles of Lambrusco Bianco

Vetch Cottage
Chisbourne

Sunday 28th November

Dear Big Brother,

Had Sunday lunch in the annexe today, where Alice and Granny were determined to out-cook each other. They are both eager to ingratiate themselves with Mum and Dad, who still haven't entirely forgiven them for The Siege of Burr Cottage and have dramatically limited their access to the drinks cabinet/video/freezer by fitting a sliding bolt on their side of the adjoining door. Both clearly want the other to move out (Alice so that she can move Scrumpy in, Granny so she can shack up with the RAF boffer). It's patently clear that Mum and Dad don't want either coming 'over the wall', as they are enjoying a prolonged second honeymoon. The way they keep kissing, whispering to each other and sharing private jokes was sweet at first but has now become frankly off-putting. They spoon-fed each other trifle today. Not so bad, you might think, but it was practically inedible because Granny had dissolved a whole bottle of sherry in the sponge and half a pint of brandy in the jelly.

No riding yesterday because Horsy Tim was out hunting, as was Jane. They are on talking terms again, which is a relief (was never really sure why they stopped). Charles followed the hunt on a pedal bike apparently – last seen free-wheeling at speed in opposite direction wearing brand new Barbour, green wellies and flat-cap. Don't think he quite blends into his rural setting yet. Can't imagine him thatching, although Bella says she's sure Jane told her he was going to forge weather vanes.

Went to admire progress on the Bs' barn conversion last night, but far too cold outside to linger long and there's only so many admiring phrases you can think up for three piles of rubble and a lot of mud. Still, the Bs seem happy enough and Mum and Dad's caravan was surprisingly toasty. Brick is teaching the guitar privately at St Cuthbert's to make some extra cash, although he has yet to find full-time work. He says he's applied to the Nilson Formula One team. I hold out no hope for a motorcycle courier and sometime rock musician. I think Mike applied once, and he's a vet.

Frankly the sheep stand a better chance (potential team mascot).

Love,

Lucy xx

Posted on the Vetch Cottage fridge:

Mike,

Newcomers alert! I've just popped home during my lunch hour to fetch a schedule I'd left behind. There are two cars parked outside Burr Cottage, one of them my ex-landlord's shiny Rover. He's showing a young family around. When they saw me, I heard them asking about the neighbours, but the landlord hustled them inside before I could introduce myself and point out that the boiler keeps packing up.

As if that's not enough, I've also spotted Granny's Dolomite careering along Chisbourne High Street. Her boyfriend was sitting in passenger seat leafing through estate agents' details.

I have to work late again tonight. Can you feed Platforms? And if you're using your computer, can you remember to plug my radio alarm clock back in this time? Thanks.

Lucy

W Microsoft Word – Marketing ideas98.doc

~~Roof-rack-Mounted Singing Santas –~~
~~the final thrust towards Christmas~~

I'm working late in order to get some peace and apply mind to orchestrating marketing department's move. Went to see new Faulkstone Business Park offices with Slave Driver today, and am seriously impressed. My office is HUGE and looks right over Nilson Formula One team HQ. Have something to thank Fruit-bat for.

Would far rather work at home, but Big Mike has taken to using his computer each evening, which is still in his old spare room, i.e. my bedroom. He claims to be designing invitations for his New Year's Eve party (I call it 'his', not 'our' advisedly), but last night I found him crouched over Crash Bandicoot, desperately trying to

jump a glacier and collect a golden key. Will demand computer be
moved this weekend.

W Microsoft Word – Lucy the lodger.doc

Am in my room with Mike, who is trying to take his computer apart
in order to move it, but has drunk at least four pints in Cow in
Clover tonight and keeps falling over the cables and bumping his
head on the desk. Thank heavens my laptop is so transportable. I
offered to help, but he insists on doing it alone. Feel a bit guilty as I
only mentioned it in passing in Cow but somehow managed to
trigger huge debate about men-and-toys around table. Bella started
complaining that Brick brings bits of motorcycle into the caravan
and Jane whinged that Charles leaves his golf clubs in the hall. After
several minutes' haranguing the men retreated to the bar to discuss
Mike's party. Bella says that Mike and I are turning into middle-
aged couple. I took great issue and pointed out that I am his tenant.
Quickly changed subject to my mad grandmother's house-hunt in
village which caused such shock that B and J needed instant refills.
Miss Bella's old pub night score sheets that she used to post up on
the Burr Cottage fridge. Tonight was worthy of one.

Must go to bathroom as Mike's trousers have just split while he
was bending over to pull out his mouse and am too embarrassed to
tell him.

Later: Mike is asleep on my bed. Can't wake him up and what's
worse, he's lying on my nightie. Will have to sleep on sofa with his
dogs, who dribble like mad. May put coat on.

W Microsoft Word – Lucy's feeling neighbourly.doc

Have just woken up on sofa to see removal van outside. New family
moving into Burr Cottage. They look nice enough – he has bright
ginger hair like Jane's and she's very small and round. They have
lots of small, round, ginger children who all look alike so hard to

count them. Maybe three. Have already spotted mountain bikes and tennis rackets, so obviously healthy, and lots of books, so clever too. Can't wait to introduce myself. I wonder if Mike's still on my bed?

4p.m.

He was, along with Platforms who was looking quite comfortable lying around his neck like fox fur stole (always terrified of letting her out on Saturdays in case local hunt mistake her identity, although Jane swears that never happens). Anyway, I clambered over all the bits of computer lying around the room and told Mike that we had new neighbours. Took a while to get message across as think he was a bit hungover.

When he came downstairs, he took one look out of the window and ducked down like a sniper, moaning, 'No, no, no!' When I asked him what was wrong he said, 'Nothing! Just dropped a contact lens' and crawled on all fours into kitchen. Very odd as a) he didn't search for the dropped lens and b) he doesn't wear lenses.

Have introduced myself to the neighbours, who are called Leslie (he) and Peta (she). Get very confused by ambiguous names. I went off them a bit when they joked that the previous tenants in Burr Cottage had terrible taste in décor. Did not invite them round for drinks as intended, especially when I saw Mike running to his car, carrying coat in front of his face and driving away at speed.

WIDGETEX LTD
Memo
To: All staff
Re: Missing Items
In the course of this week's move several items have gone missing, namely:
- All next year's promotional brochures.
- Ceri Dixon's gonk collection (approx 16 items in a cardboard box marked with the words 'Fragile', 'This Way Up', 'Live Animal Transportation' and 'The Gonk-mobile').

- Gavin Slater's office putter.
- Mona Gillespie's rubber plant (approx 4 feet, very shiny leaves, contained in red pot)
- Lucy Gordon's office computer (containing ALL marketing information for next quarter, plus irreplaceable personal files).

Should any members of staff have noticed these items, please notify Lucy immediately on Ext: 6969 (NB: do NOT email until she has been allocated a temporary computer). Many thanks.

Lucy Gordon

Written on the back of new office coffee machine instructions:

Aghhh! The move from Wexbury town centre to Faulkstone Business Park has been a nightmare. Felt very sentimental leaving old building, even though parking was a nightmare and corridors smelled musty. At least the shops were near by. Have suddenly realised that Christmas is just around the corner and I haven't bought a single present. Was planning to do a blitz this weekend, but Slavey has just announced that he wants me to come in here on Saturday to make up for lost work time this week. If his putter were handy, I'd clobber him with it. Looks like I'll have to buy everyone Widgetex products at a staff discount and count the days until they fall apart.

Christmas list:
Mum – Into cooking again. Widgetex Ultrasound Vegetable Cooker
Dad – DIY. Widgetex Shed-alert CCTV system (with optional arcade games)
Alice – Still grieving trees. Widgetex Eco-friendly RottingVegweiler®
Jeremy – (NB: missed posting date for NZ). Widgetex Novelty Musical Y-fronts

Granny – Alcoholic. Gin, sherry or vodka (can always use Drinks Direct)

Jane – Living with mad man. Widgetex Self Defence Stungun key ring (prototype)

Bella – Ultra-fashionable. Widgetex Reflexology Socks (glitter design)

Ceri – Chocaholic/man-eater. Chocolate body-builder?

Mike – Womaniser. Widgetex All-Day-Breathfresh™ Electronic dental ioniser

---

'Hi, this is Lucy and Mike's answer phone. We're not around to take your call, so leave a message and we'll get back to you.' Beep.
'It's Lucy. I'm still here at the office. All looking much better now, although computer still hasn't turned up. I was looking for it when you called; that's why you got my voice-mail. So, yes I'll pick up some wine on the way home and then help you decorate the house tonight. That makes me feel so Christmassy! I love the idea of returning home to roaring fire, twinkling tree and good claret. Guess you're out on call, so I'll see you when one of us finally gets home.'

W Microsoft Word – Lucy's baubleless.doc

Mike was in the pub when I got back tonight. Found no evidence of Christmas decorations – not even a box of dud fairy lights. Total anti-climax. Bumped into Peta, our new neighbour, and she said that she'd called around earlier to ask if we'd got a stepladder they could borrow but that no one had answered the door, even though 'I'm quite sure I saw your husband coming in not ten minutes earlier'. I explained that Mike is not my husband, and went in search of stepladder. Then I remembered I had a bottle of wine in my bag so pulled it out and asked Peta if she'd like some, but I think she got the wrong idea because she said, 'That's very kind,' and just took the whole thing back inside with her, along with the step-ladder, and shut the door on me. Think she's a bit weird. No wonder Mike's avoiding them, although he totally over-reacted when he came back from the pub and found I'd lent them his stepladder. I was decidedly ratty and tired from working so late and have stomped sulkily to bed complaining about lack of charitable spirit and decorations.

Vetch Cottage
Chisbourne

Sunday 12th December

Dear Big Brother,

Came home yesterday absolutely shattered (Slave Driver demanded) to find Mike putting finishing touches to the 'decorations' he had promised and not delivered. It turns out that he hadn't been talking about wrapping tinsel around the beams at all. He was decorating my room! That's why he needed the stepladder and was so cross when he found I'd lent it to the weird new neighbours. Ah! It looks fantastic in white, bright blues and terracotta – like sleeping in a Greek island. I suggested asking the neighbours, Leslie and Peta, around to show off, but Mike went very pale and said, 'I think there's something you need to know, Lucy.' It transpires that Leslie is fanatical about breeding reptiles. He used to bring them to Mike's veterinary practice for treatment until one of them – a rare and poisonous type of tree snake – escaped from Leslie's clutches and tried to eat a budgie with a broken leg. When Mike went to rescue the little mite, he accidentally trod on the snake and killed it. Mike says that Leslie vowed revenge. Now he's turned up in the village and Mike is certain an anaconda will pop up in his bath any day. He's even taped up the cat flap and is wearing wellies indoors.

This is awful. We're living next to a snake-breeding maniac. The only positive thing to come out of it is that telling the family about it seems to have put Granny off the idea of living in the village, at least for now.

Tell the sheep to look out for snakes.

Love,

Lucy xx

W Microsoft Word – Marketing ideas99.doc

~~Is there a niche market for Novelty Prosthetics?~~

Surrounded by debris from office party. Suspect all carpets will need to be replaced and boardroom table is beyond the skills of most French polishers. Photo-copier packed up whilst Xeroxing its fifteenth bottom (although not before everyone admired A3 colour photostat of Colin the security guard's tattoo) and Slave Driver's golf clubs have been used to fire Max Pax coffee cups from the roof onto Nilson HQ's car park. Usual office party, then. I maintained my dignity throughout, I hope, although still have pine needles in strange places from falling into Christmas tree.

More concerned by the fact my computer is still missing. Am currently 'hot-desking' on other people's workstations (not hard today as most of the department is off sick with alcohol poisoning). Latest trend is screensaver that plays this year's Christmas Hit, the 'Yodelling Gerbil' song. Now can't get it out of my head. Am writing this on Slave Driver's 600Mhz Turbo-charged Compaq because I know that he hates computers and never, ever uses it (although the odd thing is that it has loads of down-loaded Web-browsing software and a pile of .gif files, so someone else has clearly had the same idea).

Fleet manager says my car won't be arriving until the middle of January because I specified such 'extravagant extras' (hardly think air con and electric windows count as extravagance given that Fruitbat had on-board computer and multi-stacker CD in her BMW). This is a bit of a problem as I agreed to sell my car to Dad very cheaply to give to Alice as combined Christmas, Birthday and 'Well done on your re-takes' present. May be forced to catch bus into work after Christmas unless Santa brings me roller blades.

Dear Lucy and Mick(?)

(Sorry, we didn't catch your name!)

Would you both like to come for a festive drink this evening to celebrate the season of our Saviour? We must apologise in advance for the appalling decoration of the cottage – we're still 'undoing' the previous occupants' bad taste! But you would be most welcome into our humble home.

Leslie and Peta Dent and family

Christmas list: The Final Score

(Queues in Crump Hopkins Department Store = 4.5 miles)

(Number of bruises collected from fighting man for last Pokémon card for cousin's son = 6)

(Mum – Into cooking again. ~~Widgetex Ultrasound Vegetable Cooker~~ Sabatier professional sushi knife set

Dad – DIY. ~~Widgetex Shed-alert CCTV system (with optional arcade games)~~ Cordless Power Drill

Alice – Still grieving trees. ~~Widgetex Eco-friendly RottingVegweiller~~® Furry Dice and Hemp car-seat covers (purple tie-dye)

Jeremy – (NB: missed posting date for NZ). Widgetex Novelty Musical Y-fronts (sent already)

Granny – Alcoholic. ~~Gin, sherry or vodka (can always use Drinks Direct)~~ Body Shop Detox-in-a-Box gift set

Jane – Living with mad man. ~~Widgetex Self-Defence Stungun key ring (prototype)~~ Latest Jilly Cooper novel

Bella – Ultra-fashionable. ~~Widgetex Reflexology Socks (glitter design)~~ Latest Irvine Welsh novel

Ceri – Chocaholic/man-eater. ~~Chocolate body-builder?~~ Milk Tray

Mike – Womaniser. ~~Widgetex All-Day-Breathfresh™ Electronic dental ioniser~~ Jumper

Christmas shopping with Big Mike this morning. We had great fun buying him lots of silly 'neighbour disguises' including Groucho Marx moustache and cigar, and Homer Simpson mask. Love shopping with him as always such a giggle.

Got home to find Leslie and Peta had slipped card under the door inviting us around for drinks tonight. Mike went pale and decided none of his disguises would hide his identity from Leslie the snake-mad vet-hater, so he is planning to creep out to the pub and send me next door to play pet detective. Would far rather go to pub too, especially as mulled wine half price tonight and all friends will be there for carols. Will have to wear trousers tucked into boots in case loose asp is slithering around seeking warmth.

Later: Leslie and Peta offered me a very small sherry and listened to Cliff Richard song on repeated loop all the time I was there. I excused myself to loo several times in order to suss out snake population. Found no evidence of reptiles whatsoever, although almost everything covered in dust-sheets as rampant DIY in progress. Eventually asked L and P whether they were into pets, but they said their youngest is allergic to fur and feathers. Taking the cue I said, 'What about snakes? I hear they make great companions.'

I swear Leslie had tears in his eyes as he whipped my empty glass away and went to wash it up. While he was out of the room, Peta explained that he had been unable to go near snakes since he lost his favourite one in a tragic accident. 'He never got over it,' she told me sadly. 'He's been a lot better since he found God, but he still refuses to forgive Sid's murderer.' Aghhh! Escaped to pub to break the news to Mike. He took it very well, although suspect he'll be less happy when he's sober. He just put on his Homer Simpson mask and grabbed me under mistletoe for strange, rubbery kiss, wailing, 'Save me, Marge, you're my only hope.' Think he's cracking under the pressure, poor man. We sang lots of carols with the Bs, Jane, Charles and Horsy Tim, but I now can't get Cliff Richard song out of my head. Was humming it as we walked home from pub, when Mike turned to me and said 'I think I should invite Leslie and Peta to our New Year's Eve party, Lucy. It's the only way to show how sorry I am.' Before I had a chance to argue, he shoved an invitation through their letterbox. Hope they have other plans. I also hope they are not easily shocked, because Mike decided that his Bonfire design (which I thought had a tasteful simplicity) was 'totally women's bloody institute' and so has really gone to town on this one. There've already been complaints.

The Annexe
13 Roundhead Avenue
Wexbury

Saturday 25th December

Dear Big Brother,

Merry Christmas!
Mum and Dad are behaving very oddly and have shooed the rest of the family into annexe while they enjoy some 'quality time' (basically, Mum has bought Tesco's Finest mince pies and there aren't enough to go around). Scrumpy and Alice

417

don't seem to mind as Granny gave them a PlayStation for Christmas and they're currently racing each other around New Zealand courtesy of Colin McRae's Rally. Granny herself is well into her second bottle of Cockburns with her boyfriend and they're nuzzling on the sofa, both burping occasionally as result of Mum's usual fantastic Christmas feast.

Am a bit bored and lonely. There's only so much fun to be had with an electric foot spa (Mum and Dad), a Black and Decker Mouse (Granny) and a year's subscription to Greenpeace (Alice and Scrumpy). At least I can get drunk, as Dad has bought my car and given it to Alice, so I don't have to drive home. Was hoping she'd give me a lift back tonight, but she seems keener to drive computer-generated Subarus than real, rusty Citroens. In fact, think she has been a bit ungrateful as she took one look at car and said, 'Have you had the clutch fixed, Lucy?' I am trying not to think about the car *vis à vis* foot spa issue. Know Mum and Dad gave me half a horse last year, so really can't let myself be childish about it. Might just pop next door to see if there's any Bailey's left. Will finish this later.

Back at Vetch Cottage:

Aghhh! So embarrassing to discover one's parents wearing novelty underwear. I'm sorry, BB, but you have to know. Remember I told you that they have been going through some sort of second honeymoon lately? Well Mum gave Dad dreadful red-nosed reindeer posing pouch thing in his stocking, while Mum received revealing red 'Santa' teddy. I burst in to find the heating up full, mince pies burning in oven and parents wearing next to nothing as they danced to Bing Crosby's *Seasonal Hits*.

Mercifully, at that moment, the phone rang. It was Big Mike calling from M5 to wish me a Happy Christmas and ask whether I wanted him to pick me up on his way back to the cottage (he wants to go to Boxing Day meet tomorrow so left his parents straight after lunch). Was so relieved, I gasped, 'Oh Mike, my hero. I love you!' That, at least, made Mum and Dad stop flaunting themselves as they gaped at me in surprise. The line went crackly and then dead. Think I'd had too many Bailey's.

Relief to get back here and give Big Mike the jumper I bought him. He went very red, and I had to gabble that I didn't mind if he hadn't bought me anything. But then he disappeared upstairs for what seemed like ages before coming back with huge, misshapen parcel covered with ribbons. It contained tens of boxes all tucked into each other in ever-decreasing sizes. By the time the room was filled with cardboard and paper and ribbon, I finally got down to tiny, tiny little velvet box in which was beautiful hand-crafted pendant with letter L made out in amber, jade and opal. It's exquisite.

'I'm sorry it isn't a bike or something more practical,' Mike muttered when I burst into tears. 'The L stands for something, as if you didn't know that already.'

I just cried and laughed and kissed him on his big, warm cheeks, telling him over and over again how fantastic it is. I love it. L for Lucy. If Mike weren't the Womaniser of Chisbourne, I'd be madly in love with him. As it is, am hopelessly in like with him.

Put a party hat on a sheep.

Love,

Lucy xx

Written on the back of a party shopping list:

Mike is wearing his jumper, I'm playing with my pendant and we're both curled up at opposite ends of the sofa divided by snoring dogs as we plot and plan the New Year's Eve party. Can't help but be excited despite reservations (sheer numbers, the snake fanatics, possibility of planes falling on us as under Heathrow flight path). Mike says it'll be the best party ever, and am inclined to agree. Can't think of anyone I'd rather

---

W **Microsoft Word – Lucy's party panic.doc**

Big Mike has now started to regret issuing a New Year's Eve party invitation to Leslie and Peta Dent. At least that is the only reason I can come up with for his odd behaviour. I don't think he slept at all last night. When I got up, he was lying on the sofa with the curtains closed watching an old movie. I asked what it was and he said, 'I Love Lucy.' Odd, as I could have sworn it was *Some Like It Hot*. Can't fathom him out at all.

When I asked him if he wanted to come to the supermarket to stock up for the party, he sighed deeply and said that he wasn't sure he wanted to have a party and couldn't the two of us stay in like we did last night? I pointed out that he could buy some mistletoe and that way he'd get to kiss all the pretty women in Chisbourne. This perked him up a little – the Womaniser is tragically one-track-minded – but he was in a terrible grump as we cruised up and down the aisles. I think it was because when he asked who I wanted to corner under the mistletoe, I couldn't bring myself to admit that it was actually Mike himself, so I said that I'd always found Horsy Tim rather sexy. He snapped that Tim has always been mad about Jane, and then added that he would kiss Amber Gunton if he could because she looks like Joanna Lumley. I pointed out that Amber is married, whereas at least Tim is available – if love-struck. Mike suggested I dye my hair red and wear my jodhpurs in that case. I suggested he has an entire body-transplant with Brad Pitt. We didn't speak between bagging oranges for the mulled wine and selecting baguettes for the garlic bread.

Mike has dashed back to Tesco's for paper cups. There was a man selling half-price Christmas wreathes and mistletoe by the cash points earlier. Both Mike and I pretended not to see him, although a wreath might be apt right now.

420

From: Lucy Gordon (juicylucy@webbedup.net)
To: Mo Lavender (Hobo-mobo@Hotmail.com)

11.13
Subject: Eve a lot on my mind

There is only one person to write to on a day like today with heart as full-to-bursting as mine is (either that or last night's mulled wine at Yuppie Cottage has given me indigestion). Anyway, my old brainwashed ex-housemate and sofa therapist who I. Miss. Like. Mad. I need advice!!!!!

It is the eve of a New Year and my landlord/friend/man-I-secretly-fancy-although-I-know-he-is-a-heartbreaker is hoovering downstairs singing 'I Will Survive'. I, meanwhile, have been 'cleaning' the bathroom for hours. The truth is, I gave it a quick wipe around and then sat down on the edge of the bath to write you a quick Happy New Year email (not sure what time-zone you're in but you're bound to be celebrating already). But I got distracted looking at my previous emails to you. And then I started reading through my Word documents too. Only looked up once, when I heard the new neighbours' car start up and managed to catch sight of it out of the window as it sped away, its roof-rack loaded down with suitcases. Don't think they'll be coming to our party. Would have broken the good news to Mike, but was too astonished by what I was reading to tell him.

Oh God, I've been reading the signals all wrong, haven't I? I think that Mike might have been feeling the same way all along but, like me, he simply didn't know it. Aghhh! I am *so* confused. How can I tell him how I feel before he tries to seduce Amber at the party?

It's no good. I adore him. I'm going to have to say something *now*. No time to send this.

12.00:
Help! I cleaned my teeth, splashed water on my burning cheeks and took a deep breath before racing downstairs to have it out

with Mike, but just found the Hoover sucking away to itself and no sign of him. Where has he gone?

14.00:
Still no sign of Mike. Have busied myself making party food. We now have twenty loaves of garlic bread, ten massive pizzas, several bowls of salad, a stack of mince pies and a tear-stained hostess. Am going to call Mum.

14.15:
Mum says that I just have to tell him how I feel. I pointed out that I can't do this as he is not here, and could have already run to the arms of Amber Gunton for all I know.

15.00:
He is not with Amber. According to her housekeeper, she and Lord G are in Australia and have already seen in the New Year on board a yacht in Sydney Harbour. The housekeeper looked very embarrassed as she was wearing one of Amber's designer dresses, and is obviously planning to have huge, wild party in her employers' absence.

15.20:
Mike is not in the Cow in Clover either. Jane and Charles the Yuppie were there, and asked me what was wrong. I said that I needed to get hold of some mistletoe urgently and could they give me a lift to Tesco's? This was clearly a bad suggestion, as Charles seemed to have some sort of breakdown-flashback and started screaming, 'L Plates!'

17.15:
Have committed terrible sin. Stole one of the Dents' bicycles to cycle to Tesco's and buy mistletoe, but man was packing up to go home and says he has sold out. He offered me two wreathes for the price of one. Cycled back with one on each handlebar, but some of the holly fell off and bike now has punctures in both

tyres. Have hidden it behind others and hope the Dents don't notice. Mike's car is still missing.

19.00:
Guests will be arriving soon and Mike remains AWOL. Have arranged food and made punch, shut dogs in Mike's bedroom, Platforms in mine and I've made half-hearted attempt to dress up, but don't feel like partying at all. Am going to call Mum again.

19.10:
Dad says Mum is in the bath. He suggested calling Mike's mobile. Why didn't I think of that earlier?

19.20:
Mike says that he's not coming to the party. I wailed that he had to, that it's *his* party. He hung up, but not before I heard whinnying in the background. He must be at Horsy Tim's (probably warning him that I plan to get off with him tonight). I must get there! Will post this now. Wish me luck. L xxx

---

'Hi, this is Lucy and Mike's answer phone. We're not around to take your call, so leave a message and we'll get back to you.' Beep. 'Lucy! It's *Mo!!!!!!* Jesus, I finally track down your new number by ringing about fifteen people including your brother. I call from the other side of the world to wish you a Happy New Year and tell you I'm coming home and you're *not in*! Where are you? What's happening? You're supposed to be having a party. It's half eleven over there, isn't it? Are you having such a wild time that you can't hear –'

'Mo! It's Jane. I thought I was hearing things – *quieten down everyone.* I'm in Mike's hallway – you can hardly hear yourself think here. Happy New Year! We're having a fantastic night. I wish you were here. Come to that, I wish Lucy and Mike were here too – it's their party and no one's seen them.'

From: Lucy Gordon (juicylucy@webbedup.net)
To: Mo Lavender (Hobo-mobo@Hotmail.com)

23.50
Subject: Happy New Year!

It is so weird to turn up to your own party and find it in full swing,
but that's what Mike and I have just done. All my food has been
eaten, the punch drunk and the fireworks are already popping
away in the garden. But there's ten minutes to go and so I've just
got time to let you know what's happened. Jane won't let me out
of my room until I do. She says you even called! Now I know what
I have to do to hear back from you.

So here's the story from where I left off . . .

20.15:
I stole another of the Dents' bicycles. It was one of the children's
and was way too small so it took me ages to get to the stables,
especially as the hem of my dress kept catching in the chain.
Found Horsy Tim in his kitchen. He looked really surprised to see
me, and said that he had been about to set out to come to the
party and was Jane going to be there? When I asked after Mike,
he said that he hadn't seen him all day. That was when I realised
that the whinny must have come from the horse hospital at the
surgery and not Tim's yard.

22.00:
Thank goodness I didn't have to ride that stupid bike to the
surgery, as it's on the other side of Wexbury. Tim gave me a
lift and waited in the car park while I tracked Mike down to
his consulting room. Then I stopped in the door and just
stared.

I have never seen so much mistletoe in my life. It was
everywhere. Mike was looking furious.

'You're not having any!' he yelled when I walked in. 'I know
what you've both come here for – don't think I haven't spotted

424

his car out there. Well I bought the lot and you can't have any!' He started grabbing mistletoe and holding it to his chest. 'It's all mine.'

'In that case,' I tried to stop my voice from shaking, 'could you hold some over your head for me?'

The rest, as they say, is kiss-story.

Oh! They've started the count-down downstairs. Mike says it doesn't matter. If we can exchange a kiss for every piece of mistletoe he bought – as we plan to – then we'll be kissing well into the New Year, and the one after that, and the one after that . . . . Who cares whether this one starts now or later?

00.34:
Dear Mo,

Lucy and Mike are a bit distracted right now, so I'm going to post this off. Great to hear you're coming home.

Jane x

From: Mitch Bodowski (Hobo-mobo@Hotmail.com)
To: Lucy Gordon (juicylucy@webbedup.net)

03.54
Subject: Re: Happy New Year!

Dear Lucy,
You do not know me, but I just have to write and say how happy you have made me this New Years. I am so excited that you and Mike have gotten it together at last. I've been crossing my fingers all year that you would – you guys are so perfect for each other.

I hope that you don't mind that I have never written before, or explained that you were emailing my address by mistake. I'm glad your friend Mo is coming home again. I hope you guys have a great time catching up.

I feel like you have become my friend too. Will you please write back some time?

Yours sincerely,

Mitchel O. Bodowski, (aged 13) Oregon.

PS I really hope that this is not the end.